"You are doing it, Gabe."

"Doing what?"

"Seducing me."

"I hope so," he said with a soft smile. "Heaven knows you've been seducing me for weeks now." Dipping his head, he trailed sweet kisses from the corner of her mouth across her cheek until he could whisper in her ear. "Let me make love to you."

She shuddered. "I can't fight you anymore."

"I don't want to fight, darlin'. I want to love."

"God help me, but so do I, Gabe. So do I."

He wanted to shout for joy. Instead he laid her down upon the mattress like a pirate's prize and paused just long enough to savor the moment. A dozen different sensations rolled through him in that instant. Anticipation. Elation and awe. Tenderness and reverence.

Gut-wrenching, fever-hot, wild-and-pulsing hunger. . . .

Praise for Geralyn Dawson's Sparkling, Sensual, and Sensational Romances

The Wedding Ransom

"This delightful story is full of humor, good dialogue, love, and loyalty. It will touch your heart. It did mine."

—*Rendezvous*

"A fast-paced, action-packed tale. For fans of her previous novels who pleaded for his story, Rafe's romance will thrill. A great piece of work that will surely be recognized as one of the top ten romances of the year."

—Harriet Klausner, *Affaire de Coeur* (five-star rating)

"One you won't want to miss. . . . A rollicking romantic adventure that will thoroughly captivate readers and leave them eager for Geralyn Dawson's next book. A perfect book to warm your heart on a cold winter's night."

—Merry Stahel, *Calico Trails*

"Hilarious from the first page. . . . Great characters and Geralyn Dawson's wonderful sense of humor marry to make *The Wedding Ransom* a most entertaining book."

—Carrie Romero, CompuServe Romance Reviews

"If you're looking for a funny, sexy Western romance with a bit of mystery thrown in, try this follow-up to *The Wedding Raffle.*"

—Lenore Howard, *Old Book Barn Gazette*

"A wonderful blend of romance, adventure, and the best cast of humorous characters you'll ever come across. . . . This is absolutely priceless! Ms. Dawson is just what you need. Fantastic. 5 BELLS!!!!"

—Bell, Book, and Candle

Books by Geralyn Dawson

The Wedding Raffle
The Wedding Ransom
The Bad Luck Wedding Cake
The Kissing Stars

Published by POCKET BOOKS

GERALYN DAWSON

The Kissing Stars

SONNET BOOKS

New York London Toronto Sydney Tokyo Singapore

An *Original* Publication of POCKET BOOKS

A Sonnet Book published by
POCKET BOOKS, a division of Simon & Schuster Inc.
1230 Avenue of the Americas, New York, NY 10020

ISBN: 0-671-01518-4

First Sonnet Books printing April 1999

10 9 8 7 6 5 4 3 2 1

SONNET BOOKS and colophon are registered
trademarks of Simon & Schuster Inc.

Front cover illustration by Brian Bailey, tip-in illustration by
Aleta Jenks

Printed in the U.S.A.

For
Pat Cody
Lesa Raesz
and Sharon Rowe

Thanks for your time, your help, your ideas
and most of all, for your friendship.
I'd be lost without you.

Oh, and thanks for all the Rosie stuff
to decorate my office, too.

September 1889
Dallas, Texas

"This can't go on much longer. Word is getting around about Rosie."

Tess Cameron glanced at her friend Edna Starbright, otherwise known as Twinkle, and offered a reassuring smile. "It won't go on much longer. She's getting too old and besides, this is the last fair of the season."

"And the money? How are we doing there?"

"Will counted up, and as of last night, Rosie's earnings have exceeded his goal by thirty-seven dollars. Any cash he pockets today will be extra."

Twinkle brightened at the news. "Well, isn't that wonderful." Glancing at Rosie, she said, "You could retire right now if you wanted, but I don't think you do. In fact, I bet you'll miss it once you quit. You like leading men around by their noses, don't you, girl?"

Rosie snorted and nabbed the carrot dangling from Tess's hand.

"I think that's a no," Tess said with a laugh. "Rosie is a terrible flirt."

"She's a terribly fast flirt." Twinkle leaned over and cooed into Rosie's face. "Isn't that right, precious. You'll have those boys so confused they won't know sic 'em from come here."

Rosie's snout wrinkled in what looked suspiciously like a grin. She truly did appear to enjoy her work, and she was so very good at it. Greased up and turned loose in a pen of people intent upon the chase, Rosie ran fast enough to split the wind and scorch the ground. Eight times out of ten she escaped the chaser's clutches altogether. The few times she lost the contest and ended up imprisoned in the hunter's arms, Tess swore her squeals were gales of laughter.

Everyone who saw Rosie run agreed she was the fastest pig in Texas.

Tess thought she was probably the happiest pig in the state, too. She wouldn't allow Will to race Rosie if she didn't believe the animal enjoyed it. She loved the young swine. Rosie was family, and family meant everything to Tess. Maybe because she'd worked so hard to create one for herself.

Twinkle interrupted her reverie by clicking her tongue and asking, "What's keeping Will? It's not like the boy to ask you to get Rosie ready for her race."

"He's meeting us at the arena," Tess replied, a smile teasing her lips. "He managed to talk his way into judging the pie contest, and he knew he wouldn't be through in time to see to Rosie's preparations."

"Food. I should have realized. I swear the child could eat the blades off a windmill these days. Never seems to get enough to eat. He and Rosie are two peas in a pod where supper is concerned."

"More like two pigs in a pen," Tess replied dryly, thinking of how Will wore dirt like a badge of honor. Most of the time, Rosie was far cleaner.

Rosie snorted as if in agreement.

Leaning against the wooden fence rail of Rosie's small stall, Tess observed the bustle of activity as owners prepared their livestock for the judging scheduled to take place later that afternoon. She'd grown accustomed to the sights, sounds, and scents of similar barns during the past six weeks, and enjoyed being part of it.

It was a relatively new experience for Tess. Although she'd lectured at county fairs and expositions across the state since returning from her European studies four years ago, she'd never ventured into the livestock barns until this season. But Will had needed something to keep him occupied while on the fair trail this summer, and racing Rosie turned out to be the perfect solution. The boy had both enjoyed the time away from Aurora Springs and earned the money to buy his own telescope, something he greatly coveted.

Which brought her thoughts around to the new telescope she'd ordered for herself. The shipment should have arrived in Aurora Springs by now. "Oh, Twinkle, I am so ready to go home."

Her friend looked up from her task of tying a pretty red ribbon around Rosie's neck for the walk across the fairgrounds to the arena. "You are?"

"Yes, I am. In fact, I'm tempted to head back after I've given my speech this afternoon."

Twinkle gave the bow one last adjustment, then patted the sixty-pound porker on the head. "But we're not scheduled to leave until the day after tomorrow."

"I know." Tess brushed her fingers across the soft satin ribbon around Rosie's neck, then scratched the underside of her snout, just the way she liked it. "But I'm anxious to get back to work, and besides, I miss everyone at home."

"It has been a long six weeks," Twinkle agreed. "You won't get any arguments from me if our plans change. In fact, I'd feel better if we did catch an early train. I haven't wanted to mention anything, but I've been having one of my hunches."

Tess shot her friend a sharp look. "About someone back home?"

"It's nothing specific, hon," Twinkle said, shrugging. "More like a general sense of foreboding."

Tess shuddered as a chill ran up her spine. She had learned to pay attention to Twinkle's hunches because they so often proved true. "But it's about someone at Aurora Springs? You can't tell who? Doc or Andrew, maybe? The Bakers?"

Twinkle nibbled at her bottom lip and considered the question for a full half minute. "No, not Amy Baker, anyway. This is a masculine feeling, but I can't take it any farther."

"Maybe we should send a telegram," Tess said, thinking out loud.

"As if anyone in Eagle Gulch would bother to deliver it to Aurora Springs," Twinkle replied with a grimace. "This is one of the few times I dislike the fact we've made our home in such an isolated locale as southwest Texas."

Tess couldn't argue with that. Reaching down to give Rosie a comforting pat—for her own sake, not the pig's—she said, "I wish Doc had come with us this summer. He promised not to head down to Big Bend before autumn, but ever since the Rangers mentioned finding those pictographs in the caves, he's been like a kid waiting for Christmas. If he has already started down there, he could be in real trouble. I worry about him crossing the desert in the summertime. He's not as young as he thinks he is."

"And he's too stupid to realize it."

"Twinkle!"

"Well," Twinkle said defensively. "Admit it, Tess. The man is a terrible flirt despite being almost fifty years old."

Good for him, Tess thought, though she was too busy worrying to argue. She allowed the conversation to die while she considered the problem of their departure. Leaving early would take some doing, but ignoring Twinkle's hunch might be more difficult in the long run. In that instant, the decision was made. "Twinkle, after I've presented my lecture at the science hall this afternoon, how about we gather up Rosie and Will and take the first train headed west? The state fair officials can find a substitute pig to run in tomorrow night's contest."

"Say no more, dear," Twinkle replied while giving Rosie one last brushing down. "I'll see that our things get packed."

Minutes later, Tess led the pig from the barn. Stepping out into the warm September sunshine, she tried to shake off the strong sense of dread Twinkle's suspicion had draped about her shoulders like a leaden shawl. But the feeling wouldn't go away. In fact, as she crossed the fairgrounds toward the canvas-enclosed arena, it only grew stronger. Outside the temporary structure she paused and took a deep breath.

She didn't want to go inside. She really, really didn't want to step into that tent. Idly, she wondered if Twinkle's hunch-powers had rubbed off on her. Because in that moment while facing the arena doorway, Tess knew that somehow, in some way, her life was about to change.

And not necessarily for the better.

"Pig races."

Gabriel "Whip" Montana stuffed the fair schedule in the pocket of his sturdy denim trousers, then slipped his fingers beneath the red bandanna tied around his neck and massaged his tense muscles. Lifting an exasperated gaze toward the cherubs painted on the main exposition hall's ceiling, he asked, "What idiot thought up that one? And why do I have to judge the finish line? Haven't I done my part by putting ribbons on the pies? The rhubarb was so bitter it liked to have killed me. And the governor is still after me to give a speech."

Mack Hunter hooked his thumbs behind his suspenders and smirked. "It's a fair, partner, and since you're the fairest man of all at the moment, you're lucky they haven't hung an exhibit sign around your neck and set you down between the needlepoint and the quilts. You're a hero, Whip. A first-class, bona-fide hero."

As a flock of females passed by them, their flirtatious smiles reserved for Gabe alone, Mack added, "And I don't mind telling you that hanging around with a hero is playing hell with my wooing opportunities."

Gabe scowled at his friend. "I'm not a damned hero."

"Uh huh." Mack stuck his hands in his pockets and sauntered off, whistling.

Temper rumbled inside of Gabe. The emotion had been building slowly over the past three months, but all this attention today had brought him right to the edge of an eruption. He strode after his friend and nudged him roughly on the shoulder. "Put a cork in it, Mack. Davy Crockett was a hero. Jim Bowie was a hero. I'm an investigator for the railroad."

The baiting spark in Mack's brown eyes faded, replaced by a look of total seriousness. "You brought in Jimmy Wayne Bodine, the most evil sonofabitch ever to ride the roads of this state. You saved every hostage in that schoolhouse. You earned the title of hero whether it wears easy or not."

Gabe set his jaw, not willing to hear it from Mack, too. Maybe things worked out this time, but it didn't always happen that way. He knew that first hand, and the memory of it chapped like wet leather. "I did my job," he bit out. "That's all."

"And a damn fine job it was," Mack snapped back, his voice echoing in the high-ceilinged hall.

"One that should never have needed doing. The Rangers were idiots for allowing him to escape their custody to begin with. And I was simply in the right place at the right time to get him back."

"Only because you were smart enough to track him when he'd fooled the law into thinking he'd headed in the opposite direction. Quit being so stubborn and take credit where it is due."

After that, a full minute passed without either man speaking. Being two strong personalities, the partners got crossways on a regular basis and experience had taught them that sometimes a little silence prevented a descent into a full-blown argument. Not that Gabe minded locking horns with Mack; sometimes a man simply needed a good fight to get the blood flowing. But the middle of the exposition hall during the fourth annual Texas State Fair when he was an official, invited guest of honor whether he liked it or not, wasn't the time and place for a word war with his best friend.

Mack apparently agreed because he lightened the atmosphere by slapping Gabe on the back and grinning. "Well, since you're so bound by duty, I reckon it's time to ease your way on over to the swine barn. I swear I hear those little piggies squealing from here."

"Pig races." Gabe sighed heavily. "They're being held in the arena area underneath the canvas, not in the swine barn. And what could be a more appropriate venue than a circus tent?"

The two men made their way from the exposition hall and out into the sunshine. Animal odors hung heavy in the air of the unseasonably hot afternoon, along with the more appetizing aromas of fried chicken and barbequed beef. The midway was filled with bustles and bowlers and giggling youngsters lining up to ride the flying-jennies. Laughter and conversation hummed around them, punctuated by an occasional roar coming from the one-mile racetrack at the center of the eighty-acre fair site.

Gabe gazed longingly at the track as they strolled toward the canvas pavilion. "That's the finish line I wanted to judge. The horse races. Tried to talk the fair officials into letting me do it. I think I would have convinced them had Mayor Wilson's wife not been eavesdropping on my conversation."

"I saw that." Mack flashed a wide smile toward a pretty young woman walking past, then sulked when she ignored him in order to bat her lashes toward his partner. "I think Helen Wilson might have gone so far as to take a gun to you to get you to taste her Arabella's peach pie."

"It was delicious," Gabe said with a shrug. "It suited me just fine to award her a ribbon. That's all they were gunning for, unlike some of the others."

"Just how many marriage proposals did you get, anyway?"

Grimacing, he took a mental count. "Four during the pies. Six with the jams and jellies."

"Damned women are getting more forward every day. Scares me to think about what's ahead of us once the century rolls over eleven years from now."

Gabe snorted a laugh. "Don't blow that smoke my direction. I know you, Hunter. You adore forward women."

"Only when they're being forward with me, which

hasn't been happening because they're too busy making cow eyes at you. Ten marriage proposals." He shook his head with disgust. "Any others that weren't so honorable?"

Recalling Rachel Mayberry's whispered suggestion, Gabe couldn't help but crack a grin. "Just one I'd consider acting upon."

"I knew it." Mack slapped his hat against his thigh. "The delectable Widow Mayberry. Right? She had that look in her eye."

Gabe nodded. She'd also had some damned interesting ideas on how best to enjoy her blue-ribbon blackberry jam.

Tugging his pocket watch from his brown leather vest, Gabe checked the time and picked up his pace. Like it or not, he'd bowed to Governor Ross's pressure and agreed to participate in the fair. One of the hard-and-fast rules he lived by was that once he said he'd do something, he damn well did it.

Another lesson taken away from that cursed night a dozen years past when he'd failed so horribly.

Strangers hailed him repeatedly on his way to the arena, the more bold among them attempting to draw him into conversation about the events at Cottonwood Hollow school. Mack, ever his friend, ran interference for him, and thankfully he made it to his destination without having to speak Jimmy Wayne Bodine's name a single time.

Tiered wooden bleachers rimmed the perimeter of the tent, providing viewing stands for spectators. A railed fence separated them from the arena. As Gabe and Mack arrived, a group of acrobats completed their performance by building a human pyramid. Mack purchased a bag of peanuts from a vendor, then found a seat from which to watch the show.

Gabe glanced around for the yellow badge that would indicate the man in charge. On the far side of the arena, he spied a number of dignitaries including the mayor of Dallas, a couple of state senators, and to his surprise, his boss, Jared Walker. The men appeared to be in good spirits, both literally and figuratively. The jug going round clued him into that. He was surprised to see Jared take a tot because, as a rule, the majority shareholder in the Brazos Valley Rail Company didn't partake.

A gray mustached man standing to one side of the luminaries sported the yellow badge Gabe sought. He approached the fellow, gave him his name, and watched as he made a check mark on a sheet of paper. "You'll be wearing number three, Mr. Montana," the man said. "And I don't have your charity listed. Who are you representing?"

Charity? Wearing number three? "What do you mean? I'm here to judge the pig races."

"Judge?" The fellow scoffed. "What do you need a judge in a pig race for? The winner is obvious. Whoever gets the pig in the pen within the allotted five minutes gets to claim the pot for charity. No, you're not here to judge, Mr. Montana. You're down as a participant. You're racer number three. Now, what's your favorite cause?"

Absently, Gabe named a local orphan's home as he tried to think this situation through. It wasn't until he caught his boss's eyes that he knew he'd been had. He

sauntered over to Jared and asked, "Why am I thinking you're the man behind whatever is fixing to happen here?"

"I wanted it to be a surprise," the railroad owner
claimed, his broad shoulders shrugging beneath a
finely-tailored jacket. "I'm doing you a favor."

"Now why does that make me nervous?"

"No, really. You'll like this. It'll be good for you.
In one way or another you've been strung tight as a
hoedown fiddle ever since the mess with Bodine. This
pig contest might loosen you up a bit. Take a look at
the contestants, Whip. See who'll be down in the dust
along with you."

Gabe arched a brow. "Down in the dust?"

"Sawdust. That's what's spread across the arena
floor. A man tends to get down among it when he's
trying to catch a greased pig."

A greased pig. His boss volunteered him to try and
catch a greased pig in front of a circus tent full of
people? "Sonofabitch, Jared! Why the hell . . . ?"

Walker grabbed the contestant's roll from the fair
official and shoved it at Gabe. "Read it, Whip. I believe you'll see a couple of Texas Rangers' names
listed."

Gabe froze, finally getting his friend's point.
Compton and Whitaker? His gaze scanned the page
for the pair of damned fool Rangers who had allowed Bodine to get loose and go on his most recent
killing rampage.

"You know," Walker casually observed, "I hear
these greased pig races are nothing more than a melee.

No telling what kind of injuries a man might incur while wrestling for a pig in a crowd."

Spirits lifted, Gabe rolled his tongue around his mouth. "Certain to be some bruising. Maybe a broken bone or two."

Walker nodded. "A fella has to acknowledge the risk when he agrees to participate. Can't very well go whining to one's buddies to arrest somebody for assault when the injuries result from a contest at the fair."

Gabe's lips twitched with a gleeful grin. "Sure would make a man look sissified to raise a complaint." He handed the list back to the official, hitched up his britches, and strode toward the arena gate saying, "Somebody call for the hog."

One of the first lessons Tess learned on the fair trail with Rosie was to provide a specially scented grease for the races. An expert at making aromatic candles and soaps, Amy Baker had been happy to concoct a grease perfumed with the fragrance of, appropriately enough, roses. Will beamed with approval the first time they'd used it, declaring the blend "slicker than snot on a doorknob."

A packed house listened to the announcement of each contestant's name, and the excitement swelled as spectators anticipated watching stodgy politicians and other famous Texans make fools of themselves on behalf of charity. Tess paid the announcer only scant attention, so intent was she upon helping Will smear the rose-scented grease on his pig.

She had just dipped her hand into the jar for another glob of the slick stuff when the announcer called out an introduction that had her glancing up for a curious look.

"Representing the Brazos Valley Rail Company, the Hero of Cottonwood Hollow, Mr. Gabriel "Whip" Montana!"

Whip Montana. Now there was a man to admire. Courageous and daring, he'd risked what the newspapers said was certain death when he offered himself up to Bodine in place of those schoolchildren. Then he'd used his wits to outsmart the outlaw. "I'd like to meet him," she said softly. She would consider it an honor.

Her gaze scanned the arena center and halted on the man who waved his hat in answer to the crowd's salute. Gabriel "Whip" Montana. She'd never known his given name was Gabriel. As always, the name sent a pang through her heart.

She stepped toward the front of the pen and took a better look. Funny, he even resembled her Gabe a little bit.

As the announcer went on about the exploits at Cottonwood Hollow, Whip Montana ducked his head and strolled back toward the line of contestants. The sight had Tess clutching the railing, heedless of the fact that she deposited the grease on her hand onto the splintered wood. Her gaze never left the Hero of Cottonwood Creek. Her heartbeat sped up.

Whip Montana. He resembled her Gabe a whole lot.

Tess had read of Montana's exploits in the newspapers. The man had Gabe's wavy dark hair, even down to the raffish lock that spilled across his forehead. He had Gabe's height, but a thicker, more muscular build. A mature man's build.

She leaned forward, staring hard, willing him to turn her way. She wanted . . . she needed . . . to see his face.

Then he placed his hat on his head, fitting it just so, running his thumb along the edge of the brim, and Tess didn't need to see his face after all. Only one man had that same quirky habit. She'd watched him don his hat in just that manner hundreds of times.

The Hero of Cottonwood Hollow? For a time long ago, he'd been her hero. For a time, he'd been her life.

Not Gabriel "Whip" Montana. This man was Gabe Cameron. Her Gabe.

Tess closed her eyes and for a moment was transported back in time to a quilt spread across a starlit meadow. The sweet memory didn't last for long, however, and as thoughts of what had followed threatened to overcome her, she firmly pushed them away. She'd survived it, alive and healthy and for the most part happy. The hard times had made her strong and for that she was grateful.

Slowly, Tess opened her eyes and gazed out toward the center of the arena. "Oh, my," she whispered. "Oh, Gabe."

He'd matured into a devastating man. A dangerous man.

Tall and tanned and broad-shouldered, he stalked across the arena with a loose-limbed grace reminiscent of the mountain lions that sometimes visited Aurora

Springs. Tess had no difficulty imagining this man taking down Jimmy Wayne Bodine barehanded.

Her gaze never left him as he paused and spoke to another contestant. Then his lips slashed a smile—her Gabe's smile—and a little cry of loss escaped her.

"Tess?" Twinkle asked. "Is there a problem? They're waiting for Rosie."

Tess looked up to see every pair of eyes in the arena turned in her direction. Every pair, including the one slate-colored pair absent from her life for more than a decade.

Gabe's stare locked on hers. In a single, heart-wrenching moment, she saw the truth.

He didn't recognize her.

The scoundrel didn't recognize her!

Tess couldn't breathe. She heard a roaring noise in her ears that had nothing to do with the sounds the crowd made. Gabe Cameron didn't know her from Rosie. "What kind of man is he?" she muttered softly.

What kind of man didn't recognize his own wife?

So Tess, being Tess, did the only thing she could do under the circumstances. She opened the gate and hissed to Rosie, "Sic 'em, girl. Sic him."

CHAPTER

2

*P*retty woman, Gabe thought, before glancing down at the pig. He didn't look long, preferring to devote his attention to Rangers Compton and Whitaker. As the four-legged animal came barreling into the arena, he decided to take the two-legged fools one at a time, starting with Compton. He was the jackass whose brainless decision to remove Jimmy Wayne's leg chains had set up the opportunity for the outlaw's escape and those uncalled-for deaths.

The pig made its initial pass through the crowd of men unscathed, and the crowd roared with laughter as the mayor of Dallas became the first to fall in the dust. Gabe worked his way around behind Compton as a congressman chased the pig back toward the crowd of catchers. The animal streaked forward. Compton shifted. With near perfect timing, Gabe landed a nice, satisfying blow to the Ranger's kidney.

Then he started enjoying himself.

The laughter in the arena drew him into the spirit

of the game and lightened his mood, so he didn't break any bones, settling instead for bruises. Compton was so stupid he never did catch on to the fact that one man alone stood responsible for his tanning. Whitaker proved to be a little sharper, going so far as to cuss at Gabe for his "carelessness" when Gabe laid him flat with a shoulder to his gut.

"Sorry," he lied in reply, offering the man a hand to help him to his feet. At that moment, the pig doubled back and headed right for him, giving Gabe the perfect opportunity to knock Whitaker in a pile of manure he'd eyeballed earlier. Then, to strengthen the credibility of his act, he made an honest effort at grabbing the ham-on-legs, but came away with nothing more than a handful of grease.

Peculiar grease, he thought, staring down at his hands. Something about it was . . .

He lifted his fingers to his nose and sniffed. Roses? Why would anyone go to the bother to slick up a pig with rose-scented grease?

As if caught in a magnet's pull, his gaze traveled across the arena to the north gate where the woman he'd noticed earlier leaned against the railing, a splash of white petticoat visible beneath a modest peach-colored cotton dress. Suddenly, an odd sense of familiarity swept over him, and he took a couple of steps toward the fence. He narrowed his eyes and peered at the female, wishing she'd move from the shadows so he could see her better.

Somebody brushed him from behind as the melee turned in his direction, and he took a staggering blow to the ribs without looking away from the woman.

What was it about her that compelled him so? He couldn't see enough of her to tell what she looked like. Perhaps it was the way she stood, or how she tilted her head. Whatever it was, he knew he had to explore the question.

Gabe pushed past a preacher and a judge who stepped in front of him. When he was halfway to the fence, she backed away from the gate. The movement took her beyond the shadows, and light illuminated her face.

Gabe froze mid-step. His heart pounded. His focus narrowed, telescoping down until the only two people left in the arena were him and her. The old him and Tess.

Tess.

The breath left his body. Twelve years. Twelve long, lonely years.

She was all grown up now. Still beautiful, though. More beautiful. With streaks of flame in her golden hair, a field of bluebonnets in her eyes, and . . .

His gaze slid past the graceful length of her neck, lingered on the surprising swell of bosom, then traced the narrow expanse of waist and gentle swell of hip displayed by her skirt.

. . . heaven in her form.

"Tess."

She heard him. She recognized him. He could see it in her eyes.

What he didn't see was the pig which came racing up behind him, barreling into him, knocking him flat on his face. He heard an ugly crunch as his nose slapped the dirt, and he tasted the raw, metallic bite of blood. The force of the blow caused his eyes to water, and pain radiated in waves across his face. Then, just as he braced his hands against the ground to push himself up, something hit his head and his world went black.

How long he lay unconscious, he couldn't say. All he knew was that the slobber woke him up. The slobber and the snout. The snort probably had something to do with it, too.

Gabe's eyes yanked open to find the damned overgrown pork chop rooting at his ear, the pink snout streaked red with Gabe's own blood. "Sonofabitch," he muttered, grimacing, lifting his arms to push the pig away. That's when he spied the skirt swishing beside the swine's front feet. The peach colored skirt.

"Stop it, Rosie. Leave him alone."

Gabe pushed up on all fours, then rolled back onto his knees. The movement gave rise to nausea and his mind whirled dizzily. He blinked twice, swayed on his knees, and gazed up at Tess. "Hiya, honey. Your bosom is bigger than I remember."

Her voice faded as the darkness reclaimed him. "Never mind, Rosie. Go ahead and bite him."

"Hiya honey," Tess drawled mockingly, her arms folded across said bosom and her nose wrinkled in a snit. She watched from the stock pen as Gabe shuffled slowly from the arena, holding a hand to his head as he exchanged what appeared to be sharp words with the two men who had rushed to tend to him the second time he passed out. Tess couldn't tell what the men were saying, but she hoped they all realized Rosie wasn't at fault for Gabe's injury. She may have knocked him down, but one of the men kicked him in the head. "Not that a mere boot could truly damage a head that hard," she muttered.

At the edge of the arena, Gabe shook off his escorts and turned around, his gaze obviously searching. Quickly, Tess ducked down and slipped outside through a flap in the canvas. She didn't want to face him, not yet. She needed a little time to figure out her feelings.

In the past half hour her emotions had run the gamut from thrill to despair, touching on everything in between. For a dozen years she'd done her best to put Gabe Cameron behind her, and for the most part, she'd succeeded. She lived a fulfilling life with fascinating work and dear friends and far-reaching dreams. She'd learned early on it did no good to dwell on what she had lost. She went months without ever thinking of her father or the Rolling R Ranch. Sometimes she went weeks on end without thinking about Gabe.

Other times, however, thoughts of her erstwhile husband haunted her. Especially on those particular calendar days that marked an anniversary of one sort or another.

Tess lifted her face to the heat of the September sun, closed her eyes, and remembered. Oh, how she had loved him. Smart and handsome and witty, Gabe had captured her young girl's heart shortly after their initial meeting. She had a clear vision of that first day when she walked into his father's laboratory with her brother, Billy.

Gabe had been as animated as Professor Cameron when he discussed the advances in astronomical study made possible by the relatively recent invention of the spectroscope. Tess's fascination with Gabe only grew as his friendship with Billy developed. She also recalled clear as day the first time he looked at her as more than just Billy's little sister. That's when he started teaching her the stars. Soon she'd fallen in love with both the night sky and Gabe Cameron.

Her love of astronomy had survived the trials that followed. And her love for Gabe . . . well . . . some things just weren't meant to be.

"Here you are."

Tess started at the sound of his voice. Then, summoning her courage, she slowly turned around. He was mussed and dusty and devastating, and Tess was thankful her long skirt hid her shaking knees.

"Sorry for what I said earlier," Gabe said, gesturing in the general direction of her chest. "That pig knocked my senses loose." After a moment's pause, he added, "I've been looking for you. Were you hiding from me?"

Gabe couldn't have known it, but he'd managed to pick the perfect question to get her back up. "I never hid from Gabe Cameron. Never. But you're not him, are you?"

He gave her a long, measuring look, then his lips twisted in a wry smile. "Whip is a nickname I picked up over time."

"And Montana? Why change your name, Gabe?"

"Montana is where I finally sobered up. Cameron

is my father's name. Since I reject the man, I figured I should get rid of the name, too."

"Oh." Tess didn't know how else to respond, so she kept her mouth shut. That turned out to be a good thing because as the seconds ticked by, all the accusations she'd dreamed of making to his face over the years bubbled up her throat and fought for room on her tongue. If she'd tried to talk, she'd probably have choked to death.

"How about I buy you a lemonade?"

"I'm not thirsty."

"All right. How about I buy me a lemonade and you walk along? I need to work out some of the kinks that brouhaha put in my muscles."

When Tess hesitated, he stuck his hands in his pockets and rocked back on his heels. Speaking in a serious tone, he said, "Tess, I'd really like to know what's going on in your life, but if you still can't stand to talk to me, well, I reckon I understand. I think about Billy every day."

At his words, tears stung the back of her eyes, surprising her. She hadn't cried about her brother in the longest time. In a moment of clarity, she realized she hurt for Gabe's obvious pain as much as for her own loss.

Some things never change.

"I guess I would like a lemonade, after all," she said, gesturing toward the concession stand a short walk away. "Although I don't have much time to spare. I need to see to Rosie before I make my speech."

"Rosie? Is she the woman you stood with inside the arena?"

"No."

"A child, then? I saw the youngster with you in the pen. I took her for a boy, though, wearing britches like she was. The light wasn't all that good inside either, so take it as an understandable mistake, all right?" He hesitated just an instant before adding, "So, how old is your Rosie? When did you remarry?"

The pain slashed swift and deep. "Remarry?"

He shrugged. "Judging by the height of your daughter, it didn't take you long."

"My daughter?" Just saying it sent Tess reeling on her feet.

Alarm tracked across Gabe's face, and he reached out and took her elbow, steadying her. "Rosie. Isn't she your daughter?"

"Rosie is my pig!" Tess stared down at the hand that held her, trembling from the combined effects of the memory of the past and the reality of the present—her first physical contact with the man in twelve long years.

"Well, I'm lost," Gabe said, his voice melting to husky. With his free hand he reached up and touched the back of his head. "Maybe this bump scrambled my brains worse than I thought."

He smelled of arena dust and bay rum and memories. As Tess fought the urge to lean against him, Twinkle's voice provided a welcome distraction. "Honey, are you all right? Is this fella bothering you? Should I call for help?"

Tess summoned her strength and shook off Gabe's

hold, stepping away from him. "I'm fine. This is . . ." she stumbled over his name, uncertain which to use.

He solved the question by tipping his hat and saying, "I'm Gabe Montana. Tess and I are old friends. We thought we'd have a glass of lemonade and catch up with each other."

"That's right, Twinkle," Tess added, staring hard at her friend. "Gabe and I used to be very close."

Twinkle's eyes widened slightly, then abruptly narrowed. Everyone at Aurora Springs knew about Gabe Cameron. Obviously, Twinkle had made the connection between him and Gabe "Whip" Montana. After giving him a cool nod, she addressed Tess. "I'll see to Will and make sure he gets Rosie ready for tonight. Don't worry about him interrupting."

Tess sent her a grateful smile. "Thank you, Twinkle. And don't worry. I'll be fine, and this short delay won't change our plans at all."

The women exchanged a significant look, then Twinkle ducked inside the canvas tent. Gabe frowned after her. "Sounds to me like you got the names switched. Twinkle is your friend and Rosie is your pig?"

"Yes. You met Rosie earlier."

He folded his arms and shook his head slowly. "So that slobbering swine really does belong to you?"

"She's family, Gabe. Please don't be insulting."

He opened his mouth to speak, but apparently reconsidered, and slapped it shut. It was a good decision. Tess had about reached the end of her emotional rope, and another pithy comment from him might well send her screaming into waters best left unexplored for the time being.

At the concession, he purchased two lemonades, then nodded toward a tree-shaded table and chairs. "Shall we sit or would you prefer to walk?"

"I'd rather sit." It was safer that way. This encounter with her husband made her weak in the knees.

They sipped their drinks in silence for a time, Tess waiting for him to speak first. She'd never felt so tongue-tied around this man before, even when she was a nervous young girl suffering her first—and what turned out to be only—romantic crush. She excused her shortcoming. Gabe had not been nearly this intimidating twelve years ago. Not so big, so muscular, so overwhelmingly masculine. Plus back then, they hadn't had tragedy hanging between them like a black cloud.

She was beginning to wonder if he might not be a little nervous himself when he finally spoke. "You mentioned a speech. What's that all about? You talking about quilting or something?"

Tess smiled. She could talk about her work with confidence, and for the first time since gazing across that arena and spying Gabe, she felt a sense of control. And, to be perfectly honest with herself, she preened at the notion of impressing him with the expertise she'd garnered over the years. "The title of my talk is 'The Spectroscope and Saturn's Rings: How new inventions are changing old conceptions.' "

His brows winged up. "Excuse me?"

" 'The Spectroscope and—' "

"What do you know about Saturn's rings?"

Smugly, she lifted her chin. "Quite a bit, actually. I centered my studies on Saturn for four years. I've moved on to a new area of inquiry now, but I am quite capable of answering any questions the Texas State Fair crowd might ask."

"You're a student?"

"I'm an astronomer. With credentials. I spent six years studying under the tutelage of Dr. Winslow Pierce."

He reared back in his seat. "Astronomy! But you're not . . . that's my . . . I was the one . . ."

"You showed me how to fall in love with the stars, Gabe."

She spoke the truth. She'd been a girl enamored of a young man whose imagination had been captivated by the mysteries of the universe. In an effort to please him, to make herself more attractive to him, she had made his interests hers.

Looking back on that time with a woman's wisdom, it appalled her to remember how willing she'd been to change herself for him. She wondered if other young women followed the same path and if so, how well their relationships stood the test of time. Tess's hadn't lasted long enough to begin to answer that question. Luckily, though, in her case, the changes she made worked out just fine. Her fascination with the stars had outlasted her fascination with Gabe Cameron.

At least, that's what she'd told herself for years. Seeing him again, she wondered if she had fooled herself all along.

The scowl stretching across her husband's face told her his thoughts weren't any happier than hers during this pause in their conversation. But before she could question him, a well-dressed couple escorting two adolescent children approached.

"Mr. Montana?" the gentleman said.

"Yes." Gabe stood and accepted the man's handshake.

"Mr. Montana, I'm Gerald Hanford. This is my wife Martha and our sons Jim and John David. We're all just so very honored to meet you."

Mrs. Hanford beamed a toothy smile at Gabe and added, "While the boys don't attend the Cottonwood Hollow school, we have friends in the area and their children were among those saved by your heroism. We wanted to thank you personally for preserving the lives of those dear, dear babies. You are truly a hero, Mr. Montana. Dare we hope you'll quit your job as an investigator for the railroad and join the Rangers? Those boys could use a man of your caliber."

Tess's gaze flew to Gabe. A railroad investigator. Come to think of it, newspaper accounts of the capture of Jimmy Wayne Bodine had mentioned Whip Montana worked for the railroad. She wondered why the young man so interested in scientific research had turned his attention to studying crime for a living.

Gabe shifted uncomfortably and answered Mrs. Hanford. "I'm happy doing what I'm doing, ma'am."

The older child, Jim, interrupted with a question about the kegs of gunpowder Jimmy Wayne Bodine had positioned around the schoolhouse. The younger boy asked to see Gabe's scar from where Jimmy Wayne shot him.

"John David!" his mother exclaimed in a scandalized voice. "Don't be rude. Mr. Montana here isn't a fair exhibit."

"Now *that* I'm not so certain about," Gabe replied with a grin.

The Hanfords fawned over him a few more minutes before excusing themselves to find seats for the outdoor puppet show due to start soon. The slight relaxing of her husband's shoulders as he reclaimed his seat tipped Tess off to his relief, and reminded her of the young man she'd married. He'd shunned attention back then, too. Still, he deserved to be honored for his heroics.

Tess waited until the family moved out of earshot before saying, "You did a fine thing in Cottonwood Hollow, Gabe. Saving so many young lives must be terribly gratifying."

"Having to save those lives was terrible, period. It never should have gone that far. That's the kind of mess you get when you put churnheads in charge." He lifted his glass to his mouth, tilted up his head, and took a long swallow of lemonade.

Tess watched the movement of his throat and was surprised by a memory flash of her tongue tracing along its contours. She had so loved the taste of him. As heat flushed her body, she pushed to her feet. "I must go. It's almost time for my speech. I need to prepare."

"Wait a minute." He grasped her arm. "We really need to talk. You never said . . . I don't know . . ." He grimaced and muttered a low curse. "Shouldn't I have received a copy of the divorce papers? Your father told me he would see to the legalities, so I expect it's long been taken care of. But shouldn't I have signed a paper or two, or was your signature enough?"

Divorce papers? Tess sank back into her seat. Her stomach dropped clear to her ankles. "My father said he'd arrange a divorce? When did this happen?" Suddenly, Gabe's earlier remarks about remarriage and a daughter made an ugly sort of sense.

Gabe's expression grew wary. He set down his glass on the table. "A few months after the fire. He had Rangers track me to the ranch south of Houston where I was working cattle. He sent a note." After a moment's pause, he added, "I wasn't surprised you wanted to divorce me, but it's always sort of bothered me because I never saw any papers. I guess I've never felt it was finished."

Tess's mind whirled with the ramifications of Gabe's revelations. The old, bitter ache washed through her. Her father and his damnable revenge. Even years after his death, Stanford Rawlins had managed to reach out from the grave to wound.

She cleared her throat. "So you've gone along all these years assuming our marriage had ended without ever checking into it?"

"Honey," he drawled, his eyes narrowing. "We haven't seen each other in a dozen years. Our marriage *did* end."

Tess set her own glass down with a bang. "But you never talked to me about it. How could you let this happen without talking to me?"

Gabe's jaw hardened. "You told me you never wanted to see me again, Tess. I took you at your word."

"Why?" She shoved to her feet. "I was seventeen years old, Gabe. I was distraught with grief. You should have known people say things they don't mean when they are grief-stricken. How could you let my father do this to us?"

He didn't answer her right away. Tess stared at him, seeing the muscles working in his jaw, watching those gray eyes go cold. Controlled anger. She remembered that about Gabe.

His voice was low and dangerous when he spoke. "Maybe I felt the same way. Maybe I didn't want to see you again, either."

He might as well have plunged a pitchfork through her heart, so badly did his words hurt.

On watery knees, she sank back into her seat. Neither of them spoke for a time. The laughter of passing fair-goers sounded harsh to Tess's ears. Her thoughts were in a turmoil. All these years she'd wondered. All these years she'd entertained one scenario after another, instigated a search a time or two, finally deciding her husband was dead. Never once had she guessed her father told Gabe they were divorced. Never once had she considered he might have changed—no, rejected—the Cameron name.

Another thought struck Tess and her eyes widened. Gabe hadn't mentioned another woman, but what if . . .

She felt as though a noose slowly tightened around her neck when she repeated the question he had asked her earlier. "Did you marry again, Gabe?"

He glanced away from her, his lips flattening in a grim line. "No."

Thank God. A wave of relief washed over Tess as she waited for him to elaborate. He didn't.

From just beyond the fairgrounds to the south came the peal of a church bell counting off the hour. In fifteen minutes she was due to begin her speech. She drew a deep breath, braced herself, then said, "Gabe, my father banished me from the ranch two weeks after the fire. He died six months after that. I never saw him or spoke with him again. I never signed divorce papers."

His head whipped around. "What?"

Tess licked her lips. "As far as I know, you and I are still married."

He sat back heavily in his chair. "The hell you say."

Half a minute ticked by in silence before he said, "I can't believe your father would lie about this. Why would he? What was the purpose?" Before she could summon a reply, he narrowed his eyes and added, "Wait a minute. Your father kicked you out? Why?"

Tess glanced away. She couldn't answer his question. Not without thinking it all through. Too much was at stake. "Did you ever look for me, Gabe?"

"Look for you? Why would I? You divorced me, or at least, that's what I thought."

Emotion rumbled up inside her, threatening to overwhelm. What should she tell him? What would he do when he learned the rest of it?

Maybe she'd never tell him. What purpose would it serve at this late date? Tess swallowed hard. She needed some time to think about this. Everything was happening too fast.

Standing she affected an unconcerned air, even

though on the inside she was trembling. "I've got to go. I'll be late for my speech."

"But we're not finished," Gabe protested. "You can't leave now. There are things I need to know."

Tess suddenly ached with weariness. Emotional upheaval purely wore a woman down. "You're not the only person in my world now, Gabe. I don't have time at the moment. There is too much to tell. Too many questions."

"Then you'll meet me after your talk," Gabe demanded, scowling.

Tess thought of her plans to catch the evening train, and Twinkle's hunch that something was wrong at home. If she could figure out what to say to him, she'd have a little time to spare for a talk. "I'll meet you at the swine barn in two hours. That's the best I can do."

"I'll be there."

She started to walk away then, but good manners and a surprising reluctance to part from him had her pausing long enough to say, "Thank you for the lemonade."

"Sure. Anytime."

"Well, good-bye, Gabe."

As she walked past him, he reached out, grabbed her hand, and pulled her toward him saying, "That reminds me."

Before she realized his intent, he dipped his head and his lips captured hers. He tasted of lemons and sugar, and Tess wanted to weep at the sweetness of his kiss. It ended entirely too soon.

"I've always regretted not kissing you good-bye,"

Gabe said in a low, rough voice. "Figured I might as well make up for it. Of course, that wasn't good-bye, but a see-you-later kiss. Two hours at the swine barn, right?"

Speechless, she simply nodded. She couldn't have spoken had her life depended on it. Gabe picked up the empty lemonade glasses and returned them to the vendor before striding away in the direction of the racetrack, whistling as he went.

Tess didn't move, she couldn't. He'd kissed her. Gabe Cameron had kissed her. For a dozen years she'd dreamed of his kisses and now, again, she'd experienced one. In the flesh.

Kisses weren't the only thing she'd dreamed about, either.

"Oh, my." Her eyes drifted shut.

For a long moment she stood frozen in place, emotions beating at her like hailstones. Shock and bitterness, anger and grief. Joy and elation and anticipation. And, the memory of love. Such deep, soul-filling love.

It all but brought her to her knees.

Finally, she stirred herself to move, and five minutes later, she made her way into the chair-filled room that served as the Texas State Fair's lecture hall. Twinkle waited for her. "My stars, Tess, you've cut this close. I was beginning to worry."

"No need to fret. I'm here and I'm fine." More or less, she added silently.

Twinkle flipped the latch on her purse and yanked it open. Removing a small piece of paper, she handed it to Tess. "I'm glad somebody's fine. I was right to be worried, honey. A messenger delivered this telegram ten minutes ago. It's Andrew. He's taken sick again and he's running out of quinine. They need us home with the medicine as soon as we can get there. I had Will get Rosie boxed up, and they'll meet us at the train station. If you cut the last section of your speech, we should be able to make the early train. We'll reach home a full day sooner."

Tess stared at the telegram, then lifted her fingers to her lips, and murmured, "A good-bye kiss."

At that moment, the moderator introduced her to the crowd, forcing Tess to turn her thoughts away from earthly desires and toward more heavenly pursuits—namely the rings of Saturn.

Gabe stuck his head inside the pig barn. "Whew-y. I swear pigs must be the smelliest animals on earth."

"Then why the hell are we here?" Mack asked.

"I told you. I'm meeting my wife."

"Uh huh." Mack rolled his eyes. "I'd come closer to believing you're meeting those two Rangers to kiss and make up than that you're meeting a wife."

"Wanna put some money on it?"

Mack gave him a shrewd look. "What's going on, Montana? You trying to put a bluff over on me?"

Gabe simply grinned. He was feeling pretty good despite his aches and pains.

It had been quite a day. He'd damn near gotten his nose broken, been drooled on by a hog, discovered a long-lost wife, and sneaked in the back of a lecture hall to listen to the little woman give a fascinating paper on a subject that once upon a time he'd dreamed of studying himself.

Damn, but she had grown up fine. The promise of the girl had been more than realized in the woman. She was Helen of Troy, only better. A Texan beauty with brains, and a kiss that still knocked his boots off.

Still, he wondered how she could stand to study the stars. He couldn't. He hadn't stargazed once since that god-awful night when their lives blew apart. The very thought of doing so gave him the shakes.

Yes, his little wife had been full of surprises this afternoon. Now that he'd had some time and distance to think matters through, he had at least a hundred questions to ask her. Starting with this bit about her father, that bastard. Had old man Rawlins truly kicked her off the Rolling R? If so, why? Was he part of the reason?

Surely her father hadn't abandoned her entirely. He must have left her the money that supported her studies, otherwise how could she have managed?

Tess an astronomer. Imagine that. To be perfectly honest, the idea of it sort of pissed him off. She'd taken his dream and lived it.

He pulled out his pocket watch and checked the time. "She's late."

Mack cuffed him on the shoulder. "You're pretty good, Montana. You sound as if she truly exists."

Twenty minutes later, he was beginning to wonder himself. Had he been kicked in the head so hard he hallucinated her?

No. He damn well hadn't hallucinated that kiss.

Forty minutes past their appointed meeting time, he knew without a doubt that she existed. Nobody but Tess had ever made him this angry. He left Mack waiting at the swine barn while he conducted a thorough search of the fair. The woman wasn't to be found.

He was steaming when he returned to the pig palace. Mack obviously saw his temper on his face because he reached into his pants pocket and tugged out a white handkerchief, waving it in the air. "Don't light into me. I'm innocent."

"Did you see her?"

"The phantom wife, you mean?"

"Don't mess with me, Mack."

Mack narrowed his eyes and studied Gabe. "Well, I'll be good and go to hell. You are serious, aren't you? This isn't a joke you're pulling on me."

"I'm as serious as you've ever seen me."

Gravely, Mack nodded. "All right, then. What do you want to do?"

"Find her," Gabe replied. "It looks like she's run off. Surprises me, though. The Tess I knew wasn't the type to run away from her problems."

"Is that what you are to her, Montana? A problem?"

Gabe ignored the question, thinking aloud. "She owns that ham-on-the-hoof that ran in the charity race. We can see if it's scheduled for any more contests. If nothing else, the fair officials should have an address for her. Could be she lives here in Dallas, and I can track her down at home."

Mack's brow furrowed as he scratched behind his ear. "She's your wife, but you don't know where she lives. Makes perfect sense to me."

Mack followed his friend into the swine barn and they split up, Mack going right and Gabe heading left in search of one of those yellow badges. A few minutes later, Mack hailed him with a whistle. "I got your answers. Such as they are," he said when Gabe approached. "She canceled tomorrow's race and went home."

Gabe spat a curse. "Where's home?"

"A place called Aurora Springs."

"Aurora Springs? Never heard of it."

"Neither had I," Mack said. "I asked. It's a speck on the map out near Eagle Gulch."

"Where the hell is Eagle Gulch?"

Mack exhaled a long, loud sigh. "Damned if I know. But judging by the look in your eyes, I bet you're fixing to find out."

CHAPTER

3

༺๑๑༻

Gabe eyed the small grouping of adobe and stone buildings snuggled up against the canyon wall and sighed with relief. This had to be Aurora Springs. Finally. Better they had named it Back-of-Beyond. To say his wife had picked an out of the way spot in which to settle was like saying Texas got a little warm in August.

Aurora Springs was located deep in southwest Texas about a million miles from everywhere. Leaving Dallas ten days ago, Gabe had traveled south to San Antonio, then waited around to catch a westbound train for the four-hundred-mile stretch through wilderness and desert to the water-stop town of Eagle Gulch. There he left the train, bought a couple of horses, and rode north by northwest along the old Comanche War Trail to reach the tiny settlement.

He was travel-weary, tired clear to the bone. He'd love to stagger to a bed and sleep for a couple of days. But at the same time he wanted to spur his horse and gallop into the village. He had questions galore for his runaway bride, questions he'd come hundreds of miles to ask.

Gabe knew better than to barrel into town without first taking careful stock of his surroundings. Considering how Tess had ducked out on him in Dallas, he didn't figure she'd be all that happy to see him now. He didn't think she'd greet him with the business end of a gun, but he couldn't be sure. Twelve years had passed. The Tess he'd married then might have little in common with the Tess he aimed to get to know today.

Dusk crawled across the plain behind Gabe as he secured his horses, retrieved a pair of field glasses from the saddle bags, and made his way to an outcropping of rock some twenty yards to the north. Avoiding a cactus, he lay down and stretched out on his belly. Heated metal ringed his eyes as he gazed through the sun-warmed glasses. Starting at the north end of the settlement, he slowly panned the area.

The cottonwoods lining the banks of the creek caught his notice first. They were the first real trees he'd seen in better than a hundred miles. Moving on, he counted five small houses, a barn, a couple sheds, a chicken coop, a pair of camels, and what appeared to be a communal kitchen or mess hall. Abruptly, he jerked his glasses back. "Camels?"

Yep, they were camels all right. What sort of place was this? Pigs he understood, but camels?

Gabe continued his perusal. Aurora Springs resembled a ranch headquarters more than a town. He spied no stores, no churches. Hell, not even a saloon. What kind of Texas town didn't have a saloon? Maybe this wasn't Aurora Springs, after all. Maybe he'd taken a wrong turn in the desert.

Then his glasses caught a bright flash of orange against a backdrop of pink. A ribbon. A ribbon on a pig. "Nope, I'm in the right place," he muttered softly.

Tess's pig lay sprawled in the shade in front of one of the houses. As Gabe watched, its head slowly lifted and it wrenched to its feet, then plodded across the yard toward the barn where a lanky man stood tossing food scraps from a bucket into a wooden trough.

Gabe gave the man a quick study. No gunbelt. Work gloves poked into a pocket. Well-worn hat. Mid-twenties, he'd reckon.

So, two camels, one pig and one man so far. How many others?

Movement at the far north end of the compound caught his notice and Gabe refocused his field glasses. Two women carried a basin and bedding up the front steps of the last house in the row. He recognized one of them from the fair. What was her name? Twitter or Tremble? Something silly like that. A buxom lady, she was dressed in a flowing, patterned robe of purple and red. Instead of the requisite sunbonnet, the woman wore a turban like one of those Swami fellows. But this one was orange.

Gabe shifted the field glasses away from his eyes and blinked. "Enough to make a man see spots," he grumbled before focusing once again on the women.

The other female was much younger. Tall and slender, she wore a normal skirt, shirtwaist, and bonnet, something Gabe found reassuring in the face of the older woman's flamboyance.

The females set their burdens down on the porch, then Twinkle—that's the name—rapped on the door. Staring hard, Gabe saw her lips move, but he was too far away to hear what she said. The women waited a moment, picked up what might have been an empty stew pot sitting beside the door, and departed. They made their way across the yard to the barn where they struck up a conversation with the man Gabe had previously noticed.

The fellow wrapped a casual, yet possessive arm around the young woman's waist as he twisted his head and called out toward the barn. An older man stepped out of the shadows. He wore a blue uniform coat and buff-colored trousers. Sunlight flashed off rows of medals lining his breast.

As the four of them spoke, their heads turned toward the house the two women had visited. Gabe deduced their talk centered on whoever was inside.

Tess. It had to be her. He felt it in his bones. He'd bet his saddle he was right.

Summoning his patience, Gabe waited until the small gathering dispersed before slipping down to the village. Furtively, he made his way toward the cabin. Wooden shutters shielded the window on the west wall, so Gabe made his way around to the south where luckily they hung open. Easing up to the portal, he cautiously peered inside.

And damned near swallowed his tongue.

At least she has her clothes on.

Gabe swallowed a suddenly sour taste in his mouth,

unable to peel his gaze away from the scene inside the cabin. Tess was here, all right.

His wife lay sound asleep, sprawled like a blanket across a bare-assed naked man.

Tess woke abruptly, exhaustion clawing at her body even as she realized something was wrong. Immediately, she reached for Andrew's neck and felt for a pulse. Weak, but still beating, thank God.

She brushed back a lock of his carrot red hair and placed a weary hand against his forehead. Hot again, blast it. When she'd finally lost the battle against sleep, he'd been shivering with chills. Now the fever had him burning up again, and he'd kicked off his blankets. She was surprised he hadn't pushed her out of the bed like he had the last time she'd crawled in beside him to help him keep warm. She'd fallen asleep then, too, and when he got hot, he'd rolled her onto the floor.

But she wasn't on the floor now. So what had dragged her from the sleep she so dearly needed?

Brow wrinkling, she glanced around the room. Someone stood hidden in the shadows in the corner. "Jack? Is that you? What are you doing in here? You know no one is allowed inside."

"I can see why." Gabe Cameron stepped into the light and added in a hard, ugly tone, "Adultery is something better kept private."

Gabe. Tess's stomach fell like a meteor and she groaned aloud. "Well, Aries, Cancer, and Cassiopeia," she muttered. When she'd stood him up in Dallas, she'd suspected he might follow her home. But since he'd given up on her easy enough the first time, she'd figured the odds at fifty-fifty. Thank goodness she'd hedged that bet by taking precautions. As soon as she'd returned to Aurora Springs, she'd sent Will off with Doc. "I need this today like Rosie needs singing lessons."

For the briefest of moments, he appeared distracted. Then he folded his arms and sneered, "I can't imagine a time when it's handy to get caught cheating on your spouse."

"Oh, be quiet. You don't have a clue of what's really going on, Gabe Cameron."

"Don't call me that," he said, taking a step forward. "My surname is Montana now. Don't hang anything else on me."

"Fine. Call yourself whatever you want, but I'm still Mrs. Cameron."

"At least you remember the Mrs. part," he noted, pointedly eyeing the bed.

Tess sniffed. She'd bet her favorite star chart he hadn't changed it legally, but that wasn't worth mentioning. Tired, she rolled out of bed and braced herself, preparing to confront him. When she got a good look at the furious light in his eyes, she almost crawled right back in. Gabe was obviously itching for a fight and unless he'd changed significantly in the past dozen years, she could count on the battle taking awhile.

Lovely.

"You used to be smarter than this," she observed before turning her back on her husband and devoting her attentions to Andrew.

She could almost hear Gabe fuming as she retrieved

the basin of fresh water and bed linens outside her door. When she dipped a cloth into the water and began sponging her friend's overheated, freckled face, she would have sworn she heard her husband grinding his teeth.

She rinsed the towel, then stroked it across Andrew's naked chest, fully expecting Gabe to protest. She didn't anticipate his grasping her around the waist and lifting her bodily away from Andrew's sickbed, then yanking the cloth from her hand.

"So maybe I know you're playing nursemaid instead of bedmate, but that still doesn't mean I want to watch my wife performing this kind of intimacy with another man."

"Close your eyes, then," she replied, making a grab for the damp washrag. "You're acting the half-wit, Gabe. You haven't fretted over what your wife's been doing for the past twelve years. No reason for you to start now."

He muttered something she couldn't make out and held his arm out as she struggled with him, the cloth beyond her reach. Frustration welled up inside her. She was too tired for this. She wasn't prepared for him. "Please, Gabe."

After a moment's hesitation, he released her. "What's the matter with him, anyway?"

Tess pushed her hair back away from her face and smoothed her skirt as she gazed with concern at the man lying prone in the bed, "I'm not at all certain. Andrew has suffered fevers in the past, but this one is different. This one frightens me. It's worse than ever before, and we're afraid it may be contagious."

Gabe lowered his arm to his side, the washcloth dangling limply from his hand. "Contagious?" he said with a sharp edge to his voice. "This fella's illness may be contagious so they send you in to nurse him? Why not one of the men I saw outside? What is he to you, Tess? Was I right the first time?"

He sounded jealous and it surprised her. He'd never displayed that particular character trait before, and he had no right to act that way now. But at the moment, she didn't have the energy to fight that particular fight. "Andrew is my friend, and I'm here because I was with him when he collapsed the day before yesterday."

Skepticism curled Gabe's lip. Her hand tingled with the need to slap it off his face and the reaction surprised her. As a rule, she didn't believe in violence.

"I'm telling the truth," she insisted. "He suffers from recurrent malarial fevers. That's why I left the state fair earlier than planned. He needed a fresh supply of quinine."

"If you brought the quinine, then why is he still sick?"

Frustration overwhelmed her. "That's the problem. His recovery lasted only days. This may well be a different type of illness entirely. He spent a month up in the hills tracking the white stallion, and we don't know what he may have come in contact with."

"The white stallion? Oh, never mind. What does the doctor say?"

"The nearest doctor is in Eagle Gulch, and he refuses to come out here. We use our best judgement in dealing with illnesses, and in this case that includes keeping quarantine."

"Quarantine?" he croaked.

"Yes, quarantine."

Gabe glanced down at his feet, then slowly looked back up. "You and this naked guy."

"And now you."

"Me."

"Yes."

Gabe muttered an epithet, then strode over to the stack of clean bedding, retrieved a sheet, and draped it across Andrew's loins. For a moment, he stood beside the bed studying the fevered patient, his brow furrowed in thought. "Well, this isn't exactly how I had it figured, but I guess it'll give me time to ask my questions."

Questions. Wonderful. As if fighting death for Andrew wasn't battle enough, now she'd get to war over the past with Gabe. Tess closed her eyes and sighed. "Andrew comes first."

Gabe scowled and dipped the towel into the basin. He twisted it, wringing away the excess water, and turned toward the bed.

"Wait." Tess touched his arm. His muscle was steel beneath her fingers and for a brief flash she remembered what it was like to be wrapped in his arms. *No, Tess. Don't do that to yourself.* "If this fever is transferable by physical contact, I've already been exposed. You haven't. There's no need for you to take the risk."

Gabe looked down to where her pale hand rested against his bronzed skin. His nostrils flared as he filled his lungs with air. Tess fought the urge to step closer.

"Risk?" His mouth twisted into a wry smile.

"Haven't you heard? I'm a hero. Risk-taking is part of the job description."

Gabe gently removed her hand from his arm. "I'll deal with your . . . friend, Tess. Now, why don't you give me a rundown of his symptoms, tell me what I can expect. Then we can make a plan on how the two of us can work together to get him well."

The combination of too little sleep and too much Gabe Cameron had scrambled her brains. She wanted to maintain her defenses against him, but the other emotions rolling through her were weakening the walls. "I'd feel better if I took care . . ."

Gabe settled the question by dragging the damp cloth across Andrew's furry chest in a brisk, efficient manner. Watching him, Tess idly wondered if her friend would miss her gentle touch.

"The symptoms?" Gabe repeated.

She shook her head and summoned her thoughts. She could indulge anger later. With crisp, concise sentences, she explained about the fever, chills, and sweats. She told him how Andrew's periods of lucidity alternated with long stretches of delirium. "He's had bouts of vomiting, although those seem to have subsided in the past few hours."

"Sounds like your diagnosis was right the first time," Gabe observed. "It's malaria. We're not gonna catch anything from him."

"No, it's not malaria," she said firmly. "Like I said, it's different this time."

He shrugged. "Fine, I won't argue. What do you want me to do once I get him washed down? Do we need to feed him?"

"He was awake earlier, and we ate supper then." She filled a glass from a pitcher and approached the bed. "He needs water most of all. If you'll hold him up, I'll try to get some down him. Then I want to change the bedding."

Gabe appropriated the glass saying, "I'll do it. You know, he might not be hungry, but I sure am. Think you could rustle me up some groceries while I water up the patient?"

Tess rubbed her eyes. Gabe's manner made it obvious he didn't intend to allow her to touch Andrew again. Fine. As long as her friend received the care he needed, she could use the help. Besides, she needed to put some distance between herself and the uninvited guest before she lost her composure. "I don't cook here in Andrew's house, but I do have makings for a sandwich in the back parlor. You'll change his sheets?"

"I'll take care of him. My word on it, Tess. As long as you feed me, that is. And while I'm eating, I want to hear about how the divorce never happened."

The divorce. She would almost consider breaking quarantine to avoid speaking about her father's lie and its aftermath.

She'd had plenty of time to think on the train ride through West Texas, and she had spent much of it analyzing her feelings where her husband was concerned. She'd been angry with Gabe for twelve long years, and it would take more than learning that her father had lied to him to erase it. True, in her grief she had pushed her husband away, but the man had displayed his feelings with his feet, had he not? He'd left, hadn't stayed and fought for her, fought for them.

He hadn't loved her enough, and she had paid a terrible price for it. A price she'd be hanged if she would speak of while short of sleep and holding onto her control by a corset string.

Sighing, she exited Andrew's bedroom and took the outside path to the back parlor. Like all the homes here in Aurora Springs, the house Andrew normally shared with Colonel Jasper Wilhoit was built in an L-shape. In this case, an entry hall separated the two bedrooms in the front of the house. The parlor and bathroom stretched toward the back and were accessible from both the back porch and Jasper's bedroom. For the length of the quarantine, Tess and the colonel had traded beds, and as Tess buttered bread for Gabe's sandwich, she gazed longingly in that direction.

The oblivion of sleep sounded good right now. Ordinarily, Tess wasn't one to run away from conflict, but the thought of slogging her way through both lies and truth with Gabe at this particular time made her shudder. Run from conflict? Shoot, she'd fly away if she could.

She made his sandwich, then placed it and a glass of buttermilk on a table. Then, once again eyeing Colonel Wilhoit's feather mattress, she wondered if she dared lie down. She probably should return to the sickroom, but Gabe said he'd see to Andrew. She trusted him to keep his word.

She hadn't done more than catnap for the past two days. He said he wanted to discuss the past and she would certainly need all her defenses for that. *I'm not ready.*

Tess all but dove for the bed.

For the second time that day, Gabe found Tess sleeping. Fear slithered up his spine and he hurried to lay his hand against her forehead. Cool.

He breathed a sigh of relief.

Tenderly he brushed straggling strands of hair away from her forehead, then, with a will of their own, his fingers slid into the thick, silken luster of her hair. So soft. So beautiful. Warm, flowing honey that glinted with hints of fire.

Without conscious thought, he gently pulled the hairpins free. Her tresses tumbled in a shimmering waterfall, some of which he caught and lifted to his face. He knew the scent. Lavender and innocence. It swept him back to a time and place where the fragrance surrounded him by day. And by night.

They lay side by side on a quilt spread across a mattress of spring green grass in a meadow bordered by fragrant pines. Above them, the moonless sky displayed the stars in frosty splendor. Today was Tess Rawlins' fifteenth birthday and Gabe's universe had just been sent reeling with a dismaying discovery.

His best friend Billy's little sister made him horny.

Thank God it was dark.

He never dreamed anything this shocking would happen when he accepted Billy's invitation to supper earlier this evening. He was going mainly for the birthday cake. Lila Mae Wilson cooked for the Rawlins, and she baked one mean devil's food cake. Billy had promised Gabe an extra big slice.

The trouble started when Tess began opening her presents. Gabe was full as a tick on fried chicken and chocolate cake and feeling guilty that he hadn't brought a gift. So he had tossed out an offer to teach her some star lore, and Tess had taken him up on the idea. Billy had come along with them—it wouldn't be proper for Tess to meet Gabe alone—but he was propped up against a pine tree some ten feet away, sound asleep and sawing logs.

So here they were, he and the birthday girl, practically alone, her hair spilling against his shoulder and smelling like lavender. And him with a cock hard enough to drive a railroad spike.

Billy would kill him.

"I know the Big and Little Dippers," Tess said, gesturing toward the sky. "Where's Gemini the Twins? That's my astrological sign, is it not?"

Gabe cleared his throat. "Yeah."

"When is your birthday, Gabe? What's your sign?"

He closed his eyes. "I just turned seventeen, myself. On May second. I'm Taurus, Taurus the Bull."

And he knew he'd best find a distraction and get his pecker under control or he'd be one bull seeing red—red from his own bloody nose once Billy got through with him.

Stargazing. That's what he needed to think about. Hadn't the sky distracted him dang near every day of his life?

"You want me to show you Gemini. All right, Tess.

Can you see my arm well enough to follow my finger?"

"I think so."

He helped her locate the constellation she sought, then said, "The brighter of the twins is Pollux. The orange one, see it?"

"Yes. I do."

"Pollux is also one end of the necklace of jewels the sky is sporting tonight. Look. It arcs from west-northwest and ends in the southeast. Five bright jewels." He pointed to the stars as he named them. "Pollux, then Regulus, the blue-white star that's the heart of Leo the lion. Then Mars, the middle jewel of the necklace. It's the brightest."

"Do you mean that yellowish orange star?"

Dang, but she had a sweet little voice. How come he'd never noticed it before? "Planet. That's why it doesn't twinkle."

He sensed her inquiring stare. "If that's Mars, why isn't it red? I thought Mars was the red planet."

"It appears more red when it's closer to the earth."

"Oh."

"The fourth jewel is—"

"Let me guess," she interrupted, catching his hand in one of hers while her free arm drew an arc from northwest to southeast. "Is that it? That blue-white one? It's like the first, like Pollux."

"Yep, Spica. It's the brightest star in the constellation Virgo." He inhaled a deep breath of lavender-scented air. Virgo the virgin. Tess the virgin.

He sat up abruptly. "The last jewel is just above

the southeastern horizon. Look. It's Antares, in the constellation Scorpio. The Scorpion."

"Scorpions are red like that."

"In this case, the name means 'not Mars.' They say the ancients who named it thought its color made it a rival of Mars. Natural competitors, I guess."

Tess sat up, too, and when she lifted her face toward the sky, starlight cast a milky, luminous glow across her skin. Gabe swallowed hard.

Delight lit her voice. "A necklace made of stars. What a wonderful idea." Giving his hand an innocent squeeze, she added, "I'll never look at the stars in the same way again. You've given me the most wonderful birthday gift, Gabe. Thank you so very much."

She leaned over to bestow the same sisterly peck on the cheek she always gave Billy, the same kiss she'd given Gabe a dozen times before. At the last minute, without stopping to think of how foolish an act it would be, he turned his head.

Their lips touched. They both froze.

Tess pulled back. Gabe pursued.

She sighed and surrendered, and Gabe decided that kissing Tess Rawlins was a sweeter treat than Lila Mae's cake.

When she woke her brother a few minutes later and told Gabe a shy good-night, he realized he need not look above him to catch a last look at the distant suns.

Tess Rawlins had stars shining in her eyes. He reckoned a mirror would show him that his own were twinkling, too.

★　　　★　　　★

Fourteen years and a thousand heartbreaks later, Tess's husband said softly, "But the light died, didn't it, sweetheart? I killed it."

He allowed her hair to slip through his fingers and spill down onto the pillow. "Now I need to know why you didn't bury it."

Why the hell hadn't she divorced him? That question and others had plagued him ever since the fair. Had concern for public scorn stopped her? Possibly, but he doubted it. This was Texas, after all. Considering the land had been settled by miscreants and thieves, something like divorce didn't carry the social stigma here that it did in other parts of the world. Still, he wanted her to tell him why she had not acted.

Another topic Gabe wanted to discuss was why her father turned her out after the fire. The very thought of it sent shivers running up Gabe's spine and made him wish Stanford Rawlins was still alive so he could kill him. Tess had been all of seventeen years old at the time. Where had she gone? Who had helped her? Why hadn't she come to him? She could have found him if she'd tried. The name change wouldn't have stopped her for long because mutual friends had known where he was. They'd have told her if she'd asked.

You know the answer to that, Montana. She never wanted to see your sorry hide again. She told you that to your face. She hated you. Almost as much as you hated yourself.

Tess awoke slowly, deliciously. Stretching, she inhaled a deep breath, filling her lungs with air. Fragrance teased her, a spicy, musky scent she associated with happiness, pleasure, and . . . Gabe.

With eyes closed she turned her face, seeking to hold onto the aroma, the dream. Humming with languid desire, she sank into her memories.

"Someday I'm going to discover a new comet," her beau said. *"When I do, I'm going to name it after you."*

Tess glanced away from the telescope's lens and shot Gabe a scolding glare. "Now you made me lose Saturn's rings."

He grabbed her hand and pulled her into his arms. "You make me lose my head. If Billy or your father knew you sneaked out here to meet me like this, they'd have my liver for lunch."

She rose up on her tip-toes to press a quick kiss against his lips. "Let's not fight about this tonight, please? We're not doing anything wrong."

"We're coming awfully darned close, though. And it is wrong to lie to your family. I can hardly look Billy in the eyes anymore."

"Gabe, not tonight. It's my seventeenth birthday and I don't want to spend our time together bickering."

Silence dragged out. She felt his resistance, and then his surrender as the source of his tension changed. "Really? And how do you want to spend it, Venus?"

In answer, she tugged his head down to hers. Their lips met, clung together. That familiar, delicious fire began zinging through her blood.

Together, they sank to the pillow of green grass. Gabe guided her gently down onto her back, his mouth leaving hers to nibble its way down her neck. His nimble fingers worked the buttons at her bodice, then slipped inside to caress her bare skin. "*No chemise again, Tess? Naughty girl.*"

She moaned as his hands smoothed across her breasts, cupping and kneading. Tess arched her back, offering, craving to be suckled. His mouth closed around her nipple and she cried out with pleasure.

Not the memory of pleasure.

Here and now, God-it's-been-so-long-and-it-feels-like-heaven bliss.

This wasn't a dream anymore.

Tess froze. The familiar scent. The heated weight of a hard body atop hers. The rasp of bare skin against bare skin.

Gabe Cameron was really in her bed.

Keeping her eyes closed, she took a minute to consider what to do. A long, lovely, minute during which he switched to the other breast. She seriously considered stretching her internal reflection to five or maybe even ten minutes. A half an hour would be splendid.

Her dress lay tangled around her waist. By touch she determined he sported nothing more than cotton drawers. She tried hard to summon up a little shame. She failed. From the very beginning, she'd been bold where Gabe was concerned. She had loved him with every fiber of her being, and she'd never considered what they did together wrong.

But then was then and now was now. A dozen years had passed. He wasn't the same man, nor she the same woman. This couldn't be love; it had to be lust.

It had to be.

And oh, how she wanted to give in to the weakness.

But she shouldn't. Nothing between them was settled. Indulging in lust today wouldn't be honest. It might belittle the memory of their love, and those memories were too precious to taint.

Regretfully, Tess realized she couldn't take the risk.

She opened her eyes and faced the moment, or more precisely, she faced the thick mahogany waves atop Gabe's head. Her fingers itched to slide through his hair, but instead she pushed against his shoulders and affected outrage. "What do you think you are doing?"

Gabe slowly lifted his head. His gray eyes watched her with that heavy-lidded, sleepily aroused look she remembered so well. So many times during the few months they lived together they had awakened in the process of making love, one of them having reached for the other in his or her dreams. Now he gave her a drowsy, sexy smile and pain twisted through her. Oh, but she had missed that particular grin. "Wake up, Gabe. What are you doing in my bed?"

His eyes focused, and he blinked once, then twice. The second time an accompanying wince betrayed the knowledge of where he was—and when. Tess held her breath, waiting for his next reaction in order to formulate her own response. She expected him to act defensive or perhaps apologetic. What she didn't anticipate was regret. Regret and maybe even dismay.

Dismay. Well, isn't that flattering.

His reaction gouged at her vulnerabilities and pricked her pride, so she adopted the challenging, snippy tone that used to drive him crazy and demanded, "Get out of my bed. You don't belong here."

He didn't move an inch, although the flare of temper in his eyes told her he still didn't care for snippy. Anticipation skittered up Tess's spine, and in that moment, she felt more alive than she'd felt in years. Fighting with Gabe had always been stimulating; making up pure heaven.

"Where the hell was I supposed to sleep? With the pig? Sorry, darlin', but the floor is hard and cold, and this bed is big enough for two. And besides . . ." He lowered his voice to a low, silky drawl. "According to you I'm still your husband. That gives me every right to be here." His gaze dropped, made a deliberate, assessing journey that ended on her still-naked breasts. "That gives me rights, period."

Yes, screamed her body.

No, hollered her good sense.

"I'm confused," she admitted with a cry.

"I'm shocked," came Andrew's voice from the doorway.

With a yelp, Tess pushed Gabe off of her, yanked the sheet up to her chin, and stared in distress toward the crowd of people standing in the open doorway. "Andrew? Twinkle?"

"Us, too," Amy Baker said, clapping her hands over her husband Jack's eyes, her wedding ring flashing right along with her bright blue eyes. "And Colonel Jasper. I must say, I'm surprised at you, Tess."

"Well, I'm impressed," Twinkle said, fingering a dangling earring as her measured gaze swept over Gabe's bare chest.

"What's this all about?" Colonel Wilhoit demanded. His medals lifted as he filled his lungs with air. "We don't have time for any nonsense. Tell her, Twinkle."

"Let me catch my breath," the older woman replied, fanning her face with her hand. "The last time I saw a chest that intriguing I was—"

"Hush, everyone," Tess demanded, heat staining its way up her neck and burning her cheeks. She'd never been so embarrassed in her life. This was even worse than when her father discovered her and Gabe making love in the Rolling R's barn. Positive she didn't want to hear Twinkle finish that sentence, she took the conversation in a different direction. "What's happened? What about the quarantine? Andrew, why are you out of bed?"

"His fever broke about two this morning," Gabe's voice rumbled from beside her. "That's when I decided to get some sleep." He reached for the trousers lying at the end of the bed and said, "Ladies, consider this fair warning. I'm fixing to put on my pants."

At that Jack Baker mimicked his wife's actions and covered her eyes with his hands as Gabe rolled out of bed. Twinkle folded her arms, obviously impressed.

"Tess, who *is* this man?" Andrew scowled, his freckles glowing bright against a complexion paled by sickness.

Tess turned a pleading gaze toward Twinkle. "Edna?"

Twinkle grimaced. Tess only used her real name when she lost all patience. "Rosie broke the quarantine, but Andrew didn't figure it mattered because he was feeling so much better." She tossed Andrew a chiding look and added, "Without knowing you had a guest—Andrew didn't bother to tell us—we thought to let you sleep in. But then the trouble started."

"Trouble? What trouble?"

"It's bad business, Tess," Colonel Wilhoit said. "You won't be happy about this."

Sheet clutched tightly to her chest, Tess reared up and demanded. "Explain."

They all started talking at once, and Tess couldn't make any sense out of their words. When Gabe put two fingers in his mouth and blew out a shrill, ear-piercing whistle, she tossed him a grateful glance. He said, "One at a time, please. Missus Twinkle, why don't you start."

Twinkle nodded, got distracted for a moment while he buttoned his pants, then said, "Rosie got into your star shed, Tess. She ate up last month's log and made a general mess of things. Worst of all, I think she might have damaged your new telescope."

Dismay blew through Tess like a dust storm. She'd ordered the telescope months ago, and it had been waiting for her in Eagle Gulch upon her return from Dallas. Busy nursing Andrew, she had yet to have the chance to cart it up to the observation post. "Oh, Rosie."

"Don't blame her, Tess," Colonel Wilhoit said, stepping forward and squaring his shoulders. "It's my fault. I'm afraid I didn't secure the door good enough last time I went in the shed."

"Oh, enough about Rosie," Jack Baker exclaimed, tugging his wife's hands away from his eyes. "The telescope isn't the worst of it. Tess, your beau rode in a few minutes ago. Captain Robards brought word of trouble. It's serious, Tess."

Her stomach sinking, Tess ignored her husband's curious look. "How serious?"

Colonel Wilhoit harrumphed. "There's been another incidence of vandalism out at the railroad spur construction sight. A fire destroyed a tool shed. The Ranger says somebody claimed they saw an Aurora Springs wagon at the scene of the crime."

Tess hung her head and sighed. "Oh, Twink. What did you do this time?"

"That's just it," the gray-haired woman said, her voice hazy with bewilderment. "It's not me. I didn't do anything. I'm innocent."

"Innocent? You?" Tess repeated.

"Yes." Twinkle nodded briskly, then added, "The problem is . . . Oh, Tess, I hate to tell you this. . . . Captain Robards wants to talk to Doc. He said the railroad wants Doc arrested."

"Doc!" Tess froze, her heart twisting. "They want to arrest Doc?"

"Captain Robards says an eyewitness claims he set the fire."

Oh, no. Tess's breath left her body in a rush. "And Will? What about Will?"

Twinkle shook her head. "I don't know. Robards didn't say a word about Will. Surely he would have mentioned if the Rangers were looking for Will, too. If Doc did this mischief on his way to the Big Bend, he kept the boy hidden."

"That's right, Tess," Colonel Wilhoit said. "I don't believe young Will is in trouble."

For a long moment, nobody spoke and the only sound to be heard was the *tick tick tick* of the mantle clock. Tess's mind was a whirl. Doc would never destroy the railroad's property, never. No matter how appealing the idea. Nor would he put Will into harm's way. Would he?

While she thought through the problem, Gabe glanced from Tess, to the Aurorians, then back to Tess again. "So," he said, pointing a thumb toward the crowd. "Which one is Doc?"

A groan slipped from Tess's lips. For one short second she debated dumping the entire problem in her husband's lap. But Gabriel "Whip" Montana's reputation held her back. This man might go after Doc and do him in.

And if Doc has led Will into trouble, I'll want to kill the man myself.

*T*ess ordered everyone but Twinkle out of the house,
her excuse the need to put herself to rights. Her distracted air told Gabe she really wanted time to think.
He could almost see the wheels turning in her head,
but she kept her lips sealed tight as a jar of pickled
beets. Her reticence didn't sit well with Gabe. Once
upon a time, she would have shared her thoughts with
him. Now, she hustled him out the door with nary a
nod, leaving him to the not-so-tender mercies of the
inhabitants of Aurora Springs.

They surrounded him like a pack of dogs. He was
the bone.

"So you're Cameron?"

" 'Bout time you showed up."

"Nervy of you to jump right back into her bed."

Gabe ignored them as he shrugged into the shirt
he'd grabbed on his way outside. The early morning
air carried a crisp hint of autumn, and sunshine felt
good on his face as he lifted it toward the sky. Even

better was the unmistakable aroma of coffee that floated past him on the breeze. Gabe turned his head toward the scent and caught the swish of a sorrel's tail from the corner of his eyes. His?

He took a step toward the barn and peered through the open doorway. Yep, both of them. "I see y'all found my horses. Do I need to get them fed and watered?"

The young husband said, "I took care of it."

"Thanks. I appreciate it. Are you Doc?"

"I'm Jack Baker and I want you to tell us why you were 'taking care' of Tess."

His wife jumped in. "You better not have hurt her."

The uniformed gentleman swelled up like a peacock and demanded, "Who are you and what were you doing to poor Tess?"

Bunch of busy hens, Gabe thought, grimacing. He was tempted to check his ankles to see if they had "Peck me here" painted on them. He cleared his throat. "Sounds to me like we all have a question or two. If y'all will button your beaks a moment, I'll start the answers."

One by one, they quieted. Gabe let the silence rest in his ears a moment, knowing that as soon as he spoke, the noise would start up all over again. Then, tipping his hat toward Mrs. Baker, he said, "I am Tess's husband, but my name is Gabe Montana. Some folks call me Whip."

"Whip Montana?" Jack Baker repeated. "The schoolhouse hero?"

"You're not Tess's husband!" his wife exclaimed. "Gabe Cameron is her husband's name."

"I still go by Gabe. I got stuck with the Whip a

few years back when I used one to my advantage while trying to prevent a train robbery."

Andrew shook his head. "I don't understand. Tess didn't mention any name change when she said you might be visiting."

"Look, call me anything you want as long as it's not Cameron. I'm of a serious mind about that."

As the Aurorians shared a look, Gabe nodded toward the man he'd found in bed with his wife. "I could use some introductions myself. You're Andrew . . . ?"

"Ross. Andrew Ross." He folded his arms across a fringed, buckskin shirt and nodded toward the others as he said their names. "Jack and Amy Baker. Colonel Jasper Wilhoit. And Twinkle is inside with Tess. We are all very good friends of Tess's. In fact, we refer to ourselves as family."

"All right." That didn't surprise him. Tess always had been one to take in strays. "I heard a couple other names, too. Doc and Will are where?"

"Gone," Tess said from the doorway to the house. She wore a pretty blue dress that matched her eyes, and she strode purposefully across the porch and down the front steps.

Admiration and a fair dose of lust warmed Gabe at the sight of his wife. The woman was all grown up and showing a side of herself he'd never seen before. She wore authority like a mantle, determination like a lance. The air around her sizzled with energy. She was a Valkyrie prepared for battle. And Gabe all but swallowed his tongue at her beauty.

Their gazes locked and Gabe fantasized about surrender.

Amy Baker broke the spell by demanding, "Is it true, Tess? You're married to this man, to Whip Montana?"

Without looking away, Tess shook her head. "Yes, I married him. But I married Gabe Cameron."

"I'm not him, Tess," Gabe warned. "And you should be glad for it, too."

"I still don't understand," Andrew repeated.

Gabe looked away first, and Tess said, "No matter what he calls himself now, this is the Gabe you've all heard about. I see I should have provided more details when I told you he might be visiting, but in all honesty, I was more concerned with seeing to Andrew's recovery. Now, I want to think this situation with Doc through a bit before I speak with Lionel Robards, so I'll check my star shed first. Is he waiting at my house?"

"No," Jack answered. "The Ranger captain is in the kitchen. Amy fixed him breakfast."

"I wouldn't put it past him to have made this all up in order to make another run at your biscuits," Tess said, tossing Amy a smile. "Haven't you noticed how often he visits right at breakfast time? That's no coincidence, believe me."

The young wife ducked her head bashfully. "Oh, Tess. It's not that. I think he's simply so anxious to see you he makes the trip faster every time he visits."

"He does cut quite a dashing figure," the colonel observed, darting a sly look toward Gabe. "Would you like us to entertain him until you're ready to see him, dear?"

"No." She shook her head. "Just go about your

normal business. I'll check in with everyone once Lionel leaves. Then we can figure out what to do next."

Without so much as a word to him, Tess headed for one of the sheds. Gabe stood and watched her until she disappeared inside. He was entranced by this new side of Tess's personality. She'd always been confident in herself, but she'd never acted so . . . assertive. In fact, the Tess he'd married used to express her opinion, then look to him to make the decision. Now she up and told him and everyone else what to do. Damned if he didn't find the change in her intriguing. "I wonder what other surprises she has up her sleeve."

"Looked to me like you had a good enough view of our Tess's sleeves as it was," grumbled the colonel before strolling toward the barn.

The Bakers walked hand-in-hand into the house next to Andrew's, and Twinkle muttered something about fall tomatoes before striding toward the garden. That left Gabe to track down the Ranger by himself which suited him perfectly. It worked better for a man to meet his wife's "dashing beau" by himself.

He followed the scent of coffee to the free-standing building that served as a kitchen and sauntered inside. A pot of the aromatic brew sat on a stove and a pretty-boy Ranger occupied a chair at a long table eating cream gravy and biscuits with a fork.

Gabe knew a number of Rangers across the state, but this fellow was a stranger to him. Broad shouldered and blond, the Ranger had those classically handsome features that women sighed over. Gabe disliked him on sight.

"Morning," he said casually, striding toward the

stove. He poured a cup of coffee and joined him at the table, straddling a chair to sit down.

"Yes?" asked the Ranger captain. He frowned and set down his fork.

Gabe eyed Lionel Robards' plate. "You're a fork man, hmm? Personally, I always considered biscuits and good cream gravy as one of life's perfect finger-lickin' foods."

"Who *are* you?"

Gabe debated his choice of reply. Considering the stink he'd made recently about the ineptitude displayed by some companies of Rangers, his reputation might well have preceded him. This fellow would button his lips at the mention of Gabe's name. However, if Robards considered himself Tess's beau, he'd damn sure shut up the moment Gabe named himself as her husband. He set down his coffee and extended his hand. "Gabe Montana. Glad to make your acquaintance, Captain Robards."

"Montana." The Ranger shook his hand with a firm grip, then eyed him studiously and added, "Hmm . . . Whip Montana?" At Gabe's reluctant nod, he continued, "I know you. I heard you came through Eagle Gulch a few days back. You're the special investigator for the Brazos Valley Rail Company."

His moss green eyes narrowing suspiciously, Captain Robards continued, "I've been wondering what brought you to this part of the world. Not the vandalism along the rail line, surely. The Brazos Valley isn't building this spur and besides, the Rangers are on the job of tracking down the vandals. We don't require your help."

Professional rivalry. Having run into this in the past, Gabe suppressed a sigh. He was continually amazed at how men allowed their own petty jealousies to get in the way of everything from friendship to getting the job done. He had no quarrel with honest competition, but it didn't belong in every venue. If a criminal needed catching, what did it matter who did the work as long as the villain ended up behind bars? Gabe had no patience for prima donnas, but he knew when it was best to play his cards close to his vest.

"I haven't come to Aurora Springs in an official capacity. In fact, I'm on a leave of absence from the railroad. I'm here for personal reasons."

The Ranger's eyes narrowed. "Is that so?"

Gabe nodded and lied, "I'm toying with the idea of relocating from southeast Texas, and this part of the world intrigues me. I stumbled across this place yesterday. You know, these springs are the best source of water around."

It made all the difference in the world. Robards visibly relaxed and offered an indulging smile. His teeth were white and straight. Tess would like that.

He chuckled softly. "Sorry, Mr. Montana, but if you're here in Aurora Springs hoping to buy land in this canyon, I'm afraid you've wasted the trip. I had my eye on this property myself but the owners refused to entertain any offers."

"Really?" Gabe paused to sip his coffee. "And who holds the deed on these acres?"

"Well . . ." Robards paused to take another bite of biscuit. "Tess's name is on the paper, but she says it is community property. You should understand that the inhabitants of Aurora Springs are turned a bit differently than most, but then, you've probably already seen that yourself."

Turned a bit differently was a polite way to say it, Gabe thought. "I did notice the camels."

The Ranger nodded. "Castor and Pollux, named after the stars. They're descendants of Jefferson Davis's experiment with the importation of dromedaries to be employed for military purposes. Those animals fit right at home here in Aurora Springs. Now, don't get me wrong," he hastened to add, "I think the Aurorians are for the most part fine people, but one can't deny their . . . how shall I put it . . . eccentricities."

"I've never met a woman named Twinkle before," Gabe observed as he idly sipped his coffee and tried to think of a way to best broach the subject of this man's courtship of his wife. He wanted to settle this beau nonsense before Tess showed up.

Robards waved his fork. "Don't sell Twinkle short. If you can overlook her colorful dress and misguided beliefs, you'll soon realize the woman is a treasure."

"What do you mean 'misguided beliefs'?"

"Never mind. I shouldn't have said anything."

"No, please. I won't judge the woman. I'm just curious."

After a moment's silence, Robards said, "It's the . . ." he held up his hands and wiggled his fingers in the air ". . . lights."

"Lights?" The word combined with the motions grabbed Gabe's attention, diverting his thoughts from Tess.

Robards snapped his fingers and sat back in his chair.

"That's right. You're new to the area. I guess you are not familiar with the tales of the Aurora Springs Ghost Lights, or Kissing Stars like Tess calls them."

"Can't say that I am."

"It's a long story, but suffice it to say the Aurorians claim they see unexplainable bouncing balls of light in the night sky near here," said the Ranger. "Twinkle thinks they're ghosts. She says her crystal ball is energized by the stars and that's how she contacts souls on the other side."

Gabe scratched his chin. "I saw her séance tent at the Texas State Fair. I thought she did all that as an act—not that she believed it."

"Oh, she believes it. Everyone around here believes something foolish about the Mystery Lights. Take the Yankee colonel, for instance. He's a water witcher and he told me that the magnetic energies put off by the stars empowers his divining rods. He believes the star-charged rods will lead him not to water, but to diamonds."

"A treasure hunter," Gabe said, wondering what life path took a much-decorated soldier in such a direction.

"Not just any treasure. It must be diamonds. Why, the man happened to stumble across a cache of stolen gold—stagecoach robberies were regular occurrences in these badlands until recently—and the colonel brought it back to Aurora Springs as an afterthought. He wasn't looking for gold, you see. Just diamonds."

"Interesting approach," Gabe observed. He thought of the other residents of Aurora Springs, the Bakers and Andrew Ross, and wondered about their beliefs concerning these so-called stars. And Tess, of course. Surely she had professional reasons for being here.

Robards must have followed his line of thinking. "As far as I can tell, Miss Cameron is the only one here in Aurora Springs with a sane approach to the story. She claims to be searching for a scientific explanation for the lights' presence."

Gabe nodded. That fit with what he knew of Tess. "Have you seen these spooklights?"

The Ranger scoffed, but his gaze shifted away from Gabe. "Of course not. There is nothing out there to see. It's just a bunch of foolishness that I am afraid is causing trouble."

Gabe polished off his coffee, then rose to refill his cup. "What trouble?"

"Oh, I don't think I should go into all of that."

"You mean the fire at the rail yard?"

The Ranger's eyes narrowed, but before he could reply the door swung open. Tess swept inside, still in her warrior goddess mode. She halted in the middle of the room, leveled a frown at Gabe, then turned to Robards. "Lionel? What's this nonsense about a fire?"

The Ranger stood, his mouth stretching into a smile. "Good morning, Tess. May I say you look exceptionally beautiful in that dress. The shade of blue is a perfect match to your exquisite eyes."

She waved off the compliment. "Doc didn't do anything and you know it, Lionel."

He sighed. "Honey, I'm sorry, but an eyewitness claims he saw Doc at the scene of the crime."

Gabe frowned. *Honey?*

"Who?" she snapped, bracing her hands on her hips.

He glanced at Gabe and said, "Perhaps we should discuss this in private?"

Gabe settled back in his chair and stretched out his legs, crossing them at the ankles. He wasn't going anywhere. Tess either knew it or didn't care because she glossed right over the objection and asked, "Who is the eyewitness?"

Shrugging, the Ranger captain gave in. "Lizard Johnson."

Tess scoffed. "Lionel, be serious. Who says he saw Doc at the railroad spur?"

"I told you. Lizard Johnson." The Ranger set down his fork and pushed away his plate. "I interviewed him myself after the sheriff questioned him. You know I'm always trying to look out for you, Tess. Lizard says he saw Doc at the supply yard just minutes before the fire broke out. The man even carried a torch." Sympathy dimmed his eyes as he added, "I knew how much this would upset you."

Tess started shaking her head and didn't stop. "He didn't do it. This charge is ridiculous and you know it. Poor Lizard hasn't had a sober day in the past six months, perhaps even the past six years."

Robards said, "I know, honey. And I'll admit I have my doubts about his claims. That's why I came right away to warn you. I'd expect the sheriff later this afternoon."

Tess grimaced, sighed, and sank onto the bench that ran along one side of the table. She rubbed her forehead. "He really intends to make an arrest?"

"Yes, he does." The Ranger rose from his chair and walked around the table. He met Gabe's gaze, threw a pointed look from Gabe to the door—a look Gabe ignored—then he took Tess's hand in his and lowered his voice. Gabe pointed his ear their direction.

"Please, Tess. Don't you think the time has come? Let me protect you. Even if you're not ready for marriage, let me and a couple of my men move out to Aurora Springs. I'll be able to prove you and your friends' innocence if and when more trouble happens. And, if I'm headquartered here, I know I can convince the sheriff to hold off on moving against Doc. I can keep him out of jail, Tess. Let me."

The corners of her mouth lifted in a brief smile. "He's not here. He's safe."

"What?" The Ranger froze.

"Doc is making another trip down to the Big Bend area, down near the Dead Horse Range. Will went with him."

"The Big Bend?" Now the captain reared back. In an incredulous tone he asked, "Why did he go there? That place isn't fit for living."

As Tess launched into a story about cave paintings and the mystery lights, Gabe watched Robards closely. Tess's news had disturbed him more than just a little.

Gabe snagged a biscuit off a serving plate in the middle of the table and took a healthy bite. Curious reaction, he thought. Robards wasn't telling all. He'd bet another biscuit on it.

"I need to get a message to them," Tess finished. She reached out and rested her hand on the Ranger's forearm. The warrior goddess turned manipulator, both her eyes and voice pleading as she asked, "Could you do that for me? That's how I could use your help."

Robards winced and cut a quick glance toward Gabe. "Uh, I'm scheduled to patrol the northwest for the next few weeks."

"I know it is asking a lot, Lionel, but it would mean so very much to me if you could see a way to juggle your schedule. If your offer to help is sincere . . . ?"

"I do want to help you. I just don't know if I can get away to the Big Bend."

Her voice was soft and haunting as she said, "But I must warn Doc."

"And just who is he, Tess?" Gabe interrupted. She glanced in his direction briefly, exasperation and a flash of guilt obvious in the look. The guilt made him uneasy. "I thought you said Aurora Springs doesn't have a doctor?"

"He's not a medical doctor. He's a scientist like me. Doc is a nickname, a joke that stuck." She refocused her attention on the Ranger. "Perhaps some of your men could go?"

While Tess tried to convince the other man to do her bidding, Gabe pondered the facts he had picked up. That led to more questions. He'd gathered that Will was a boy, but who was this Doc? Why the guilt? Could he be Tess's lover?

He rolled the idea around his brain. Tess and another man. His wife and a lover. Gabe grimaced as the sour taint of jealousy coated his mouth and a burning sensation stabbed his gut. His gaze focused on Tess, then shifted to the Ranger, then returned to Tess again. Was that why she high-tailed it away from him at the state fair? Did she have a guilty conscience?

Gabe hadn't been celibate during the past dozen

years, but then he'd had every reason to believe him-self divorced. Tess didn't have that excuse. Tess knew she was a married woman.

Tess knew she was a married woman.

Gabe dragged a hand along his stubbled jaw and considered the willful beauty engaged in hammering out a concession from the enamored Texas Ranger. He'd known her inside and out twelve years ago, and he simply couldn't picture her character undergoing that enormous a change. Nope, Gabe would bet his favorite pair of boots that ol' Doc wasn't his wife's lover. Tess wouldn't commit adultery.

However, twelve years was a long time to do without.

Nagged by doubts, he raked her with his gaze. Tess and another man. The idea made him want to puke.

Then she glanced in his direction and the doubts faded away. Nah, Tess was true blue. He'd still put his money on her faithfulness.

Honesty was something else. It hadn't escaped his notice that she wouldn't look him good in the eyes. He tuned into the conversation. ". . . pay you for your effort. The pictographs are in the caves up in the mountains."

The captain nodded reluctantly. Tess flashed a beau-tiful smile and leaned over to kiss his cheek. Gabe's grip tightened on his coffee cup.

His wife stood and crossed to a shelf in one corner of the room. She took down a jar and removed a wad of cash. Slipping a sealed envelope from her pocket, she handed both the note and the money to the Ranger. Robards slid them into his pocket.

Gabe was disgusted. The man took money for doing his job? What a pig. Just another example of the depths to which some outfits in the Ranger corps had sunk.

"I'll ride back to Eagle Gulch and outfit myself and a few of my men for the trip. I'll deliver your note, honey. And when I get back . . . well . . . we'll talk." He reached out and touched her cheek. "You know my feelings for you. You know how much I care. Say yes this time. Let me take care of you, watch over you. You know you need a man."

Gabe had had enough. "Isn't it handy that she already has one, then?"

Tess fired a warning glare. "Yes, I have Andrew and the colonel and Jack to watch over matters here."

"And me," he shot back, not quite ready to give up.

"Temporarily," Tess assured Lionel Robards. "Mr. Montana is just passing through."

Gabe just about chewed a hole in his tongue trying to keep quiet. Then when his wife stood on her tiptoes and kissed the Ranger full on the mouth, his hand automatically went for the whip he often carried coiled on his hip. It wasn't there, of course, because he'd quit carrying it after that last tangle with Bodine. Rage had gotten the better of Gabe then, and afterwards he'd decided a clean gunshot to the head would have been better for everyone all around. *The Ranger doesn't know how lucky he is,* Gabe thought. He wouldn't kill a man for kissing his wife, but a whipping wasn't out of the question.

Then, not a second too soon, Captain Robards took his leave. Tess heaved a sigh, turned, and made a beeline for the coffee pot. Gabe slowly shook his head. "I must say you've surprised me, *honey*. He's not the type I'd have figured you'd want courting you."

"I don't invite him here, Gabe."

"Good," he replied, satisfaction washing through him. "I'm glad to know you have better sense than that. The man is a Texas Ranger. I can't believe he took money from you to play pony express. And what message was so all-fired important anyway that you felt you had to pay the man to deliver it, anyway? Who is this Doc person, Tess? What is he to you?" And then, because he wanted to hear her denial, he couldn't help but add, "Are the two of you more than friends?"

She slammed the coffee pot down onto the stove, then whirled to face him. "Don't you try to make this something dirty. Doc is . . ."

She broke off abruptly. The flames of anger burning in her eyes died, replaced by something that made Gabe's stomach take another sinking dip. Guilt again.

Sonofabitch. He should have stopped while he was ahead. He didn't like this one little bit.

Distrust nagged at him. Resentment coiled in his gut. Dammit, she'd run him off once, ran off from him once, but this time they would have it out. They had unfinished business and she owed him answers. Gabe set down his coffee. "Tess, you're not putting me off any longer. We've gotta talk."

Tess heard the steel in his voice and knew her moment of truth was upon her. On the train home from Dallas, she'd spent some time debating how to face this man and his questions if and when this moment ever arrived, so she was prepared. More or less.

At least she'd had a good night's sleep. She was in control of herself. She could face the questions he would throw at her, and hopefully toss a few back at him herself. First, however, she needed to determine just how much of the truth to reveal.

Whip Montana wasn't Gabe Cameron. The years had changed him. The tragedy of Billy's death had changed him. How would he respond to the tales she had to tell? Despite the grief he'd caused her, Tess didn't want to cause Gabe needless pain. He had been hurt enough.

True, but your world had been rocked, also. Tess had been forced to deal with matters no woman should endure.

Recalling those months that followed her brother's death still made her shudder. Looking back, she recognized the trials had made her stronger, but while she lived it—during that awful, horrible time—she'd sometimes wanted to lie down and die.

Tess didn't want to put Gabe through that, not if she didn't have to. So she'd decided to pace her revelations. She'd start at the beginning, but rather than throw everything at him at once, she'd dribble out the story and use his reaction to judge just how far to go.

She cleared her throat. "Yes, Gabe, you're right. I'll be happy to address your questions, but first I need to check on Andrew and make some arrangements with the others."

He narrowed his eyes. "I don't think so. The last

time you put off talking to me I had to travel to the end of nowhere to find you again."

"You have my word I won't run this time," she promised. "Look, I'm hungry. Let me speak with my friends, then I'll pack up a cold breakfast and we can hike up Paintbrush Mountain. The view is peaceful up there, and we won't be interrupted."

Gabe studied her for a moment, then abruptly nodded. "That sounds good. The biscuits took the edge off my appetite, but I could stand something more substantial. How about a sandwich? Ham and cheese sure sounds good."

Tess chided him with a look. "We don't eat pork here in Aurora Springs."

"No pork?"

"No pork."

He glanced around the kitchen, his brows arched. "No ham or bacon or chops?"

"Not even any drippings to flavor the beans or fry the eggs."

He reared back, appalled. "Why?"

Tess rolled her eyes. "In a word, Rosie. It wouldn't do to offend her sensibilities." When her husband's chin dropped in shock, she hastened to add, "I can't give you ham, but I can offer something else I think you might like better. I made cardamon rolls day before yesterday."

Gabe's dark eyes sparked with interest. "Two-day-old cardamon rolls? That means today they're at their prime."

Tess nodded. He'd always loved the bread she

baked, and the cardamon rolls had been his particular favorite.

He strode toward the door. "The day's a-wastin'. Let's gig this horse to a trot, shall we?"

Twenty minutes later they were headed up out of the canyon. Gabe carried a basket filled with bread and cheese and a jug of fresh milk. Tess toted along a quilt and a good dose of nervousness.

Halfway up the hill Gabe paused and gazed out over the flats. "That has to be the most desolate, lifeless place on earth."

Tess lived just beyond the northern edge of the Chihuahuan Desert. The majority of the land was rocky and sparsely vegetated, with little water and almost no trees out on the flats. Her canyon was fertile, however, fed as it was by the springs, and in the higher elevations, piñon and ponderosa pines covered the mountains.

She followed the path of Gabe's stare out across the desert where visibility stretched for miles on end. Where he saw desolation, she spied a wild, rugged beauty.

"Actually if you look closely you'll see this part of Texas is teeming with life. I can't count all the varieties of cactus and succulents, and we have plenty of animals. Jackrabbits and coyotes. Antelope. And don't forget the scorpions, snakes, and horned toads."

"Desert critters," he replied, dismissing her argument with a shake of his head. "You grew up on the edge of the Big Thicket. Don't you miss the trees?"

"Some. But the sky makes up for it. Day and night there's not a prettier sky anywhere in the world." She glanced at him, and spoke in a voice animated by the topic under discussion. "You must have noticed. Have you ever seen the stars appear so close? Some nights it feels like you could reach out and touch them."

For just a moment, she forgot his purpose for being here, recalling only the shared passion of their past. "Wait till you get a peek through my new telescope. Thank goodness Rosie didn't hurt it. I'm so anxious to get it all set up. You'll be amazed, Gabe. The view I get of Saturn even with the smaller mirror is superb. Dr. Pierce said the clarity is due to the quality of air here."

Gabe jerked as if something had poked him, and a peculiar, almost bitter look seeped across his face. "Don't, Tess. I don't want to hear it." He resumed the climb up the hill.

Taken aback, she scrambled after him, wincing when she slipped on a pile of pebbles and twisted her ankle. "Ouch. That hurt."

He stopped and turned. "You all right?"

"Yes." She pushed the hair that had spilled over her shoulder out of her face. "What is it you don't want to hear? I don't understand."

Frustration flowed across his features before he resumed the upward trek, batting harshly at a tree branch hanging low across the path. "I came to this godforsaken place for answers, not to stargaze," he snapped. "So don't talk about it. It's not going to happen."

"Leo, Lynx, and Lyra," Tess grumbled. "The man is acting strange." If she didn't know better, she'd think he was running away rather than climbing Paint-brush Mountain.

Under other circumstances, she probably would have let the subject drop, but she was nervous about the upcoming conversation, and Gabe's unusual reaction offered a timely distraction. Calling up to him, she asked, "Why would looking through a telescope put a burr beneath your saddle?"

"Forget it, Tess."

"No. I don't want to forget it. What's going on, Gabe?"

"Would you let it go?"

"What's wrong with stargazing?"

He halted abruptly. Frustration rolled off him in waves and he wrenched off his hat and raked his fingers through his hair. "God, I'd forgotten what a nag you can be. All right, Tess, you want the story? Here it is. I don't look at the stars anymore. It's a quirk of mine. One I developed a dozen years ago. Now do you see?"

"No." She'd forgotten her bonnet, so she shielded the sun from her eyes with her hand and stared hard at him. He looked so handsome, so powerful. So miserable. "I don't understand."

"You don't connect the two in your head?"

"The two of what?"

"You don't look at the stars and remember that damned night?" he asked, his tone sharp and a little wild. "You can look at the night sky without being haunted by what you were doing when the lab exploded and turned our lives to hell?"

"Oh, Gabe." Tess's heart seemed to freeze. "Are you telling me—"

"I'm saying that just the thought of studying the stars makes my blood curdle. Frankly, I'm surprised you've made a life of it. I make it a practice never to look above the treeline at night. When I'm not careful and catch a occasional glimpse, it plunges me right back into that nightmare all over again."

Tess's stomach hung somewhere around her knees. "You mean Billy."

Gabe visibly shuddered. "Yeah, I mean Billy."

He stalked off up the mountain then, but Tess remained where she stood, her breathing labored as if she'd run for miles. Troubled thoughts stung her mind like a swarm of wasps as Gabe's words cast her back to that night, that awful, horrible night.

"Look, bride-of-mine," Tess's young husband said, pointing toward the sparkling night sky. "It's a shooting star. You know what that means. Time for a little more stargazing."

Gabe caught her around the waist and lifted her feet from the ground. He nuzzled her neck as he carried her over to the quilt spread across the ground. "Gabe," she protested weakly as he lay her on her back. "We can't. We don't have time. Don't forget you promised to show Billy how to use the spectroscope."

Gabe glanced toward the sky as he stripped off his shirt, revealing a muscled torso that still took her breath away after two months of marriage. "He'll just have to wait," Gabe said. "Look, there's another. Two more. I think we're fixin' to have a full-blown meteor shower. And you know what shooting stars do to me."

When he turned his wicked gaze her way, she dismissed her feeling of apprehension and laughed. "Everything makes you randy, Gabe Cameron. You got frisky watching me peel a yam yesterday."

"It was the way you were holding it, darlin'. It got to me."

As he reached for her bodice buttons, Tess said, "You have the dirtiest mind."

"Aren't you glad?"

When he successfully bared her breasts, Tess silently admitted that, yes, she was glad. These past two months had been the most wonderful time of her life. Happier, in fact, than she ever would have dreamed considering their rocky start.

Though Gabe had never said it, Tess knew he hadn't wanted to get married quite so soon. The choice had been taken from their hands the morning her father discovered them in the barn at the Rolling R. They lay naked in each other's arms, Tess having offered up her virginity a week earlier when Gabe finally lost his ability to resist her seduction.

Her father and brother had a preacher to the house by noon, and relations between the three men she loved most in the world had been strained ever since. In fact, this meeting tonight was the first friendly overture Billy had made toward Gabe since the wedding.

"I love you, Gabe."

He trailed his tongue up between the cleft of her breasts then murmured. "I love you, too."

"You don't mind being married anymore?"

His hands stopped tugging at her skirts. "Ah, Tess. Don't. That's not how I felt. I decided to marry you when you were fifteen years old."

"But Billy and my daddy made you do it now."

"Darlin', don't insult my manly pride. Had I not wanted to marry you, your brother and your pa would have needed the ghosts of every brave hero who died at the Alamo to wring the words out of my mouth. And I'm not entirely certain they'd have managed it then."

She brushed a hand down his bare chest, desperately needing reassurance, and finally brave enough to ask for it. "But that day . . . I seduced you, Gabe. It was all my fault."

He rolled onto his back giving a hoot of laughter. "You were a hussy that night, weren't you? And I was so danged easy."

She punched him in the side, recognizing well when Gabe was teasing. "There wasn't anything easy about it. As I remember, you were very hard."

"Mrs. Cameron!" he exclaimed in a falsely scandalized voice. "You wicked woman, you."

"I'm a wicked wife."

"That you are," he said. He flashed her a pirate's grin. "And thankful I am for it." Then he rose up on one elbow and his gaze captured hers. Slowly, the teasing light died, replaced with a solemn, serious look. "Sweetheart, I want you to listen to me."

She thought she could drown in the dark pool of his eyes.

He grazed a thumb across her cheek. "I love you.

I'm very, very happy to be your husband. You are in my blood, Tess. You're my home. I wish I'd married you a year ago, two years ago."

"Oh, Gabe. Stop it or I'll cry."

Then he delved beneath her skirt, and Tess lost all ability to think, she could only feel. He made love to her with his hands, his mouth, his words, driving her higher and higher and higher. When finally he joined his body with hers, she thought she'd hitched a ride on the shower of stars shooting through the sky.

When her tremors subsided, he smoothly reversed their positions until Tess lay atop him. Gabe urged her hips closer, and she held him deep within her body. "Let me fly the stars with you, baby. Take me there."

She rode him, her eyes opened, their gazes locked, until he thrust with his hips and threw his head back with a groan. She felt the pulse as he erupted inside her. She watched the starlight glimmer in his eyes.

They drifted back to earth slowly, together. Like one.

And then the night exploded.

A thunderous boom ripped the sky as bright light burst above the trees. Fire. An explosion.

Oh, God.

She knew. Somehow, she simply knew.

The lab. Billy.

"Gabe!"

He was already scrambling from beneath her. "Where are my clothes, goddammit! My clothes!"

Precious seconds ticked by before he located his pants and yanked them on. He took off running barefoot and shirtless. Tess paused long enough to pull on her dress and shoes, then followed her husband as fast as she possibly could.

Heat hit her like a fist as she arrived. Flames roared from the pile of rubble that once had been Gabe's father's laboratory. The whooshing, crackling, crashing noise screamed in her head. She ran forward, horror consuming her. "Billy?" she shouted. "Billy!"

She gazed frantically around the gathered crowd. "Billy, where are you? Where's my brother?" She spied Gabe. He stood facing the burning ruin, his hands clenched at his sides. His shoulders heaved with the force of his labored breaths.

She dashed toward her husband and grabbed his arms. The tears slipping down his cheeks shot another arrow of fear through her already wounded heart. "Gabe, where's Billy?"

His voice was strained and raspy. "They saw him earlier. He's inside. Oh, God." His entire body shuddered.

Tess whirled around to dash into the lab. Gabe caught her around the waist. "No, darlin', don't."

She clawed at his hands, wriggling in his confining embrace. "Let me go! We've got to save him!"

He turned her around and stared down into her face. "We can't, Tess. It's too late. We're too late."

"No-o-o!" she screamed, fighting harder, fisting her hands and beating at his chest. "Let me go! We can't be too late. We have to save my brother."

A part of her knew that hysteria had overtaken her, but she couldn't stop it. She couldn't stop anything about this nightmare. She yelled and hit and kicked, but Gabe held her tight.

Then a second explosion ripped the night.

Tess's knees turned to water and she collapsed, sobbing, into Gabe's embrace. She could deny it no longer. Her brother was gone.

Minutes ticked by, dragging like years, as grief consumed her. Gabe held her gently, tenderly, even as he rattled off a string of ugly epithets. "I'm so sorry, darlin'. God, I'm sorry." He paused a moment, then added almost to himself. "I should have been here."

He should have been here.

His words burrowed through her pain like a bullet, leaving a streak of rage in its wake. Tears streamed down her face as she wrenched away from him. "You told him you'd be here. He didn't know your father's laboratory. He didn't know how to work the spectroscope and if he lit the Bunsen burner . . ." The image of her brother being blown to bits flashed in her mind. "It's your fault!"

Gabe flinched and closed his eyes.

He didn't try to deny it and that only increased her rage. "It's your fault! You were late because you had to 'stargaze' some more. That's all you think about. You should have been here to help him."

"God, I know." He looked at her then, the firelight clearly revealing the anguish and misery in his eyes. Tears rolling down his cheeks. "Please, Tess . . ."

But she was seventeen years old and in terrible pain, so she struck out at the nearest target. "You killed him, Gabe. You killed your best friend. You killed my brother. I hate you." Her voice broke on a sob. "I hate you!"

With that, and one last glance at the haunting inferno, she ran off into the night.

When Tess's mind returned to the present, she discovered her cheeks were wet with tears. She brushed away the wetness and gazed up toward the top of the mountain where her husband stood like a statue facing away from her.

She'd been cruel that night. Cruel to someone she loved. Shame washed over her like a cold December rain.

But fate had been cruel, too. Cruel to both of them.

She closed her eyes. She owed her husband an apology for her actions and accusations that night, but what else did she owe him? How much of the truth did he need to know, did he deserve to know?

She'd told him to leave her one time. Once. Once, when she was mindless with grief.

And he'd gone. No argument, no resistance. No fighting for the love she had thought they shared. He'd left her to face her father, face her trials, all alone. "Maybe I don't owe him anything more than an apology."

Tess drew a deep breath and resumed her climb. She'd find out how much of Gabe Cameron remained in Gabriel "Whip" Montana.

Then she'd know whether or not to tell him about Doc and Will. And about sweet little Rachel.

CHAPTER
5

ꙮ

*A*t the crest of Paintbrush Mountain, Gabe dropped the picnic basket, then bent and scooped up a handful of pebbles. One by one, he chucked them, absently aiming toward a cactus some fifteen yards down the hill. He stared out over a West Texas landscape that seemed to go on forever, his thoughts as bleak as the view.

Why had he bothered to make the trip to Aurora Springs anyway? So what if he and Tess were still married? Having answers to the questions tumbling around in his brain wouldn't change anything. Time couldn't change anything.

Billy's death would always divide him and Tess.

The intensity of his reaction to her idle talk about stargazing had caught him by surprise. Funny how a couple of questions or a particular word or two could wipe out a man's maturity, shooting him right back to boyhood in the blink of an eye. In that moment, all those old emotions came roaring back brand new again. The intervening years might well have never happened. The grief and anguish and shame. That soul-eating sense of loss.

He believed he had dealt with Billy's death and its aftermath years ago, that he'd put it all behind him and moved on. Now he had to admit he'd lied to himself. He should have realized it. His quirk of avoiding sight of the stars was a hell of a clue, one he'd gone out of his way not to address. When he fessed up to Tess, he'd put his feelings into words for the very first time.

But maybe in his heart, he'd known it all along.

He took the last stone in his hand and pinged it against a ponderosa pine. Maybe some part of him had recognized he had some old ghosts to face. Maybe that had fueled his urgency to follow Tess from Dallas. Maybe it wasn't answers he searched for, but absolution.

"Gabe, I owe you an apology."

He stiffened. He hadn't heard her approach. The way he'd barked at her, he had expected her to run back to town. *Instead she offers me an apology?*

Slowly, he turned around and faced her. The anguish painted across her face cut him to the quick.

She took a step closer. Earnestly, she said, "I know you're not responsible for what happened to Billy. It was a dreadful, horrible accident. An *accident*. It was no one's fault, and it was wrong, terribly wrong of me to blame you."

Gabe drew a deep breath. Absolution. Well, if that's what he came here for, she'd laid it right out for him. He waited for a sense of relief. Nothing, nothing at all.

It made him angry.

His gaze followed a sparrow flitting from tree to tree. With a bite to his voice, he challenged, "Figured that out, did you? When? Just now?"

"No, Gabe." She clutched the brightly colored quilt tightly to her chest and shot him a chastising look. "I've known it all along."

He recalled her hateful accusations the night her brother died. In a tone as dry as the Chihuahuan in July, he observed, "Not quite all along."

Guilt flashed across the summer sky blue of her eyes. "I was confused at first. Grief does that to people. I was wrong. I'm asking for your forgiveness."

He scooped up another handful of stones and resumed chucking them one by one at the cactus. *Sonofabitch.* Guess he hadn't come here for absolution, after all. Here she was offering it up to him on a platter, and instead of easing him, hearing her humble herself like this only made him feel worse. His anger evaporated, leaving weariness behind. "You don't need to ask, Tess," he told her honestly. "There's nothing to forgive. You were grieving, and a person has trouble making sense under those circumstances. I was the same way."

"You were?" Hope brightened her face.

She's so beautiful. Looks like an angel.

Gabe nodded. "I wallowed around in guilt for a good while after the fire, but once my mind cleared and I understood what had happened, I started thinking straight. I realized I wasn't to blame for the accident that took my best friend's life."

She licked her lips, then shot the question like a bullet. "Then why didn't you come home?"

Gabe lowered his head and rubbed the back of his neck. "That's a complicated question."

Regally, she drew herself up. "No, I think it's quite simple. You didn't want to come home."

The accusation in her tone pricked his temper. "Damned right I didn't. You sent me away, Tess. You told me you hated me. I thought you were divorcing me." Seeing the stricken look on her face, he muttered a curse, then added, "And besides, if I'd have come home I'd have murdered my father. I figured patricide was best left out of the equation."

She closed her eyes and allowed her head to drop back. "I knew it. You blame him still, don't you?"

"Of course I blame him," he replied, furious. "Monty Cameron might as well have killed your brother himself."

"That's lunacy," she scoffed. "It was an accident. You said it yourself not two minutes ago."

"An accident caused by negligence on that man's part. Monty ignored the need to repair the faulty valve on the Bunsen burner, and he failed to secure volatile chemicals. Monty and his cursed carelessness did poor Billy in."

"I knew it," Tess muttered, whipping the quilt into the wind. It opened and floated to the ground in a vibrant splash of reds, blues, and yellows, the bright colors shocking eyes accustomed to the monotony of West Texas. She dropped to her knees and smoothed away wrinkles in the cloth with a harsh stroke of her hand. "I knew you wouldn't listen to reason where your father is concerned."

"There is nothing reasonable about my father's actions. You and I were young, Tess, and young folks just act stupid. That's one of nature's rules."

He sighed heavily. "Look, I know now that I should have tried harder to see you, especially after you returned my letters unread. But you should have read them. You should have let me know if you wanted me to come home. But my father wasn't young; he doesn't have that excuse. He's the one who truly deserves our wrath."

"Letters?" She jerked her head up. "What letters?"

Gabe went still. "What do you mean 'what letters'? I wrote you at least twice a week for a month. All of them came back unopened."

She sank all the way to the ground. He saw her throat bob as she swallowed hard. Softly, hurtfully, she said, "I never got them. They were never delivered."

"Oh, they were delivered." Gabe folded his arms. "A friend of mine laid the three I sent that first week in your daddy's own hand. They came to me packed inside another envelope along with the letter your father sent about the divorce."

Tess shut her eyes. "My father never gave them to me. He never told me." After a moment's pause, she added, "Oh, Gabe. My father was truly a wicked man."

God damn Stanford Rawlins. Bitterness rolled through Gabe like a tumbleweed in the wind. "Fathers," he said with a sneer. "Reckon you and I were both lucky in that regard."

"No." Tess reached irritably for the picnic basket. "Your father isn't wicked at all. He's a good man, a loving, caring man who made a mistake. He deserves forgiveness from you, not rancor."

"Forgive Monty Cameron?" With one, powerful swing of his arm, Gabe threw the pebbles remaining in his fist. "When your pal Rosie flies. The man is a killer and I'm not gonna forget it."

She rolled back on her heels and gazed up at him, her mouth tightened in a grim line. "Gabe, an accidental explosion killed Billy. It wasn't your fault. It wasn't your father's fault. Monty is—"

Gabe rounded on her, furious. "Remember, Tess, Billy isn't the only person Monty Cameron killed. My own mother and infant brother died needless deaths because he was too wrapped up in one of his stupid scientific searches to take my laboring mother out of the Florida swamp."

Her eyes snapped with temper and she shoved to her feet. "Gabe, you're not being fair!"

"Fair?" He burst out with a laugh. "Darlin', fair is where you run your pig. It has nothing to do with real life. Why are you defending him anyway?"

Tess braced her hands on her hips and shot him a glare. "Your mother wasn't due to deliver for two months. There should have been plenty of time to get back to a town. And your father's searches weren't stupid. You can't blame him for seeking the truth. That's what scientists do."

"He wasn't a scientist, he was a reckless adventurer who used science as an excuse."

Her jaw worked as if she were swallowing her words. Then she drew a deep breath and exhaled it loudly. "I swear, Gabe Cameron, your head is so hard it could etch glass. Maybe it's best we don't talk about your father right now."

"Try 'ever' and I'll agree with you."

Kneeling, she reached into her basket and pulled out a cardamon roll. She chucked it at him saying, "Stuff this in your mouth. I don't want to listen to your yammering."

He caught the roll and held it. Slowly, the anger drained out of him. The girl had always had a backbone, and she hadn't left it behind when becoming a woman. He took a bite of his roll and flavor exploded in his mouth, washing away the lingering bitterness of his anger.

Damn, but he'd missed this taste. Among others.

Gabe cleared his throat. "So, since we're not gonna talk about my pa anymore, let's get on to what brought me here, shall we? I want to understand this divorce-that-wasn't, Tess. Tell me why you left the Rolling R."

"Oh, damn." She sank down onto her seat, folding like a bad poker hand.

Damn? Out of Tess's mouth? This explanation must be worse than he'd figured.

He watched silently as she took a moment, obviously gathering her thoughts. It required such an effort that Gabe decided to sit down, too. The seconds ticked slowly by, and he began to wonder why he'd ever asked his cursed question. And he'd bet money on the fact he wouldn't like the story she had to tell one little bit.

Tess poured herself a cup of milk, took a sip, then said, "As you know, after the funeral I went back to live at the ranch with my father. You also know how he felt about Billy. My father wouldn't speak to anyone but the ranch foreman, so deeply did he grieve. I think he went a little crazy holed up in that room. When he finally called me to the library to talk with him two weeks after the funeral, he demanded I leave."

"Why?"

She hesitated, obviously searching for words. Finally, she said, "My last name was Cameron. He demanded I change it, to divorce you. I refused."

"So he decided to take care of ending the marriage himself," Gabe replied, drawing the obvious conclusion.

"Maybe he intended to at first, but he never followed through."

Gabe nodded. "We didn't sign divorce papers."

"Oh, I wouldn't have put it past him to sign our names for us." She gave a small, unamused laugh. "In fact, that's what I would have expected him to do. But because of a copy of the will I received upon his death, I know that didn't happen."

Gabe fastened his gaze on the feather of white smoke rising from the chimney of Aurora Springs' communal kitchen. He damned sure wouldn't partake of anything they were cooking up there this morning, and not because Tess had thought to feed him from a picnic basket, either. This story she was telling had curdled his stomach. "So you inherited the Rolling R. Is that how you financed your studies?"

She took a long time to answer. "No, Father left the ranch to his foreman."

"He what?" Gabe jerked his head around, pinning her with his stare. "He disinherited you?" When she nodded, he clenched his fists. "Damn that man! What happened, Tess? How did you live? How did you support yourself?"

She shut her eyes and a moment later, tears began to trickle down her cheeks. Gabe melted. This woman's tears had always knocked his legs right out from underneath him. Probably because she so seldom cried.

He took a couple of awkward steps in her direction, uncertain how to respond. When the little whimper escaped her lips, he knew he'd had enough. "Never mind, darlin'. That's enough. Don't cry. We can talk about this later. I think we've both had all the revelations we need for now."

She looked at him, then, the film of tears sparkling in the morning sunlight. "Gabe, I—"

Squeal.

The animal's pain-filled shriek halted Tess midsentence.

Squeal. Squeal. Squeal.

Sounds like the butcher is getting to that hog, Gabe thought.

"Rosie!" Tess cried, shoving to her feet. Without so much as a word to him, she ran for the path down the hill hollering.

Gabe remained seated, his gaze trailing his wife's mad dash. "Saved by the pig," he observed, relief washing through him. It wasn't like him to run from problems, but this situation was different from any he'd experienced before.

Discussing the past with Tess was like strolling across a desert filled with cactus. One misstep could result in a nasty stick.

Down in town, the pig squealed again and Gabe rolled to his feet to watch the action. Then, to his utter surprise considering recent events, he started to laugh. Soon he found himself laughing so hard he couldn't have run ten yards to save his soul.

What else was a fellow to do when he watched the citizens of Aurora Springs chase a pair of camels loping after a fleet-footed pig coated in molasses and feathers?

"I'm not giving that pig a bath."

The afternoon sun and Gabe's indignant voice filtered through the window of the pig-ravaged storeroom. In the midst of the cleanup, Tess couldn't help but smile. God bless Rosie. The pig's antics had pulled Tess from the nightmare conversation with Gabe up on Paintbrush Mountain and restored Tess's good humor. She considered the mess that had awaited her in the storeroom a fair price to pay.

After she had managed to catch Rosie, but before Gabe dragged himself howling with laughter down the bluff, she had spoken with her Aurora Springs family and impressed upon them the importance of keeping certain details about their community quiet. Twinkle, who knew more of the details about Tess's relationship with Gabe, stepped up and declared her intention to take the man beneath her wing—whether he liked it or not.

From the sounds of it, he didn't care for the job she had in mind for him at the moment.

"Now, Gabe-dear," Twinkle scolded. "One of the few rules we have here in our community is that everyone pitches in to help. I don't know what's gotten into Rosie today; she's normally quite well-behaved. First Tess's star shed and now our storeroom—we need the extra pair of hands to help."

"I don't mind helping. I'm just not scrubbing down that undercooked roast with lavender soap."

"It's honeysuckle soap, not lavender. I alternate fragrances on a weekly basis. I think variety in a soap adds a touch of excitement, a little allure to one's life. And everyone else has other chores that need doing. You're the only one here with extra time on your hands."

"Better time than a sudsy porker," Gabe grumbled.

"Would you rather see to Castor and Pollux? The dromedaries. I'll warn you, they do like to spit."

Gabe muttered something Tess couldn't make out. Wanting to hear better, she deposited glass from a broken jar of canned peaches into her box of trash and moved a little closer to the window.

"Ma'am," Gabe said. "This ham-on-the-hoof stinks. A little scent in the soap isn't going to make it any nicer to be around. The only thing that will make the animal smell alluring is a frying pan and a fire."

Tess scowled. Twinkle inquired, "Frying pan and a fire?"

"Bacon, ma'am."

Tess heard a gasp, then a grunt.

"Ouch!" said Gabe. "You kicked me."

"You deserved it, saying such a thing in front of

Rosie. Now pick up the scrub brush, Gabe-dear, and get to work before I change my mind about you."

Tess listened intently for his response as she stooped to right an overturned basket of sewing supplies. It might be better for her in the long run if her friend did change her opinion of the man. Romantic that she was, Twinkle had decided Gabe's trip to Aurora Springs was the work of Billy Rawlins's ghost in a beyond-this-world matchmaking effort. In fact, she intended to conduct a star-séance this very evening to personally offer her thanks.

"I don't even want to think of how Gabe will react to that," Tess murmured, going down on her hands and knees to retrieve a jar of canned peas that had rolled behind a barrel.

She heard him ask, "Why don't I help Tess clean up the storeroom? She'll likely need some help with the heavy stuff."

Accusation gave Twinkle's voice a razor's edge. "Your wife has made do without a man around to help for years, hasn't she? The girl has learned to adapt. She doesn't need you."

Tess rolled her eyes and made room on the shelf for the jar of peas next to the canned beets. Twinkle was lying like a rug. She constantly harped at Tess about how she needed a man in her life, and when Tess discussed her connection to Gabe during the train trip back from Dallas, the woman had all but done somersaults up and down the aisle.

"Now, here's the brush," Twinkle continued. "Have at it. I need to look in on Andrew, and I'll check back with you in a little while. Make sure you scrub the folds of her skin good. That molasses will attract ants and we don't want that."

"I don't know," Gabe said. "Seems I heard somewhere that ant stings tenderize meat."

Twinkle's outraged gasp nearly rattled the walls, and Tess made a mental note to explain to the woman how Gabe liked to focus in on a sore spot to tease a person. Obviously that hadn't changed over the years.

She waited for her husband to argue with Twinkle some more, but apparently he'd ceded the battle. From outside the window, she heard the unmistakable sound of a scrub brush rasping across Rosie's hide. Twinkle had talked Gabe into washing Rosie. This Tess had to see.

She paid for her curiosity. The man had stripped off his shirt for the wet and messy work.

Peeking through the window at him, Tess felt a stirring of desire. He rolled his shoulders and her breath caught. Hunger cut like a knife. "Pisces, Pegasus, and Polaris," she grumbled softly. So much for not needing her husband.

She couldn't believe she reacted this way, especially on the heels of that scene this morning. Maybe all that emotion had stirred up her juices.

Actually, she'd been fighting these feelings ever since seeing him at the state fair. That's when her womanly needs had reasserted themselves. She sometimes felt as though she were rousing from a twelve-year hibernation.

Gabe wore the years well, his body hard and handsome and corded with muscle. His biceps flexed and bunched as he worked, and the sight of his wet, soapy hands stroking over Rosie made Tess think of other times and other baths.

Apparently anger didn't interfere with a woman's feminine cravings. She pushed the shutters open wider for a better view.

Sunshine sparkled in droplets of water that had splashed across his skin. Tess's gaze skimmed across his broad shoulders, paused on the contours of his chest, then continued down to where ridged muscles kept his stomach flat. Visually tracing the arrow of dark hair down to where it disappeared into his pants, she sucked in a breath, then sighed at the sheer beauty of the man.

Despite all that divided them, Tess imagined herself marching out to where he stood and demanding he fulfill his husbandly duties.

She groaned and turned away from the window. She'd finished her work in the storeroom but for the sweeping, so she reached for the broom and tried to banish the picture of a soap-splattered Gabe from her mind. The task was more difficult than sweeping up talcum powder. Sometimes—like when she couldn't reach the highest shelf in the storeroom—a woman needed a man. Other times she *needed* a man, whether she had a storeroom or not. This was one of those other times.

"Dear heaven, I am losing my mind."

From outside came a squeal, a clunk, then a splash, followed by a stream of profanity hot enough to singe the hair off Rosie's hide. Twinkle must have forgotten to warn Gabe about Rosie's predilection for dust. The sweetheart could only stand being so clean, and once she'd reached that point, well, it was best to get out of her way.

Tess hoped Gabe managed to get most of the molasses off. Chances were neither her husband nor her pet pig would be up for another bath today.

She started to check, but stopped herself in time. Rosie might have drenched Gabe's pants. Wet, they would lie plastered against him. She didn't need that particular torture.

She held out for an entire thirty seconds. "Tess Cameron, you're a brazen woman," she muttered, going to the window.

His pants were dry. More or less. He lay flat on his back—still cursing—while Rosie rolled in the dirt nearby. Tess had a sudden memory of a time when he'd started a mud fight that led to slick, slippery lovemaking.

Gabe broke off his cursing abruptly when he spied her watching from the window. Their gazes locked. He levered himself to a sitting position and Tess's world ground to a halt. *Dear Lord, I've missed him so.*

Some of what she was feeling must have shown in her expression because after a long, lovely minute, his lips spread in a slow, seductive grin. He lifted his hand and he gave her a muddy, two-fingered salute.

Tess actually licked her lips.

Mortified, she whirled away from the window, propped the broom against the wall, and fled the storeroom. She hurried across the compound, seeking the comfort of her own house. Chores could wait for a little while. At the moment, her mental health needed tending.

Hurrying up her front steps, she wondered what in the world was happening to her. Since awakening this morning her emotions had run the gamut from joy to lust, anger to lust, embarrassment to lust, fear to lust, and . . .

It had to stop.

She made a beeline for her favorite chair, a teakwood rocker Doc had sent to her while on his trip to South America a couple of years ago. Curling up in the seat, she pulled an afghan around her and closed her eyes.

And pictured her half-naked husband.

Her eyes flew open once again. With her blood thrumming through her veins, and a hollow ache consuming her feminine parts, she allowed herself a little whine. She'd gotten along fine without much of a sexual drive for the past dozen years. Why did it have to kick in now?

Gabe, of course.

It was understandable she'd feel an attraction. She'd loved him desperately back then, and she wasn't certain she didn't love him still. But with the hurts and betrayals and secrets still lying between them, nothing could or should come of this. At least, not anytime soon.

"Isn't that right?" she murmured.

Maybe. But maybe not.

She sat up straight and stared unseeing at the mantle clock. They *were* still married, after all. What would it hurt? Judging by his actions, she doubted Gabe would raise any objections.

She shifted in her seat. Was it just this morning she'd awakened in his arms? The day had lasted as long as a month and it wasn't even suppertime yet.

Maybe I could sleep in his arms tonight.

"No." Indulging would only complicate an already complex situation. Besides, she couldn't ignore the very real risk one took with such activity. She'd learned that particular lesson once already, and although she didn't regret it, the experience liked to have killed her.

"I can't believe I'm doing this," she said with a sigh.

The line between the passion of anger and the passion of lust must be thinner than she'd thought.

Desperate for a distraction, she rose from the comfort of her chair and crossed the room to her desk. She pulled out a star journal and picked up a pencil, her intention to bury herself in work. She needed to not think about Gabe for a little while, or for a long while if that's what it took to get her wayward desires under control. In fact, now that she thought about it, rather than work, she just might take a nap.

She was worn out. The rush home from Dallas, taking care of Andrew, fretting about Doc, missing Will. Dealing with Gabe and all the memories and all the emotions he inspired. She needed a few hours' rest from it. She needed a little oblivion.

But when she crawled between the sheets and shut her eyes, sleep refused to come. She lay in her bed and ached, wishing her husband lay beside her.

Just when she started to cry, she couldn't say. All Tess knew was that at some point, the aching turned to grief, and tears overflowed her eyes. She wept for her husband, for the dreams the two of them had lost, for the family stolen from them.

Tess wept for the loss of a love that had once burned brighter than the Kissing Stars that danced in the West Texas sky.

CHAPTER
6
❧⟨≋⟩❧

Sunset teased the western horizon as Gabe pounded the hammer down on the head of a nail, driving it through a shingle and into the decking on Twinkle Starbright's roof. An overnight rain had revealed a leak, so earlier this afternoon Twinkle had set Gabe and Jack Baker to task. He didn't mind the work. Sharing a house but not a bed with Tess for the past five nights wore on a man, made him need an outlet for his frustrations. Hammering helped. So, taking the place of convalescing Andrew Ross, Gabe had partnered with Jack to tackle the projects requiring brute strength—and hammering—around the community.

Community was a good word to describe Aurora Springs, he thought. This place wasn't a town or a ranch headquarters or even a railroad water stop. Gabe figured Aurora Springs was as close to a commune as Texas had seen since the La Réunion society disbanded back in the fifties. The folks who lived here shared their meals, their efforts, and even their wealth in an effort to further the cause that appeared to unite them. From what Gabe had discovered, everyone who lived here had a stake of one sort or another in these spooklights or Kissing Stars, to use Tess's term.

He wondered why she used that name. He decided he didn't want to ask.

Jack interrupted his reverie by asking, "Toss me another shingle, would you?"

Gabe did as requested, then puzzled as the young man eyed the sunset with what was best described as a wistful expression.

Young and with a gentle, almost innocent manner about him, Jack was the only member of Tess's little clan who didn't strike Gabe as three-quarters tetched. Of course, Gabe had yet to pry from Jack his reasons for living in Aurora Springs, so that opinion could always change.

The Ranger had been right on the mark about the Aurorians. These people were as strange as a tail on a tree. Why, in the short time he'd been here, he'd already witnessed more examples of peculiar beliefs and behaviors than a man would see in a month of saloon-spent Saturday nights. Take Colonel Wilhoit, for instance. Every day at noon he loaded up one of the camels and, armed with his divining rods, headed up into the mountains to look for diamonds. One day he came back with a strongbox filled with gold. Now the typical man would do handsprings over finding a cache of what was obviously stolen loot, especially since he mentioned more gold sat waiting to be retrieved. But the colonel wasn't happy. He went witchin' for diamonds in the hills each day because he believed the spooklights were mineral markers. Stashed outlaw gold wasn't good enough for Jasper Wilhoit. He wanted a vein of riches to dig out of the ground.

It worried Gabe a bit that he almost understood how the colonel and the other Aurorians felt.

Handing Jack the requested shingle, Gabe observed, "I haven't seen your wife this afternoon. Is she helping Twinkle in the vegetable garden?"

Jack took a nail from his pocket and positioned it on the cedar shake. "No. Amy has starwatch this evening."

"Starwatch?"

Jack nodded. "We take weekly shifts."

Gabe debated taking the matter any further. He didn't want to discover that Jack was as cockle-minded as the others, but his curiosity got the better of him. "And what is it exactly you're watching for? The spooklights I've been hearing about? Have you seen them, too?"

"Not recently," Jack grumbled, his expression dipping in a scowl. He brought his hammer down extra hard and muttered something beneath his breath that sounded like "too damned long."

Gabe rolled back on his knees. "But you *have* seen them?"

"Yeah. Three weeks ago yesterday was the last time they showed up. It's a longer dry spell than usual, and I don't like it." He pounded another nail all the way into the roof with a single stroke.

"Why not? Are you here to study the lights like

Tess?" Gabe asked hopefully. "Bet the delay frustrates your research, huh?"

"I'm not here for research," Jack admitted. "But I'm sure as hell frustrated. However, I want the best for my family and Amy is certain this is it. I can be a man about it. I just don't have to like it."

Now that didn't make a lick of sense. "I don't follow you."

A bashful smile accompanied the ruddy flush of Jack's cheeks. Rather than answer Gabe's questions, he gestured toward the stack of shingles. "Hand me another one, would you?"

Gabe chose to let the matter drop, a reaction that had become somewhat of a habit of late. Despite having traveled hundreds of miles to ask questions about the past, he'd quit pestering Tess for more answers ever since their exchange up on Paintbrush Mountain. In fact, since then they'd hardly spoken at all.

It didn't mean that Gabe hadn't learned a thing or two. Twinkle had provided the information he'd wanted about the mysterious Doc and Will. Getting that had turned out to be easy. All he'd had to do was ask. She'd told him right out that Will was her grandson and Doc her beau, and that their trip down to the Big Bend area had something to do with a search for ancient cave paintings that portrayed the spooklights. The woman had hedged when he tried to get her to talk to him about the railroad vandalism accusation, but Gabe hadn't pressed the issue. He was too busy being glad he'd been right that Tess and this Doc weren't lovers, after all.

With that question settled, and on the heels of that

rugged first day in Aurora Springs, Gabe had decided to slow down a bit. He'd had a lot to mull over in the wake of his chat with Tess up on Paintbrush Mountain. He still had a few questions, but he figured they'd get around to talking their way through in time.

Gabe was in no particular hurry to head home. Except for the sparseness of trees, he liked it here in Aurora Springs. He was glad to have left his notoriety back on the other side of the Pecos, and since he'd taken a leave of absence from his job with the railroad, he had plenty of time to kill. And ever since a certain blistering look they'd shared after that ham-bath, he'd been mulling over the notion of spending that free time courting his wife.

The idea had a certain appeal. Tess had a definite appeal. She made him randy as a goat in springtime, and from what he'd observed, she wasn't immune to him either. Since it looked like their knot was still tied, he didn't see why they couldn't take advantage of the fact. He'd more than welcome a little—or a lot—of relief in that area, and he reckoned she could use some, too. The physical part of their marriage had always been spectacular. He didn't doubt Tess had missed it as much as Gabe had. Why, it'd be doing them both a favor.

Of course, before he could get her to *bed* him he needed to get her to *talk* to him again. Tess had always liked being seduced with words, and chances were that hadn't changed. Still, he'd take this slow, too. He'd start off with general topics of conversation, then work his way up to the good stuff. *Maybe when*

I go home tonight I'll pay a compliment to the pig. She'd like that.

Gabe rolled back on his heels and swiped his bandanna across his sweaty brow, his gaze skimming across the landscape in search of the porcine princess. He finally spied her plopped in a sunny spot in Twinkle's flowerbed. He gestured toward the pig. "Look at ol' Rosie. She's just bacon in the sun."

It got a laugh out of Jack Baker, but Gabe didn't figure it was quite the right kind of compliment to impress Tess. For the next five minutes he mentally examined possible pig praises. Then, while he and Jack worked together to hammer on the last shingle, the faraway call of a musical instrument—french horn, he believed—was acknowledged by the blare of a trumpet coming from right below Gabe. The shock of it damn near knocked him off the roof. "What the hell?" he muttered, his sliding feet finally finding purchase on the rooftop. Glancing down, he saw Colonel Wilhoit draw a breath to blow again.

Weooooeeeooooee.

The sound grated on Gabe's ears. He opened his mouth to complain, but the look on Jack Baker's face stopped him short.

Joy. Pure, unadulterated joy with a sprinkling of anticipation and relief.

"What's going on?" Gabe asked as Jack tossed down his hammer and scrambled toward the ladder.

"That was Amy. It's the signal."

"Signal?"

"The stars are out."

The sudden bustle of activity below told Gabe the

young man probably wasn't talking about the evening star or something else that mundane. For the first time in years, Gabe was tempted to lift his gaze to the heavens to investigate the matter himself. He couldn't do it.

He followed the younger man to the ground, wincing when the colonel trumpeted right next to his ear. "All right, already," he said. "I think everyone has heard your signal."

For the next few minutes he watched the Aurorians' bizarre behavior in wonder. The colonel shoved the trumpet into Gabe's hands then dashed for his cabin. Seconds later he reappeared carrying a pair of divining rods. Twinkle and Tess ran from the communal kitchen to their houses. In a few short minutes, Twinkle reappeared wearing a purple and green gypsy skirt, white blouse, a turquoise turban, and enough jewelry to open a shop. In her hands she cradled a crystal ball.

Tess emerged right after Twinkle. She hadn't changed her clothes, but she now carried a small leather valise. "She packed?" Gabe muttered. "What? Does she think these stars are taking her to study Saturn's rings in person or something?"

Considering the company she kept, she might be eating a little loco weed mixed with her oatmeal after all.

Without a word to him, they hurried toward the trail leading up out of the canyon toward the hill they called Lookout Peak which rose higher than Paintbrush Mountain. Gabe propped the trumpet against the wall of Tess's cabin and headed out after them. A few steps down the path, he heard footsteps coming up fast behind him. Simultaneously, he caught a strong whiff of bay rum.

"Hey!" he hollered as Jack barreled into him.

"Sorry. Didn't see you."

He tried to dart around, but Gabe caught his arm. "Hold on, there, Jack. Real quick now before the toilet water fumes knock me out, care to tell me what has you in such an all-fired hurry? I thought you were one of the sensible ones in this crowd."

Jack wasn't putting up with any delay. He shrugged off Gabe's hold. "I told you. It's been three weeks."

"So?"

"So I finally get to be with my wife again."

"Be with your wife?"

"Sex, Montana! I'm not like you. I don't go a decade without making love with my wife." With that, he was gone.

And not a moment too soon, to Gabe's way of thinking. Scowling, he shoved his hands in his pockets and continued up the trail. What did these spooklights have to do with sex? Just how did the colonel use those divining rods of his with stars? What would he find when he reached the top of the hill? An orgy?

He wouldn't put it past Twinkle, but not Tess. She hadn't changed that much. Of course, he wouldn't have expected her to share intimate details about their marriage with her friends, either. The Tess he'd known a dozen years ago would never have spilled those particular celibacy beans.

This Tess apparently didn't think twice about it. At the end of his first day in Aurora Springs when he went looking for a place to sleep, she'd made sure everyone knew he'd be staying in her spare bedroom, not her own. The men of the village had offered him sympathetic looks. Twinkle's and Amy's expressions had told him he deserved what he had coming.

Small town life. Where everyone knew your business better than you did. "Hell."

Gabe followed the sound of excited voices to the top of the hill. Instead of an orgy he found his wife standing behind a telescope making notations in a notebook. Jack and Amy were headed back down the hill by a different path, walking hand in hand. Jack held a quilt tucked under one arm. The colonel held his rods to the sky. Twinkle appeared to be conjuring, her crystal ball set atop a makeshift table, her hands outstretched over it as she gazed out over the West Texas plain.

Then he heard a sound that stopped him in his tracks. Tess was laughing, that delighted, delightful music she'd once shared with him. Back then, it made him feel ten feet tall. Now it twisted his heart. He'd never thought to hear that particular song again.

As always, her laughter cast a spell over him, drew him like the sparkle of moonlight on water. "What is it?" he asked.

She turned. Her blue eyes glowed. Her smile shined like a sun in the gathering dusk. "Look at the colors. Look at them dance!"

"What colors?"

"The lights, Gabe. The Kissing Stars." Tess laughed again and reached for his hand. "Look. You have to look at them."

His heart seemed to stop as a bittersweet yearning

filled him. Her laughter, the music. Happiness lost long ago. His mouth went dry as sandpaper.

Maybe he could do it. Maybe now was the time, here with Tess at his side. Maybe now was the moment to lay the ghosts to rest.

Gabe drew a deep breath, then exhaled loudly. Then, swallowing the sudden lump in his throat, he tightened his grip on Tess's hand and slowly lifted his eyes above the horizon.

"Do you see them?" Tess asked. "Aren't they beautiful? Tonight they're blue and green. Some nights they're red, and other times yellow. I think blue is my favorite, though. What do you think?"

He stared at the sky for a long minute without speaking. Then abruptly he released her hand and turned away, headed for the path leading down to Aurora Springs. "What do I think? I think you're all lunatics, that's what."

Emotion churned like sour milk in his gut. Gabe had faced an old ghost and look what it had got him. Nothing. He'd looked into the sky. He'd searched for Tess's Kissing Stars.

And he hadn't seen a goddamned thing.

A multitude of stars pulsed in a black velvet sky, aiding the yellow glow of the lantern lighting Tess's way down Lookout Peak. She made the trip alone at half past two in the morning, the others having sought their beds hours earlier. The chilled night air nipped at her skin, but the excitement thrumming through her blood helped keep her warm. *It has been*, she thought, *an exhilarating night.*

For months now she'd mapped the paths the Kissing Stars took as they bounced and hovered over the distant desert, and she'd come to suspect she'd uncovered a pattern to their movements. Tonight's show had blown that theory to bits.

For the first hour, the lights played back and forth across the flats in their customary north-to-south, east-to-west pattern at a distance of approximately five to ten miles from Lookout Peak. An exact measurement remained impossible to obtain because whenever anyone went out onto the desert to track them, they acted like mirages, migrating farther away. Always moving in pairs, the lights had separated, then come together, fusing, then splitting again. Hence the name, the Kissing Stars.

But shortly after the second hour began, the lights acted in an altogether unusual manner. They moved close to Lookout Peak. Extremely close. Within half a mile, Tess would guess. And then they'd hovered. For seven straight hours they hovered, never moving, never once changing color, but slowly growing steadily bigger. Six individual stars, glowing an angry, orange color.

The effect on the Aurorians had been significant. Colonel Wilhoit charged his divining rods until his arms gave out. He left the mountain elated, certain that now his tools finally contained enough starpower to locate his dream. Twinkle had spent hours hovered over her glass globe, positive that this time enough energy flowed into the sphere to call the individual spirits she wanted to summon. And finally at half past one, Jack and Amy had dragged through camp on their way home, exhausted but hopeful that the night's efforts had achieved the desired results—the conception of the gifted child Amy's dreams foretold.

For her part, Tess spent the hours captivated by the stars' unusual actions. She'd occupied her time by taking measurements and recording observations in her journal. And, despite her best intentions, wondering about Gabe. She didn't know which to consider more of a puzzle—her husband or the Kissing Stars.

Why had Gabe stormed off after looking at the lights? Surely the sight of the lights hadn't reminded him of Billy's death. A sky full of stars had shined above them that night; strange balls of fire didn't bounce above the horizon. It was ludicrous to think the lights might have frightened Gabe, but they obviously disturbed him in some way. He'd all but kicked up dust in his rush back down the hill.

His response proved to her how much her husband had changed. The Gabe Cameron she'd married would have stood and watched, enthralled, until the stars disappeared.

Having reached the bottom of the trail down Lookout Peak, Tess sighed and firmly turned her attention away from her husband and back toward the Kissing Stars as she made her way into Aurora Springs. Intent upon the mystery, she paid little note to the fact that lamplight lit up her house. "A three week absence, then this unusual appearance," she murmured aloud as she climbed her front steps. "I'll need to go back through my books and see if I can find a reference to a similar phenomena."

Gabe's gruff voice loomed from the porch swing. "First I want you to tell me about the lights."

Tess tripped on one of the steps and teetered, almost falling. "Gabe Cameron, you scared the stuffing out of me!"

"Montana."

"Did you change it legally?"

"Doesn't matter. The name is Montana."

Orion, Aries, and Gemini, I'm not up for that name fight tonight. Tess smiled grimly and walked into her house. He followed her inside and right into her bedroom, something he'd never before dared.

"Sorry I surprised you, Tess. Now tell me about these lights. Tell me what people see, what your studies have shown."

Tess lit her bedside lamp before turning to face him. *He looks tired,* she thought. Weariness shadowed his eyes and the slight slump to his shoulders was unusual. What was wrong with Gabe?

He shoved his hands in his pockets and glared at her. "Talk to me. I want to know about these damned lights of yours."

The impatience reverberating through his voice reassured her, and a small seed of hope blossomed. He'd shown little interest in her work up until now and it had hurt her.

"Tess?"

"I'm trying to decide where to start."

"Try the beginning."

She smiled. "You'll need to speak with the Apaches if you want to go that far back. I'm told their legends concerning the lights have been repeated for generations."

"You followed an Indian legend here?"

"No." She smiled. "Actually a friend sent a newspaper article about the lights to me. I had just finished my studies with Dr. Pierce, so it was perfect timing to begin a new project. We made the trip to this canyon after interviewing the rancher who first reported the lights. After seeing them for ourselves, we decided to settle here. We made the rancher an offer for his land and Aurora Springs was born."

"We? Who's we? You and Twinkle?"

She cursed her choice of pronouns and sidestepped the question. "Twinkle owns a large section. She was attracted by more than just the stars. Twinkle suffers respiratory difficulties and the climate here is good for her."

Gabe obviously didn't want to hear about Twinkle's health. "This rancher. What was it he saw?"

"It was back in '83. Mr. Henderson was moving two thousand head of cattle through Snakeater Pass which is just south of here. One of his hands riding herd brought the lights to his attention. When I interviewed him he told me he saw strange, starlike flickers of light, and he assumed they were Apache campfires burning at the base of the distant mountains. But when he and his men went to investigate, they didn't find a single sign of any Apache. For months afterward the stars appeared every night."

"But what was it that he saw? Just flickers?"

Tess shook her head. "He saw the same thing then that we see now."

"Which is . . . ?"

"Usually something different than what I saw tonight," she replied, her brow dipping in a perplexed frown as she recalled the evening's entertainment. "It was after you were gone, Gabe. You saw the Kissing Lights as colored spheres, like slow-bouncing balls, right? The tones were soft, more like distant stars than brilliant balls of fire. That's what we see most often. But after you left, one of them did something I'd never seen before. It started swinging in an arc." She made a motion with her hand like the rocker on a rocking chair to illustrate.

Gabe walked over to her bed and sat down. He appeared attentive, but not at all pleased with her explanation.

Her imagination caught with the retelling of the puzzle, Tess didn't stop to wonder why. "Next it did a whole loop and another half loop, and then it stopped. It hung suspended for a moment before bursting into six small stars. Those stars in turn flashed a brilliant white and moved in close. They started growing and turned orange and hovered. They just hung there, Gabe, for hours. Growing bigger and brighter by the minute. It was truly the strangest thing, and it completely ruins a hypothesis I had developed about the phenomena."

Gabe dragged his hand down his jawline. "And the others. They saw the same thing?"

She nodded. "All except for Andrew, of course. He came up the hill—against my instructions, I might add, since he's still recovering. But Andrew never sees the lights."

Gabe's hand fell back into his lap and he leaned forward. "He doesn't?"

"No. He only sees the horses. When the lights shine a herd of wild horses led by a beautiful white stallion sometimes comes out of the hills into the flats. It's the only time any of us has ever seen the stallion. Andrew wants to catch the horse. He feels an affinity with it; some sort of connection. He's determined to at least get close enough to touch it, even if they decide he shouldn't try to keep it."

"They?"

"He and the horse."

Gabe shook his head. "I'll leave that be for now, but don't you think the other is strange? That he doesn't see these stars that the rest of you see, I mean."

Tess shrugged. "I think everything about these lights is strange. We don't know what they are, Gabe. At this point we can't say they're not some type of optical trick that our eyes see when atmospheric conditions are a certain way. If that's the answer, maybe Andrew and the others who don't see them have a different eye shape or lens dimension that prevents their seeing the illusion we see. That's something I'm attempting to study."

"But you're an astronomer, not a physician."

"I know," she replied almost ruefully. "The entire phenomena is fascinating and quite frankly, has captured my interest like no other work I've ever done. For instance, Amy Baker sees the stars, but she never sees the colors. They are always white to her. Why is that?"

Gabe let out a breath, and she detected a sense of relief in the action. He reached around and propped her pillows behind him against the headboard, then he swung his legs up on the bed and leaned back, his hands linked behind his head, elbows outstretched. "I didn't see them, either."

Tess swallowed her demand he get his boots off her bed. "What?"

"I didn't see the spooklights."

She felt a wrench of sorrow as she recalled what he'd said about stargazing in the aftermath of the explosion. "Oh, Gabe. You couldn't look at them?"

"Oh, I looked. I just couldn't see them."

Her eyes widened. "Why didn't you say something?"

"I'm saying something now. So, Amy isn't color blind in other areas?"

"No."

"This is all very curious." He focused his gaze upon her, and the intrigue glowing in their steel gray depths caused her breath to catch. This was the Gabe she remembered.

He slowly nodded. "You might be onto something by considering differences in eye shape. This group of yours is a small sampling of the population, and if two of them see the events differently than others, it lends credence to the hypothesis of a physical anomaly."

"It could just mean they are nearsighted and need spectacles," Tess replied. "But I do see something out there, Gabe. The Kissing Stars exist. And I want an explanation for it."

He stared vacantly at a spot over her shoulder, his

lips twisted in a contemplative frown, one foot rhythmically tapping the air.

Watching him, Tess melted. This was the Gabe she fell in love with. She'd seen him sit exactly that same way so many times while he pondered the possibility of life on Mars or the number of galaxies in the universe. He was a man whose mind lent itself to puzzles, and for the first time she recognized the connection between his current occupation of railroad investigator and his previous interest. He'd abandoned celestial enigmas for earthly riddles.

"You considered St. Elmo's fire?"

Tess shook her head. "Of course. I don't think that's it. The flat has no obvious source of such electricity."

"Wouldn't be swamp gas in this part of the world. What about minerals? Could it be moonlight reflecting off large veins of mica?"

"This region doesn't have large veins of mica. Besides, I personally have seen the lights on cloudy and moonless nights. I've documented such conditions in my journals. Let me show you." She walked over to her desk and removed a trio of bound books. Returning to the bed, she sat beside him, feeling like a child at Christmas for having Gabe join her in an intellectual discussion again. She had missed this so much.

Opening the earliest volume, she said, "I've kept a daily journal since moving to Aurora Springs. Perhaps you'll see a pattern I have missed." Sighing, she added, "For all the facts I've gathered, I've not come up with a theory any better than Twinkle's belief in the supernatural."

Gabe pinned her with a gaze. "You believe they're spooklights?"

"No, not really. I don't believe in ghosts." She gave a half-smile as emotion stabbed like a dirk at her heart. Softly, she added, "Now, angels are another matter."

His eyes narrowed, but thankfully he didn't pursue that question. He took the journal from her hands and resettled back against the pillows. "Let's take a look at your journal."

He absently patted the space beside him, and Tess didn't hesitate to settle in there. They'd always studied this way, side by side. It felt natural. It felt . . . wonderful.

They sat for some time flipping through the pages. Tess drew his attention to the notations she considered interesting, and he paused over some others all on his own. In answer to his queries, she went into some detail about the beliefs of the other Aurora Springs residents concerning the stars.

"And what about this Doc fella? What does he think?"

Shrugging, Tess replied, "He is undecided. That's one reason he's so intent to study the pictographs in the cave. He hopes they will yield new evidence."

Gabe nodded. "And what about the boy? What does he think? You know, you hardly ever mention him."

Tess took a moment to answer, licking her dry lips and swallowing hard. "Will wants to believe in ghosts like Twinkle, but he needs proof. Will is big on proof."

Thankfully, he went on to another subject. As they talked, Tess found herself leaning toward him. He smelled woodsy and familiar and ever so appealing. She filled her lungs and sank into the scent, floated in it. She remembered and she yearned. And she leaned a little bit closer.

"Have you heard of a similar phenomena occurring in other parts of the world?"

"Hmm . . . ?"

"Surely you've looked into that."

She blinked back to attention and mentally reviewed his question. "Yes, I have. So far I haven't found anything. Just last month, though, I hired a librarian based in Boston to do a periodical research study."

His hand reached out to turn the page. Big hands, she thought. Soft in places, rough and calloused in others. Scars both new and old. Talented hands. He'd always known just how to touch her.

She shuddered as his finger skimmed down the journal page. All thoughts of the Kissing Stars and scientific research evaporated as she recalled how that same finger used to skim down her breast. Her throat tightened against a little whimper of need.

His movement froze. A dozen seconds dragged by. Had he heard her? Had she given herself away? Did he sense the tension that hummed in her veins? Did he feel it, too?

His breathing sounded harsh, the only sound Tess could hear above the rush of blood pounding through her veins. This was dangerous, this sea of emotion. A dozen years divided them. Twelve-year-old wounds healed over with a scar tissue of secrets.

She was afraid to look at him. She couldn't stop herself from looking.

Oh, God.

The sum of every sun in the universe blazed in his eyes. Fire and heat. Desire.

"Tess."

Her name sounded wrenched from his mouth. Torn from a memory.

He lifted his hand, brushed his thumb across her lips. He muttered a curse, harsh and low. "God help me. God help us both."

Then Gabe leaned over, cupped her cheek in his palm, and pressed his lips against hers.

CHAPTER

7

$\mathcal{G}$abe fell into the kiss like a man stumbling off a cliff. At the first brush of her lips, a small part of him sensed danger, but in that particular moment he simply didn't give a damn.

She tasted like home.

Tess's lips were soft and warm and wet. Her mouth sweet and . . . familiar. Oh, so familiar. The years had dimmed the memory, but he'd never forgotten. Yearning seeped into his chest, filling it to near bursting. In Tess's kiss he tasted the wonder of first love, the time before the shadows, his youthful hopes and dreams and desires.

Her mouth opened in welcome and he deepened the kiss. His tongue gently played with hers, conveying thoughts and feelings he could not put into words. Tess moaned softly as her hands snaked up around his neck to pull him closer. Her response both rocked him and soothed him. He'd long thought he'd never know this delight again.

He inhaled her soap-fresh scent and recalled the pleasure of seducing Tess in her bath, of lying beside her on a padded quilt and letting the silky strands of her hair glide through his fingers, of pinning her soft, lush body beneath him and thrusting home.

His fingers wove into her hair, his thumbs stroking gently across her temples while his mouth feasted on hers, Gabe hovered somewhere between the past and the present. He held her, tasted her, and burned hot and bright.

Like her stars.

Finally, as they approached the point where the choice must be made to take this farther or pull back, Tess wrenched from his arms. She rolled across the bed and went up on her knees. "Why? Why are we doing this? What is it you want from me, Gabe?"

"Other than the obvious?" he replied, his voice emerging rough and raspy. "Damned if I know."

He sighed and shut his eyes, then threw his head back against the pillow. "I toted a boxcar full of questions out here to West Texas, but now I can't work up a good curious about the answers. Why is that, do you think?"

Tess sat back on her heels. She nervously rubbed her hands across the tops of her thighs. Gabe wanted to mimic the motion with his tongue.

"Seeing each other again . . . the revelations . . . all this has been a shock for both of us," she replied slowly. "We've gone along for more than a decade believing one version of events, and now all of a sudden we learn our truths were nothing more than lies. I think we're both a little confused."

"A *little* confused. Darlin', I haven't been this addled since that rack of bacon of yours rang my bell at the fair."

"Talk nice about Rosie, Gabe," Tess chastised.

"Hey," he protested. "She started it."

He opened his eyes to find a smile playing about his wife's lips. He grinned in response, and the smiles served to sever the threads of sexual tension stretching between them. The atmosphere grew comfortable, friendly. Gabe relaxed for the first time since the trip up Lookout Peak to check out the spooklights.

Then Tess had to go and ruin it. "Gabe, I've been thinking about the divorce."

Sweet land of liberty. After *that* kiss? She might as well have slapped his face. A hollow pang of emotion yawned in the vicinity of his heart. His voice came out harsh. "Is that what you want, Tess? A divorce?"

"Is it what *you* want?"

The childish words, *I asked you first*, collected on his tongue, but he swallowed them and shrugged.

"Gabe, I . . ."

He saw something in her expression. He couldn't put a name to it, but it was enough to loosen his tongue. "I didn't want one twelve years ago, and I can't say that's necessarily changed. How 'bout you?"

She licked her lips. "I don't think I do, either."

"But we're not sure?" he asked, halfway hoping she'd tell him how she felt. Other than bedding her, he didn't know what the hell he wanted.

Her voice was small and she didn't look at him as she spoke. "How can we be sure, Gabe? We're all but strangers. I know I've changed in the past twelve years, and I don't doubt you have, too. Maybe what we need is a little time to get to know each other again. We should talk more. Like we did tonight."

"We can do that," he responded. His gaze drifted to the milky soft spot of skin at the base of her neck and he added, "We can do more of the other, too. This separate bed business is a waste."

She shot him a droll look. "I don't think we're ready for that."

"Oh, I'm ready, Tess. I'm definitely ready. And I got the impression that you were ready, too."

Pink stained her cheeks. She looked so damned pretty it was all he could do not to scoop her up and lay her down right then and there.

"I don't believe . . . it's not enough . . . there has to be . . ." Her sentence trailed off.

Despite the years apart, Gabe knew this woman well. He heard the one word she didn't say like a clarion call.

Love. She was saying lust wasn't enough. There had to be love

Well, hell.

He wasn't truly surprised. Tess never had been one to settle for less. The woman wanted courting, just like he'd been thinking earlier that day, only she'd taken the idea beyond the marriage bed. Something he hadn't bothered to do.

It was a basic difference between male and female, he silently observed. He thought courting. She thought commitment.

Gabe rolled the thought around in his mind. He'd had a gun to his back when he'd committed himself the first time, but he hadn't really minded. He'd taken her virginity and marrying her had been the right thing to do.

Of course, back then he'd loved her with his whole, eighteen-year-old heart. He couldn't sit here now and say he still felt the same way. The past twelve years had changed him; he wasn't that green boy anymore. And life had made its marks on Tess, too, during that time. He knew this woman like the back of his hand, but at the same time, he didn't know her at all.

Still, he couldn't honestly say he *didn't* love her, either. The fact that he'd never allowed another woman into his heart told him Tess likely had a hold on at least a portion of it to this day.

Tess broke the silence languishing between them by asking, "You weren't planning on leaving Aurora Springs anytime soon, were you? We're not in any rush, are we?"

Gabe took note of the lingering pressure in his loins and thought, *speak for yourself.*

"A person can't put aside a dozen years of hurt and misunderstandings in a week, Gabe," she continued. "It wouldn't be honest for us to . . . well . . . to make love now. You and I were always honest with one another. And we always made love when we were together. I don't want to cheapen that by simply scratching an itch now."

Damn. Because he wanted her to know exactly where he stood on this issue, he said, "It would be more than scratching an itch with you, Tess. I could bed down with you right now in clear conscience."

"But it wouldn't be lovemaking. Not like it once was."

"Does it have to be that way? Maybe this way would be better."

Sad, somber eyes met his. "Nothing could be better, Gabe. We loved."

Gabe sighed. He had no argument with that. "All right, Tess. As much as it pains me, if you're not certain, then it's probably not the right time. Not now. We can take this slow, and work our way toward . . . whatever it is we're working toward." After a moment's pause, he added, "I don't want to hurt you."

"I know," she agreed, backing off the bed. "I don't want to hurt you, either. If I even could, that is."

Oh, she could. Gabe suppressed another sigh as her falling hem hid her shapely leg from his gaze. *She definitely could.*

Tess smoothed her skirt and asked, "So, how would you suggest we go about getting to know one another again?"

"Like you said before. We need to talk." Gabe pinned her with a stare. "Avoiding each other doesn't get us very far."

"I know," she said with a sigh. "I guess I evaded you because I was scared. I was afraid you'd bring up the divorce. I wasn't ready to talk about it, Gabe."

"But you were ready tonight?"

She met his gaze briefly, then her eyes skidded away and she shrugged.

"Anything else have you worried?"

She licked her lips, then offered him a hesitant smile. "Actually, if it's all the same to you, I'd rather not talk about any of the hard stuff—about our fathers and the past and all of that. Not right away."

Gabe ran his palm down the rough stubble of his jaw. Funny, they were both thinking along the same lines, both of them running from that desert full of prickly pear. Why was that? Were they both cowards?

Or did they each want a chance with the other?

He cleared his throat. "All right, Tess. Why don't we declare the past off limits for the time being. My questions can wait, and I'll give you warning before I ask them. All right?"

"Excellent."

The smile she beamed his way got his blood heating all over again. He figured it was time to make a not-so-hasty retreat. Gabe swung his legs off the bed and stood. "Now, since we're laying our cards on the table, there is one more thing I'd like to discuss. I need something to do around here, and I've been thinking about this vandalism business. I thought I might ride into town and nose around a bit. I am an investigator, you know. Pretty good one, if I say so myself."

"That's all I need," she muttered softly.

"What's that?"

Tess scooped her journals off the bed and returned them to her desk. "I know that tone of voice. We don't need you stirring up trouble, Gabe. Captain Robards will get to the bottom of it. He's a friend."

"He was after something other than the truth when he rode in here. That's as plain as the turban on Twinkle's head."

She wrinkled her nose and folded her arms. "Besides, do you really need something to do? Haven't we given you a big enough list of chores to keep you busy here in Aurora Springs?"

"Yes, you have. And that's why I'm looking for something else to do." His gaze fastened on her hands and the graceful bend of her long, slender fingers. He imagined them stroking his chest. Then, because he needed a distraction, he added, "I don't like chores. I'm a hero, remember? Not a handyman. Heroes don't do chores."

"Maybe not." She flashed him a smile. "But husbands do."

The words formed, then flew off his tongue before he had the good sense to stop them. "Husbands are good for indoor jobs, too, you know. Indoors, in bed."

Her gaze drifted toward the piece of furniture under discussion, and she winced. "You are a dog with a bone, aren't you. Now go on, Gabe. It's late. I need to sleep."

His grin was wry and his step was light as he retired to his room. Even tired as he was, he didn't flop right down on the mattress. He was too worked up to sleep. He moved to his window and gazed outside. Despite the lack of a moon, he could pick out a shape here and there. Must be a bunch of stars in the sky.

Briefly, he considered lifting his gaze to take a look. Nah, knowing his luck, in addition to not seeing Tess's spooklights, maybe he wouldn't see regular stars anymore. He wasn't up to testing that theory tonight.

Gabe sighed heavily. Spooklights. Mystery Lights. The Kissing Stars.

Tess. His wife. In bed, alone, a few steps away.

What a night.

For a time, he stood looking out the window, not thinking of much at all. Then his mind drifed back to the word play at the end of their conversation, and he reached into his back pocket and removed a folded sheet of paper, Twinkle's list of chores.

Clean chimney. Caulk windows. Replace fenceposts. He grinned. If he had a pencil handy, he'd write in bedroom work.

Turning away from the window, he sat on his bed and pulled off his boots. He shrugged from his shirt, and tossed it onto a chair. Then, barefoot and bare chested, he walked silently back to her bedroom. Tess stood at her desk, her index finger resting on a page of an opened book. But she wasn't reading. She was staring blindly off into space.

"Darlin'?" he said softly, summoning her attention. "One more thing, just so you know. This indoor work? It won't be a chore."

His hard, naked body rose above her, gleaming in the silvered light of a gibbous moon. Yearning consumed her. She craved his touch, deep inside her. Filling her.

His lips spoke words of love and desire as he came to her. At that first, probing touch, she arched up. Offering. Begging.

Swat. "Rise and shine, woman."

The dream disintegrated and Tess groaned into her pillow, "Ow!" She'd hardly felt Gabe's slap to her rump—a quilt, blanket, sheet, and her flannel night-gown provided plenty of protective padding. The sting came from the shock of waking from the fantasy-Gabe to the reality-Gabe. It made her grumpy.

"No, go away, I don't want to get up," she complained, even though she'd made him promise to wake her at dawn before heading up Lookout Peak for the starwatch the night before. "I'm too tired."

"Doesn't matter."

"But the Kissing Stars didn't blink out until two A.M. last night. That's nine straight nights in a row they've shined past midnight. I'm sleep deprived and exhausted."

In a voice completely devoid of sympathy he told her, "Would you like some cheese with your whine this morning, my dear?" She growled at him and he laughed. "It's a four hour trip into town. You can sleep in the wagon."

"I don't want to sleep in the wagon. I want to sleep in my bed."

"Suit yourself. We're leaving in twenty minutes whether you're loaded up or not."

She rolled onto her side and lifted her head enough to glare at him. "And who made you trail boss?"

He slashed her a grin. "You did when you asked me to drive y'all into town to pick up your monthly supplies."

"I didn't intend for us to leave this early. Don't forget that the rest of us keep late hours, Gabe."

"I can't forget. Y'all wake me up every night when you come down the mountain."

She wrinkled her nose. "Well, you wake me at the break of dawn each day when you go out to work."

"Somebody has to do the chores around here.

You'll be glad I don't go spooklight-looking with the rest of you when winter comes on and my repairs on your roofs and windows and doors keep the cold out. Now, quit stalling and get out of bed. Daylight is wasting."

"You just want to get to the café before they stop serving breakfast."

He gave an unabashed nod. "Darlin', I have bacon on the brain, and I won't apologize for it. However, I've also had an idea about a possible source for your lights. I thought we might discuss it on the way to . . ."

When his voice trailed off, she saw his attention had drifted, and she realized her nightgown had slipped from one shoulder, baring her skin to the swell of her breast. She yanked the gown back up and stared at him. He met her stare with a heated look of his own, and the moment spun out like a web.

They'd suffered these spells of awareness off and on during the days since the Kissing Stars returned to the sky, and Tess knew that at some point, one of them would break. With the effects of the dream still lingering in her body, she halfway hoped today would be the day. But she knew it wouldn't happen. Today they had to go to town. Closing her eyes against the vital, masculine bundle of energy standing beside her bed, she said, "Go on, Gabe. I'll meet you at the wagon."

The son-of-gun whistled as he left her bedroom and her house.

Tess dragged herself from the bed and availed herself of the facilities, then splashed cold water on her face in an effort to wash the haunting remnants of her dream from her system. Returning to her bedroom, she lit a lamp. Pale yellow light chased the darkness from the room, and she glanced at her clock to check the time. Almost dawn. Less than four hours of sleep. A four-hour wagon ride into town ahead of her. It was going to be a very long day.

Wearily, she sighed. Between studying the lights, lying awake in bed worrying about Gabe and their situation, and dreaming these dreams when she did get to sleep, she hadn't had a good night's rest in what felt like forever. It was wearing her down. "I'm going to start taking more naps," she muttered.

She poured herself a cup of water and quenched her thirst, wishing it were coffee. A sensitive man would have woken her with a nice hot steaming cup of the brew. Her husband did it with a swat to the rump. *There's a lesson in there somewhere,* she thought.

Knowing she must get a move on, she tugged up her hem and pulled her nightgown up and over her head. Then, unfortunately, she happened to glance toward her vanity table and got a glimpse of her nude self in the mirror.

She froze and stared at herself for a long minute. Dismay hit her first, but anger blew in hard and furious on its heels. She'd been eighteen years old the last time he'd seen her naked. She wasn't eighteen any longer. Time had changed her body.

Time and childbearing.

"Plague take you, Gabe Cameron. Plague take you for not being here while I was still at my best." Bracing herself, she turned and fully faced the mirror, attempting to superimpose the memory of her body then, upon the reality of her body now. What would he think if he saw her like this? Would he realize what particular state of nature had brought about most of these physical differences? If so, how would he react?

The changes went beyond the wrinkles beginning to web out from the corners of her eyes, the most obvious contrast being in her bosom. She'd blossomed with the pregnancy, and while some of the plumpness faded when she quit nursing, she still ended up bigger than she'd started out. Bigger, and not as perky, and marred by faint white lines streaking each breast.

She had a few of those same lines across her belly, too. A belly that was thicker than it had been at eighteen. Her whole body was thicker. Look at her legs! All that up and down the mountain the last few years had laid down a layer of muscle.

So much for soft, feminine curves. She was firm as a mattress made of rock. Another wave of anger surged through her as she mentally added, *so much for these darned lusty dreams of late, too.*

She wouldn't get naked in front of Gabe on a bet.

Whirling away from the mirror, she went to her bureau and snatched up underthings and brooded as she donned them. It would be different if he'd been there to share the changes pregnancy brought to her body. The Gabe she had married would have loved watching her stomach stretch and grow. He would have done handsprings over the increase in her bust.

She'd been self-conscious about the smallness of her breasts when they married. He'd soothed her fears by telling her more than a mouthful was wasted anyway.

She'd known better, however. When she was fourteen and flat as a flapjack, she'd eavesdropped on a conversation between Gabe and Billy where they discussed women's cleavage. Gabe had been quite vociferous in his fascination with an ample bosom. That obviously had not changed. The first words out of the man's mouth upon seeing her for the first time in twelve years called attention to the size of her bosom.

"I'm darn sure ample enough now," she muttered. But ample before pregnancy and ample after nursing a child were two different amples all together.

Moving to her wardrobe, she yanked out a dress and started grumbling. "Why do you even care? This is shallow thinking, and as a scientist, you don't indulge in such. Think of how backward this world would be if scientists thought no deeper than desert dirt."

She stepped into the dress, slipped into the sleeves, and pulled it on, arguing to herself all the while. "But I'm a woman, too. Aren't women supposed to be shallow? Maybe I'm not shallow. Maybe I'm vulnerable, did you ever think about that?"

Her fingers worked her buttons. "No, I didn't think about being vulnerable and I don't want to think that now because vulnerable is weak and you swore off being weak the day your father threw you off the Rolling R because you carried Gabe Cameron's child."

She startled at the sound of Twinkle's voice. "You're not vulnerable or weak, Tess," her friend declared as she swept into Tess's bedroom. "Now, you may be well on the way to tetched, talking like that to yourself. What's this nonsense about vulnerable and weak?"

In that moment, all the troubles and the worries and too few hours of sleep caught up with her and Tess lashed out, passion ringing in her voice while pain twisted her heart. "That's how I feel, Twinkle. He makes me feel that way. He gives me these long, smoldering I-want-you-naked looks, but I'm afraid that when he gets me that way he'll throw my clothes back at me and tell me to put them back on!"

Twinkle's mouth dropped open in shock. "But, honey, why would you say something silly like that? Why, you're beautiful. You're the kind of girl men fantasize about. What brought all this on?"

"A dream. A month full of dreams. Oh, Twinkle," she held out her arms and looked down at her body. "I feel closer to a nightmare than a fantasy."

The older woman shook her head and clicked her tongue. "I swear, if you're not acting like a silly schoolgirl."

A geyser of emotion frothed and churned in her stomach, feelings Tess didn't understand. "He makes me feel like a silly schoolgirl. That's who I was when he knew me before. But back then I was a pretty, silly schoolgirl."

"And now you're a beautiful woman and your Gabe knows it. I've seen the way he looks at you."

"That's 'cause he hasn't seen me!"

"Why, hush your mouth, Tess Cameron. If you're not wallowing in a slop of pity today. What's the matter with you?"

Tess sank down upon her bed with a sigh. "I don't

know. I'm tired. The lights keep me out late, then once I go to bed I don't sleep well. He bothers me, Twinkle."

Twinkle folded her arms and projected an air of protectiveness. "Bothers you how?"

"Oh, Twink. He fills up my night dreams and my day dreams and makes me want the things I gave up on having years ago."

"You mean a husband, home, and family?"

"Yes!" Tess felt the swell of tears in her eyes and got angry all over again. "I hate being weak."

"Weak? Honey, honey, honey." Twinkle took her arm and led her over to the bed. Both women sat. "You have survived trials that would destroy a weaker person. You're one of the strongest women I've ever known. It's not weak to want love, to want a family."

"I have a family. I have you and Will and Doc and the others."

"Yes, we're all family of a sorts, and we certainly all love you. But extended family love can't substitute for the warmth of a loving husband's arms holding you through the night or the fulfillment of cradling his child to your breast. You should have that, Tess. You deserve to have that."

"But I had it once and look what happened. I had a husband's arms to hold me but I lost him. I had his child to nurse, but I lost my baby, too. The experience all but killed me. I couldn't survive going through that again."

Twinkle wrapped her arms around Tess in a comforting hug. "You are like a daughter to me, Tess, and it hurts me to see you so upset. Since we are family, I'm going to give you a mother's advice." She pulled back and looked deeply into Tess's eyes. "Remember back when we first met? Remember what a watering can I was, unable and unwilling to put my dear Herbert's death behind me?"

"I remember," Tess said, nodding.

"Do you also remember the advice you offered me? You said that on the scale of life, grief and good memories hung opposite each other. You told me—"

"Minutes are grains of sand added to memories first to balance, and then outweigh the pain," Tess completed on a sigh. "I got that from Doc. It's what he said to me after . . ." She allowed her voice to trail off, still reluctant to say the words out loud.

"Well, Doc was absolutely right." Twinkle grasped Tess's hand and squeezed. "Time heals. The pain of loss dims. But if you tend your memories, you can keep them fresh. Do you remember what else you told me, dear?"

"Not to be afraid."

Twinkle touched the tip of her finger to Tess's nose. "Exactly. And fear is what I hear coming from your mouth this morning. You said it yourself. But I have a hunch that it's not the fear of baring your body that has you in a dither. It's the fear of baring your soul."

Tess considered the notion a moment, resisting. "I don't think that's it. My body has changed in twelve years, Twinkle, and not for the better."

"Honey," her friend drawled. "I've seen you undressed. Take the word of experience. Clothed, you could attract the eyes of every man in West Texas.

Naked, you'd start a riot. You won't disappoint your Gabe."

"He's not 'my Gabe.' He hasn't been for years."

Twinkle stood, then reached for Tess's hand and pulled her to her feet. "He's yours. Signed, sealed, and delivered. All you must do is open the door for him. And, I'm not talking about your bodice and corset. I'm talking about your heart. Don't be afraid. Let him back inside again, child."

"How can I, Twinkle?" Tess scoffed. "With our past looming and lurking and ready to pounce? With the secrets I'm keeping? Believe me, Gabe is far from 'delivered.'"

Twinkle's mouth flattened into a frown. She dropped Tess's hand and folded her arms. "I've been warning you for days now. Tell him. You must."

"But I don't want to." Tess whirled and started pacing. "I have no clue as to how he'll react. I know this is selfish of me, but it's been so nice. We're getting along so well. I'm having fun for the first time in the longest time. He's fun. I love finding out so much about him, about the man he's become. I don't want to ruin that."

"Every day you wait is a betrayal."

"But every day I have now might be all I ever have, Twinkle. Doc and Will will come home before long, and I'll have to take action then." Tess halted and lifted her hands to her eyes, rubbing them. Thinking. Finally, she looked at her friend and pleaded, "I miss Will so much, I truly do. But is it so wrong for me to steal a little time for myself?"

Twinkle watched her sadly, for once saying nothing.

"I want to love Gabe again, Twinkle. It's waiting here inside me, building a little every day. But I can't let it happen. If I made love with him, I wouldn't be able to hold him out of my heart. And if I let myself love him again and he turns against me . . ." Tess inhaled a shaky breath and felt the sting of tears at the back of her eyes. Furiously, she blinked them away.

Clicking her tongue, Twinkle said, "All right, honey. I think I understand. I don't necessarily agree, but I do understand. And, since you're not ready to surrender the walls of your heart, you'd best see about deserting the walls of your home. He sent me in here to get you. He is out there chomping at the bit to head into town. We'd best get moving."

A few minutes later they walked outside to greet a glorious pink and purple dawn and a man whose flint-colored eyes flashed with impatience. "I swear you women move slow as short-legged turtles in a molasses spill. It'll be noon before we get to town."

"Oh, hush," Tess said, accepting his assistance into the carriage. "And watch what you say from now on. If you'll notice, we are still waiting on a male member of our party." She glanced toward Twinkle. "Where is Andrew, anyway?"

"Fetching Rosie."

Gabe's head whipped around toward Twinkle. "Doing what?"

"He's going after Rosie."

"That ham is not coming with us. I'm not driving that ham into town. It's strange enough you people own your own personal stagecoach, but taking a pig along as a passenger? I'm telling you, folks will think you're crazy."

"So what else is new?" Tess observed. "Fine, then. Let Colonel Jasper drive the stagecoach. It's ordinarily his job, anyway. You can drive the supply wagon."

A little over three and a half hours later, the Aurora Springs stage approached the town of Eagle Gulch. Tess had managed to sleep two hours of the time, and as a result felt more rested than when she awoke that morning. Andrew and Jack had spelled Gabe and Colonel Jasper with the driving chore about twenty minutes earlier, and while they were stopped, her husband had watched as Tess removed Rosie's best red grosgrain ribbon from her pocketbook and tied a go-to-town bow around the pig's neck.

"Darlin'?" Gabe asked with a roll of his eyes, "haven't you ever heard the expression 'like putting a silk purse on a sow's ear?' Well, bows are just as bad."

Tess shot him a chiding look. "You have the saying wrong. It's 'can't make a silk purse out of a sow's ear.' "

"Whatever. All I'm saying is . . ." His sentence trailed off when something else grabbed his attention. Sitting up straighter, he pointed east and asked, "Is that a train or a brush fire?"

Tess's gaze followed the path he indicated. A line of hazy white smoke floated against the horizon. "It's the train. With the land as flat as it is, you can see it coming for a long way."

"I see it coming in my nightmares," Colonel Wilhoit commented, his tone bitter and his face screwed up in a scowl.

"Now, let's not get into that, Jasper," Twinkle said, patting his knee. "It'll just get us all worked up and that's not the kind of attitude we need to be taking to town. Not after what happened a couple months ago."

Gabe asked, "What happened?"

"The colonel indulged in fisticuffs with the owner of the barbershop, that's what." Amy sniffed with disdain. "Mr. Wilson is a good twenty years younger than he is."

"I held my own, though, you must admit."

Andrew nodded. "You dusted his knuckles, Colonel. I was right proud for you. But Twinkle is right. We don't need any trouble this trip to town. Probably would have been better if some of us stayed home this time, but I know we all have business in town today. Now, I like a good fight as much as the next man, but we should keep in mind that we're pressing our luck with the law in Eagle Gulch."

"Why did you fight?" Gabe asked, eyeing the colonel's scowl with interest. "I take it had something to do with the railroad?"

"You know how T&NO wants to build a spur across the flats near Aurora Springs?" Tess asked him softly. In order to avoid an escalating scene, she considered it best to deal with this topic quickly and quietly. "There is some question about whether the coming of the railroad might drive the stars away. Tempers have run a little hot in the past over the subject."

Gabe glanced toward the east where the puffs of

locomotive smoke grew closer every minute. "That's why your Doc is a suspect in this sabotage they talked about. What are they—"

Tess interrupted when she saw Colonel Wilhoit cock an ear their direction. "Please, can we put this off until the trip home? I promise I'll explain everything then."

Gabe twisted his lips and considered. "Only if y'all stop and let me out on the edge of Eagle Gulch. It would ruin my reputation to be seen driving into town with a pork chop in my lap."

Tess offered him a smile as sweet as sugar on the cane. "Her name is Rosie and she's riding in the supply wagon. I think on the trip home, you and she should switch places."

Gabe playfully narrowed his gaze. "Is that a roundabout way of calling me a pig, woman?"

"If the snout fits, Gabe."

The Aurorians riding inside the stagecoach then commenced making snorting sounds.

When the coach paused on the outskirts of town, Gabe bid the Aurorians a "See you later" and hopped over the side intending to go the rest of the way afoot. He'd used Pork Ribs Rosie as an excuse, but in truth he hoped to ask around about the railroad vandalism before townsfolks connected him to Aurora Springs.

First off, however, his agenda included a stop at the bath house for a soak and a shave, then a visit to the café for a platter full of bacon and sausage to go with his fried eggs. "Might even get a slice of ham or two," he mused aloud. After that he intended to look up the sheriff here in town and dip his boot into this railroad trouble, test the waters a bit.

An hour later he was halfway through a stack of bacon and pondering the piece of sausage on the end of his fork, wondering why it didn't taste as good as he'd expected, when he overheard a woman seated at the table behind him mention Aurora Springs.

". . . folks cause nothing but trouble when they come to town."

"At least Doc isn't with them this time," a male voice replied. "They're all half a bubble off plumb, but the doctor is the one who truly gets violent. Why, I've never seen such an overprotective male. All a man had to do was look crossways at that pretty little Mrs. Cameron and the fella was ready to fight."

"I know. He did two hundred dollars damage in the mercantile when he dusted the floor with Johnny Wainwright last spring. I hear Sheriff Marston and the Texas Rangers are looking for him. I hear he's the one who started that fire up along the Aurora spur last month."

"That's Lizard Johnson talking. Do you believe him? I was with my Nellie over to the livery right before I came in here. She up and asked Mrs. Cameron if Doc was guilty. The woman denied it, and I'm inclined to take her word over Lizard's any day."

"A pretty face always fools you."

"Then it's a good thing you're so ugly, ain't it?"

Gabe ate the sausage, chewing slowly as he pondered that bit of news. Doc was protective of Tess, hmm? Protective to the point of violence? As soon as he finished his breakfast, he figured to head over to the barbershop and get in line to get his ears lowered. Experience had taught him that barbershops provided better information than saloons. That's where he'd start his behind-the-scenes investigation into good ol' Doc and the railroad shenanigans.

At that moment, the saloon doors swung open to reveal a new visitor, and all thought of Doc and haircuts disappeared from Gabe's mind. "Mack?"

Mack Hunter strolled into the café like he owned it. "Hey, Whip. I figured I'd find you either eatin' or cheatin' at cards. Guess you haven't made it as far as the poker table yet." Motioning to a pair of men seated at the table nearest the door, he said, "Just a warning, folks, but I wouldn't recommend dealing cards with this shark. He actually plays fair, he just wins so much it makes you think he must be cheating."

"What are you doing here?" Gabe asked, dropping his fork onto his plate. He sat back in his chair, folded his arms, and narrowed his eyes in suspicion. "You told me you wouldn't make this trip for all the bad whiskey in a Hell's Half Acre saloon."

"Speaking of which . . ." Mack turned to the waitress. "Can I get a whiskey here or do I need to go to the saloon for that?"

The woman provided him with two glasses and a bottle of whiskey which he took to Gabe's table. He poured them both a drink, then sipped his with a sigh. "I'm not here by choice. Jared sent me."

Gabe lifted a brow. "Looking for me?"

Mack tugged an empty chair closer and propped up his boots. "And I have a letter for you from him. I thought I'd have to travel to this Aurora place to deliver it, so when I spied that Sparkle woman I met in Dallas down the street and she told me you were here, I was right pleased as a pig in slop."

Gabe lifted his hand, palm out. "Don't bring up pigs. Or camels for that matter. And it's Twinkle, not Sparkle. Tell me why you've come."

Mack scowled, took a sip of his whiskey, then said glumly, "Actually, I'm just passing through on my way west. Jared has loaned my services to the T&NO Railroad. Their people have hit a wall trying to flush out a gang of train robbers causing havoc in these parts. Since I was going to be in the neighborhood and Jared had a letter to send you, we decided I should deliver it in person." Eyeing Gabe's plate he added, "Are you going to eat all that bacon?"

"Help yourself." Gabe pushed his plate toward his friend.

Mack helped himself to two slices. "So, tell me what is up with you? Did you find your runaway wife?"

"I found her."

"So what's the story?"

"You know, I've been here for a while now, and I guess I'm still not certain."

Mack gave him a measuring stare. "That doesn't sound like you, my friend."

Gabe had to agree. Seeing Mack again caused him to recall the sense of urgency that had gripped him in Dallas to hash out the past with Tess. Funny how that feeling had faded. Reckon that proved physical demands beat mental compulsions hands down. Uncomfortable with that thought, he asked his friend for the letter.

Mack slipped a hand inside his jacket and removed an envelope from the inner pocket. He tossed it to Gabe.

Recognizing his boss' distinctive scrawl, Gabe experienced a sudden and surprising sense of dismay. He eyed the letter like a bowl of cold grits. If Jared had summoned him back to work, what would he do?

He wasn't ready to leave Tess.

He picked up the missive and started to read. "He says there's a letter from the governor?"

Mack removed a second paper from his pocket. "He told me to give you his first."

Gabe nodded. Apparently the governor had made a request of Gabe, and Jared wanted to reassure him that whatever his decision, he always had a job with the Brazos Valley Rail Company. The railroad owner also devoted a paragraph to scolding him for running off without providing the low-down on the pig-racing beauty. That was only to be expected. Jared was a nosey sonofabitch.

Gabe held out his hand and wiggled his fingers for Mack to hand over the governor's letter. What he read ignited a spark of excitement inside him. "He wants me to report to Austin after the first of the year," he told an obviously curious Mack. "He's offered me the task of designing legislation to revamp the Texas Rangers, then sell the new plan to the state legislature."

"Well that job should suit you like a broke-in pair

of denims. You've been griping about the Rangers for years."

"Not the Rangers themselves," he protested. Then, recalling the captain come a-courting to Tess, he added, "Not all of them, anyway. It's the organizational structure of the corps that is the problem. Times have changed. The Indian wars are over. Texas is heading into a new century with new problems and a population that continues to grow. Its institutions need to recognize the world has changed."

"You don't have to lecture me, Montana. I've never argued with you on this subject, have I?"

"Yes, you have. You resist change like Tess's pig resists the skillet."

A grin split Mack's face. "And how is the fleet porker? You turned her into barbeque, yet?"

"Careful, there, Hunter. Your northern roots are showing. Texans barbeque beef, not pork. We pan-fry pork."

"And how about the pig's protectress? Have you put her on to sizzle, yet, my friend? That's the question that truly brought me out here, you know. I might have talked my way out of this job for the T&NO if I weren't dying of curiosity about your wife."

Gabe eyed his friend, then purposely glanced back down at the letter. "The governor says he thinks I'm the perfect choice to tackle this task because of the notoriety the schoolhouse incident gave me, and the fact I've been stringent in my charge that the Rangers have allowed incompetent agents into its ranks in recent years."

"I get the distinct impression you are trying to avoid talking about the lady."

"I'm not answering the question you asked, no."

"Still pretending to be a gentleman, I see."

Gabe gave his friend a pointed stare. Mack was a rogue of the first water, and he'd long taken much pleasure in needling Gabe over his discretion where the women in his life were concerned. Mack never knew the reasons behind Gabe's reticence—at least, not until now.

Gabe might have left Tess physically, but mentally she'd remained right there with him. As a result, whenever he'd taken a woman to his bed, he'd made love to a memory. Using women that way shamed him, and he tended to avoid the exercise except when his body got the better of him. Mack, being Mack, had long questioned Gabe's reluctance to take advantage of the amorous opportunities that came his way. He'd dubbed his partner's behavior "gentlemanly." Gabe never bothered to correct him.

"So," Mack continued. "What do you think about Governor Ross's proposition? You ready to dismantle the Texas Rangers?"

Gabe tossed the letter onto the table and shook his head. "I wouldn't think of it. The Rangers still have a place in the law enforcement hierarchy in this state. But like I said, times have changed. The frontier is disappearing. Our citizens have different needs than they did twenty years ago."

"So you're gonna take the job?"

Gabe thought of Tess. He couldn't float along forever. Hell, except for his goal of bedding his wife, he'd had about as much purpose of late as those damned stars of hers. The governor didn't want him in Austin for another three months. By then, he and Tess surely will have worked something out. Either that or all this pent-up sexual frustration will have driven him crazier than even the Aurorians. "Guess I'll have to get around to asking the rest of those questions."

"What questions?"

"Never mind. Yes, I'll take the job. It'll be good for me."

"It'll be good for Texas," Mack replied seriously. "You'll do the state more good doing this than by bringing in train robbers and other nefarious outlaws."

Gabe shrugged, then asked Mack about the gang of robbers he'd traveled this far to apprehend. They discussed the string of robberies taking place for a time and then, when Mack mentioned vandalism, Gabe's ears perked up. "That's been happening not far from here," Mack said. "You know anything about it?"

"Not really." Gabe relayed the little he knew about the storage shed fire and Captain Robards's accusation.

Mack nodded. "I was told about the fire and a few other instances of trouble."

"What other trouble?"

"Minor things for the most part. Tool theft, malicious pranks. I dismissed them as having anything to do with my robbers. They told me the ranchers in this area blame that mischief on a religious sect who've made a home out in the desert."

"The Aurorians aren't a religious sect," Gabe corrected.

"Well, all I know is that the ranchers accuse these folks because they recently waged and lost a legal battle against the T&NO to prevent the building of the spur. Seems they feared the railroad would interfere with whatever it is they are doing out there in the desert."

"Actually, it's a pretty little canyon." Gabe murmured. He recalled Tess's question to Twinkle and the older woman's response his first day in Aurora Springs. Tess had asked Twinkle what she'd done now. Twinkle replied she hadn't done anything wrong *this time.* "Well, hell."

"Well, hell what, Whip? Are they guilty?"

Gabe rubbed his hand along his jaw. "I do know that during my time here, I've not seen any indication of their involvement in any type of sabotage. I don't know what happened before I came. I hope they haven't done anything stupid. I like these people. They're good folk. Eccentric as all git out, but that's not criminal behavior. I may not share their beliefs, but as long as they don't hurt anyone in the pursuit of them, I see nothing wrong with how they choose to live. It's not a crime to be different."

"But it is a crime to burn out a supply depot or take a sledge hammer to machine parts."

Again, he heard Twinkle's voice in his head. *I didn't do anything this time.* "Well, like you, I don't work for the railroad building the spur so I guess it's not my concern."

Mack studied his fingernails. "Never knew you to let a skirt convince you to duck your head on justice."

Gabe leaned back in his chair and took a defiant bite of bacon. "If I didn't know how much you like to badger a person, I'd deck you for that."

Mack laughed. "One of these days I'm gonna get you good and riled, Montana. It's a goal of mine, you know."

"I suggest you concentrate on your train robbers instead," Gabe dryly replied. "Your investigation might take more effort than you anticipate. From what I've seen it's a hard-scrabble life out here in West Texas. Men who live in this part of the world are bound to be tougher than most. You may have to don your spurs to dig your way to the bottom of this particular pile of trouble."

"And what are you going to be doing while I'm busy cozying up to murderers and thieves?"

"I'm going to look into that recent fire." Then, because the governor's request established a deadline for him to leave Aurora Springs, he thought about his wife and added, "And I'm going to start one of my own."

"What?" Mack reared back in shock.

Gabe's lips twitched with a grin, but before he said any more, a disturbance at the door grabbed his attention. *Twinkle?* "Hold on a minute, Mack."

The woman dashed into the café as Gabe pushed to his feet. Beneath her multicolored go-to-town turban, her face was pale, and she literally wrung his hands. "What is it?" Gabe demanded.

"Oh, Gabe, it's terrible. You've got to get them out."

"Get who out?" Gabe replied, already headed for the door. "What happened?"

Twinkle launched into a tale that slowed his steps and soon had him biting the inside of his mouth to keep from laughing. Poor Tess, all in a tizzy about that damned hunk of ham. "Tell you what," he said when the older woman finally wound down, "You see about getting one of the wagons hitched while I see if I can't free the prisoners. We'll likely need to head home early after this."

She sagged in relief. "Thank you, Gabe-dear. I knew you'd help. I'll go for the wagon."

When Twinkle rushed off in the direction of the livery, Gabe returned to his table where he retrieved his hat and paid his bill.

"What's going on?" Mack asked as Gabe motioned for him to join him. "Seems that my wife and her friends have stirred up a little trouble."

Mack polished off his drink and stood. "Where we going?"

"The jail."

Mack's eyebrows arched. "One of those Aurorians been arrested?"

"In a manner of speaking." Gabe snagged his hat from the rack by the door and sauntered outside.

CHAPTER

8

*A*fter years of living in the wide open spaces of West Texas, Tess didn't cotton to small, enclosed places. Five steps by three steps. There was room for a fourth, but the foul smelling bucket in the corner kept her turning around before she took the final step.

Tess paced the confined area, careful not to trip over her four-legged cellmate who had plopped herself down on the floor in front of the barred and locked door. "It's a case of false arrest, that's what this is. It has nothing to do with assault and everything to do with one hardheaded, mean-spirited man. I'd like to tell that Bart Collins to go sit on a cactus."

On the other side of the bars, her Aurorian family nodded in agreement. Jack's expression dipped in a scowl. "I never liked that man. There's something sinister about him."

Andrew folded his arms and grunted. "His eyes are too close together, have you noticed that? I don't trust a man whose eyes are too close together. Bad confirmation, don't you know."

"He is somewhat beady-eyed," the colonel observed, thumbing his lapels. "I wouldn't want him standing with me in battle."

Andrew reached through the bars and took hold of Tess's hand, giving it a reassuring squeeze. "Bart Collins is trouble, no doubt about that. I'm sorry none of us were there to help you when it happened. It wouldn't have gone so far if we'd been with you."

"Why did you go off on your own?" Colonel Jasper asked.

A new voice entered the fray. "That's a good question, Colonel," Gabe said striding into the jail. "Darlin', why were you in the alley between the whorehouse and the saloon with nothing more than a pig for protection?"

Tess drew herself up and folded her arms. She wasn't about to reveal her private vice, not to him and not under these circumstances. Adopting a false air of bravado, she did her best to change the subject. "Gabe, I'm glad you're here. Please tell me you have enough money with you to bail us out of jail. We've already spent most everything we had on supplies, and considering the circumstances, I doubt Bart Collins would give us a refund anyway."

Gabe chastened her with a gaze, letting her know he was aware she hadn't answered his question. She looked away from him when another man, a stranger, entered the small jailhouse behind her husband. He snapped his fingers and said, "Now I place the face. The peach colored dress at the pig race at the fair.

You're the phantom wife?" Then he slapped Gabe on the shoulder and said, "You sonofa . . . uh . . . gun. No wonder you 'bout tore up the Texas State Fair looking for her."

Obviously, a friend of her husband. The smile she aimed at Gabe dripped sugar. "Phantom wife?"

He arched a brow. "An alley?"

Darn the man. He had the tenacity of the dromedaries on the trail. Tess thought it best to move on. She turned a genuine version of her smile toward the stranger. "I'm eager to meet a friend of my husband's, but I hope you'll understand I prefer to be out of jail for proper introductions."

He swept his hat off his head and gallantly placed it over his heart. "I shall count the minutes."

"If that's the case, then your friend best be counting out his cash so you're not counting minutes for days," grumbled Jack Baker. He stepped toward Gabe, held out his hand, and rubbed thumb and fingers together.

Ignoring him, Gabe looked at Tess. "Now, let me get this straight. You belted this Collins fellow because . . . ?"

"He fired a gun at Rosie because she was rooting through his trash."

Gabe froze. "A gun? This incident involved a gun?"

The stranger exclaimed, "Collins shot at another lady and they arrested you for assault?"

"Rosie isn't a lady," Gabe said, his glare locked on Tess. "She's a pig."

"Dang, Montana. That's a little personal, isn't it?"

Ignoring his friend's question, Gabe pushed his way past the Aurorians and stopped directly in front of the cell door, his hands braced on his hips. "Tell me exactly what happened. Every little detail."

Tess didn't care for his autocratic attitude, but since she was at the mercy of his wallet at the moment, she chose to comply. "I was visiting with a friend and not paying attention to Rosie. She wandered down the alley a bit. First thing I know, she's snorting and squealing and Bart Collins is kicking her in the ribs."

"He's the swine, not our Rosie," Colonel Jasper declared.

"Where does the gun part come in?" Gabe asked, a muscle working in his jaw.

Anger washed through Tess anew as she remembered the events. "Of course Rosie didn't like being kicked, so she turned to run and that's when she knocked him down. At that point, he lost all control and started shouting and swearing, and then he pulled the gun and pointed it at Rosie."

"So, you attacked him?"

"I don't know that *attack* is the best term. I hit him, is all. I defended Rosie."

Gabe's voice climbed with every word he spoke. "You defended your pig by attacking a man holding a gun."

Indignant, she drew herself up. "I couldn't let him shoot Rosie."

"So you thought you'd offer yourself as a target." His harsh bark of laughter held no tone of amusement. "Well, lady, I reckon those spooklights sucked up all your brain power, because that was nothing short of—" he shouted the final word "—stupid!"

Tess knew that charging Collins wasn't the smartest

thing she'd ever done, but she thought "stupid" went a little far. Her chin went up. "I will defend my family under any circumstances."

"It's a pig!"

"She's family!"

Just then Twinkle swept in through the front door. "All is ready, Gabe. Don't worry everyone, I have a hunch everything will turn out fine."

"Good."

"I don't think *good* is the word," Jack said, having edged over to the window and turned his gaze outside. "Let's get 'em out of jail and away from town before Collins incites a riot. He's chewing the sheriff's ear and a crowd is gathering. Looks to be some of the same folks who jumped into the colonel's fray last time."

"Oh, no." Andrew winced with disgust. "The last thing we need is another riot."

"Riot?" the stranger asked.

Tess answered. "We're not especially well-liked in town these days. Some of these ranchers around here think we're behind the pranks being played up along the railroad spur being built out of here."

"Are you?"

Catching the significant glance the fellow darted toward Gabe, she declared, "No, we certainly are not."

Twinkle, being Twinkle, said, "Well, that's not quite true, Tess. Remember how I—"

"Andrew, why don't you take Twink outside," Tess interrupted. "You know how the old souls around jails distracts her. I'm sure she can use some air. Gabe, are you going to bail me out of here or not?"

"Oh, I'm gonna get you out," he replied, saying it like a threat as he reached for his wallet. "How much does the sheriff want? Five or ten dollars?"

"Fifty."

"Fifty!"

"Twenty-five for me and twenty-five for Rosie."

"Twenty-five dollars to take home bacon I can't even eat?"

The Aurorians turned toward him and as one protested, "Montana."

"Watch your language, young man," the colonel added.

"Touchy bunch, aren't they," the stranger observed.

"Just get her out of here, please?" Andrew said, escorting Twinkle toward the door. "The sheriff is still right outside, but the crowd is growing. We need to leave."

"Run out of town again," the colonel said with a sigh. "This is getting to be a habit."

Gabe murmured something to the stranger, then stormed from the jailhouse yanking bills from his wallet. Jack watched through the window and provided Tess a running commentary while Gabe forked cash over to the law. "Looks like Sheriff Marston is headed this way. Wake up Rosie, Tess. It's time to go home."

"Yeah," Andrew agreed. "I don't like the sounds that crowd is making. They're saying some bad things about Rosie. They're as wrong as they can be. All she did was defend herself. Besides, she didn't know she was knocking that Bart Collins into a pile of dog sh . . . uh, stuff."

But as the sheriff led Gabe inside the jailhouse, Jack tossed them a problem. "We can't leave yet. Amy won't be through with her doctor's appointment for a good half hour."

Sheriff Marston cleared his throat, spat and missed the spittoon in the corner, and said, "Half an hour's too long to let that animal hang around. If you don't fancy seein' a hog slaughtering this afternoon, I suggest you get it on out of town."

"I'll take them back," Gabe said, his gaze on the cell door as the sheriff inserted the key and the lock clicked open. "We'll take the supply wagon and y'all can follow later in the stage."

"That will work," Twinkle replied, nodding with satisfaction. "The wagon's all loaded and ready. It's parked in front of the mercantile."

Gabe nodded, then said, "It would probably be best if Tess and the pig went out the back way. Mack," he said, addressing the stranger who stood just inside the front door. "Would you go get the wagon and drive it around back?"

"Sure, Gabe." The stranger tipped his hat toward Tess, and said, "Looks like we'll need to catch that introduction later." Then he exited the building.

The sheriff snorted. "This is a jail. There ain't a back door."

"You've got a window," Gabe explained as Mack departed.

The sheriff's bushy salt-and-pepper eyebrows arched

as he eyed the narrow window skeptically. "You're gonna shove the pig through that? This I gotta see."

Shaking his head, Gabe took hold of the lawman's arm and led him toward the door. "But what you don't need to see is what's beneath my wife's petticoats. You're going to go out there and distract the crowd."

"Now, wait a minute. I'm the sheriff."

"And you have both bail money and a bribe in your pocket, so I suggest you help us out here."

Tess vacillated between relief and trepidation while she watched Jack and Colonel Jasper escort the sheriff to assist in creating a diversion, leaving her and Rosie alone with Gabe. Although she was happy to be out of that cell, she dreaded the ride back to Aurora Springs. Her husband looked mad enough to chew bullets. "I knew I should have stayed in bed today," she muttered.

Gabe fired a glare her way and she recognized the look. He'd heard her, and he had something he wanted to add. Tess knew that something wouldn't be anything she wanted to hear. In the old days, that particular look always precipitated a particularly sarcastic remark. It was enough to get her back up under the circumstances, and she shot a scowl of her own right back at him.

The air between them all but crackled as they stood without speaking, waiting for the man he'd called Mack to arrive with the wagon. Gabe faced the window, leaned his arm against the wall, and stared outside. She kept quiet when he started drumming his fingers against the plaster. When he added a toe-tapping thud against the floor planking, she reached her limit. "I don't know why you're in such a snit."

His fingers stopped mid-thrum. "Pardon me?"

"Bart Collins is the one at fault here, not me."

"Uh huh." He slowly turned his head to look at her. His narrowed eyes glowed like hot coals. "You did nothing wrong by throwing yourself at a bullet to save a rack of ribs waitin' on the barbeque."

She wrinkled her nose in a snarl. "If I've told you once, I've told you a hundred times. Don't call Rosie names."

"She's a pig. You risked your life for a pig."

"I don't believe it was that big of a risk. Bart Collins would not have taken a shot at me. Rosie, yes. But not me. The lawmen around here may not hold those of us from Aurora Springs in high regard, but they couldn't ignore us being shot at. Collins must know that."

"Dammit, Tess, you don't mess around where guns are concerned. Bad things can happen too easily. I can't believe you were this stu—"

Luckily for him, he bit off the word when the noise of a wagon rolling up filtered in through the back window. Tess was willing to concede he had a point about the danger of firearms, but she wouldn't allow any man to call her stupid.

Gabe pointed at Rosie, saying, "Stand by to help me with this overweight, stinking sausage-on-feet if I need it."

Tess clamped her teeth against commenting on the name calling and positioned herself to assist if needed. Rosie, bless her heart, squealed and snorted but didn't squirm overmuch when he hefted her up and out into Mack's waiting arms. Now her turn, Tess felt his hands grasp her waist. Expecting him to lift her feet first through the window, she was unpleasantly surprised to find herself pointed head first. His helpful shove to her bottom felt entirely too much like a swat, and if the stranger hadn't been there to help she'd have dropped in an undignified heap. Cognizant of the value of picking one's battles, Tess chose not to mention her thoughts on his high, or more aptly, low-handedness, when he followed on her heels, literally, a moment later.

Gabe set about shifting boxes and unfolding a tarp and soon had created a hiding place for her and Rosie for the flight from town. "Think you can keep the porker quiet as we head through town?" he asked as Tess settled in beside Rosie. "I'd rather not fight off a rioting crowd this afternoon."

"Rosie won't be a lick of trouble," Tess replied with confidence she didn't honestly feel. Rosie had been acting especially ornery of late, and Tess believed the dear was pining for Will.

A particularly loud snort reinforced her unease.

Tess scratched Rosie's snout as Gabe bid his friend good-bye. "Sorry we didn't have more time. Make sure you look me up on your way back."

Mack glanced at Tess, then said, "This assignment may take awhile. Don't know that I'll finish by the first of the year."

Now, Gabe looked at her. "In that case, check with the governor."

Tess realized the men had passed some sort of message, but she didn't have the energy to try to figure it out at the moment. Gabe gave a farewell wave to his friend, then climbed up into the driver's seat. Just before she pulled the tarpaulin over her and her pet, she said, "Gabe? On the way out of town you need to take us by way of the bordello."

He fumbled the reins. "Come again?"

"I left something there I need to get."

"At the whorehouse?"

"Yes."

"I thought you were at the saloon when the trouble started. That was bad enough but now you're saying you were at the whorehouse?"

"Actually I visited both establishments. And I left a package behind the bordello that I must have before I leave town, so I want you to drive down the alley so I can retrieve it."

He lifted his face toward the sky and she heard him murmur, "She is not the woman I married."

You have that right, she silently fumed.

"What the hell." Louder, he said, "All right, I'll lead you down the garden path, madam. I reckon I'm anxious to see what's in this package of yours."

Over my dead body. She flipped the tarp over her head with flourish.

As he pulled the wagon out onto the dusty main street, she peeked between the tarp and the sideboards and observed the crowd. She spotted Andrew's hat at the center of things and she was certain she heard Twinkle's voice, wailing about some nonsense or other. The diversion had worked. Nobody noticed the departure of the Aurora Springs supply wagon. Almost nobody, that is. The stranger called Mack stood at the edge of the crowd, and Tess grinned when he stared right at her and winked.

He seemed like such a nice man. She hoped a time would come when she could meet him properly.

At the far end of town, Gabe guided the wagon onto a side street and then into an alley. A few minutes later, the wagon wheels rolled to a stop. "Tell me where it is and I'll get it."

"Not necessary," Tess said, throwing back the tarpaulin. "I'll get it."

She scrambled from the wagon and retrieved her brown-paper wrapped package from where she'd stashed it inside a broken flower pot on the bordello's back steps. Upon returning to the wagon, she spied the curiosity in her husband's gaze and clasped the package tightly to her chest. "Don't even try."

She crawled back into her hiding place with her package and Gabe signaled the mules forward. She bounced along in the back of the wagon for a good ten minutes until he told her they'd made it safely out of town, apparently without being followed. At that point, she joined him up front.

One glance at Gabe's face made her reconsider. Maybe she should ride all the way with Rosie. Time had not soothed his temper. If anything, the set to his jaw looked harder than before. *Wonderful. He's been brooding.*

Some men should never be left alone with their own thoughts.

Rosie chose that moment to snort, as though she agreed with her mistress.

"Oh, let's get it over with," Tess said, exasperated. "Go ahead, Gabe. Rant and rave and tell me how stupid you think I am. That's the word you were going to use before, am I right? You think I'm stupid for saving Rosie."

He spat an oath and yanked back on the reins until the mules lumbered to a stop. "Yes, I think you're stupid. Stupid and stubborn and pigheaded."

"Watch what you say, Gabe Cameron."

For once he didn't object to her use of his real name. He was too busy fuming and gripping her shoulders as if to shake her. "You risked your life, Tess." His voice sounded wrenched from his soul. "You went and risked your life when . . . when . . ."

"When what?"

He blew out a harsh breath once, then twice. "When I've only just found you again."

And then he kissed her. He pulled her against him, took her mouth, and plundered. She tasted his frustration, tasted his fear. Tasted his passion.

Oh, Gabe.

Tess melted and surrendered, matching him kiss for kiss. Caress for caress. Groan for achy, need-filled groan.

This explosion had been building for days. For years. Her bodice draped open by the skillful work of his fingers. Her laces loosened, her corset fell away. His hands tore her shimmy and she was free. Free, to arch and offer. Free to sigh as he accepted and kneaded and took her nipple into the heaven of his mouth.

She didn't care that she lay across the hard pine

plank of a wagon. She didn't care that they lost themselves out in the open exposed to the gaze of anyone who happened by. All she cared about was Gabe and the magic he conjured with his mouth and hands and body.

"God," he prayed as he dragged his mouth from one breast to the other, suckling, feasting. Hungry.

She was hungry too. She'd missed this, missed him. *So long. It's been so long.*

And she was so ready. They'd been headed for this since Dallas.

His hand delved beneath her skirts. His fingers found her, explored her, caressed her. Slipped inside to stroke that place untouched for what seemed like forever. She moaned aloud and he answered with a low, rough growl. Moments later the orgasm rolled over her like a gentle wind.

"Oh, my stars," she breathed, gasping at the pleasure, wondering at the speed of it, wanting it to go on and on and on.

Her words seemed to call him back to earth. His hand stilled and he lifted his head. For a long, lovely moment he looked deep into her eyes. "Damn, Venus, what are we doing?"

Venus. The old nickname was music to her ears.

Breathing heavy, he sat up. He swallowed hard and braced his hands on his knees, hanging his head, shaking it. "In the big middle of the desert. In front of the damned peeping pig."

"Are you stopping?"

He hesitated just a moment, then nodded.

"But I . . . don't you . . . you didn't . . ."

"Not like this, darlin'. We both deserve more. Forgive me, I treated you poorly."

Putting her clothing to rights, feeling the warmth stealing over her cheeks, she couldn't stop the little laugh. "Poorly? That's not exactly the term I'd use."

He jerked his head up, studied her, and the familiar, wicked gleam took light in his eyes. A smile played at the corner of his mouth. "Not poorly, huh?"

She fanned her face. "Not poorly at all."

The grin broke out and he made a show of shifting uncomfortably on his seat. "Well, at least one of us is feeling . . . uh . . ."

"Not poorly." Tess bit the inside of her mouth. Otherwise she'd giggle and she really didn't want to take it that far.

He sighed heavily and grimaced. "I don't suppose there's any whiskey stashed in those supplies back there. I sure could use a drink."

Tess considered just a moment before replying, "No whiskey, but I do have something." Reaching into the back of the wagon, she retrieved her private package, pausing long enough to scratch Rosie behind the ears when she snorted for attention. Tearing open the paper, she reached inside and felt the smooth, cool surface of the bottle. She pulled it out and handed it to him.

Gabe took her offering and his eyebrows winged up, then down, and he sympathetically said, "Elderberry wine. Still have trouble with the monthlies, do you?"

An hour earlier, she'd have died before admitting it. Now she simply nodded.

Gabe pulled the cork from the bottle with a pop. He stared at the label, grimaced, then lifted it to his lips for a long pull. Then he shuddered. "Bleh. Nasty sweet stuff. I'd forgotten just how awful this is."

Then he took another long sip, repeated his shudder, and eyed Tess with a considering stare. "You got wine from the saloon, and from the whorehouse . . ." He reached for her package.

"I prefer bordello," she held it away.

"Give over, wife. I know what it is."

"You don't know anything."

"Yeah, I do."

"Then you know I don't want to share."

"Give it up, Tess." Grinning, he lunged for the sack. She squealed and held it away, to no avail. She couldn't fight the man's superior strength. She couldn't withstand the wicked twinkle in his eyes or the way his fingers knew just where to tickle. "Oh, all right," she said, laughing. "Here." She shoved the package at him.

He reached into the paper and removed the box. "Tess, you hoarder you, you haven't changed a bit." He lifted the lid and grinned. "It's been years since I've plundered a box of chocolates."

Gabe unloaded the last box from the supply wagon and toted it into the storeroom. Setting his burden down beside a sack of flour, he stretched his aching back muscles and sighed with the relief of a job completed. Next time he'd make sure not to get stuck doing this task by himself.

Not that he hadn't enjoyed the time alone with

Tess. He wouldn't trade that wagon ride home for all the tumbleweeds in southwest Texas. It was more than just the sex play they'd shared, although that had been downright delightful. Something had changed for them out there among the cactus and the sagebrush. They'd talked to one another all the way back home. Small talk, friendly talk. Intimate talk. Hopeful talk. And underneath it all, desire hummed a constant, muted tune.

It had been nice. Damned nice. He hadn't enjoyed an afternoon this much in longer than he could remember.

Gabe stole a peppermint from the candy jar sitting next to a stack of canned beets and popped it into his mouth. Stepping outside the storeroom, he was careful to pull the door shut behind him in order to protect the day's purchases from patrolling pigs and other pests. The evening air had a welcome crispness to it, and Gabe lifted his face into the gentle breeze, appreciating the drop in temperature. Maybe fall had finally arrived. For a while there he'd thought it might stay summer forever.

Heaven knows he was accustomed to run-on seasons. Hadn't it been winter in his heart for going on thirteen years?

But after today, he wondered if the ice wasn't starting to melt, if winter wasn't preparing to slide into spring. Spring, that time of rebirth when color burst across the barren landscape as life flowered and flourished.

Gabe took a gander into his future and thought he just might be seeing a few shoots of color pushing their way up through the dead, dry dirt that had been his life of late. If it were so, Tess was the reason for it. Tess was the reason for the change.

Losing her had drained the color from his life. Finding her was bringing it back.

"Damned if you aren't waxing philosophical tonight," he grumbled to himself. "Would be a better use of time to wax up your boots. You're starting to sound like a woman."

He sighed and started moving toward the communal kitchen where Tess labored to prepare supper for him and the rest of the Aurorians upon their return. His steps were slow but steady, carrying him ever closer to his wife. Despite his effort to shake it, his contemplative mood hung on like a squirrel climbing a window screen.

If this time with Tess was a season, how long would it last? How long did he want it to last? How did he feel about this woman, his wife?

The light shining in the kitchen beckoned his gaze, and he stopped his forward movement when his position allowed him to observe her through the window. How did he feel about Tess? She'd scared the peewaddling out of him today with that gun foolishness, and she'd stirred up his lust like a high wind stirs up dust.

He watched her look down and speak to someone—something—and scowled at the idea that she let that damned pig in the kitchen. The woman went her own way in life, that's for certain. She was independent and strong. How many women—or men for that matter—would have had the sand to leave home and pursue studies like she had, or build a home out here in the middle of nowhere like she had, or create a family from a band of eccentric stargazers like she had? How many women would face down a six-shooter to rescue a pig, for goodness' sake?.

Tess Rawlins Cameron scared him. She stirred him. She made him yearn.

"I love her," Gabe said softly, closing his eyes at the admission, a truth he'd denied for years. He loved her. He'd never stopped loving her. That's why he'd thought of searching for her so many times over the years. That's why he'd worked so hard to talk himself out of doing just that. He loved her. That's why he'd made this trip to southwest Texas. That's why he'd hung around Aurora Springs. That's why he had not pressed her for answers to questions he wasn't certain he wanted to ask.

He loved her.

So what did he want to do about it?

With the question, in that moment, all his senses crystalized. The faint chatter of a roadrunner holed up in a bush to his right sounded like the *crack crack crack* of train robber's gunshots pursuing their prey. From the aroma of roasting beef riding the air, he separated the scent of burning cedar and the bite of peppercorn used to season the meat. The breeze stroked his skin and the remnants of the peppermint slid across his tongue, tickling his mouth with its tangy sweetness.

And the vision of his wife filled his eyes like the answer to a prayer. Bright and beautiful and alive.

In that magnified moment, Gabe realized what he wanted. He wanted his wife back. He wanted her back in his life for good. He wanted the color and the laughter and the joy. He wanted the fussing and the fighting and the making up. He wanted hearth and home and family. Children. Tess would make a wonderful mother.

He blew out a breath, then inhaled a deeper one, filling his chest with air. *Whoa, nothing like having a club of self-revelation whomp you upside the head.*

Exhaling loudly, he dragged his hand down along his whisker-nubbled jaw. He knew he wanted his wife, so what was he going to do about it? What was standing in his way?

She swore she didn't hold him responsible for Billy's death and from her recent actions, he was inclined to believe her. The physical attraction between them sure as hell hadn't dimmed.

Location might be a problem, though. The governor's offer required Gabe's presence in Austin which was a good piece from the place where her spooklights shined. He knew better than to expect her to pick up and leave her studies just because of him. The woman who helped build Aurora Springs would never hold for that.

But, he did have the lure of children to dangle at her. The girl he'd married twelve years ago used to rattle on about children all the time. He didn't figure she'd changed her thinking in that regard.

Yep, they'd have to dicker a bit about location, but he figured they could make it work. So, what else might interfere?

As he asked himself the question, she glanced outside and their gazes met and held. Wordlessly, she drew him toward her, and as he entered the kitchen,

Gabe's heart seemed to swell to twice its size. For the first time in a dozen years, he felt as if he'd come home.

"Hi," she said shyly.

"Hello."

"Supper's almost ready."

"Good. I'm hungry."

"Me too. I had thought to wait until the others get back from town, but they're taking longer than I expected. I hope they didn't have any more trouble."

"I'm sure they're fine." For something to do, he crossed over to the stove and lifted the lid from a pot of boiling potatoes and sniffed. Why the hell was he feeling so awkward all of a sudden?

Tess tossed him a curious look, then opened the oven and checked the roast. "So you don't want to wait? Shall we go ahead and eat our meal?"

"Mmmm . . ." he murmured, his gaze focused on her behind as she lifted the pan from the oven. The meal. Tess. A meal of Tess. The question burst from his lips like a prayer. "Darlin'? Tell me I'm not sleeping in the guest bed tonight."

CHAPTER

9

$\mathcal{T}$ess dropped the roast beef.

The pan banged against the floor and the juices sprayed but, thankfully, the meat remained in the pan. Rosie was up on all fours in an instant, but Tess moved quicker. With the beef safely placed on the cutting board, she ushered the pig away from the juice splatters and out the door saying, "You'll burn your snout, sweetheart. I love you dearly, Rosie, but I don't believe a pig belongs in the kitchen. I think this is a bad habit Twinkle allowed Will to start, and I intend to put an end to it."

Tess was proud she managed to keep her voice level and nonchalant. Inside, she was quaking.

"Tess? How about it? Haven't I worked my way down that list of chores well enough?"

Gabe's questions sent shivers of anticipation up her spine. What should she say? What should she do? Why did she feel so ill at ease with him now when the trip home had been so . . . so . . . wonderful. Bracing herself, not knowing how to reply, she turned to face him. Looking at him, she knew how she must answer.

Honestly.

"I don't know what is best, Gabe. I know what I want, but I'm not sure I'm brave enough to let it happen."

"Brave enough?" His brows dipped in a frown.

She waved her hand, uncertain how to put her feelings into words. It was more than the feminine insecurity that had brought her to tears early this morning. She chose her words as if she were walking through a field strewn with raw eggs. "What happened between us this afternoon caught me by surprise. You swept me away, Gabe. But for us to take it further, well, to me that would be a commitment of sorts. We have so many issues between us left to settle. Would it be right for us to ignore them and . . ."

"Make love?" He said it baldly, forcefully. "Hell, yes. Maybe that's just what we need to settle these 'issues' that have you in knots."

Her cheeks warmed with a blush. "I don't think problems can be settled that way."

"I think you'd be surprised." He took a step toward her. "What problems do we have anyway, Tess? You told me you no longer hold Billy's death against me. We've spent some time getting to know each other again. You can't deny you want me. I knew that even before today. Am I wrong about any of this?"

She couldn't lie, not about this. "No, you're not wrong. But you don't know everything, Gabe. I haven't told you everything."

"So tell me now."

"I can't. Not like this."

He raked her with a measuring gaze. "Are you in love with another man?"

She shook her head forcefully and said, "No."

"Then I can't think of anything else important enough to stand between us."

Which just goes to show how much you know. Suddenly, he was standing in front of her, his face intense, his gaze heated. "Gabe, I . . ."

He lifted his hand and traced her cheek with his thumb, staring at her mouth. She smelled the hint of peppermint on his breath.

"Oh, Gabe. I can't think."

"I've decided that's the problem dividing us, darlin'. Thinking. But you don't need to think, not anymore. You need to be loved."

Oh, yes.

"No." She couldn't help but sway toward him. But knowing this man as well as she knew him, aware of how betrayed he might feel when he learned all her secrets, she forced herself to add, "Not until I've told you everything."

"Everything?" He slipped his arms around her waist. "Like how your body aches for my touch? Like how your blood is running hot? Like—"

She moaned his name. "Stop. Please. I can't think."

"Good. I don't want you to think. I want you to feel."

"I am and I can't. I can't lose again, Gabe. It'll destroy me."

He waited a long beat and when he finally did

speak, his question was hesitant. "What do you mean?"

She pulled away from him, whirled and paced across the room to stand beside the kitchen window. Staring outside, she folded her arms against the shivers racking her body, tremors having little to do with the chill in the early evening air. "I'm afraid, Gabe. If I drop these last few barriers . . . if I let myself love you again and then I lose you, I . . ."

When it finally became obvious she didn't intend to finish the sentence, she heard him clear his throat. "Why would you think you'd lose me, Tess? I don't understand."

The windowpane reflected Tess's bittersweet smile. *That's because I've kept things from you.*

She turned and faced him. "We've danced around this long enough. I need to tell you what happened after Billy died."

He grimaced and hung his head, scratching the back of his neck. "Darlin', look. I know this isn't what I said when I first came out to Aurora Springs, but I've given this quite a bit of thought. I've realized that for me, the past is best left in the past. We've been apart twelve years. I imagine we both have done things we'd just as soon the other didn't know. Confession may be good for the soul, but I'm not so certain it's good for a marriage."

Conflicting emotions buffeted her. He'd said marriage like it was something he wanted, but he didn't want to confess his past sins. He was thinking of romantic liaisons, and she agreed with him in that regard. She didn't want to know.

And she didn't want to tell him her secrets tonight.

Fatigue rolled over her like a hurricane's breaker. It had been an eventful day, to say the least, followed on the heels of a dream-haunted night. She needed a break. She needed a little peace.

She shook her head and said, "No. Not tonight. I can't do this right now, Gabe. I'm not ready."

He scowled, looking every bit the little boy whose candy had been snatched away. "You were ready enough this afternoon."

"And you feel cheated because you didn't get a turn?" she replied, frustrated at the . . . the . . . maleness of this man. "We're not seventeen anymore. That argument won't—"

"That's not what I meant." Anger bristled in his tone. "I just don't see why you're backing away from me now, not after this afternoon."

"This afternoon was a mistake, Gabe."

His chin jerked up and his jaw went hard. His eyes all but snapped as he said, "Now you're making me mad. How can you say something that . . . wonderful was a mistake?"

"I'm sorry. That's not what I mean to do. It's just that . . ." She closed her eyes and gathered her thoughts, searching for the right words to express the emotions rioting through her. "Remember our first time? Do you remember how you felt afterward?"

He folded his arms. "Yeah. I felt good, real good."

"You felt guilty. You told me so later. You said you felt guilty as sin."

Gabe shrugged, and Tess pressed on. "But I didn't

feel guilty. Not at all. That's because I was one hundred percent certain of my love for you."

"Tess," he said, a warning in his tone. "You're not making this any better here. I loved you, too."

"*I* know you did, but I don't believe *you* knew you did. Not at that moment. If you're honest, you'll have to agree." She paused, and when he didn't argue, she thought she might have gotten through to him. "Gabe, I want to be just as certain this time. What we had was special. I couldn't bear it being anything less than that now."

"Are you so certain it would be less? At the risk of bringing up a sore subject, I have learned a thing or two in the past few years. I can play your body like a fiddle, Tess. Don't doubt it."

Her head dropped back and she railed toward the heavens. "You are such a *man!* I'm not talking about sexual prowess, Gabe. I'm talking about my heart. I won't give my body unless my heart comes along with it. Right now . . . tonight . . . I'm simply not positive it does."

For one, brief, unguarded second, she saw anguish and pain reflected in Gabe's eyes. Her heart twisted. She hadn't wanted to hurt him. She guessed she hadn't realized she had the power. Then as quickly as the emotions appeared, they vanished. His gaze shuttered, but he pasted on a wry smile. Even before he spoke, Tess braced for the blow. She knew this man. Knew he'd defend himself by lashing out.

"Hell, Tess. I wasn't asking for your heart. I just need to get laid." He gestured toward the stove. "Don't worry about me for supper, after all. I've a hankering to ride back into town. I'll satisfy my appetites there."

The next afternoon Gabe lay sprawled across the bed in the most expensive room of Sally McGuire's Gentleman's Club in Eagle Gulch, Texas. "Fancy name for a whorehouse," he muttered, pouring the last of a bottle of whiskey into a glass. Especially a whorehouse as sorry as this.

Counting Sally, the house had four working girls and not a one of them was tempting enough to put the lead in Gabe's pencil, so to speak. "Almost enough to make a man doubt his vigor," he grumbled, tossing back his drink. He'd be worried except that every time he thought about his wife, his prick got hard enough to drive a railroad spike. "Maybe I should get a job up there building the spur. That'd show her."

Only problem was, he didn't want to show her. He wanted to love her.

Gabe reached for another bottle of rotgut, pulled the cork with his teeth, spat it out, then took a long draw. He choked and coughed hard, then lifted the bottle to the light and stared at it. Too much of this brew would damn sure kill a man, so he'd be careful to stop at just enough.

Gabe wasn't ready to die. He just wanted to act stupid for a bit. A man had to do that now and again. Animals licked at their wounds, and a man had to act stupid.

"Which is why I'm in a whore's bed when I want to be in Tess's," he said to the stone spittoon in the corner. Of course, he was alone in the bed and had been since his arrival. He hadn't crossed the line from stupid to idiot, and he hoped like hell he never would. A man had standards he simply had to keep, even when he was acting stupid. "Especially then."

The problem with standards was that the backfire could be deadly. Like now, for instance. He was in between drunks, but lit enough so as not to be laid out from the last hangover. In this state it was possible for a man to think. Not a good thing for a man who was drinking to forget.

Under the circumstances, Gabe had to admit he was wrong to hold his hurting against Tess. She hadn't known he'd just figured out he loved her. She couldn't know how her disavowal of love cut him like a red hot bowie knife. It wasn't fair of him to expect her to reach the same conclusion at the same time as he. But he damned well expected her to figure it out sometime.

"Because she does love me," he told the spittoon. "I know it as sure as the walking porkchop likes mud." He punctuated his statement with one more glug of booze.

That proved to be a mistake. What it did was lower his defenses just enough to get him thinking about things he didn't want to be thinking about. Those damned secrets she wanted to tell him. They were the problem. They drove her to doubt. *And me to a soiled dove's empty bed.*

Gabe didn't want to think about any secrets. If he did, he'd wonder what they were, and then he'd be in even bigger trouble. He'd changed some in the last dozen years, but the basic core of him and his beliefs had remained the same. So, if Tess worried the secrets might drive him away, she stood a chance of being right. Gabe didn't want to know because he didn't *want* to be driven away. Not now.

He'd brought the bottle back to his mouth for a full tumble into idiot when the door to his room burst open. He dropped the bottle and the whiskey spilled, soaking both his britches and the bed. Gabe barely noticed. He was too busy being shocked sober. "Tess? What the hell are you doing here?"

She drew herself up, arrowed a glare his way, and stepped inside, slamming the door behind her. *Uh oh*, Gabe thought. His wife was wearing her warrior goddess persona again.

"Get up and get dressed, Gabe Cameron or Montana or just plain Idiot."

Ooh, had he crossed that line after all?

She continued, her voice razor sharp, "You are leaving this place here and now. I won't put up with this, Gabe. You won't shame me this way. You and I are married for better or worse, and I won't have you using some two dollar pleasure bunny just because I am trying to do the right thing."

Two dollar pleasure bunny? "I ordinarily spend more than that, darlin'."

Her glare was hot enough to set the alcohol afire, and Gabe thought he'd better get moving before he got burned to bits. "All right, I'm getting up. Fair warning, though. In case you haven't noticed, I'm naked."

"It's nothing I haven't seen before."

He considered that. "No, that's not totally true,

Tess. You're bosom isn't the only thing that grew in the past twelve years."

Damned if it didn't work. Her gaze dipped to his crotch, then shot back up again. "Give me half a minute and I'll be even bigger, sweetheart," he said with a wicked grin, watching the pretty blush spread across her face.

"Just put your pants on. We're leaving."

"Where we going?"

"The hotel. I took a room so we can have some privacy to talk. After that, you can either come home with me, or hop a train. But we're not leaving matters in limbo any longer. I can't go on this way. We must choose one or the other. Marriage or divorce."

If Gabe hadn't already sobered up, that would have done it.

Hell. The woman is bound and determined to spill her damned guts. Glumly, with a headache beginning to pound at his brain, he dressed. The sense of impending doom that settled on his shoulders had him grabbing up the bottle of whiskey as he followed her from the room.

Sally met them in the hallway. "Winnie told me you were here, Tess. I guess you didn't come for more chocolates, hmm?" Then she laughed and said, "Now I understand why what happened happened. Just so you know, he turned down every one of my girls. Your man was faithful to you, missy. You have yourself a good one, there. I'd hold on to him if I were you."

Tess eyed him sharply, and he sent her that sheepish, boyish grin that he saved for getting out of trouble with women. She reacted to his smile and Sally's information with a lifting of her chin and a smile of feminine confidence. "I'll give the matter some thought."

Damn right she will.

They didn't speak as they made their way to Eagle Gulch's lone hotel. Gabe collected the room key from the front desk and ordered a bath.

"But Gabe," she protested. "I want to talk."

"Well, right now I'm going to clean up. Surely you can wait another half hour to say your piece, can't you?"

She obviously didn't like it, but he didn't care. A man didn't fight the battle for his heart when he smelled like a still.

"Get some supper, Tess. I'll be back down as soon as I wash the stink off."

She lasted twenty minutes before invading the room. By then Gabe had bathed, shed his headache, donned and halfway buttoned his pants, and started shaving. He watched her in the mirror and took her obvious distraction by his bare chest as a positive sign.

"Gabe, I need to tell you what happened when Billy died."

He nicked himself and grimaced. "Don't you believe in easing into anything?"

"Isn't that what we've been doing for these past few weeks?"

"Well at least wait till I finish shaving," he grumbled. "I'd just as soon not have a straight razor near my neck while we chat about how I killed your brother."

"Oh, Gabe." She sank down onto the bed as the

air drained from her sails. "That's the one topic we *have* covered. Let's not go into it again. You and I both know you didn't kill Billy."

Gabe shrugged, then finished shaving. When he'd rinsed his face, he reached for a towel and turned around. His wife was sitting cross-legged in the middle of the bed, her jade green riding skirt spread around her like leaves framing a flower.

It was all Gabe could do not to lay her back then and there.

He wiped the moisture from his face, then tossed the towel away. Padding on bare feet across the room, he sat on the end of the bed and said, "Quit plucking at the loose threads. You'll unravel the bedspread."

"Since I feel like my life is unraveling, I guess it's only appropriate."

Her sadness was painful to watch. "Tess, listen. I owe you an apology for last night. Not for wanting to make love to you—I'll never apologize for that—but for how I reacted when you refused me. It wasn't fair of me, and I'm sorry for it."

Her spine straightened and she looked him in the eye. "You shouldn't have tried to blackmail me into your bed, Gabe. Such behavior is beneath you."

"Yeah. But what I want is *you* beneath me, Tess. I wanted it so badly that I lost my good sense."

"Oh, Gabe."

Silence fell like a mist between them. He could tell she was working up to her revelations. He wasn't inclined to help her at all with that task. Instead, he quietly studied her, watched the lamplight dance across the streaks of fire in her old gold hair, wondered at the thickness, length, and curl of the lashes framing the bluest pair of eyes in Texas. He was, as always, struck by her beauty. "I always knew you'd grow up pretty, but you outshine my expectations. You are breathtaking."

"Don't try to distract me, Gabe."

"How about I seduce you instead?" He reached out and pushed a stray curl behind her ear. "Do you know that you are the only woman I've ever truly wanted? I've dreamed about you for twelve long years. It's killing me for us to be apart."

She shut her eyes and visibly shuddered. "Don't. Please."

"Did you ever dream of me, Tess?"

"Always."

"Then let's forget about everything else and live our dreams, even if it's just for a little while. What would it hurt?"

He felt himself drowning in her eyes as she looked at him and said, "I tried to tell you this the other night. I don't want it to be a mistake."

Tenderness washed through him. "Aw, darlin'." He stroked a thumb down her cheek. "You and me will never be a mistake. Not when we were little more than kids and not now."

"But first I should tell you—"

Now he lay his thumb against her lips. "I don't want to know, Tess. Not tonight. Right now, all I want to hear is that little kittenish sound you make when you climax. I want to play like we did on the way back from town the other day, only take it all the way this time. I want you naked and hot and hungry, Tess. Like you used to be for me. Like we used to be together."

"But it hurt so bad when you left me before. It destroyed me, Gabe. I couldn't live through that again."

"You're the strongest woman I know. But who's to say it will come to that? We might make it this time."

"But we might not."

"Such a pessimist." He clicked his tongue. "Tell me, sweet, was the pain so bad that it wasn't worth the memories? It wasn't for me. The pain of losing you was dreadful, true, but the joy of loving you . . . well, it's kept me warm for a full dozen years." Wetness pooled in her eyes; a single drop overflowed. He leaned down and kissed the tear away. "I used to pull my memories of you out one by one and savor them like a peppermint stick. Let's make a new memory tonight, Tess. Let's give ourselves that gift. Let's give ourselves tonight."

She swallowed hard. He could all but see her walls tumbling. "You are doing it, Gabe."

"Doing what?"

"Seducing me."

"I hope so," he said with a soft smile. "Heaven knows you've been seducing me for weeks now. Please, Tess." He pulled her into his arms. Dipping his head, he trailed sweet kisses from the corner of her mouth across her cheek until he could whisper in her ear. "Let me make love to you."

She shuddered. "I can't fight you anymore."

"I don't want to fight, darlin'. I want to love."

"God help me, but so do I, Gabe. So do I."

He wanted to shout for joy. Instead he laid her down upon the mattress like a pirate's prize and paused just long enough to savor the moment. A dozen different sensations rolled through him in that instant. Anticipation. Elation and awe. Tenderness and reverence.

Gut-wrenching, fever-hot, wild-and-pulsing hunger.

"Remember what it was like, V-for-Venus?" he murmured, following her down, determined to take it slow despite the insistent demands of his body. He wanted it to last. He wanted it to be perfect. "Remember how we kissed?"

Sprawled across her, he lowered his head and pressed his lips to hers, soft and gentle. Testing. "Remember this?"

He spent a moment savoring, moving his lips over hers, brushing, rubbing, seducing. Then with his tongue he traced the outline of her mouth, coaxing it to open as her arms finally lifted and wrapped around him. He growled in satisfaction and deepened the kiss, his tongue delving into the slick wet of her mouth. He drew a breath, caught hers, and tasted elderberry wine and Tess. The flavor took him home to the Big Thicket, home to happy times. Home to his wife.

Then her tongue began to dance with his and Gabe abandoned all thought of the past in favor of the present. Arousal twisted through him, hard and hot, and he wanted—no, he needed—to touch and feel naked skin against naked skin.

He ended the kiss and rolled back on his knees above her. His fingers moved to the buttons on her bodice and one by one he worked them, pausing to kiss each inch of skin he bared. With determination and skill he hoped escaped her notice, he soon stripped away her riding skirt, unhooked her corset, and unbuttoned her camisole leaving her bared to his gaze.

Gabe drank in the sight of her. She was exquisite, even more than he remembered. Lush breasts beckoned him, their coral peaks hard. "Beautiful. God, Tess, you take my breath away."

She allowed him no more time to savor the view. "Don't," she murmured, before pulling him down to her and demanding his kiss. Gabe obliged, thrusting his tongue into her mouth, taking it, a carnal prophecy of the mating to come. Tess tugged at his pants, wordlessly demanding them gone. Swiftly, he granted her wish, and when they lay together, flesh to flesh, he sighed with pleasure. "I remember this," he murmured, smiling against her neck. He nipped her just below the ear where he knew she liked it. She groaned and trailed a teasing fingertip down his spine, just how she knew he liked it.

He rolled onto his back, pulling her atop him. His hands slicked up and down her back and over her buttocks. He cupped her, kneaded her, squeezed her. He pressed her against his arousal.

"Oh, Gabe," she gasped.

He wanted her breast so he lifted her forward and took it. He fastened his mouth around the turgid nipple and sucked hard over and over and over. She whimpered with need, arching up to him, rolling her hips. Her fingers wove into his hair, and she held him to her. He scented her passion, recognized her desire. While treating her other breast to the same delicious pleasure, he slipped a hand in between their bodies and found her wet and ready.

But Gabe wanted her fevered, so he replaced his hand with his mouth. Though she gasped a protest, her legs parted, revealing herself to the onslaught of his tongue.

While he attended his thirst with the taste of her sweet honey, she sobbed his name again and again, a chant of driving need. She pounded his shoulders. "Damn you, Gabe. Not by myself. Not this time. You come with me." And she wrenched her hips away.

Even as he groaned a protest, she reached for him. Her lips pressed fervent kisses across his chest and her small hand wrapped around his pulsing shaft.

Gabe shuddered. He was breathing hard, his chest heaving. Her gentle touch was pure torture, and he gritted his teeth as he strained for control. Her fingers teased and played; her lips kissed and licked. Sweat beaded on Gabe's brow, and his muscles quivered from the effort of resisting the urge to give up, to give in. He both wanted to end it now and have it go on forever. "God, Tess, I've missed you. I've missed you so damned much."

She lifted her head and their gazes met. What he saw in the depths of her deep-ocean eyes stole his breath.

"Then show me, Gabe," she said, her voice sweet and needy. "Show me."

His control hanging by a thread, he slipped into her, easing forward inch by delicious inch, until he was buried up to the hilt, their bodies fully joined, their souls united.

He kissed her with all the love in his heart, gently, hotly, purposefully. "You are my heart, Tess. You have always been my heart."

She lifted her hips, urging him, and so they moved together in the age-old rhythm, their lovemaking at the same time both old and new. She closed her eyes with his name on her lips. Gabe watched her. Her face, her breasts, the point where their bodies converged. This woman. His wife. His love. His need grew more urgent; his thrusts drove deeper. He felt his control start to give.

Then without warning, she came apart in his arms. She cried his name out wildly and strained against him. Deep within her body, her muscles milked him. And Gabe could hold out no longer.

He threw his head back and erupted, shooting his seed in short bursts of pleasure. Losing himself in the hot surge of satisfaction.

Then exhausted, he collapsed. Just like the old days, she pushed against his chest. "Lift up, I can't breathe."

And, just like the old days, without opening his eyes, Gabe rolled onto his back and smiled. "I'm numb from the waist down. Thank you, wife."

Then, just like the old days, he started to snore.

Snuggled against him, Tess smiled smugly. She hadn't felt this good for twelve years. Physically, anyway. Mentally was another matter altogether.

But she wouldn't think about that now. She'd take this moment like Gabe said. As a gift. A little holiday from the realities of life. For as long as this interlude lasted, she wouldn't mention Doc or Will or Rachel.

It's my time, she thought. *Mine and Gabe's. I'll be selfish about it.*

And she wouldn't feel guilty about it, either. After all, he'd given her permission.

She sighed and snuggled a little closer. Gabe gave a satisfied groan.

"Still take your three minute naps, I see," she said, drawing circles with her finger in the whirls of dark hair dusting his chest.

"I'm older now. Think it's stretched closer to five."

"I used to hate when you did that. It made me feel like you lost interest in me. You never started falling asleep until after we were married."

He snorted. "Tess, that's because we made love in haystacks, not a bed." He shook his head and frowned. "Remember how itchy that was? Never could get comfortable."

She laughed. Then, reminded how their pillow talk often took wild and curious courses, she indulged herself by asking, "Where is the most uncomfortable place you've ever slept? Alone, mind you."

"That's easy. I was on a stage from Montana to Idaho. Sat next to a woman with digestive problems and an aversion to baths. That was the longest month I ever spent."

"A month to go from Montana to Idaho?"

"Well, this trip was three days. It just felt like a month. So how about you? What's the worst place you ever slept in?"

The smile faded from Tess's face. The worst place was their bed once he'd left her. "The most uncomfortable place was the telescope tower at Birr Castle."

"Birr Castle?" He lifted his head from his pillow. "You went to Ireland? You saw the 'Leviathan of Parsonstown'?"

She nodded. "The biggest telescope in the world. I wish you could see it, Gabe." She described the huge, seventy-two-inch telescope and told him of her studies. "Actually seeing the pinwheel swirl of a nebula with my own eyes was such a thrill." She also mentioned the constant wet chill of a winter spent in an Irish castle. "That's what convinced me to come back to Texas," she added. "I couldn't wait to be dry and hot again."

"Living out here I expect you got your wish."

"Yes, I warmed up quite nicely, thank you." Then, before he could voice the suggestive comment she saw forming on his lips, she asked, "How about you, Gabe? You've mentioned Montana and Idaho. How did you end up back in Texas and working as a railroad investigator?"

"It's a long story and not all that interesting. My partner and I hooked up in Nevada—Mack Hunter, the fella you sort of met here in the jail. Anyway, he had a friend who had money and was fixin' to buy into the Brazos Valley Rail Company. He wanted men he could trust when problems arose so Mack and I signed on to help."

Though she knew she should hold them back, the questions slid from Tess's tongue anyway. "You like the work? Is it something you'll want to keep doing?"

His chest rose as he drew in a deep breath. She

leaned over and kissed it. He said, "Actually, I've had another job offer."

He explained about the letter he'd received from the governor. Tess was torn. She felt proud for Gabe, but concerned for herself. He intended to leave Aurora Springs by the new year. So where did she fit into his plans?

He must have seen the doubt upon her face because he rolled over on top of her and said, "Don't." His gaze delved deeply into hers. "Let's save tomorrow for tomorrow, all right? For now, for tonight, I want to focus all my energy on making love to my wife."

Her breath caught as he eased her legs apart and slipped into her again. He was hard. Hot and pulsing, like the Kissing Stars, she thought. He moved within her, stroking that fierce, fiery need back to life. This was the gift, what she needed now, tonight. Gabe's love. She had it tonight. Tomorrow was a long time away.

Tess arched her hips, moved with him, and gave herself up to the pleasure of loving her husband.

Gabe wanted to stay in Eagle Gulch another day or ten and stretch their "tonight" into a few tomorrows. Tess refused, albeit reluctantly, because of an event due to happen that very afternoon.

"Today is a holiday at Aurora Springs," she told him as they dressed to leave the hotel. "We'll have a celebration this afternoon. I can't miss it, and you won't want to."

"Want to bet?" he responded, giving the bed a significant glance.

She grinned and playfully batted his shoulder. Her flirtatiousness stirred him, and Gabe surrendered to the desire to swoop down and steal another interlude of bliss with his wife. Her protest didn't last past the first kiss, and when they rose to dress again forty-five minutes later, he felt smug and deliciously sated.

The day was bright, filled with sunshine and the promise of pleasant temperatures. Texas and October were a good fit, and Gabe's mood was high as he escorted his wife toward the livery at the edge of town. Then she had to go and open her mouth. "What do you mean you didn't bring a buggy?"

"I rode Pollux."

He stopped short. "No, you didn't. Tell me you didn't ride a camel to town."

She fiddled with the bow on her sunbonnet. "I could tell you that but it wouldn't be the truth."

"I don't believe this." Gabe removed his hat and rubbed his brow. "Why in the world would you do something like that?"

"I happen to like riding Pollux. Her gait is gentle and she's sweet as can be. And since she hasn't been away from Aurora Springs for a while, I thought she'd enjoy the exercise." She shot him a quizzical look. "Why does it matter to you what I ride?"

He ducked his head and grimaced. "How much cash do you have with you?"

"Less than five dollars."

His stomach sank. "I was afraid of that," he muttered. "How about the bank? Do you have an account at the bank?"

"No, I don't. Gabe, what is going on?"

He lifted his hat from his head and raked his fingers through his hair. "When I left home the other night, I wasn't exactly thinking straight. I didn't bring any cash with me." He drew a deep breath, then blew out a sigh. "I sold my horse to buy my room and booze."

"Not very smart of you."

"Nope. I only have three dollars left."

Tess's eyes twinkled. "Can't buy a horse for three dollars. Guess you'll have to hitch a ride with me."

"This is terrible, just awful," Gabe lamented. He figured he must look miserable as hell because at that point, Tess burst into unbridled laughter. He shot her a scowl, then closed his eyes and groaned when she led the dromedary from the livery wearing the strangest looking saddle Gabe had ever seen. "I can't do this, Tess. Texan men do not ride camels. It's not dignified."

Damned if the woman didn't just giggle harder. "Don't be afraid, Gabe. I know camels are often illtempered, but Pollux is an exception. She is well trained and cooperative. And, she's accustomed to riding double."

"I'm not afraid." *But I'd rather share tea and crumpets with Jimmy Wayne Bodine in his jail cell than fork this particular saddle.*

He eyed the ugly animal with distaste. The split upper lip brought to mind the devil's cloven hooves. "Honestly, I'd rather ride a mule than ride that shaggy beast. Hell, I'd rather ride Rosie."

Tess rolled her eyes. "Rosie isn't here, Gabe, so you might as well climb aboard." She directed the camel to kneel down, then gracefully mounted. Pinning him with an expectant gaze, she waited.

Gabe folded his arms and walked in a wide circle around the animal. This old gal had a bad case of the uglies.

"Jefferson Davis imported camels to Texas as pack animals, not mounts. Why would you go and train them for riding?"

"In the heat of the summer, the water between here and Aurora Springs dries up. Castor and Pollux can make the trip to town without needing water, so it makes perfect sense to use them instead of the horses."

Gabe thought of the trip into town the day before yesterday. "Tell me these animals don't pull a stage."

"No, we don't ask that of them, although I do think Pollux would do it for me. Castor can be more cantankerous. He is a male, after all."

Gabe just shook his head. He took another circle around the camel, stopping at its head to look past the long, double-fringe of interlocking eyelashes and into its eyes. She blinked twice and moved her mouth, revealing her teeth. Gabe snickered. She looked like she was flirting with him.

Then, before he realized what was happening, Pollux let fly a wad of spit that struck him right in the face.

Sonofabitch! He'd have shouted the word aloud except that he was afraid the camel spit would dribble into his mouth. Yanking his handkerchief from his pocket, he wiped his face. "You sorry, hump-back, stinking piece of—"

"Gabe," Tess warned. "Don't. It's her way of saying hello."

"—sand-loving ugly, I'm gonna—"

"Gabe! I'm sick to death of you insulting my animals. Now, unless you want to walk home, get on up here. If you don't like it, well, you have no one but yourself to blame. You're the one who stomped off in a fit, and you're the one who sold your horse for whiskey money."

"A spit and a scolding," he grumbled, hitching up

his pants as he prepared to climb into the so-called saddle. "Not exactly an auspicious start to the trip home."

A smile as pretty as sunshine lit Tess's face. When he settled in behind her, she twisted around and planted a pucker on him hot enough to make him see stars. *Now those are the kind of Kissing Stars I want to see.* "What's that for?" he asked. "Not that I'm complaining, mind you."

"You said 'the trip home.' You called Aurora Springs home."

So he had. Uncertain how he felt about that, Gabe chose not to respond. Instead, he held on for dear life as his wife commanded the camel to rise.

And so, Gabe rode out of Eagle Gulch for the second time in as many days. This time, literally, on a spit and a prayer.

Tess spent the first half of the ride home in an exuberant mood. Gabe kept her laughing with his carrying on about the indignity of riding Pollux. Really, from the way he talked one would think a man's entire masculinity was wrapped up in the kind of horse he rode.

"Nah," he replied when she made that observation. "If that were true we'd all ride stallions and not a man jack among us would get within a mile of a gelding."

Eventually, conversation lagged and Tess took to thinking. That, in turn, dampened her mood. She needed to confess her secrets.

Half a dozen times she attempted to bring the subject up. Half a dozen times she couldn't get the words past her lips. It was a relief when Gabe asked about the Aurorians' holiday she'd mentioned earlier.

"Ah, yes. Today is a special day."

"No kidding," her husband drawled. "It's not every day I parade around on the back of a dirty dromedary."

She elbowed him in the ribs and continued, "We are due to have a partial solar eclipse this afternoon. We always try to make days like this a little extra special."

Gabe was pleased to hear of the pending event. He told her of witnessing the total solar eclipse while in central Texas back in 1878. Out of the country at the time and never having witnessed such a phenomena first-hand, Tess listened to his descriptions with rapt fascination, and truth be told, a twinge of jealousy.

"About a minute before the total eclipse began, I got to see Baily's Beads."

Tess knew he referred to the necklace of brilliant points caused by mountain peaks along the moon's edge, the phenomenon named for the English astronomer, Francis Baily, who first described the spectacle in the mid-seventies.

"During the last fifteen seconds or so," Gabe continued enthusiastically, "one bead shone more brightly than the other—the diamond ring effect—and after that, the western sky went dark. It was amazing, Tess. The moon completely masked the Sun, and it was twilight in the big middle of the day. You could see bright stars and planets."

"You looked?"

He nodded, the expression in his eyes conveying

the rueful acknowledgment of this deviation from what had become his norm. "I did then. Guess my idiosyncracy doesn't extend to daytime stars."

"So how long did this last?"

"The totality?" At her nod, he said, "Over five minutes. I could see the sun's corona. A white halo of light. It was fascinating to watch."

"What about the chromosphere? Could you see the red layer?"

"Yep. Saw prominences, too, the red flame-like extensions. Then came the flash of diamond ring and Baily's Beads and the total eclipse was over."

Envious, Tess said, "That must have been the most exciting sight of your life."

"Nah," he replied, shaking his head. "Seeing you naked last night in my bed was infinitely more thrilling."

"Oh, Gabe." She rolled her eyes, but couldn't stop the small smile of pleasure. She asked how the people and animals around him reacted to the unusual event. The discussion carried them to the very edge of Aurora Springs, and Tess realized she had been granted yet another reprieve.

They arrived home to find the Aurorians all prepared for the coming celestial event. Twinkle wore her brightest, sunflower yellow robe and orange turban. The colonel brought out his dress uniform, including all his medals and ribbons, and his dress sword. Upon seeing the display, Gabe expressed admiring surprise that the man could walk upright.

"Strong abdominals," the elderly man replied.

They had set the long table from the dining hall

outside, taking advantage of the moderate fall weather to have an outdoor community picnic. "We'll have a taffy pull later," Tess told him. "Will just loves it, and we started doing the pull for him."

"Oh?" Gabe glanced around curiously. "So he's home? The boy and your Doc returned while I was away?"

Tess shook her head and wished she'd never brought up Will's name. There wasn't time to get into everything now. "No, I doubt they'll be home for weeks yet. We'll pull the taffy because it's become tradition and because it's our way of including Will even though he's not with us today."

"I'll bet Twinkle misses having him around." Gabe gave Tess a sidelong look and asked, "Whatever happened to his parents? How did he come to live with his grandmother?"

Her stomach took a dive. "Family troubles," she vaguely replied. "Twinkle loves him. Everyone here in Aurora Springs loves him. This is a good place for him."

"How old is the boy? What do you do for schooling?"

"I teach him. Oh, look, Amy has made her chocolate cake. You'll think you've died and gone to heaven when you get a taste of this, Gabe." She flashed him a smile, then melted with relief when Jack waved her over to ask where in her star shed he should look for the heavy white paper they would use to safely observe the eclipse.

Excitement swelled as the time for the event approached. Even Rosie sensed the party atmosphere, reacting by dashing around the picnic table in circles reminiscent of her racing days. Gabe's dry observation that the ham was trying to knock the baked beans off the table drew a scolding finger-shake from Twinkle. He laughed and kissed her cheek which set Twinkle to blushing, an event almost as rare as a total solar eclipse.

Obviously caught up in the anticipation, Gabe entertained the Aurorians with his total eclipse story as he pitched in to help with last minute preparations. The animation on his face drew Tess's gaze time and time again. The man was so darned handsome. Too handsome for *her* own good. Her gaze drifted over the thick waves of doeskin-colored hair, past his gleaming, flint gray eyes, sculpted cheekbones, and strong chin to those shoulders as broad and as wide as the West Texas plain. She recalled how arms like steel had held her so gently. How his big hands had swept across her skin in a path that sparkled and burned like a comet's tail.

As if he felt her stare, Gabe looked up. He slashed her a grin, that quick, infectious, just-a-little-bit wicked smile. At this moment, he reminded her of the Gabe she'd married, and the memory of the love she'd felt for him swelled in her heart.

Then, like the flash of a shooting star, came the knowledge that this was not the memory of love, but the here-and-now variety.

She loved him.

Tess's throat tightened, and she was filled with a sense of bittersweet. It was true. She couldn't deny it any longer. She had fallen in love with him as a young girl, and that love had never died. Not when they lost Billy. Not during those desperate months that followed. Not over the course of the years that came after, when she'd picked herself up and put herself back together. She'd loved him then and she loved him now. She'd probably love him always.

And, oh God, it would hurt if he left her.

I knew this would happen if we made love.

So wrapped up was she in her musings that she didn't even notice the onset of the eclipse. "What are you doing, woman?" Gabe demanded, shoving a square of paper into her hands. "You're gonna miss it. Here, you and I can share. I already poked a pinhole, a real tiny, sharp one, I'm proud to say. I'll hold the second sheet a couple of feet away."

As the sky over them slowly darkened, Tess stared at the small, inverted image of the Sun's disk projected onto the card Gabe held in his hand. All in all, she'd have felt just as involved had he held a poker hand rather than an eclipse viewing sheet. Her mind was occupied with more earthly problems at the moment.

I realize I love him just as the sun goes dark. Is there a message in there somewhere?

Moments later the eclipse ended and the celebration began. After the *oohing* and *ahhing* was done, Andrew brought out his accordion and the colonel tuned up his trumpet. When Gabe asked if anyone had a guitar, she looked at him in surprise. "Mack taught me," he told her. "Nothing much else to do when you're cabin-bound during a Montana blizzard."

"Want me to get him Will's, Tess?" Jack asked.

She nodded, wondering how Will would react if he

knew. The boy was awfully particular about the guitar Doc had given him for Christmas a year ago. But Tess wanted to hear Gabe play. She wanted to watch his fingers pick out the chords. She wanted him to do it with that specific instrument. It just felt right.

For the next hour, the Aurorians ate and drank and danced. Even the animals got into the spirit of the day, Castor and Pollux having wandered out of the barn and plopped down just outside the kitchen—downwind, thank goodness. Rosie for some reason chose to sit at Gabe's feet and wouldn't move. As a result, he strummed the guitar and sang a song he titled "Pickled Pig's Feet in a Mason Jar."

Amy Baker chucked a roll at him. Rosie went for the bread, then returned to her position at Gabe's feet, only this time she managed to lie *on* his feet which amused everyone but Gabe.

Soon the colonel leaned back and patted his stomach, declaring himself full near to busting. At that point Amy glanced at Jack and he nodded. Tess's instincts went on alert. Something was definitely up.

The young man excused himself, then returned a few moments later carrying his humidor. The box containing Jack's favorite smokes. The one thing he refused to share with the community. "What's up, Jack?" Andrew asked.

Tess knew. She could tell by the look on Amy's face.

Jack said, "I've been saving these for a special occasion and this is as special as they come. I have an announcement to make. Our efforts have met with success. My wife is expecting a child."

A baby. Tess listened to the news with mixed emotions. Fierce gladness rushed through her like water through a bursting dam. But wrenching regret rode as driftwood beneath the surface, battering both her heart and her soul.

Summoning her grit, Tess did her best to lock any sad thoughts firmly away as she joined her friends in offering the happy couple their congratulations. "Amy," she said, giving the beaming young woman a hug. "I am so thrilled for you. Are you feeling all right?"

"Thank you, Tess." Amy's hand drifted down to hover over her womb. "It's such a grand thought. And I know she's a girl. I sense it. We'll have a beautiful little girl and she'll grow up to make a grand scientific discovery one day. I just know it."

"A girl?" Tess repeated. "Do you really think you'll have a girl?"

Jack slipped his arm around his wife and beamed. "A bright-eyed little girl just as pretty as her mama."

Instinctively, Tess's gaze sought Gabe. He was busy selecting a smoke from the box and didn't catch her look. "Congratulations, Jack," she told him. "This is truly wonderful news."

The lump in her throat prevented Tess from speaking any more, so she wrapped her arms around Amy and gave her another hug. When she pulled away, Andrew stood at her back. He wrapped his arms around her and leaned down to whisper in her ear, "You're a good friend, Tess, and you're a strong woman."

"Thank you, Andrew."

Along with Doc and Twinkle, he was the only other resident of Aurora Springs who knew all the relevant details about her past. She allowed herself a moment of rest in the comfort of his embrace, and said a quick prayer of thanks for friends like Amy and Andrew.

Then, she pasted on a smile and called, "Colonel, if your accordion is handy, how about a waltz? I think Jack should dance with the mother-to-be, don't you?"

And so the dancing resumed and merrymaking recommenced. Tess tried, she tried hard, but the past had charged in and caught her unaware. Knocked her flat. Grief welled up inside her.

Needing some time to herself, she watched for a chance to slip away unobtrusively. Her opportunity came a short time later when Gabe asked Twinkle for a dance. Tess gave no conscious thought to where she was going, but her feet carried her home and into her bedroom where she retrieved a key from her jewelry box. She climbed the stairs to the loft and made her way toward the farthest, darkest, dustiest corner where a trunk sat against a rafter. Tess sank to her knees, inserted the key, and unlocked her past.

Gabe wondered what had come over Tess. It wasn't like her to get so down in the mouth, especially not during a party. She'd hid it well, and he didn't think anyone else had noticed. But he'd watched her closely and something was definitely bothering her.

Half a dozen times he'd started to ask her what was wrong, but he'd always stopped. She wore a hands-off sign as obvious as the bow around Rosie's neck.

He was willing to wait her out until she up and

sneaked away. Once he realized she'd disappeared from the festivities, he knew he had to track her down. Because Andrew had been hugging on her, Gabe approached him first. "What's the matter with Tess?"

"What do you mean?" He tried to look surprised, but he couldn't manage it.

"She's upset. Why?"

Andrew wouldn't meet Gabe's eyes. He did, however, keep his lips zipped tight, so Gabe turned to Twinkle next. "Where is Tess?"

She glanced around and frowned. "Oh, dear. I was afraid of this."

"Afraid of what? What's the matter with her?"

He startled in surprise when she reached up and grasped his chin, then pulled his face around so she could look into his eyes. She studied him long and hard, and Gabe felt as if she peered straight into his heart.

Maybe there was something to this crystal ball stuff of hers after all.

Abruptly, she gave a satisfied nod. "She's more to you than just your past, isn't she?"

Gabe drew a deep breath, then let out the air in a rush. "Actually, I'm hoping she'll be my future."

"Then go to her, Gabe. Go to her and make her tell you what happened. She can't be yours until she does. But I caution you to be gentle with her. These moods don't come on her often, but when they do, she isn't herself. She's fragile. Make sure you keep that in mind."

The warning sounded ominous. "Where do you

think she went? Up Paintbrush Mountain? Lookout Peak?"

Twinkle thought about it a moment, then shook her head. "Try her house first. Knowing her, you'll find her up in the loft. She keeps a trunk up there, and I bet my orange turban that's where she went."

The orange was Twinkle's favorite. Gabe would start with the house. Sure enough, he found her seated on the floor, folded squares of cloth of some sort in her lap. "What is the matter? What's wrong, darlin'?"

She looked up at him then and he saw an ocean of grief floating in her eyes. "Her scent is gone. It stayed for a time, but it's all gone now. All gone. Oh, Gabe, I miss her so much."

He knelt beside her and took one of her hands in both of his. "Miss who?"

"Rachel. Rachel Elizabeth." As tears overflowed her eyes to slip down her cheek, she added, "She was our daughter, Gabe."

Everything inside him froze. "Daughter? I have a daughter? Where is she?"

"She was born too early, and she wasn't strong. She couldn't fight hard enough. But she tried. Oh, she tried so hard. I had her two weeks before I lost her."

Baby clothes. Those were baby clothes packed away in that trunk. Gabe dropped her hand and sat back on his heels. He dragged a hand down his face as he tried to comprehend what she had told him.

A baby. A little girl.

Dead.

"Oh, God." He worked to draw a breath.

Tess gently unfolded one of the squares in her lap. It was a gown. A tiny little pink baby sacque.

"She was so beautiful," Tess said, her smile bittersweet. "A full head of hair. It was red, Gabe. She had a tiny little head just full of red hair. There was this place . . ." She tilted her head to one side and pointed at a spot. "It was a swirl, a little nebula of downy red hair. Her eyes were blue, of course. All baby's eyes are blue when they're born. But Rachel's didn't muddy. They were still true blue when she died."

Gabe flinched at the word.

"She didn't have any eyelashes that you could see, but she did have all her fingers and all her toes." Tess stared at the tip of her finger, using her thumb to mark a spot not even halfway down her index finger. "Her entire hand was hardly bigger than this. It never had the chance to grow any larger. Her voice was little, too. A tiny kitten voice. It broke my heart. I used to worry so when I heard her cry, but at the same time I worried she wouldn't. One day she didn't."

Shit. Shit. Shit. Gabe rocked back and forth. His feet went numb from sitting on them. His whole body was numb. A baby. A daughter. A death.

Tess suddenly set aside the baby clothes and went digging in the trunk. She removed a gold locket that dangled from a chain. She held it out to him saying, "I saved a lock of her hair. You can see the color."

His hand trembling like a palsied old man, Gabe reached for the necklace. He didn't open it. He couldn't.

"And I have a portrait," Tess continued, returning

her attention to the trunk. "I usually save it to look at last. It's not a painting, just a charcoal drawing the doctor's wife did for me. She was something of an artist, and I think he must have told her Rachel wouldn't live long because she showed up with a sketch pad when Rachel was three days old."

She withdrew a folded photographer's mat from the trunk and tried to hand it to him. He wouldn't take it. He still hadn't opened the locket. Forcing the word through the noose of emotion strangling his throat, Gabe spoke for the first time since Tess told him he'd once been a father. "No."

She straightened her arm, holding it right in his face. Silently demanding.

"No," he repeated, staring with something akin to horror at the folder. This news had slain him. He had to prepare himself.

"Yes," she hissed, leaning toward him. "Yes, you will, Gabe Cameron."

His gaze flew up to meet hers and what he saw there took him aback. Her eyes were glittering blue diamonds, hard and cutting and filled with fury. Her voice trembled with the force of her emotions. "You *will* look at her and you will listen of her and you will touch her things and do everything you should have done eleven years ago. You weren't there for her when she needed you. You weren't there. She needed you. We needed you. You weren't there!"

She swung her hand and slapped him.

Before he could absorb the blow, she threw herself into his arms. She clutched the portrait to her heart as grief poured out. She wept violently, passionately; her bereavement a bitter, unconsolable despair.

And Gabe couldn't breathe. Something was crushing his chest. He panted, trying to . . . survive.

Oh, God. A baby. A daughter.

He hadn't been there.

How long Tess cried he couldn't say. It might have been minutes or days for all he knew. He held her until the storm of tears rained itself out, and she fell into an exhausted slumber in his arms. And then he continued to hold her.

Eleven goddamned years too late.

Tess awoke at sunset. She was in her own room, tucked into her bed. Her body felt battered, but her mind and her soul were at peace.

Then she turned her head and saw her husband.

He sat in the hardwood rocker staring out the window. Rachel's picture lay in his lap. He held the locket, the chain looped around his right hand, his thumb stroking the pendant.

His face looked ravaged.

Tess closed her eyes, haunted by the sight. Shame nipped at her, its teeth razor-sharp. She'd been cruel in the telling of it. Cruel with her accusations and omissions. She'd shared only the bad and none of the good.

Bedsheets rustled as she slid to a sitting position. While she searched her mind for the right words with which to begin. "Gabe, I've tried to tell you a number of times."

He cut her off with a question. "Why was Rachel born early?"

"The doctor said it sometimes happens that way when a woman . . ."

"When a woman what?" he prodded, his expression stark, his sorrow so raw it bled from his voice. "Is all alone? Has no man around to help her?"

"Gabe, I—"

"Your father threw you out because you were carrying, didn't he? Because she was *my* baby. He hated me because of how Billy died, so he hated you, too."

She nodded.

He shut his eyes. "God, Tess. Your father was as worthless as mine." Then he let out a chuckle that sent shivers racing down her spine. "And I'm as worthless as Monty Cameron. Like father, like son. I followed in the old man's footsteps without even knowing it."

"No, Gabe," she protested her fists clutching at the bedcovers. "I'm sorry I said what I did earlier. I'm sorry I slapped you. It wasn't your fault you weren't there. You would have been had you known. I know that; I knew it then. It was wicked of me to accuse you like that. It was the grief talking. I get that way sometimes and I'm sorry. I'm so sorry I told you about Rachel in that way. You deserved better."

He spat an oath. "Not my fault? You mean like it wasn't my father's fault he left my mother to die giving birth in a swamp? Where did you give birth, Tess? Out here in the Chihuahuan Desert?" He lifted Rachel's picture and asked, "Where did my baby die?"

She chose her words carefully. "I think this would

be easier for me . . . for us both . . . if I started this story from the beginning."

He stood and walked toward her, placed the picture and pendant carefully on the bed. Then, without speaking he turned away and returned to the rocker where he sat, resting his elbows on his knees, his hands loosely clasped. He stared at the ground, his entire being braced as if anticipating a blow. "Let's hear it."

"You already know the worst of it," she said softly. "Nothing I have to say will be any worse than hearing about Rachel."

He shrugged in reply. Tess took a deep breath and began. "As you know, after Billy's funeral my father invited me back to the Rolling R. When he found out I was getting sick in the mornings, he guessed the truth. His fury caught me by surprise. He was so full of hate. He said no Cameron spawn would ever get a hand on anything that should have belonged to Billy. He cursed the Cameron name. Cursed me."

Gabe's features hardened like mortar. "Did he hurt you? Hit you?"

She shook her head. "He wasn't physical. Not much anyway. Nothing more than a shove or two."

Gabe's grip on his hands tightened, his knuckles growing white with the strain.

Tess pressed on. "The problem was, he sent me away without any money. All I had was what you and I had saved in our biscuit tin at home."

"That couldn't have been much more than forty dollars."

"Twenty-seven fifty, to be exact."

He turned his head away from her, staring out the window. "So how did you get by?"

"The first couple months were all right. I was careful with what I spent and the townspeople were kind. I took in some sewing and got by. Then the rumors started."

"Rumors?"

Tess debated how much to tell him. On the one hand, he didn't need to know all the details, but on the other . . . well . . . it might make the going easier if he knew just how much Doc had helped her. "Word got around town that I was whoring."

"What?"

"My father made it known that he'd disowned me. Do you remember Lester Woods at the Rolling R? I've always believed he was the one who started the talk. He came by our cabin one day with a wicked glint in his eyes. I sent him on his way. Shortly after that, word got around that I was supposedly making my living on my back. Men took to coming around night and day. It became rather . . . ugly. Someone burned me out."

Across the small bedroom, Gabe sucked in a harsh breath. "They burned our home?"

She nodded. The horror of those old memories washed over her, forcing her to collect herself before continuing the tale. "The following day the sheriff came around and suggested I move on to another town where I could make a fresh start. He gave me twenty dollars and a stage ticket west. I got lucky when we arrived at a stagecoach inn only to find the owner's wife had traveled back East for a family visit and the cook had quit the day before. I got the job and that lasted for almost three months until the wife returned."

Gabe lurched from his chair and started pacing, a panther on the prowl. Or a man trying desperately to run from the reality of the past.

"After that is when I had a run of bad luck. I took a job as a seamstress in San Antonio. One of the other employees resented me and . . . well . . . to make a long story short, I ended up in jail charged with theft."

He braced both hands against a wall at shoulder level, his head hanging, one knee bent, his weight resting on the other leg. He gave the appearance of an animal in pain, and Tess hated to continue, but she knew she must. Better to cauterize a wound quickly. "They didn't listen to me when I tried to explain what had happened. I was in jail for six weeks."

Gabe reared back and put his fist through the plaster wall, his curses steady, low, and furious.

Tess shook her head at the sight of his scraped and bleeding knuckles. "Now what good did that do, might I ask?" she said, getting up to wet a cloth from the pitcher of water on her bedside table. She crossed over to him, intending to tend his hand, but he flinched away from her. "Don't. Don't bother."

"But you need—"

He yanked the cloth away from her and wrapped his hand. "Finish it, Tess. Tell me everything."

"Why?" she replied angrily. "So you can run off and break your leg next? I'm not doing this to hurt you, Gabe, and I won't have you hurting yourself, either."

He clenched his jaw and said, "Fine."

She sighed heavily. "Don't lock up on me now. I want you to listen hard to what I have to tell you next."

"I'm listening."

Like a man headed to the gallows, she thought. *Fine, then. I'll give him the noose and we'll see what he does with it.*

"I was in jail when Doc found me. He'd been looking for me, trailing me across Texas. He convinced the other seamstress to confess to the theft, got me released from jail, then found a house to rent and a doctor to monitor my pregnancy."

As she spoke, Tess watched him grow tense, his body going stiff like wet rawhide drying beneath the desert sun. But she was determined to mention every single thing Doc had done for her. Gabe needed to hear them.

She continued. "Doc stayed with me, took care of me. When I went into labor, he went for the doctor. In those first few minutes following Rachel's birth when she almost died and the doctor was busy saving my own life, Doc tended Rachel and pulled her through the crisis. He was there for me that night and the night she died. When I felt so sad afterward and wanted to give up and die myself, he reminded me of all the good things I had to live for. He wrote off and got me the fellowship with Dr. Pierce, then saw us safely to Europe. When it was time, he brought us home and found us a place to settle, a place to build a home."

"What a paragon," he drawled. "So what will he

think to learn you've been bedding down with me, Tess? Do I need to watch my back?"

With a penetrating stare, Tess studied her husband. He was good at hiding his emotions, but when she looked past the gray glaciers that were his eyes she saw flickers of what he was feeling. Fury and jealousy. Shame and self-contempt. It was time to finish it. Time to finish so the healing could begin.

Her mouth as dry as the Chihuahuan in summer, she drew a deep breath and said, "He is a treasure. I never would have made it without Doc."

"He took the place of your husband."

"In a manner of speaking, he did. He filled in for you. For *you*, Gabe. Everything he did for me, he was doing for you."

"Oh yeah? I can't wait to hear how you're gonna reason this one out."

"You've never asked his last name." She waited, watching, hoping he'd work his way to the truth himself. But from the set of his jaw and the steel in his stance, she realized he wasn't thinking, simply absorbing. That and waiting for the next blow.

She hoped the last one wouldn't fell him.

Tess licked her lips, then said, "Doc stood in for you like any good father would do. Like any good father and grandfather."

His gaze jerked up to meet hers then, his eyes round and glittering. Like an animal caught in torchlight.

"Yes, Gabe," she said. "Doc is the name we call Monty Cameron. Doc is your father."

CHAPTER

11

For three days Tess watched the canyon trail waiting for Gabe to come home. For three nights she studied the Kissing Stars, wishing she believed in their supernatural powers like her friends so she could ask them to lead her husband back to where he belonged. With her.

He'd left without a word once she told him the truth about Doc. He'd left, fled, before she could confess her last secret, the one that might have soothed some of his pain.

As the first day passed and then the second, she came to believe events had worked out for the best. As much as she loved him, if Gabe wanted to be part of her life, part of her family, then he must reconcile with Doc. She refused to turn her back on the man who'd walked with her through fire.

Then, too, she had her more selfish reason for keeping the last bit of news to herself. She loved her husband and she wanted his love in return. She wanted him to want *her*. And she needed to trust in the knowledge that he wanted her as much as he wanted what she could give him.

The fact that she had intended to tell him and was prevented from doing so by his flight assuaged any guilt she might have felt for deciding to keep her secret a little while longer. "Not that it makes any difference," she grumbled. "The man might never come back."

Tess turned her attentions to her studies, once again using astronomy to distract her from the mess of her personal life. Early on the fourth afternoon as she left her star shed carrying the Birr Castle notebook containing her notes on stellar parallax, she noted the rider making his way down the trail into the canyon.

Her heartbeat sped up as anticipation swept over her. Then she identified the horseman and anticipation melted into disappointment. Captain Robards. Not Gabe.

Oh, well. Maybe he brought a letter from Will.

The Ranger smiled broadly as he rode into town on a bay mare. Dismounting, he greeted the Aurorians and spent a few moments talking to Andrew, discussing a herd of wild horses he'd run across on his way down to the Big Bend. He accepted Andrew's offer to see to his mount, then he turned toward Tess, tipped his gray felt hat, and said, "Hello, honey."

"Lionel." She nodded and hoped her return smile didn't look as letdown as it felt. "How was your trip? Did you find Doc and Will?"

He nodded. "I did. And I must admit, it took some doing. Thankfully, they camp outside the caves Doc is studying and I spotted their smoke. It's a wicked land down there, Tess. I'd hate to get stranded there alone. Doc and the boy said to tell y'all they were fine and working hard. They send their hellos to everyone."

"No letters?" Tess asked.

He snapped his fingers and delved into his saddle-bags, withdrawing a pair of envelopes addressed to Tess. She grinned with delight and tucked them into her pocket, choosing to savor them later in privacy.

Amy invited him to stay for supper and promised to make her biscuits to go along with it. Andrew offered his extra bed and the Ranger accepted their hospitality with grace. Tess was anxious for more details about her loved ones, so when he invited her to take a walk with him, she readily agreed.

He asked to see her telescope, so they climbed up Lookout Peak. As they walked, she inquired about Doc and Will, and listened attentively as he described what he'd found along with her family down near the Rio Grande.

"Spiders," she repeated, shuddering. "For the most part, I truly love the desert. But I have to say tarantulas frighten me half to death. I'm not surprised to hear of Will's collection, however. He's always been fascinated by the creatures."

As the path grew steeper, the lawman took the lead. Tess couldn't help but notice that Lionel Robards cut a fine figure. Broad of shoulder and slim of hip, he did the Texas Rangers proud. She felt a rush of gratitude that the people of Aurora Springs had such a man looking out for them. "How did you come to be a Ranger, Lionel?" she asked. "Did you always want to be a lawman?"

For just a moment, her question appeared to take him aback. Then he chuckled. "No, I didn't. What I truly wanted was to grow up and play games."

"Pardon me?"

"Chess, my dear. I've always wished a man could make a living playing chess. It was such a disappointment to learn as a boy that it couldn't be done."

Tess thought about that, then observed. "You must have an analytical mind, Lionel. I would think that serves you well with the Rangers."

"It does." He paused to take her hand, offering her balance as she stepped over a fallen log. "Tracking down criminals is often a case of out-thinking them. How about you? Did you always want to study the stars?"

She thought of those late night "stargazing" sessions with Gabe and shook her head. "No, I guess you could say I fell into it. But I love astronomy. It's a beautiful, fascinating science that is peaceful, considering one is studying distant explosions."

They reached the crest of the hill and Tess's work station. There she showed him her new telescope and explained a little of how she tracked the Kissing Stars' movements.

"The Kissing Stars. I must admit, Miss Tess, I like the sound of that much better than Ghost Lights, which is what I hear them called most." The Ranger sent her a sidelong look, then winked. "If a fella were up here watching the Kissing Stars with you, would he be allowed one or two himself?"

The blatant flirtation caught her by surprise and she didn't know how she should react. Evading the question, she donned an act of dim-witted innocence and replied, "You're welcome to use my telescope to look at the lights any time."

The fact that her reply didn't address his question apparently didn't bother him. Nor did it do much more than buy her time to figure out how to react to him because she hadn't discouraged him. To the contrary. Lionel's remarks grew more suggestive and his pursuit more overt as the minutes ticked by.

This wasn't at all like him. Lionel Robards had long pursued a mild flirtation with her, but it had remained just that. Mild. What in the world had gotten into him? What was different about today?

In an effort to change the direction of their conversation, Tess swivelled her telescope away from the flats and around toward Aurora Springs. She focused on Castor and Pollux as they chewed their cuds, then motioned for the Ranger to take a look.

"Not one of God's prettiest creatures, is it?"

"Now don't go maligning my animals, Lionel. I get enough of that from Gabe."

"Gabe. Ah, yes. Whip Montana, the estimable Hero of Cottonwood Hollow. And where is the man? I didn't notice him in town."

"He left," Tess told him simply.

"Did he go to Austin?"

"No," Tess said, thinking of his guns. Gabe hadn't packed a thing when he left her house that day. Along with his personal possessions, he'd left a pair of Colt revolvers behind. She'd taken comfort in that fact. Gabe might take off without taking his pants, but he'd never skip out on a fine pair of pistols. "He didn't mention Austin when he left."

She saw no reason to mention that he hadn't spoken at all.

"Good," the Ranger forcibly replied. "Glad to hear it."

His reaction surprised her and it must have shown on her face. Robards explained, "I heard through the ranks that Governor Ross has asked Montana to come to Austin and revamp the Texas Rangers. The rumor is he wants to put all the Indian fighters out to pasture now that they succeeded in driving the Indians out of Texas. They say he'll bring down the corps."

Tess felt compelled to defend Gabe. "I don't think he's the type of man to recommend any action that isn't warranted."

Lionel wanted to argue—she could see it in his expression—but he chose not to. Instead he reached out and took her hand. "Enough about Whip Montana. I'm just glad he's gone from here. I didn't like the idea of him being around to spark my woman."

Spark his woman? Tess's unease escalated into full discomfort. Taking a step away from him, she reclaimed her hand. "Lionel, please. I've told you in the past there can be nothing between us."

He nodded. "I understand, Tess. You are trying to protect the boy and everything."

"No, you do not understand, Lionel," Tess insisted. "I'm not trying to protect anyone. It's the truth. I'm *married.*"

"Uh huh." He grabbed her hand again. "This isn't exactly how I wanted to get into this, but I can see it is time. I know there is no Mr. Cameron. You've no need to be ashamed of being a grass widow with me, Tess. I'll be more than glad to make your make-believe husband a reality. I want you to marry me, my dear, and along with my proposal, I'm offering the promise to stay here in Aurora Springs. I will not ask you to move away from your home."

Tess wanted to groan aloud, but she managed to stifle the impulse. A marriage proposal from Captain Lionel Robards of the Texas Rangers. Rather than being flattered, Tess was ashamed.

Though she had always presented herself as a married woman, she had to admit she'd enjoyed his attentions. She'd been alone a long time and his admiration had appealed to her femininity. It had been nice to be reminded she was still a woman. It had been nice to be shown a man could still want her. But today, under current circumstances, it wasn't so nice after all.

Shame nipped at her like kitten's teeth, and she began, "Lionel, please. You must—"

"Get down on my knee," he interrupted, dropping to one knee with a flourish. "Tess Cameron, would you do me the honor of becoming my wife?"

Oh no, oh no, oh no. Mortification heated Tess's cheeks and she knew they must be as pink as Rosie's tongue. She grabbed Lionel's arm and tried to tug him to his feet. "Oh, I'm so sorry. Please Lionel. I'm so very sorry, but you've misunderstood. I truly *am* married."

He frowned and finally rose to his feet, thank God. Surely he believed her now.

"No, you're not married," he answered, dashing her hope. "I know you're not. I've asked around. No one has ever met your husband. You are just trying to protect your bastard."

"What?" she shouted sharply, her guilt melting in a flash of anger. "I have no bastard."

"The boy. Will. He's your son. He calls you mama."

"He does call me mama, but he also calls Twinkle mother and Amy mommy. It's the way we do things here in Aurora Springs. We are all one big family."

"Are you denying him?"

"The only thing I'm denying is my marital status. I'm married, Lionel. I'm sorry if you feel as if I've led you on, but the fact of the matter is, I am not free to marry. You have met my husband, Lionel. Last time you were here. It's Gabe. I'm married to Gabe "Whip Montana" Cameron, and I have been for going on thirteen years. I told you from the first that I was married, and I'm sorry if my actions—innocent though they were—led you to think otherwise. I won't blame you if you are angry, but I must insist on something. You won't *ever* use that distasteful term in connection with our Will again."

For a long moment, Lionel Robards stood completely still. Then he shook himself and gave her a sad little smile, and the tense moment was past. "I apologize, Tess. In my disappointment, I spoke out of turn. It's true, you always told me you were married, and it was wrong of me to doubt it. I guess I simply didn't want to believe you weren't free to be mine."

Honestly, Tess said, "You've been a special friend to me, Lionel, and I hope that won't change. If things had been different . . ."

He leaned over and tenderly kissed her cheek. "Well, Tess, I have to tell you, I'm not giving up hope. Things can always change, can't they? And while you might be married to him now, who's to say what will happen in the future? After all, Whip Montana isn't here, is he?"

Tess closed her eyes. Lionel was right. Gabe wasn't here.

So what else was new?

Gabe returned to Aurora Springs at dusk. He'd timed it that way, hoping to find the spooklights shining and the place deserted. His next conversation with his wife would be better held in private.

He'd spent the first day of his exodus into the desert in a haze of grief and despair. The second and third day he raged in anger. The fourth he planned his revenge. Monty Cameron would finally get what he had coming. Because Gabe, unlike Tess, knew the extent of Monty Cameron's sins.

Once a year for the past four years, Monty had tracked down Gabe for a visit. Never once during those tense, angry hours had he mentioned Tess or the fact that Gabe's marriage was still valid or the detail that, for a short time anyway, Gabe had been a father.

For that alone, Gabe could kill the man.

That Monty had denied any knowledge of Tess on those occasions made him want to cut out Cameron's tongue before doing him in.

After careful consideration, Gabe decided against patricide, mainly because he thought of something much better—or worse, to his daddy's way of thinking. It was just that plan that led him back to Aurora Springs.

As he had hoped, the village was deserted. Good. Glancing up toward the setting sun, he figured he had time to scrape some of the dirt off, too. Even better. Smelling like a horse as he did at the moment likely wouldn't help his cause, and he didn't want to give Tess any excuse to say no.

Because one way or another, by fair means or foul, trickery or truth, he intended to win her away from her damned precious Doc.

Tess was his wife, his responsibility. His joy. Monty Cameron had stolen that joy away from Gabe for years. He couldn't have her any longer.

At the house, Gabe bathed, shaved, and donned fresh clothes. Then, suitably armored both mentally and physically, he headed for Lookout Peak.

Total darkness came slowly in this part of the world, and although the sun had dipped below the horizon, fingers of brilliant red and gold light stretched from the horizon into the sky, lighting his way up the hill. He found Tess seated on a thin, multi-colored quilt near her observation point overlooking the flats. She was alone, none of the other Aurorians in sight. Her telescope stood abandoned while she sat with her arms wrapped around her knees. Her manner was that of someone lost in thought rather than study, and Gabe wondered if the spooklights were not glowing tonight after all.

He purposefully rustled a bush or two as he approached, not wishing to startle her. She didn't speak, but he could tell she knew he was there. He drew a deep breath, let it out in a rush, and said, "Hello, Tess."

"So, you came back," she said flatly, not bothering to turn around.

Gabe grimaced. Not exactly an auspicious start. Maybe he'd best ease into the topic another way. "What are the spooklights doing tonight?"

She waved her hand toward the flats. "See for yourself."

Gabe figured this was as good a place to start as any. Tess always had been a sucker for vulnerability. "I would if I could, but you know I don't see your stars, Tess."

She didn't respond.

Gabe scooped up a handful of pebbles and started launching them one by one out into the air. "I wish I did see them. I wish I could share that with you." He sent her a sidelong look and thought, *What the hell*. Then he laid his heart right out between them. "I want to share everything with you. I love you, Tess. I always have. I imagine I always will."

Gabe waited for her reaction. Then he waited some more. Silence stretched between them like miles of empty desert.

A serrated blade of emotion twisted in his gut. Gabe

had not honestly expected her to return his declaration, but he had hoped. *Sonofabitch.* This war might be harder to win than he'd thought.

Tess shut her eyes and said softly, "I'm so angry at you."

Well, it wasn't exactly the response a man likes to hear following a declaration of love, but at least she was talking to him. "Do you want to push me off this hill?"

"Part of me does, yes."

"In that case I reckon I'll take a seat." He sat beside her, legs crossed at the ankles, and leaning back on his hands. "But part of you still wants to keep me around."

"That's the problem, Gabe." She turned her head and looked at him, her eyes round shimmering pools of blue. "You're not around. You're never around."

Tess always had been one to cut right to the nut.

Gabe let another rock fly and debated the best way to respond. "I have lots to feel guilty about where you're concerned, but I do have a defense in this case. Remember, Tess, I wasn't around because you sent me away. Back then I believed you meant it."

"And now?"

"Are you trying to send me away?"

She sighed. "No."

"Good. No way in hell I'd go, but I wouldn't want to have to fight you on it." After a moment's pause, he said again, "I love you, Tess."

The wicked woman ignored him again. Even worse, her next comment involved another man. "Lionel Robards paid me a visit yesterday."

The Ranger. He must have brought word about Monty. Wonderful. Gabe took a cue from his wife and didn't respond.

She didn't seem to care. "He asked me to marry him. Do you know that it was the fifth such offer I've received in the past twelve years?"

Gabe felt torn. Which got to him worst? Robards or the four unknown suitors? He shot her a disgruntled look and said, "I trust you told the Ranger to fork his saddle and hit the trail. Who were the others, Tess? You never mentioned any others."

She gave a frustrated groan. "You are such a man, and I mean that in the worst sense of the word. What does it matter who the others were? Isn't it enough to know I've had to put my life on hold because I'm married to you?"

"If you've had five marriage proposals it doesn't sound like you were holding on all that tight." When she didn't reply, he clamped down on his irritation and grumbled, "I love you, Tess."

"You are starting to sound like Twinkle doing one of her spirit-summoning chants."

Gabe's temper flared. "That's a helluva response, woman."

"What do you expect from me, Gabe? Do you want me to bow at your feet and say I love you, too? Well, guess what? It's not gonna happen. I waited for you for a dozen years, and what good did it do me? At the first sign of trouble, you leave."

He uncrossed his ankles and sat up straight. "At the first sign of trouble *you lash out and tell me to leave*."

"I can't trust in your love, Gabe," she said bitterly.

"I've finally figured it out. I can't trust in your love, and it's an anchor around my neck keeping me from living my life."

A tremor of something that might be related to fear rumbled around in Gabe's gut. This wasn't turning out at all like he had planned. He'd figured Monty to be the stumbling block. Hell, he could declare war against that man, but how could he fight Tess? He couldn't fight her. He loved her.

And apparently, she couldn't care less.

Shoving to his feet, he began to pace. With every step, the knot in his stomach grew harder. "Are you telling me you wanted to marry the others? Do you want to marry Robards?"

She didn't answer.

Gabe halted abruptly. Fury whipped over him like a brush fire. Had he been totally mistaken? Had it truly come back to this? "Are you asking me for a divorce?"

"It depends."

"It depends? What kind of answer is 'it depends'? Do you love him? Is that the problem?"

"I'm not in love with Lionel, although this would all be so much easier if I were. Then I wouldn't care if you breezed in and out of my life."

"So you do care about me."

"I never said I didn't."

"Well, you never said you did. Not tonight, anyway. I thought you did, you know. We made love the other night. You know we did. It was more than just scratching an itch. A helluva lot more. And then you poured your heart out to me. And I listened and I—"

"Left," she snapped. "You left again, damn you."

It was the cuss word that did it, that clued him into the real problem. She'd said it before but fool that he was, he hadn't picked up on it. Tess didn't want a divorce to marry that slick, smarmy Ranger. What she wanted was a fight. Tess was spoiling for a good, old-fashioned Pecos promenade. And because Gabe remembered just how his little wife went about fighting, he was more than happy to oblige.

He dropped to his knees on the quilt and got right in her face. "Yeah, I left. I left and I stayed away a whole four days."

"You always leave."

"Uh huh. But I always come back."

"No, not always. Four days could have been four years just as easily. Fourteen years."

"I love you, Tess."

She balled up her fist and hit his arm. Gabe wanted to laugh out loud. Yeah, he remembered these fights. Tempestuous Tess. "You can do better than that. I hurt you, didn't I? You opened up your heart to me. You shared your feelings."

Her chin came up. "And you ran away. Like a coward."

"Like a man." It earned him another punch, this time to the stomach. He might have felt that one had he not been prepared. "Tell me, darlin', do you get this angry at anybody other that me?"

"No!" she said, her tone sharp as the stone digging into his kneecap.

"So what does that tell you?"

Anger blazed in her eyes and she spoke through gritted teeth. "It tells me that you're loathsome."

"No, it tells you that you love me." He flashed her a victorious grin, leaned forward, and whispered, "I win."

He read the reaction in her eyes before she moved. *Damned if I can't play this gal like a hundred dollar fiddle.* Then she was flying toward him, fuming and fussing and falling into him. She took him down and he reveled in it. Her mouth seized his and he surrendered gratefully.

Tess in high passion was a glorious being. Her kiss was aggressive; her hands bold. Her hunger savage.

Her tongue invaded his mouth, plunging and plundering, even as she grasped the neck of his shirt and tugged, yanking the buttons free and baring his skin. With rough hands, she pushed his shirt from his shoulders and her mouth—her wet, warm, magic mouth—trailed kisses down his chest before capturing his nipple in her mouth.

All sense of victory, of smug triumph, went up in flames beneath the hot, primitive arousal Tess incited to life inside him. He went hard as the rock here on Lookout Peak, and his senses grew sharp even as the heat pulsing through him clouded his ability to think. When her wicked, wonderful hands swept down his torso, tore at his pants and found his aching, throbbing shaft, he groaned aloud and relinquished the last threads of his control.

Primal need fueled him. He had to get inside her. Now.

Gabe's hands went to work. With Tess's anxious assistance, he freed himself from the restriction of his pants, then reached for the final barrier between them. The sound of tearing cotton ripped through the air and finally he had access.

Shuddering, his breaths coming in harsh pants, he attempted to roll her onto her back. But Tess resisted.

"No," she said in a harsh, raspy whisper. "My way. I want you my way." Her skirt billowed around them as she straddled his thighs.

Gabe arched upward, seeking, desperately needing. Finally, she took him in her hand, positioned him at the entrance of her warm, moist channel, and took him. A wild, guttural groan wrenched from his mouth as her slick sheath surrounded him.

He thought he might die from the pleasure of it.

She rode him hard and fast and furiously, battering him with greedy, delicious demands. Tension coiled in his loins, the pressure building . . . building . . . building. "No," he moaned urgently. Too fast. It was happening too fast. He wanted it to last, to last forever.

The orgasm exploded through him.

"Damn," he muttered, gripping her hips and grinding her hard against him, wringing every last zing of pleasure from the moment. "Damn.

And Tess, the dratted woman, laughed. She laughed even as she shuddered with her climax, her muscles contracting and releasing, milking him.

Then, still holding him deep inside her, she threw back her head and lifted her face toward the heavens.

"Oh, Gabe," she said breathlessly. "The Kissing Stars. They're above us. Look."

And, depleted and replete, he forgot his own rules. Lying on his back on a quilt beneath the wide Texas sky, his body still joined to the woman he loved, Gabe forgot not to look.

Above them, moving in tandem, two brilliant balls of ethereal gold light danced across the sky. Gabe's heart pounded. His mouth went dry as old dirt. He could see them. The spooklights. And behind them, surrounding them, a sky full of stars.

Stars. He was actually looking at the stars.

His chest went tight with emotion. He blinked, clearing his vision. Golden Kissing Stars against a midnight sky.

"Do you see them this time?" Tess asked, her face still lifted toward the heavens. "I want so badly for us to share this."

He cleared his throat. "They're gold."

Even as he acknowledged them, the two lights moved together, fusing into a single star that glowed bigger and brighter for a good ten seconds. Then in a brilliant flash, the Kissing Stars disappeared.

"Oh." Tess gave a disappointed sigh.

Gabe didn't share her disappointment. He was too enthralled by the sky the spooklights left behind. "God, Venus, look at all the stars." He mentally named the constellations he drank in with his sight. Hercules, Cepheus, Cassiopeia. He gazed from Vega to Polaris across the Capella, then to his old favorites, the Pleiades.

He felt such wonder, such youth. A sense that he

had reclaimed his place in the universe, that the world was once again complete.

Now he needed to do what he could to keep it this way.

He blurted out, "Tess, come live with me and be my wife. Come to Austin with me, would you?"

CHAPTER

12

❧❧❧

"*G*o to Austin with you?" Tess repeated, her tone incredulous.

"Yeah. While I do the job for the governor. It shouldn't take more than six months or so."

She rolled away from him, sat up, and began to right her clothing. "You want me to leave Aurora Springs? Leave my work?"

"Just until my job is finished." He paused long enough to get his pants back on, then continued, "And I'll bet you have six months worth of analysis to do on your data, anyway. I'm not asking you to give up your work, Tess. Don't think that. I know how important it is to you."

"What about my family?"

"Let me be your family. They've had you for years. Can't they spare you for six months? I love you, Tess. Make a family with me." He reached out and took hold of her hand. "If we're lucky, we can make another baby. Maybe we already have."

Another baby. Tess yanked her hand away. As if she didn't have enough trouble as it were. "I don't need another child to raise on my own, Gabe. Thanks, but no thanks."

"Tess. You won't be on your own this time. I'll be with you."

"Uh huh." Doubt dripped from the two words. "For how long? A week? A month? Until the baby gets sick and you run off rather than face an illness?"

"Dammit, Tess. I ran off to deal with the fact my wife had borne then buried a child I didn't know existed. Now, unless you have another secret of that magnitude up your sleeve, I don't foresee anything making me leave you again."

She clamped her teeth against a bitter laugh. *No sense giving away the game at this point.* "What about Doc?"

Gabe was but a shadow in the darkness, but the stars and slivered moon cast enough light upon his form to illuminate his flinch when she mentioned his father's name. "What about him?"

"Doc is part of my family. Where I go, he goes. Are you prepared to accept that?"

"You are *my* wife, not his."

"I love him. He stood by me." She felt Gabe's sharp, frustrated gaze, but she refused to capitulate and say what he expected of her. The stakes in this battle were high, and if she needed to use the love she felt for Gabe as a weapon, then so be it. And she wouldn't feel one bit guilty, either.

"Tess?" he said, a slight note of hurt in his voice. *Well, maybe just a little bit guilty.* "Your father earned my love and loyalty, Gabe. I told you everything he did for me."

He snorted. "The man used you, Tess, and he's slick enough to hide the fact from even someone as smart as you. Monty always did want someone else taking care of him. I'm sure you've suited his purpose just fine."

"He didn't use me. He saved my life. When, I might add, you weren't there to do it."

"I wasn't there because he killed your brother. Have you forgotten that little detail?"

"Doc didn't kill Billy. The explosion did."

"And Monty's carelessness caused the explosion. How can you disregard that, Tess? How can you forgive him?"

"It was an accident, Gabe. A terrible accident, but an accident nonetheless. We put it behind us years ago and so should you."

"Why should I? He cost me so much. My mother, Billy. You. We lost twelve years together, Tess. I never got to see my little baby girl. And while I'm glad Monty was around to help you, I can't forget the fact that you wouldn't have needed his help if it weren't for him to begin with. Besides, he may have told you he came looking for you, but I'd put my money on the notion he just stumbled across you. Monty Cameron isn't as good a friend to you as you think."

"Oh really? And why do you say that?"

"Because if he truly cared about you, he'd have told me about you when I asked."

"When you asked? You've seen Doc?" Alarm

whipped through her. "He's home? He's come home with Will?"

"No. This was before now. I saw him last spring. In fact, I've seen him once a year for the past four years. Has he bothered to mention that to you?"

Her stomach felt queasy. "No."

"I didn't think so. I asked him about you. Every time. He told me he hadn't seen you since Billy's funeral."

Tess's stomach dropped. "What are you saying?"

"The man looked me up. I saw Monty on eight different occasions, and each and every time, I asked about you. He denied having seen you."

"No, you're wrong."

"Tess," he chided. "I'm lots of things, but I've never been a liar. You know that. I'm telling you the gospel truth. Monty Cameron claimed to know nothing about you. He sure as hell denied living with you. And he does live with you, doesn't he? That's his bed I've been sleeping in?"

"How did you . . . ?"

"One of the books stacked on the bedside table has a note written on the title page. It's his handwriting. I put the two together once you connected your Doc and Monty."

Tess shook her head, baffled by Gabe's claims. She didn't understand. "Why would Doc do something like that?"

"I don't know. Does it really matter? He lied, Tess. I looked for you. Every city. Every town. I was always on the lookout for your face, even when I denied it to myself." He again reached for her hand.

"Now that I've finally found you, finally figured out what I want, I don't intend to let you go again."

"But—"

Leaning over, he gently kissed her lips. "Come to Austin with me, Tess. I love you."

She wanted to run. She was ready to run or fly or fall off this mountain to get away from Gabe and all the turmoil he'd planted in her mind. Instead, she stood and wrapped her arms around herself. "I have to think about this. I have to ask Doc. I don't know. . . . There are things you don't know."

"I know I love you and that whether you'll admit it or not, you love me, too."

"No, I can't." She backed away from him. She believed Gabe. He'd told the truth when he'd said he wasn't a liar. But as far as Doc was concerned . . . well . . . she needed the chance to think it all through. Surely Doc had a reason for what he'd done. He would explain if she asked. Then everything would come clear. "I need to go," she said to Gabe. "To go home. I need to think this through."

She was ten steps down the path when he called out for her to stop. "What are you feeling right this moment?" Gabe asked.

Confused. Disillusioned. Worried as all git out.

Although she didn't reply, he continued with his point. "Think of how you feel, then ask yourself what you are doing."

"What I'm doing?" she repeated.

"You're running away, Tess. You're upset and bedeviled and you're running away." After a brief pause, he added, "So I'm not the only one who runs, am I?"

Huntsville, Texas

Tinny piano music drifted from the tavern's outer room as the prison guard carefully counted a stack of bills. After starting over twice, he finally worked his way to the end. He folded the notes, tucked them into his jacket pocket, then flashed a toothy grin. "Paper money sure carries easier than coin. I miss the *chink*, though. Love that sound."

"Quiet," replied the visitor. "You worry about doing your job, not the money I'm paying you. Otherwise, you'll end up dead."

"Nah, I'll be fine. I make sure to buy 'em a round of drinks every Saturday night." Reaching for a bottle of whiskey, the guard added, "They won't fire on me."

The visitor grabbed the fellow's arm short of the bottle. "Maybe not, but I will."

The guard scowled, but wisely made no further comment. Nor did he make another try for the liquor in the face of the visitor's coldest stare.

Lips twisting in a sneer, the visitor gestured toward the door. "Shall we?"

The two men made a stealthy departure from the tavern through the back door, then snaked their way through the deeply shadowed alleys headed for the "Walls."

A fiddler's waltz drifted on the crisp winter air, a pleasing contrast to the stench of refuse rising from waste pits and corners. The visitor picked up his pace, anxious to put this part of the mission behind him. He didn't like exposing himself to danger this way, but as usual, he'd been the best man for the job. Less than ten minutes after leaving the tavern, he spied the intimidating walls of the Texas State Penitentiary.

The prison sat smack dab in the middle of Huntsville. The red brick walls were thirty-two inches thick and varied in height from eighteen feet to twenty-six feet above ground. They surrounded a yard of sufficient size to accommodate cellblocks that currently housed around three thousand prisoners, a cotton mill, wool mill, warehouses, outbuildings, a library, and a chapel.

Thin clouds drifting across the moon cast eerie shadows on the prison walls. The visitor shuddered. He had long nursed an aversion to jails, and the thought of entering one—even voluntarily—created a nauseous sensation in his stomach.

"Ready?" asked the guard.

The visitor yanked his hat down low on his brow, then pulled a badge from his pocket, and pinned it to his vest. He nodded at the guard and together, they sauntered toward the prison gate.

The guard vouched for him to the gatekeeper and moments later, the men were inside. Sweat trickled down the newcomer's spine, but he hid all outward sign of nervousness. Twice he made a point of stopping for an introduction to other guards, once to a prison official. Come morning, he'd be well-remembered.

Come morning, he wouldn't look a thing like he did now.

According to his research, the man he had come to see currently and conveniently resided in solitary confinement. Without further delay, the guard led him to cell block eight and his quarry.

The solitary cells were small, dark, and primitive, and the stench of urine and hopelessness permeated the air. As he walked down the cell block corridor, his boot steps echoing off the cold brick walls, he once again shuddered. *Better to die than live like an animal in this place,* he thought. Then, his gaze snagging on the guard's back, he silently added, *and what a horrible place to die.*

The prisoner whom he had come to see lay snoring in his cot. Setting his lantern down on the dirt floor, the guard rattled the iron bars before sliding the key into the lock. "Wake up. Got a lawman here to see you."

The prisoner rolled over. "Like I give a good goddamn."

As the door swung open, a rush of excitement flowed through the visitor's veins. Danger always aroused him. He fed on it, reveled in it. Gloried in it.

He followed the guard into the cell, reached down and drew the cudgel from his boot, then blithely whacked the man across the back of his head. When the guard slumped to the ground, the visitor bent over and struck the man hard four more times until the skull cracked.

"Shit!" exclaimed the prisoner, scuttling to sit up. The visitor laughed softly. Power surged through his body like a current and as he slipped the small metal club back into his boot, he regretted that the prisoner wasn't a woman. He was hard as a fence post; he could use some relief.

"What the hell is going on?"

"Your language offends me," said the visitor. "I suggest you clean it up."

"Who are you?"

The visitor retrieved the stack of bills from the dead man's pocket. He tossed the currency to the prisoner. "As of this moment, I am your employer. I'll have twice that amount waiting for you when the job is done."

The prisoner stared at the money lying in his lap. "What job?" he croaked.

The visitor pulled a folded newssheet from his pocket. Paper crackled as he shook it open and turned it toward the light. "I trust you are familiar with this story, Mr. Bodine? He read the headline aloud. "Hero of Cottonwood Hollow Brings Criminal to Justice."

Jimmy Wayne Bodine sputtered in anger, "That godda— . . . I mean that goldarn Whip Montana. I'd like to kill that sonofabitch. I dream about it."

"I thought you might. In fact, I am counting on it."

Eyes lighting, Bodine asked, "Are you saying Montana is here at the Walls?"

"No." The visitor shook his head. "He's in southwest Texas. I want you to go there and kill him."

"You mean you're breaking me out of here?" Bodine shoved to his feet.

The visitor nodded toward the body on the floor. "Put his clothes on. We'll need to time our departure carefully."

Bodine grinned a hungry coyote's leer and started stripping away the dead guard's clothes. "Sprung from the Walls to go after Montana. A man cain't get luckier than this."

"Hurry," said the visitor. As the thrill of murder faded, the prison walls started closing in on him.

The two men hoisted the dead guard onto Bodine's cot and yanked the thin blanket over the body. Then, after instructing Bodine how to act on the way out, the visitor led him from the cell block and into the prison yard. There they paused while the visitor lit a cigar, taking the opportunity to check the position of the guards.

One of the men he'd spoken with earlier stood speaking to the guard at the front gate. The visitor waited until the man moved on, then motioned for Bodine to follow him. They made the front gate without incident, at which time Bodine pulled a handkerchief from his pocket and started blowing his nose as instructed. The visitor exchanged goodnights with the gatekeeper, and moments later, they exited through the huge iron gate.

The jailbreak was a success. Now to get safely out of town.

He'd stashed horses in the stable of the First Baptist Church earlier that evening, so he led Bodine in that direction. Ten minutes later, they mounted their horses and headed out of Huntsville. They rode west for almost an hour before reaching a fork in the road. The visitor called for Bodine to halt. "This is where we split up," he said, withdrawing an envelope from his pocket. "Here is your train ticket and detailed instructions on where to find Montana and how to deal with him." He paused a moment, frowning. "But you don't know how to read, do you? That's a problem I didn't anticipate."

Bodine took the envelope saying, "I've got a good memory, though. Tell me what you wrote, and I won't forget it."

Seeing no other way around it, the visitor verbally relayed the contents of the envelope. When he was done, Bodine cocked his head to one side and inquired, "Aren't you worried I'll run out on you?"

"No, Jimmy Wayne, I'm not. I know enough about you to be certain you want your revenge upon Montana. I also believe you want to stay alive. Kill Montana and you're a rich man. Cross me and you're a dead man. It's a simple choice."

Bodine stuck out his chin and attempted to act tough. "What makes you so certain you could find me?"

"Jimmy, Jimmy, Jimmy. Don't be a fool. It's not my nature to boast, but I can track a minnow through a swamp if I so choose." He turned his horse toward the north road, saying, "Once you can prove Montana's demise, leave word for me at the Cactus Café in Eagle Gulch. I'll find you."

As he nudged his horse forward, Bodine called out, "Wait a minute. You never told me who to ask for. Who are you, mister?"

The visitor smiled and said, "Well, Jimmy Wayne, since we are now partners, you can call me Doc."

Aurora Springs

"Gabe Cameron is a dead man." Tearing her gaze away from the window, Tess stormed from her star shed mad enough to out-spit Pollux. Trailing on her heels, like a pair of chicks running to keep up with mama hen, came Jack Baker and Colonel Jasper.

"Now Tess," said Jack, hurrying to catch up as she marched across the yard toward the barn. "No sense getting all huffy."

"That's right," added the colonel. "We're just looking out for you."

She stopped abruptly. "Looking out for me? As if I can't look after myself?" The afternoon breeze whipped her hair into her eyes, and she shoved it impatiently out of the way.

Jack gave a frustrated sigh. "Of course you can look out for yourself. The problem is you don't because you are so busy taking care of us."

"That's not true."

"Yes, it is, Tess." The colonel folded his arms and frowned. "Montana is right about that. You've taken care of us for years now and it's time you did something for yourself."

"Fine. Then the thing I'm going to do for myself is to kill my husband."

"Tess!" Jack and the colonel said simultaneously.

She threw out her arms. "I can't believe he went to you, too. When he talked to Amy, I gave him what for. When he bent Twinkle's ear, I warned him to keep his mouth shut. The man completely ignores me."

"The man loves you."

"I'm going to kill him. I'm going to make him listen to me this time if it's the last thing I do." Changing directions, she headed for her home.

Jack and the colonel followed, arguing on her husband's behalf all the way. At least they stopped short before they entered her bedroom. Tess didn't know how she'd explain her anger in the light of Gabe's very obvious presence in her bed. She couldn't even explain it to herself.

Sixteen days had passed since her husband asked her to leave Aurora Springs with him. Sixteen days since he'd made his accusations against Doc, accusations that baffled Tess, confused her. Charges she simply didn't want to believe. But despite her doubt and bewilderment, she had allowed the man to spend the past sixteen nights in her bed.

Sexual relations might be a glorious boon for the body, but they certainly had a deleterious effect on the mind.

She threw open the lid of an old trunk and dug to the box in the bottom. Inside lay the few keepsakes of her brother's that she'd managed to acquire before her father threw her off the Rolling R. At the bottom she found the pistol she sought, an old double-barrelled flintlock Billy claimed had been used at the Battle of San Jacinto. He'd kept the gun for its historical value, not for its usefulness. The pistol didn't work. Still, it would suit Tess's purpose as a prop because even though Gabe most likely would recognize the gun, in that split second before he did, she would snag his attention.

The man needed to listen to what she had to say. She was determined he'd do just that.

She stuck the pistol in her skirt pocket and exited her bedroom. Jack and Colonel Jasper waited in her parlor. Seeing her coming, they jumped in front of the doorway, blocking her exit.

Jack held his hands palms out signaling her to stop. "Tess, don't be angry with us. We're simply trying to help. Besides, it'll upset Amy if you're angry and that's not good for the baby."

"Jack, I—"

Colonel Jasper interrupted, "We are thinking of Will, too, Tess."

Her heart clutched. "You haven't said anything . . . ?"

"No, of course not. That's not our place. But the boy needs—"

"Will doesn't need anything. He has Doc. Doc has always been there for us both, and I won't do anything to ruin that. It wouldn't be right."

A troubled frown creased Jack's handsome face. "Was it right for Doc to keep your whereabouts a secret from your husband? I don't think so. As a husband myself, I have to side with Gabe on this one. I think Gabe has every right to his upset."

"I agree," the colonel said with a definite nod. "I sure would like to know what Doc was thinking when he paid all those visits to his boy and kept it a secret from you and kept you a secret from Gabe."

Me too, Tess silently agreed. "I'm sure he had a good reason. Gabe on the other hand has no good excuse for pestering you all like he's done."

"He hasn't pestered us."

"Hah!" She stepped forward, brushing past them. "He has sung his tune to everyone but Andrew, and the only reason Andrew has missed out on it is because he's been away from home on the trail of the white horse."

Outside, her gaze went immediately toward the barn where Gabe was tackling another task on Twinkle's list of chores, the construction of new stalls for Castor and Pollux. The mule-headed fool. Maybe she should suggest that Gabe "Whip Montana" Cameron build himself a new place to sleep right alongside the camels. He might smell better, but heaven knows he was just as stubborn. When Castor or Pollux got it into their heads to sit down and stay down, nothing and no one could change their minds. Gabe was acting just the same way with his idea for her to move away with him. "If he tells me he loves me one more time, I'm going to shoot him dead," she muttered.

Somewhere deep inside, Tess knew she wasn't being exactly rational about this situation. Being told she was loved by the man she loved in return wasn't a good argument for murder. But her emotions were in a turmoil; her mind in a dither.

He wanted her to postpone her studies. He wanted her to leave her home and her family. What kind of love was that?

One thing the past dozen years had taught her was the value of extended family. True, the Aurorians weren't family by blood, but they were by choice. Every day one of them added a little gift to her life and to Will's. Gabe thought to deny them that treasure. He thought his love should be enough. But why should she settle? Why couldn't she have both?

"I can have both," she muttered, stepping around

a "gift" Rosie had left in the yard. "We can all have so much if only Gabe will let go of his anger."

But at the moment, it was Tess's anger that needed tending to.

She reached the barn and stepped inside. What she found brought her up short. Gabe stood shirtless and sweaty, hammer in hand. He wasn't working. He was talking to Rosie.

". . . you'll agree that female human beings know how to be stubborn. Well, Tess has stubborn down to a science. You'd think she studied it just like astronomy."

Rosie, the traitor, snorted as if in agreement.

Then Gabe turned to Castor and Pollux. "What's a man to do? The woman has always been smart as a fox. Why, you should have seen the way she used to wile her way around me and Billy years ago. From the time she turned fifteen I have found her irresistible, and now that she's all grown up I damn near swallow my tongue every time I look at her. Not only is she a vision to look at, she's a vixen in bed, too. Such talented hands. Why, last night when she—"

"Don't you dare." she exclaimed, her anger once again nursed to a fevered pitch. She drew the gun from her pocket and demanded, "You shut your mouth. And keep it shut. I am at the end of my rope with you, Gabe. It's not enough you go after my family, now you try and corrupt my animals, too. Maybe I should shoot you and put us all out of our misery."

He eyed the flintlock and arched a curious brow. "Do you always carry a pistol in your pocket, darlin'?"

"Only during times of elevated stress."

"You know, of course, that you won't be shooting anybody with that particular weapon. It's Billy's old San Jacinto gun, isn't it? I doubt that flintlock has been in firing condition for half a century."

"And you should be glad of it," she grumbled. "The fact this pistol won't shoot is the only thing keeping you alive at the moment."

He grinned with delight and said, "I love you, Tess."

She cried with frustration and flung the gun at him, missing by a hair. He glanced down at Rosie and said, "Did I mention cantankerous?"

Tess ran at him, her hand curled in a fist and ready to sock him in the stomach. She knew all she'd do was hurt her hand, but she was too frustrated to care.

Gabe reached out and grabbed her arm at the wrist, then he pulled her close, wrapping his arms around her. "Ah, darlin', don't be mad. Or else get really mad and tumble me here in the straw."

He nibbled at her neck even as she pounded weakly on his back. "You don't play fair, Gabe."

"I've told you before that fair is the party they throw in Dallas in the fall. And I'm not playing at anything, angel. This is serious business."

She arched her neck in offering. "I can't believe I let you do this to me."

"You love me, Tess. That's why. You want me to wear you down and make it easy to say yes."

"It's more complicated than you think, Gabe. Besides, bothering my family won't do you any good. Our problem isn't my family. It's yours. You're going to have to make your peace with Doc for us to have a future."

At that, Gabe let her go. Scowling, he looked at Pollux and said, "Stubborn."

The dromedary batted her eyelashes and spat. Tess glared at her and said, "Traitor."

Gabe turned his attentions back to the stack of lumber he was using to build the camels' new shelter. The set of his jaw and the jerk in his movements proved the man to be far less than happy. Well, good. If she had to be upset, she thought it only fair that he be aggravated, too.

"You're not being sensible about this, Tess." He placed the point of a nail against the pine board and brought the hammer down with a whack. "There is enough water under that particular bridge to turn all of West Texas into a swamp."

"No, Gabe," she said, raising her voice to be heard above the pounding. "You are the one talking nonsense. All you have to do is to let go of your anger and give your father a chance. He's a good man, Gabe. Truly he is."

He cut her a stare as hard as the head on the hammer. "And you define 'good men' as liars, thieves, and killers?"

"He's not a killer or a thief."

"Depends on one's point of view. But even you can't deny the lying, though, can you?"

Tess closed her eyes, totally sick at heart. "Gabe, we must stop this. We keep going round and round with the same argument and it never gets us anywhere."

"So give it up." He gave the nail one last pound, then tossed the hammer to the ground, braced his hands on his hips, and turned toward her. "Give it up, Tess, and come be my wife. I love you. I want a future with you. I want a home filled with children."

Her heart started pounding and the words formed on her tongue before she had time to consider them. "Aurora Springs can give you that if you'll only let it happen."

"I told you I don't mind living in Aurora Springs part of the year. Give me six months in Austin to revamp the Rangers for Governor Ross, and I'll be happy to come back here and live with you. All I ask is that you send that old worthless rogue packing."

It hurt Tess to hear the vitriol in his voice, and it was that hurt that kept her from elaborating on her previous statement. That and the need to protect the one person she loved in this world as much as she loved Gabe.

Jack Baker's excited shout grabbed both Tess's and Gabe's attentions. Gabe grabbed the rag hung over a nearby railing and wiped his hands as he headed for the barn door. Tess stepped around Rosie and followed, stepping out into the mid-morning sunshine.

The sight that met their eyes left Tess gasping. A slow smile spread across Gabe's face as he folded his arms and said, "Well, I'll be a suck-egg mule. Look at that."

Andrew Ross rode proudly into Aurora Springs. Atop a snow white stallion. Bareback. Without a bridle.

"It's Pegasus," Tess breathed.

The white horse stood sixteen hands high, had a long mane and tail that flowed like the sweep of an eagle's wing. He was without obvious blemish, his muscles powerful and his coat sleek. He held his head high as though he knew what a magnificent animal he was.

"Finest damned horse I've ever seen," Gabe observed.

As the citizens of Aurora Springs surrounded him, Andrew slid off the horse. Ignoring the buzz of questions the Aurorians posed, he patted the beauty's neck, then whispered something in his ear. A ripple passed across the horse's skin like small waves in a pond, and his ears perked forward as if he were listening intently and understood Andrew's every word.

Tess felt a nudge against her legs and looked down to discover Rosie hiding beneath her skirts. "Now, now. Don't be afraid. It's just a horse." Throwing Gabe a questioning look, she said, "Right? It's just a horse?"

He stuck his hands in the back pockets of his pants and studied the stallion. "Calling that animal 'just a horse' is like saying the Chihuahuan gets a tad bit hot in August."

"But he is real, right? Not a figment of our imagination?"

Gabe nodded. "I reckon so. Otherwise, wouldn't our minds have gone ahead and given Pegasus his wings?"

Finally, Andrew quit communing with his horse and turned to face the crowd. "Not Pegasus," he corrected, a beatific smile spreading across his face. "Regulus."

"The heart of the Lion," Gabe observed, referring to the constellation Leo.

"Regulus does have a lion's heart. He also has the strength of a bull, the ferociousness of a mother bear protecting her young, and the canny intelligence of a coyote."

Jack Baker appeared skeptical. "If that's the case, then how come he let you catch him."

"He didn't. He caught me. Saved me, actually." When the Aurorians demanded an explanation, Andrew continued. "I had followed a trail deep into the Chihuahuan. I was three days from nowhere when the fever came back."

"Oh, Andrew, no," Amy said. "Was it the normal malarial fever? Tell us it wasn't the strange fever you had last time surely."

"Oh, Amy, yes," Andrew replied, teasingly. "And it was that new, wicked fever, not the old familiar one. It damn near killed me this time."

At first Tess couldn't speak because her heart was in her throat. Finally, she forced out, "You did take your medicine with you though, right?"

Andrew nodded. "I felt the fever coming on, and I was trying to reach shelter. But I got too sick too fast, and when I slid off my horse, I didn't have the strength to stand up and grab my saddlebags. The mare ran off, taking my quinine with her."

"Trouble, that," said Colonel Jasper.

"To put it mildly, I'd say," added Jack.

"But the quinine didn't work on that fever," Tess

said. "What happened? How did this horse save your life?"

Andrew told them a fantastical tale of dreams so real he refused to name them hallucinations. He told of how the Mystery Lights came to shine and hover above him. He spoke of how Regulus nuzzled him awake and kept on pushing and nipping until in one of his lucid moments, he was able to climb upon the stallion's back. "That's when my adventure took a strange twist. Regulus took me to a valley, much like this one, only more green and lush. Flowers bloomed everywhere and the season seemed springlike rather than fall. And, Colonel?" Andrew turned and looked at Colonel Jasper. "I saw diamonds lying in the brook. They sparkled like stars."

"I must find this valley," the colonel replied.

"Diamonds in southwest Texas?" Gabe leaned over and spoke softly to Tess from the side of his mouth. "Obviously, he was delirious with fever."

"Next thing I knew, I was surrounded by strange and mysterious creatures. They weren't human, but they weren't animals, either. They had these great big heads and thin, stick-like bodies. With a touch as soft and gentle as a butterfly's wings, they laid their hands on me and healed me."

"Space travelers," Twinkle declared. "Do you think that might be what we're dealing with here? I've had suspicions along those lines for some time now. The way the lights have been shining . . . their strength. I figured I should have had contact with the spirit world by now."

She turned to Tess. "It's a possibility, dear. Your

Kissing Stars could actually be visitors from one of those stars you study. Could be they talk to horses and heal the sick. Why, maybe the valley Andrew saw was actually their ship. They could have put a spell of some sort on him to make it appear to be a beautiful spot here on earth."

"That's a wild notion, Twinkle." Gabe folded his arms. "Too wild, I'm afraid. Andrew here had a fever dream, that's all. I've had 'em a time or two."

Twinkle tossed her head so hard her pink and green turban teetered. "And did you wake up on the back of a fabulous horse sent to take you home?"

"No, but I—*uumph*" Tess's elbow in the stomach ended his argument.

"It doesn't matter," she said, warning Gabe with a glare.

He made a snorting noise, but refrained from further comment about space travelers and instead asked Andrew questions about the horse.

"He rides like the wind," Andrew replied. "But his gait is as smooth as Amy's vanilla pudding; I had no trouble at all staying on."

Jack asked, "So now that you've caught him, what do you do with him?"

Andrew gave a rueful smile. "The more proper question is what is he going to do with me. I can already tell that he is not what I had thought. I think I'm going to need some time to figure out what part, if any, Regulus will play in my life in the future."

"While you figure all that out," Colonel Jasper said, "could you ponder a bit on this valley? I sure would like to learn more about those diamonds you spied."

The conversation then turned to Colonel Wilhoit's hunt for diamonds and the Aurorians each had an opinion or twelve to add to the discussion. All the Aurorians except for Tess, that is. Her attention was caught by the spit of dust rising from the trail into the canyon. A rider was coming. A rider was coming fast.

Somehow, she knew. Long before she could see him, she knew. Automatically, her hand reached out and took hold of Gabe's. Then, her heart pounding fiercely, she swallowed hard and said, "It's Will. He's come home. Look, everyone. Will has come home."

The boy galloped the horse into Aurora Springs. She spied the panic in his expression and her heart caught. Dropping Gabe's hand, she took one, then two steps toward him. Their gazes locked and he cried, "Help! Everybody help. It's Doc. An outlaw kidnapped Doc!"

CHAPTER

13

Chaos reigned.

Gabe watched with a curious detachment as the dust covered boy threw himself from his saddle and hit the ground running. *This has to be Will*, Gabe thought as the boy streaked passed him.

He glanced at Twinkle, expecting to see her waiting with open arms, but found her clutching her hands in worry instead. Maybe that's why the boy chose to head for Tess's hug rather than his grandmother's. Of course, any male with any intelligence at all would make that choice.

Gabe tried to tune into the babble, but Rosie drowned it out with her squeals as she came racing by, reminding Gabe of her state fair run. The boy wrenched away from Tess's arms and dropped on one knee to hug the ham.

Maybe the kid wasn't so smart after all.

Twinkle shouted to be heard above the uproar. "Enough of this. Will, what's this you're yammering on about? Oh, I've a feeling in my bones that this is bad news, *bad* news. Will, tell us about Doc."

With the boy's attentions, Rosie's squeals faded to grunts. The Aurorians all looked anxious. Tess appeared downright fearful. Had the subject of her fear been any other man than Monty Cameron, Gabe would have gone to her and held her, offering his comfort and support. As it was, he remained rooted to his spot.

"I didn't know what to do," the boy said, an audible quaver to his voice. "I didn't know if I should try and find him myself or what."

Tess said, "You did the right thing coming home, Will."

The small shoulders shrugged and he dipped his head. He kicked at the dirt with the toe of a boot as he confessed, "It's been the awfulest week. I realized I needed help and I wasn't sure I could find my way home. The stars got me here. I figured out real quick that in the daytime I was lost, but once the sun set, I knew exactly where to go."

Amy Baker said, "Are you saying you made the trip by yourself? All the way from the Big Bend?"

He nodded and his hat slid even lower on his brow. Gabe resisted the urge to thumb it back so he and everyone else could better see the boy's face. He wanted to know if the kid was as scared as he sounded.

"That's where he took him," Will said. "Snagged him right out of our camp up in the Dead Horse basin." He glanced around the circle of concerned Aurorians, his gaze passing right over Gabe who stood outside the circle. "We'd had a black bear messing with our supplies and we'd decided to move camp. I'd taken a load of foodstuffs to the new place, and when I came back, Doc was gone. The letter was sticking out from under the coffee pot."

"The letter?" Jack Baker asked.

Will's head bobbed rapidly up and down. He tugged absently, nervously, on the cuff of one sleeve. "The outlaw left a letter. He gives us ten days. I've used a chunk of that already coming home." The boy hurried to his horse, unbuckled a saddlebag, and threw back the leather flap. Removing an envelope, he handed it to the closest adult, Andrew Ross. "It's all here."

While Andrew read the note, the boy glanced at Tess and explained. "It says we have to give all of Colonel Wilhoit's gold in return for Doc's safe release. That's not the hard part, though. The worst is we're somehow supposed to get Whip Montana—you know, the Hero of Cottonwood Hollow school—to deliver the gold to a place up on Dagger Mesa."

Colonel Wilhoit said, "I shall be happy to donate that gold to the cause. However, I can't help but wonder how this outlaw knows of my discovery."

"Those men from the J-Bar ranch were here the day you brought the gold in, remember, Jasper?" Twinkle said. "And that was right before the big dance they had down in Marfa. Why, I imagine all it took was for one of those cowboys to mention seeing you lugging in that gold."

Gabe folded his arms and added to the conversation for the first time. "In that case the whole territory has heard about your find by now, Jasper."

The boy twisted his head around. Though his eyes were shadowed by the brim of his hat, his stare was intense. "Who are you, mister?"

Tess appeared to sway on her feet and her face went a shade green. *Guess the boy's news about her beloved Doc is just now sinking in.* Gabe opened his mouth to answer Will's question, but Tess beat him to it. "This is Whip Montana. He's here in Aurora Springs already, and obviously the man who took Doc knows it."

Admiration rang in the youngster's voice. "You're him? The Hero of Cottonwood Hollow school? I'm right pleased to meet you, sir. How come you're visiting Aurora Springs?"

Gabe motioned to Tess and said, "Well, actually—"

"Oh no-o-o-o," Twinkle cried, drowning out his reply while stepping forward. She bumped into Rosie, lost her balance, and tumbled face first into the dirt. Coins, a pair of thimbles, two seed packets, a pipe, and a pocket-sized Bible spilled from her pockets.

"Twinkle!" the Aurorians cried as one.

Squeal squeal squeal, added Rosie.

"Are you hurt?" Amy asked, hurrying to her side.

"My knee. I think I have twisted my knee."

Rosie waddled over beside Gabe, then promptly sat on his foot. "Get up, you old salt pork," he grumbled, yanking his boot from beneath her.

"I'll need one of you men to carry her home," Amy said, frowning as she gently felt for swelling in Twinkle's knee. Gabe kept waiting for Tess to take control and direct their actions, but she remained frozen in place, a strange look on her face.

"I'll take her," said Andrew.

"Let me," Jack said, stepping forward. He motioned to the white stallion. "Regulus could probably use some water and grain, don't you think? Why don't you see to him while Amy and I get Twinkle settled at home. Colonel, if you would support her leg it might cause her less pain."

"You can't carry me, young man," Twinkle scolded. "You'll break your back trying to tote me around."

Jack scowled at her. "Hush and let me help. Amy? You run ahead and open the doors, please."

"Oh, dear. I hate to be such a bother," Twinkle said as Jack lifted her gently. "And what about Doc? We've got to figure out how to save him."

"Let's take things one step at a time," replied Colonel Wilhoit as he helped support her injured knee. "Let's reassemble in Twinkle's parlor in . . . say . . . ten minutes, shall we? That should give Amy enough time to see you settled, Andrew the chance to see to this wonderful stallion, and Tess to . . . well . . . to do what she needs to do."

The Aurorians all shot Tess a significant look. She shut her eyes and hung her head.

What the hell is going on here? Gabe narrowed his eyes. His wife was acting downright peculiar.

As the two men carried her off, Twinkle called back. "Will, be a dear and stop by the kitchen and grab up a snack for the both of us. I do believe Amy made a chocolate cake this morning."

"Yes, ma'am."

The smile that winged across the boy's face gave Gabe a pause, but he couldn't quite grasp why.

Will continued, "First, though, I'd better gather up your belongings before Rosie takes the notion to eat them. You know how she is." As he spoke, the boy knelt and whipped his hat off his head. With quick efficient motions, he set about retrieving his grandmother's things.

Gabe spied a dime that had rolled his way and he bent down and picked it up, then carried it to the boy. "Here you go, son. This ended up over by me." He tossed the coin into the hat.

"Thanks, Mr. Montana." Will tilted his head up when he spoke, giving Gabe his first quick look at the boy's face.

And something inside of Gabe went brittle.

Will stood and looked at Tess. "Would you see to Starfire for me? I know he'll be glad to get rid of the saddle. Hurry back to Twinkle's, though, all right? We don't have any time to waste. Doc is counting on us."

"Sure, Will," Tess said, her gaze cutting across to meet Gabe's. "I'll take care of your horse and everything else. First, though, I need a welcome home hug."

As the boy stepped into Tess's embrace, Gabe watched the moment unfold as if observing a play from the top row of the balcony. He felt detached from the scene, an observer rather than a participant. Numbed. Yet at the same time, the churning in his gut hinted that life as he knew it had unalterably changed.

The actors moved in slow motion; seconds dragged by like minutes. *Look at her eyes when she looks at me.* Cautious. Pleading. Protective. Fiercely protective. And, a little fearful. Tess was afraid.

God, so was he.

Gabe couldn't look at the boy. His eyes wouldn't lower past the tuft of chestnut hair brushing Tess's cheek. He couldn't yet face the truth he'd glimpsed a moment before.

The boy is almost as tall as she.

Had his heart ever pounded this hard? Had his mouth ever been this dry? Had his lungs ever struggled this much to draw a breath?

Yes. Once. Once, not long ago. He'd felt like this the day Tess had told him about his baby girl.

Hell, man. You're a damned coward. Yellow as mustard but missing the bite. Well, it's time to get over it. Live up to your reputation, why don't you? Just rustle up some guts and do it. Look at the boy.

Gabe turned his head away and dragged a hand over his jaw. Breathing deeply, summoning all his courage, he braced himself and looked.

The boy was looking back.

He gazed at Gabe through storm cloud gray eyes. A light dusting of freckles stretched across a straight and sun-reddened nose. Boyish lips twisted in an uncertain grin.

A steel band of emotion wrapped around Gabe's chest, and he lost the ability to breathe. Looking at this boy was like looking in a mirror, one that had somehow frozen time at a date some eighteen-odd years earlier. Gabe was looking at a younger version of himself.

A son. I have a son.

He tore his gaze away from the boy long enough

to throw a look toward Tess. *How could you keep him a secret?*

Her chin came up and she faced him without flinching, her eyes flashing a warning as bright as the Kissing Stars at night. No apologies there, just a blaze of maternal protection, a vixen baring her claws in defense of her kit. How like Tess. Despite his inner turmoil, Gabe couldn't help but feel a spark of admiration.

With a nod in Gabe's direction, the boy took his treasure-filled hat and stood. He walked passed Gabe on his way to the storeroom. Gabe wanted to tell him to stop; he wanted to reach out and touch him.

My son.

Now he stood alone with Tess in the yard. Alone except for Rosie, that is. Funny thing about that, he was almost glad for the company.

Gabe looked at his wife and repeated the words that he'd said when he first arrived in Aurora Springs. "Tess, we've got to talk."

Now he'll leave.

It was her first thought when enlightenment dawned across his face. Then her motherly instincts kicked in and filled her with determination to protect her son at all costs.

"Tess, we've got to talk."

She wiped sweat-dampened palms on her skirt and said, "Let's go . . ."

"No, not again. Here. Now."

All right. Here and now. Why not? *At least he won't*

kill me out here in the open. His gaze bore into her, as hard and cold and gray as a January norther.

Gabe said, "Rachel had a twin."

Tess licked her lips. "Yes."

"Will."

"William Gabriel Cameron. After Billy."

A muscle worked in Gabe's jaw. "He's eleven years old."

"Almost twelve. They were born a month early."

Now standing halfway between Tess and Gabe, Rosie snorted and rooted at something in the dirt, and reminded Tess of the most important issue in the emotional slop currently being spread between them. "Gabe, he doesn't know. Please, please don't tell him, not right now when he is so desperately worried about Doc."

Fire shot from his eyes at that, and Tess felt the burn of his fury. Fine, let him scorch her with his temper. Let him burn her to a crisp. Just don't let him hurt his son.

He bit off his words. "So you've kept the fact that the boy has a father as quiet as the fact that I have a son?"

"He knows Gabe Cameron is his father. Whip Montana . . . even Gabe Montana . . . isn't enough for him to make the connection."

"Yeah? What about the fact that we look so damned much alike?"

She looked away. "He didn't know you when you were a boy, Gabe. He'll never see the resemblance."

"You did though, didn't you? Bet you saw it every

time you looked into his face. Sorta makes me feel good to think I haunted you that way."

She shut her eyes, reeling on her feet, and he followed that blow with another. "Why didn't you tell me?"

"I've explained this all before, Gabe. I didn't know where you were."

"You've known where I was for the past six weeks. You knew where I was when you managed to tell me about my baby who died, but not about the baby who lived."

Her eyelids lifted and her chin came up. "The time wasn't right then. Rachel is no less important than Will. One child is no substitute for another. She deserved your full attention. She deserved to be mourned."

"I'll give you that," he said, with a grimace. "But no more. You've had plenty of time since then to mention the little detail that I have a son. Were you ever going to tell me, Tess? Was the time ever going to be right for that?"

"I don't know!" she snapped. "I was waiting on you."

"Waiting on me? For what?"

"To make peace with your father, that's what."

He snorted. "Well if that's the case you'd have been waiting until the Rangers wear dresses for uniforms."

Tess wrapped her arms around herself. "We're a family, Gabe. Me and Will and Doc. Doc has been part of Will's life since the day he was born. He kept him alive those first days when I was too sick to tend him. Doc diapered him and taught him to fish. He held him when he cried and punished him when he misbehaved. He's given our son his love, a love Will desperately needed. He—"

"Stole my place," Gabe shot. Tension swirled in the air, billowing and brewing like a violent thunderstorm. He stood clenching his fists then releasing them, over and over as he spoke. "Those are all the things I should have done with my boy. All the things my father never did with me."

Tess's heart broke at the pain in his voice, pain she knew he tried to hide. "I know, Gabe. But don't you see? That's why he did those things for Will. He knows he failed you, and this is how he tried to make up for it. You couldn't care for your son, so he did. He did the very best he could."

He gave an acidic laugh and glanced away from her. "How do you manage to study the stars wearing blinders like you do?"

"What do you mean?" She stepped back, hurt and confused.

"It's the same tired question we've been batting around for a while now. Tess, if that man was trying to do what was right, then why the hell did he lie to me? Monty lied, goddammit! Why didn't he tell me, at least about you? He's known for the past four years that I go by the name Whip Montana. So why did he keep y'all secret?"

"I don't know," she moaned.

Fury whipped through his voice. "I'll tell you why. He wanted to keep you for himself. He was being the same old selfish sonofabitch he's always been."

"Gabe, that's not true," Tess protested. But deep

inside herself, she asked if maybe there wasn't something to his argument after all.

He shot her a dry, pitying look. "You're smarter than this, Tess."

"Well, there's one way to solve the question, isn't there? We will have to rescue Doc and ask him."

"Define *we*."

Tess froze. Her stare locked on the mean look in his eyes. *Oh, Gabe. Don't do this.* "You have to help rescue him."

He shook his head. "No, I don't. In fact, I'd rather eat a coil of barbed wire than go one step out of my way for Monty Cameron."

Catching a movement out of the corner of one eye, Tess turned to see her son darting across the yard toward Twinkle's house, his hat filled literally to the brim with what had been the contents of Twinkle's pockets. In that instant, she knew she had an argument he'd be hard pressed to ignore. "He'll never forgive you."

"Like I give a damn?"

She shook her head. "Not Doc; Will. If you run away from this, he'll hold it against you forever. Our son is a lot like you in that regard—he can hold a grudge like nobody's business."

"Our son." Gabe's eyes drifted shut and he drew a deep, ragged breath. "That just sounds so . . . wonderful." Then he looked at her and announced, "I want him to know I'm his father. I won't be denied on this, Tess. How do you want to tell him?"

"Aren't you listening to me, Gabe? I know the boy. If you go up to him right now and tell him you are really Gabe Cameron, but you're not going to lift a finger on your own father's behalf, then he will hate you every bit as much as you hate your father. Is that what you want, Gabe? Is it?"

"The name is Montana!"

"Well, your son's name is Cameron!"

Gabe spat a curse and stabbed his fingers through his hair. "I wouldn't tell him like that. What is it you want, Tess? Do you want me to keep this a secret? Well, I can't. I won't. Secrets are your style, not mine."

Tess covered her face with her hands and said a quick prayer for guidance. Wearily, she rubbed her eyes, then spoke to him. "I'm asking that you give Will a little time. I'm asking that you give yourself a little time. I don't want to keep this a secret, Gabe. I've never wanted that. One of my favorite fantasies has been introducing you to our boy. He needs you in his life, Gabe, but he needs his grandfather, too. You saw how upset he is. What you don't know is that your son is ordinarily a champion at hiding what he feels."

"Well, he sure doesn't get that trait from you," Gabe drawled.

That's when Tess knew he finally was listening. Gabe often used sarcasm as a defensive measure. "Look, Gabe, I'll admit I'm very upset that Doc kept your whereabouts a secret. I can't imagine what his reasoning might have been, and I'll be first in line to give him a piece of my mind if he can't justify it to my satisfaction. But what you must realize is that Doc isn't truly the problem here. The problem is the future of your relationship with your son. Take some time and get to know him before you tell him you're his father. Knowing Will, he'll take the news better if you are his friend before you become his father."

She breached the distance between them and laid a hand against his chest. "Be a hero, Gabe. Be Will's hero. Put aside your anger at Doc, and do this for your son if you won't do it for yourself."

When he started cussing, Tess knew she'd convinced him. It took him a good two minutes, but he finally filtered through a repertoire blue enough to make a bullwhacker blush, then ended by covering her hand with his and asking, "Will you tell me about him in the meantime? Stories of when he was little?"

"I'll tell you anything you want to know."

Gabe nodded and gazed toward Twinkle's house. "I reckon we should go hear the rest of this tale."

"I reckon we should."

Hand in hand, they started for the house. Halfway there, Tess tugged his arm and pulled him to a stop. "I probably shouldn't do this, but can I ask you one question?"

"Sure."

"Why are you holding my hand? Why aren't you angry at me, storming around, and yelling and cursing me for keeping Will from you as long as I did? Why aren't you leaving?"

He arched a brow. "*One* question, darlin'?"

She rolled her eyes and waited.

The smile spread across his face like a love song. He reached up and brushed a thumb across her cheek. "I can answer your singular question with a singular reply. I don't need to explain that I feel like I've been given a very, very special gift. I don't need to say that I understand why you've handled this situation the way you have, I'd have probably done the same thing. I certainly don't need to address the fact that leaving you and our child is absolutely, positively the last thing I'd do. All I need to say, my dear Tess, is that . . ." he leaned down and pressed a tender kiss against her mouth. "I love you."

This time, for the first time, she began to believe it.

Tess floated the rest of the way to Twinkle's house. As she placed her foot on the bottom step of the porch stairs, her husband tugged on her arm. "Wait a minute. I have one question *I* want answered, too."

"Yes?"

He inhaled a deep breath, then exhaled in a rush. "If we're not telling the boy he's my son, then I assume we're not telling him you and I are married, either."

Tess blinked. "Well, I hadn't thought about it, but he wouldn't like the idea that I married a stranger. Not at all. And if we tell him we married years ago, he'll figure out who you really are. We can't tell him, can we?"

"That's what I was afraid of." When she shot him a curious look, he elaborated. "What does this do to our sleeping arrangements."

"Oh." Tess's stomach sank.

"Yeah, oh." Gabe sighed heavily. "You know what? Motivation is a powerful thing. All of a sudden I want to get Monty Cameron freed in a double-geared hurry."

Me too, thought Tess. Aloud, she said, "Don't pout, Gabe. You'll give the game away. You and your boy look too much alike when you do."

He sighed again, then together they climbed the porch steps, prepared to talk with their son. More or less.

He's got my mother's nose.

Leaning against the wall in Twinkle's comfortable and colorfully decorated parlor, Gabe listened to the story Will told with half an ear, caring little for the story, but enthralled by the sight and sound of his son. If anyone thought it curious that Gabe stood grinning while the boy told a tale of kidnapping and mayhem, they didn't go out of their way to react. Will himself didn't notice. He was too busy fretting.

It stuck in Gabe's craw that Monty had so completely sold the boy a possum hide for a rabbit fur. Of course, that didn't mean his son was soft in the head or anything. Monty had been fooling people his entire life. Hell, he'd fooled Tess for years now, and she was one of the smartest people Gabe knew.

He continued to watch the boy, barely listening, until one particular name in the conversation seared into his consciousness like a hot brand. "Jimmy Wayne Bodine? What was that about Jimmy Wayne Bodine?"

Colonel Wilhoit waved a sheet of paper. "He's the one who kidnapped Doc."

"He's the man who left the letter," added Will.

Gabe's heart skipped a beat. *Jimmy Wayne Bodine within spitting distance of my son?* Then reality reasserted itself and he said, "No, that can't be. I delivered him to the Walls myself."

"His letter says he broke out of prison, Mr. Montana. Says he killed a guard by breaking his neck with his bare hands. Then he dressed in the dead man's clothes and walked right out the gate, slick as bullsnake dipped in hot butter."

Gabe dragged a hand along the side of his jaw. Surely his son was mistaken. Surely whoever was behind this simply sought to take advantage of Gabe's history with Bodine. "You never got a glimpse of this man, son?"

Tess shot him a glare, but Gabe ignored her. He always called boys "son." Lots of men did. Will wouldn't think anything of it, and Gabe would get a hell of a lot of pleasure from it. Sure enough, Will didn't so much as pause, simply started talking.

"No sir. I didn't. But the letter says if you question his identity to tell you he thinks of you every time the scar on his right cheek gets to itching."

Oh, hell. Gabe had given Jimmy Wayne that knife wound while wrestling with him during that last capture.

The thought that Bodine had the opportunity to take his son as hostage turned Gabe's knees to water and he had to sit down. Since the parlor chairs were all taken, he slumped to the floor. Will gaped at him, and Gabe would have laughed had he not been so busy fretting. Guess the boy hadn't expected this reaction from the so-called Hero of Cottonwood Hollow. "Let me see the letter."

Colonel Wilhoit handed him the page and Gabe

quickly scanned it. Quickly he realized that Jimmy Wayne—or whoever had penned the paper—wanted two things from this plot of his: gold and Gabe's hide. "This doesn't prove anything except that the author knows a little of my history with Bodine. Anyone could have written this. He could have learned about the scar from a number of places. Hell, we don't even know that Bodine can read and write."

"Were details like the scar ever written up in any of the newspaper articles about you and that outlaw?" Tess asked hopefully.

"Not that I remember," Gabe admitted. "I didn't read all of them, of course. Maybe this fellow went and spoke with Bodine at the Walls. That makes more sense than Jimmy Wayne killing a man in a prison break, tracking me to out here, and creating this elaborate plot."

"You don't think he could escape the Walls?" Jack asked.

"That's the only part I can believe. Bodine is a violent man; an evil man. But he's stupid. Dumb as dirt. If he came up with a kidnapping and blackmail plan all on his own, then you can shoot me for a squirrel and call me dinner. Nope, I'm willing to bet that Bodine is still behind the Walls and someone else is pulling our strings."

Twinkle pushed up from her chair and started pacing the room. "Your theory makes sense. If Bodine wanted to kill you and he knew you were here in Aurora Springs, all he needed to do was wait with a rifle up on the canyon rim and pick you off at his leisure. And if he wanted Jasper's gold, he could easily have sneaked in here and stolen it. We're not much on guarding our belongings."

"We don't guard them at all," observed the colonel in a rueful tone.

"Twinkle, what about your knee?" Will asked.

"Oh." She stopped abruptly and pink stained her cheeks. "Isn't that wonderful. Amy, your chocolate cake worked miracles. I've always been a believer in the healing powers of chocolate, and this certainly proves it." With that, she took her seat and folded her hands primly in her lap.

Busy thinking during the nonsense, Gabe said, "Even if it is Jimmy Wayne, he has a partner. I'm certain of it."

"Who could it be?" Tess asked.

"Well . . ." Gabe drummed his fingers against the wooden floor. "Could be whoever is behind the railroad vandalism. Could be this is connected to that gang of thieves my friend Mack has come out here to deal with."

"That makes sense," Amy said. "Maybe the same person or group of people is behind most of the trouble happening in southwest Texas these days."

"That's a good point, Amy." Twinkle tapped her lips with a forefinger.

Another possibility occurred to Gabe, and he opened his mouth to say it, then stopped himself when he caught sight of his boy. Frustration painted Will's face.

"What does it matter who's behind it?" his son demanded, throwing out his arms. "Let's just get the gold and do what he says. It's a long ride to the

Big Bend. We don't have time to waste. We have to save Doc!"

Maybe or maybe not. Gabe had a bad feeling that Monty Cameron might just be the man behind this and all the other trouble.

The idea made a scary sort of sense. Despite his failings, the man was smart. Monty possessed a mind sharp enough to develop and implement a plot of this intricacy.

"Our young man is right," Colonel Wilhoit agreed, pulling out his pocket watch. "We can discuss the ins and outs of this and formulate a plan of action on the way to Eagle Gulch. I suggest we ready our things and meet at the wagon in say . . . half an hour. That should allow sufficient time for us to make the trip into town before dark."

That brought Gabe back to his feet. "Hold on just one minute. *We* aren't going anywhere. It's me he wants. I took care of Bodine by myself once before and I can do it again. I'll go alone."

"No, you won't," the Aurorians spoke as one.

Gabe's mouth gaped open in disbelief as Amy added, "Doc is family. If he's in trouble, we'll all do our part to help him. And Gabe you are . . ." Her gaze cut to Will and she amended her statement. "You are already one of us. We wouldn't think of letting you do this alone."

"*Letting* me?" Gabe sputtered, searching for words tame enough to say in polite company. The best he could come up with was, "But Amy, you can't go. You have a baby on the way."

"You do?" Will broke out in a smile. "That's great!"

"Montana is right, sweetheart," Jack said, frowning. "I'd worry myself sick if you made the trip with us to the Big Bend. It might be better for you to stay here, or at least in Eagle Gulch."

"Now, why would she stay in Eagle Gulch?" Twinkle asked.

"So she isn't alone in Aurora Springs," Jack replied.

"She won't be alone in Aurora Springs." Gabe glared his way around the parlor, skipping Will, but giving Tess a double dose.

She stepped forward and said, "You need someone to take the gold or at least act as a decoy for the gold. You need someone to watch your back. You need someone to show you where to go."

"Don't insult me. I track folks for a living, remember?"

"But you've never tracked anyone into this part of the world. The land bordering the bend in the Rio Grande is as rough and primitive as any you'll ever see. I'm not doubting your abilities, Gabe. I know you could rescue Doc on your own. But why should you? You don't have to do everything by yourself anymore. You have us to help you; you're not alone. We're your friends, and if you'll but allow it, we can be your family."

Family. He gazed slowly around the parlor. Colonel Wilhoit stood, looped his thumbs around his suspenders, and nodded sagely. Jack and Amy Baker rose, linked their fingers, and nodded. Andrew rolled to his feet and braced his hands on his hips. And nodded. Twinkle sailed across the room, grabbed him by the shoulders, and planted a fat kiss on his mouth.

Recovering, Gabe looked at Tess. She went and stood behind their son, placed her hands upon his shoulders, and offered a smile of such hope and encouragement, of such love, that his heart all but cracked right in two.

Family. Damned if the woman didn't cut right to the nut. Damned if she didn't fight dirty. She knew that having a real family had been a secret wish of his. Now she offered him one—a strange one—but a family nonetheless. Too bad these poor, innocent Aurorians didn't realize they'd taken a skunk into their midst when they made Monty Cameron one of their own.

Gabe had no choice but to chase down the truth of this kidnapping plot. And it looked like the liberty of going alone on the trip had been taken from him, too.

Next thing you know, they'll want to bring the pig.

"First thing we'll need to do is find out whether Jimmy Wayne has escaped. Since we must go to Eagle Gulch anyway, I won't argue with y'all coming along that far. What we discover there will determine whether I allow you to go any farther or not."

Twinkle swelled up to argue, but Tess stopped her with a gentle squeeze of the older woman's shoulder and a wink. She might as well have come out and declared they would win that battle later, the hell of it being the woman was probably right.

Disgusted, Gabe turned to Andrew. "I've an idea in mind for you and your Regulus if you would consider it." After explaining how Mack Hunter's skills could be extremely useful in this situation, Gabe asked Andrew if he'd be willing to ride out immediately in the hopes of catching the westbound train due to come through Eagle Gulch that evening. Andrew readily agreed and Gabe addressed his son. "I know you must be plumb wore out, but I need to ask you some questions. I need to know more about your campsite and what Doc had been doing shortly before he disappeared."

"I'll do anything I can do to help, Mr. Montana. We've gotta save Doc. I'd lay down and die if something happened to him. You see, Mr. Montana, he's the only pa I've ever had."

"One problem at a time, son," Gabe said with a sigh. "I gotta take 'em one problem at a time."

CHAPTER

14

❦

*D*amned if they didn't bring the pig.

And, as if that wasn't bad enough, they loaded up the camels and brought them along, too. One would think they were off to join a circus rather than track down a criminal. At least bringing Castor and Pollux along made sense. The dromedaries were perfect for toting the colonel's gold, although Gabe thought having Rosie ride atop Castor in a Bedouin basket was a bit much.

A seasonal chill nipped the late afternoon air as the Aurorians rumbled into Eagle Gulch. At the livery, Gabe was dismayed not to see Regulus in a stall, and he asked the owner about Andrew and the white horse.

"Took him on the train, he did," said the gray bearded, grizzly man. "Damnedest thing I ever saw. You'd have thought the two of them were having a conversation. He tried to leave the horse here, but that stallion followed him right to the station and bellowed at the boxcars. When the train pulled out a couple hours ago, both the man and that white beauty were aboard."

Gabe thought it curious, but he wasn't about to question anything to do with Andrew and his mystical Regulus.

Tess kept the livery man distracted while the men stealthily unloaded the gold and hid it in the camels' stall. With that chore accomplished, the Aurorians split up and went about their business as planned. With promises not to start any fights or cause an uproar, Amy and Twinkle headed for the hotel to secure rooms for the night. Jack and the colonel took off for the mercantile with a supply list and their pockets full of cash.

Gabe, Tess, and their son walked along Main Street toward the sheriff's office. Halfway down the first block, Gabe realized he was strutting. Pride had puffed out his chest and lifted his chin. He'd bet every dime he'd earned that not a man in Eagle Gulch could boast of such a fine family. Tess, mind reader that she was, gazed at him with knowing eyes and smiled. Surreptitiously, he reached over and caught her hand, giving it a squeeze.

They arrived at the sheriff's office only to find it closed. A sign on the door referred all inquiries to the Texas Rangers, headquartered out of an office on First Street. Tess glanced up at Gabe. "Will the Rangers have information about a jailbreak in Huntsville?"

"They should. Wanted posters go out to all the peace-keeping organizations in the state."

"Good," Will said. "Maybe I'll get to see Captain

Robards again. Have you met him, Mr. Montana? He sure is a mighty fine man."

"Yeah, I've met him." Gabe left it at that.

They found the "mighty fine man" in his office finishing up a supper of stew and cornbread. He glanced up as they entered and a smile blossomed across his face. He dabbed at his lips with a napkin, then stood. "Tess. Will. Now isn't this a nice surprise. Please, come in and have a seat. May I offer you some stew? It's delicious and I'd be happy to send for more."

Gabe didn't mind being ignored, but he drew the line at watching another man tousle his son's hair, then drool at his wife. "This isn't a social call, Captain. We have business."

Robards finally looked at Gabe. "Business?" he repeated, his brows arching up. He sent Tess a smile filled with flirtation and regret. Gabe restrained himself from punching the man, then scowled at the way Will watched the proceedings with interest. Surely the boy hasn't been encouraging this sort of eyelash-batting behavior.

Maybe he has. Maybe he is pining for a father.

Well, by God he has one. Gabe decided right then and there to see the truth revealed at the earliest possible moment.

"We're not here to socialize," he said gruffly. "We need to know if you've had a report out of Huntsville regarding Jimmy Wayne Bodine."

The Ranger nodded. "I thought you might be interested, considering the history between you two. When did you hear about it?"

Tess whipped a fearful glance at Gabe, then asked, "Hear about what?"

"The prison break."

Gabe said a mental epithet as Captain Robards stood and crossed the room to where a wooden filing cabinet sat against one wall. He slid the drawer open, reached inside, and removed a stack of papers two inches thick. He handed them to Gabe saying, "You'll find a poster on Bodine and also one on his accomplice. Happened the last part of September. Should be toward the front of the stack."

Bodine's poster was the fourth one down. Loathing filled Gabe as he stared at the outlaw's familiar likeness. He read the brief description of the breakout with disgust. The prison officials weren't any better at taking care of Jimmy Wayne than the Rangers. Maybe the penal system needed overhauling, too. He handed the poster to Tess to read and asked, "And who was his accomplice?"

"We don't have a name. Got a good drawing, though. In fact, I have the nagging suspicion that I know him from somewhere." He snapped his fingers. "Wait a minute. I forgot I took his poster out of the stack. I studied it a couple days ago." He opened a drawer of his desk, then handed over a folded sheet of paper.

Will looked over Gabe's shoulder as he opened it. *Well, I'll be damned.* The boy's quick gasp verified what Gabe suspected.

"Do you know the man, Will?" Robards asked.

"No, sir."

"But you made a noise like you did."

"No, sir. I mean, I did make a noise, but that was because I just then realized I forgot to bring some corn for Rosie."

Gabe couldn't tell whether or not Will's fib fooled Robards, but it didn't come close to bluffing his mother. Tess took one look at her son, then gazed at the wanted poster Gabe held in his hand. She went pale as moonlight on a cloudy night.

"You *do* know this man," Robards accused hotly. "Who is it?" He yanked the page from Gabe's hand and gave it another look. "He must be one of your . . ." Then he jabbed the drawing with his index finger. "That's who it is. Your Doc. I knew I recognized the face, but I let the big hat and the spectacles and that mustache throw me off. Must have been a false one. I can't believe I didn't put it together, especially since he's the one responsible for all the trouble along the railroad spur."

"No," Tess snapped. "Doc didn't do that, and he is not the man in that drawing. It's mere coincidence that they look alike. Doc would never have done anything as wicked as free the Cottonwood Hollow school killer from prison. Never. Besides, when was he supposed to have done this evil deed? The man can't be in two places at once. He's been with Will down in the Big Bend area since mid-September. You know that yourself." She motioned toward Will. "Tell him, son. Tell him Doc was with you. . . . What was the date? The end of September?"

"The twenty-second," Gabe said, reading off the poster.

Will's eyes went round as a telescope mirror, and

he threw a panicked look toward the Ranger. Apprehension crawled up Gabe's spine. What the hell was going on here?

"Cap'n, Doc would never do anything bad like that. This man isn't Doc. He's not."

"Will?" Tess asked, a question in her tone.

The boy sent a pleading glance toward Robards, and the Ranger answered. "When I delivered the message you sent to Doc, Will here told me he was bored to death from searching for pictographs. I had some personal time coming, so I took a couple weeks off duty, and Will and I spent it together. He taught me about the constellations, and I showed him how to hunt javelina and coyotes through the mountains."

"Hunting?" Tess rounded on her son. "Hunting!" She shot a befuddled glance at Gabe. "He's never killed an animal in his life. You know how he is about Rosie."

"Mama, all I did was track 'em. Drew a couple of pictures, too."

"Why?" She looked at the Ranger. "I didn't say he could go with you. I didn't give my permission. What made you think you could take my son away from his grandfather and teach him to hunt?"

"It wasn't my idea. His grandfather was the one who suggested it and now we know why. He needed the time to break a killer out of jail."

"No!" Will cried, his eyes snapping anger.

"I have to ask myself why he'd go to all that trouble. Is there a connection between your Doc and Jimmy Wayne Bodine?" Gesturing toward Gabe he added, "Beyond the one that involves you, of course."

That floated right over Will's head, thank goodness. Gabe didn't know what he would have said if the boy had questioned the remark.

Tess stood staring at the wanted poster, her expression troubled and shaken. "I can't believe this. I simply can't. Why would he do it?" She looked up at Gabe. "Why?"

Had his father been within shooting distance Gabe would have killed him on the spot for putting that pain in Tess's eyes. "Who's to know why Monty Cameron does anything, Tess. I do think the gold probably has something to do with this kidnapping scheme, though."

Robards snapped up straight. "Kidnapping scheme?"

Gabe wished he'd bitten off his own tongue. After that there was nothing to do but to tell the entire tale. The tricky part was relaying the facts without revealing too much to Will. He managed to get the job accomplished, however, and to his dismay, but not to his surprise, Robards declared his intention for the Texas Rangers to join with the Aurorians in the hunt for Monty "Doc" Cameron.

Through it all, Will protested the very idea that Doc was in the wrong, Tess acted stunned and uncertain, and Gabe refrained from expressing his opinion. Finally, when the boy appeared on the brink of tears at the defense of his grandfather, Gabe reached out and put his hands on Will's shoulders. "Listen, Will. It's a good thing to stand up for those you believe in. I hope you're right about Doc. More than you can ever know, I hope he hasn't let you down. But if things don't work out your way and you find out

Monty Cameron isn't the man you think he is, I want you to remember one thing. You still have your family. Your mother, Twinkle, the Bakers, and Colonel Wilhoit. You've even got Rosie. They'll all stick by you. And, even though you don't know me from Adam yet, I want you to know that I will help you in any way, shape, form, or fashion. You just say the word."

"I don't understand."

"You don't have to understand right now. Just accept it. I'm here for you if you need me."

"Thank you, Mr. Montana," the boy said hesitantly. He sent a questioning look toward his mother, but all she did was stand by with tears in her eyes.

Gabe nodded toward the Ranger. "I'm going to see Tess and her son settled in the hotel. We intend to leave at first light. If you still plan on trailing along, we'll meet you at the south end of town at daybreak."

Tess tossed and turned most of the night. She couldn't believe Doc would do anything so vile. She wouldn't believe it. But deep inside her a little seed of doubt began to sprout. Doc had lied to Gabe about her whereabouts; he'd kept Will's existence a secret. All the while, Doc had known of Tess's wish to speak to her husband again and see if there might be something in their relationship to salvage. If Doc lied about something as important as that, what else was he capable of? Was Gabe right? Had Doc kept an evil side of himself hidden from her? She hated to think so. She hated to think she'd been that blind. She didn't believe that, not really.

But the doubt had been planted.

When she dragged herself from her hotel room and assembled with the others downstairs, she learned that with a little help from Mother Nature, Gabe had won the first battle of the day. Following the bumpy trip in from Aurora Springs, Amy Baker suffered an uncomfortable night so neither she nor Jack would join them on the trip. Gabe's victory wasn't complete, however, because neither Twinkle nor the colonel paid heed to his request to remain behind safe and sound. Tess wouldn't consider it, herself, and she knew her son well enough not to waste her breath insisting he hole up in Eagle Gulch like Gabe demanded. They'd have to lock him in jail to keep him from coming along, and even then she couldn't be certain the boy wouldn't wiggle his way out of the cell and follow. Will Cameron was a stubborn young man. *Takes after his father,* she thought, watching Gabe give his argument one more try with Twinkle.

Twenty minutes later than he had intended, Gabe led their party south. Lionel Robards and two of his men joined them a half hour into the trip. Up until that point, the mood among the Aurorians had been subdued. The accusations against Doc hung over them all like a gray winter day.

If nothing more, Lionel's presence managed to dispel the gloom somewhat. The interplay between the Ranger and her husband proved downright entertaining. Tess didn't like to be vulgar, but men used a term that perfectly defined the nonsense Gabe and Captain Robards spouted throughout the day. The term was "pissing contest" and the person they attempted to impress was her son.

For every story of personal bravery Lionel told, Gabe had a subtle, but stronger tale of his own. For every act of physical strength performed by one man throughout the day, the other made sure to find some task requiring even more effort. It got to be so silly that at one point, the men decided to snack on chili peppers and darned near ruined their mouths by eating one too many of the extra-hot habanero peppers.

By the time the caravan halted for the night, Tess was disgusted with both men. Will, on the other hand, was enthralled. When after-dinner talk turned to an arm wrestling contest, Tess reached her limit. "Will, come with me. I want to climb that hill and see if the Kissing Stars might make an appearance this far from home."

Both Gabe and Lionel pushed to their feet. "I'll go too," said Gabe.

"So will I," replied Lionel.

"Absolutely not," demanded Tess. "I require some time alone with my son."

Both men advanced a protest. Tess quelled it with a glare as hot as the habaneros burning their stomach linings. "It's been a long day. Why don't you men turn in, and Will and I will see you both in the morning."

Robards tried to protest further. Gabe knew when to cry off.

Tess and her son climbed the nearby rise and sat side by side gazing out over the desert just like they'd done so many times before. It was comfortable and familiar and oh, so needed. "I've missed you so much William Gabriel Cameron. Remind me never to let you go off for an extended length of time like that again."

"Come on, Mama. I wasn't gone that long. Besides, it was your idea I go with Doc."

Speaking the name seemed to dull the stars starting to pop out against the gathering darkness. After a few moments of silence, Will asked, "What do you think about all this, Mama? You don't think Doc did what they say he did, do you?"

Tess didn't want to lie to her child. Keeping the secret about his father was twisting her in two as it was. She wanted to deal with that particular situation as soon as possible. For that reason, among others, she chose her words with care as she responded to his questions. "Your grandfather has done so much for you and me over the years, honey. I can't see his being involved in a plot that frightened you, much less put you in physical danger. He loves you desperately. That much I do know."

"Mama, why do I think the next word you're gonna say is *however?*"

She reached over and ruffled his hair. "How did you get to be so smart?"

"I take after you."

"No, you take after your father."

Will gave her a curious, sidelong look. Although Tess always answered the questions her son asked about his father, she rarely brought up Gabe's name to him on her own. "He's the one who originally sparked my interest in the stars, have I told you that before?"

"No."

Tess spent the next ten minutes sharing stories about Gabe and his interest in astronomy. "He's the one who first pointed out the celestial necklace to me."

Will hung on her every word. "Doc told me a lot about my pa, but he never said he studied astronomy."

"Doc talked to you about your father?" Tess was surprised. The only time Doc ever mentioned his son to her was when she brought up his name.

"All the time," Will answered, nodding. "He talked about all the traveling they did when my father was young like me. He talked a lot about how honorable my pa was, and how he believed in law and order and Texas. Said he thinks my pa might have grown up to be a lawman of one sort or another."

"He did, did he?"

"Yeah." He scooped a doodlebug into his hand and watched it crawl across his palm. "That's why I went off with Captain Robards, Mama. I wanted to get to know him better because I can tell he's sweet on you. I needed to see what kind of man he is, figure out whether he's good enough for you." After a moment's hesitation he added, "I figured if you liked my father and he was the lawman type, then you might like the captain. It's not right for you to be alone, Mama. I'm growing up fast, and you'll need somebody to take care of you."

"So, in essence, you were interviewing Captain Robards as a potential father."

"And husband for you."

Her heart broke. "Will, you can't forget I'm already married."

"To who? A ghost? He might as well be. We would be better off if he was dead."

"Will Cameron! You watch your mouth."

"Well, it's true, Mama. Fact is I'd rather be a bastard than Gabe Cameron's son. At least that way you wouldn't be tied to the man who threw us away, and you could marry somebody good like Captain Robards."

"Your father didn't throw us away, Will. I've told you about the explosion, and how I sent him away. It's my fault he left, not his."

"Why didn't he ever come back? If he'd cared about us one little bit, he'd have come back."

"He cared, Will. He cared so very much. And you don't know that he didn't try to come back. Maybe he did and my father wouldn't let him see me. Maybe he did, only it was too late and by then I'd left home. Maybe all these years he's looked for us but he didn't know to look in Ireland or here in southwest Texas. You must admit we've been living in out-of-the-way places."

"That's no excuse," Will said angrily. "If he really loved us he wouldn't have left you in the first place, no matter what you said. If he really loved us, he'd have found us no matter where we lived. A real father wouldn't have rested until he did. He wouldn't have just abandoned his son."

"But honey, Gabe didn't know he was a father, remember? I didn't even know I was expecting when

I sent him away. I'll tell you this. If Gabe Cameron had known I carried his children, he would have stuck to me like glue whether I wanted him there or not. You can believe that. That's the kind of man your father is."

The boy shrugged. "Or was. It would be nice to know. I like Captain Robards, Mama. Look." He pointed toward the horizon. "I never figured we'd see the Kissing Stars this far south. I didn't see them before, either on the way down to the Big Bend or on the way back. But there they are. Maybe they are following us."

"I'm not about to put any limits on what the lights can and cannot do," she replied, watching the balls of light dance across the darkening sky.

"I missed seeing them. Wish I had a telescope. That's what I missed most about being away from home. Saturn just isn't the same if you can't see her rings."

"Don't let Rosie hear you say that. She'll eat my telescope."

Will cracked a grin that was a replica of Gabe's. "Oh, I didn't mean Rosie or any of the rest of the family. You know that."

"True, but I also know how much you enjoy our work in Aurora Springs. I know you love the sky. So being away from the Kissing Stars, and away from our astronomical studies made you unhappy, did it?"

Will picked up a stick and started drawing lines in the dirt. "Not really. I knew I'd be coming home and it wasn't like the stars were going anywhere or anything. The regular stars, I mean. Not the Kissing Stars.

Who knows what they'll do. I liked getting out and seeing something different. As long as I know I can come back home, well, I think that sounds perfect." He glanced at her and said, "Maybe after we rescue Doc the three of us can take a trip. I'd like to go someplace that has a real honest to goodness forest. Think we could do that, Mama?"

"Maybe."

He allowed a full minute to pass before he said, "Mama, you never answered my question."

"What question?"

"You never said for sure if you think Doc helped Jimmy Wayne Bodine break out of jail. If you think he's faked his own kidnapping."

"Oh, Will." She sighed heavily and wished the Kissing Stars would provide the answer. "You would have to force the issue, wouldn't you?"

Accusation colored his voice. "You think he's guilty?"

"No, I don't. But the truth is, I don't think he's entirely innocent, either. I've learned something that causes me to question Doc in ways I've never questioned him before. There is something you don't know, honey. Something I need to tell you."

"What about?"

"Well, your grandfather. And your father. You see, sweetheart—"

"There you are," Gabe's voice boomed from the shadows. He strolled up before them saying, "I've been wondering where you were. Will, Rosie is making these pining sort of noises and the look on her face is downright lonely. I think she might be afraid you've left again."

"Oh, dear," the boy said, pushing to his feet. He dusted off his behind with his hands, adding, "Guess I'll have to drag out my guitar and calm her down. I never expected her to be so sensitive. She's been awful clingy since I got home. I'm hoping she gets over it soon. As much as I love her, she isn't all that pleasant to sleep with."

Gabe nodded sagely. "It's the perfume. Pigs tend to over apply the stuff."

Tess watched father and son share a mirrored grin, then the boy headed down the hill. When Gabe took Will's seat beside Tess, she asked, "Why did you stop me? I was going to tell him. Isn't that what you want?"

"Yeah. No. Not like that." He sighed heavily. "I eavesdropped on the two of you. It was some damned hard listening."

"You know the old saying about eavesdroppers never hearing good of themselves."

"Now that wasn't all true. You said some mighty fine things about me. Made it easier to hear that my son wished me dead."

"Gabe," she said reproachfully.

He reached out and took her hand, threading his fingers through hers. "You were right about me getting to know him before we tell him."

"No, I was wrong. I feel like we're lying to him, and I don't like it. I never have before, and I don't intend to start now."

"I don't think it's lying. I think it's doing what's

best for the boy. After today—especially after what I heard tonight—I can see how he'd take the truth better knowing I'm more than just the fellow who ran out on you."

"Gabe, I didn't mean for him . . . he didn't know the circumstances. Please, don't let what he said—"

"Hush, darlin'." As the soothing strum of a guitar floated up from below, he brought her hand up to his lips for a kiss. "I can't change how he felt in the past, but I'll do my all to see that our future is square." Gabe paused and Tess could hear the frown in his voice as he added, "It would help a lot more if Ranger Robards wasn't horning in and trying to out-do my every overture toward the boy. What's his problem, anyway? You told me he knows what I am to you and Will. Does he think he still has a chance with you? Is that what this is all about?"

"I think Lionel is a lot like you. He's a strong man, a competitor."

"He's a pain in the butt."

"Never mind Lionel. What shall we do about Will? How and when do we tell him you are his father?"

Gabe rolled to his feet, then pulled her up beside him. "Let's give it one more day. Just see how it goes between us. Maybe I'll get lucky and ol' Lionel's horse will throw a shoe and he'll have to walk."

"I could try and keep Lionel occupied," she said innocently.

He answered by taking her mouth in a fierce, breath-stealing kiss. "Over my dead body, woman. Over my dead body."

★   ★   ★

The accident happened mid-afternoon on the third day out of Eagle Gulch. Captain Robards had led his pair of Rangers ahead to scout out the route through the line of craggy, fractured mountains that rose before them like the gateway to hell, brown and barren and forbidding. Tess and Twinkle traveled inside the stagecoach being driven for the afternoon shift by the colonel. Rosie continued her ride in Castor's basket.

Glad for a respite from the Rangers, Gabe rode alongside Will who regaled him with tales of his porcine friend. One hour stretched to two during which Gabe discovered a pleasant fact. His son was fun to be around.

The boy was witty, intelligent, and could spit a watermelon seed with dead-eye aim. Will seemed to like him, too. He was quick with a grin and the questions he asked showed honest interest in the answers. Gabe's work impressed him, and with every "wow" and "who-eee, mister" Gabe sat a little straighter in the saddle. A time or two he tested the waters about the fatherhood question and took encouragement from the answers his son offered.

All in all Gabe's day looked pretty bright as the stagecoach led the way down a moderately steep incline. A flash of sunlight on water grabbed his attention, and he had just lifted his hand to point out the spring off to their left when he heard the ominous wrench of tearing metal and saw the stagecoach pitch wildly to one side.

The next few moments passed in a panicky blur. Even as Colonel Wilhoit struggled for control, the stage slammed into a boulder, then tumbled on its side and started to roll. Above Twinkle's scream and Rosie's squeals, Gabe heard Tess shout his name.

Fear gripped him. He spurred his horse forward as the colonel went flying off the driver's seat, landing hard at the base of an ocotillo cactus. The stagecoach rolled side over side. Supplies sailed and crashed; wood and metal twisted and snapped. The horses tumbled, too, screaming and pawing. Then one got loose, got back on his feet and ran, trailing broken harnesses. The other went abruptly silent.

Seconds later, the stagecoach did too, crashing to a halt in the shallow water at the bottom of the gully.

"Mommy?" Will said in a little voice.

He hung back as Gabe slid off his mount and side-stepped double-time down the hill toward the coach. Gabe glanced back over his shoulder. "Will, check on Colonel Wilhoit. If he's bleeding, staunch the flow, but otherwise don't try to move him." When the boy didn't move, he called again. "Will! Shake a leg, son. We need your help."

The battered coach lay on its left side, the right front wheel missing, the back wheel slowly spinning. Gabe's stomach sat somewhere around his ankles, his heart smack dab in the middle of his throat as he climbed up on the coach, wrenched open the door, and peered inside.

At first all he saw was the blood.

Horrible streaks of red stained Twinkle's bright yellow dress. She lay atop Tess and neither woman moved. At first glance, Gabe couldn't determine the source of the terrifying stain. "Tess? Sweetheart?" He sucked in a breath. "Twinkle?"

Nothing.

Gabe started praying.

Water was starting to seep into the coach and Gabe's sense of urgency accelerated. A person could drown in those two inches of water if their head rested just so.

Please, God, let them be alive for drowning to be a concern.

He eased himself down into the coach, grimacing when the conveyance shifted. Twinkle's pain-filled moan was music to his ears.

Finding footholds, he considered how best to act. He hated to move her without first determining the state of her injuries, but he had to risk it. The blood had come from somewhere and Tess . . .

As gently as possible, he slid his arms beneath Twinkle's unmoving form and shifted her enough to get his first look at Tess. Everything in him froze. Blood streaked her face and she lay crumpled like a doll in the bottom of the coach. Her head rested in the rising water; her opened mouth half-filled.

He licked his dry lips, then slipped a hand beneath Tess's oh-so-still head and lifted it out of the water. Her head rolled, dead weight. His heart raced. With trembling fingers, he felt for a pulse. Faint but steady. "Thank God."

Then his boot slipped and he almost dropped her. Damnation, there wasn't room to move in here.

Where were the goddamned Rangers when he needed them? Gabe couldn't get them out of the coach by himself. "Will! Jasper! Can you hear me? I need help!"

"Mr. Montana?" his son called. "I'm here. The colonel is just starting to wake up. I think he'll be all right, but he isn't gonna be much help. Not for awhile, anyway." The boy paused a moment, then asked in a trembling voice, "Mr. Montana, how's my mama?

"She's alive, son. She has a gash on the side of her head, and this kind of wound bleeds a lot."

"She'll be okay, though, won't she?"

Gabe cleared his voice to speak. "I won't lie to you, Will. She's unconscious and that may be simply from the gash on her head or it might be something worse. I can't tell much more without getting her out of here."

A silent moment passed as the boy absorbed the news. Then he asked, "What about Twinkle?"

"I think she'll be all right," Gabe replied, relieved to see stirring that signified the older woman was coming to. "Any sign of Captain Robards or his men?"

"None, sir."

Hell. Gabe tried to figure out what to do next. Ordinarily he was a quick thinking man, but the sight of Tess's blood made his mind as sharp as cornmeal mush.

"What are we going to do, sir? Do you need the ladder?"

Ladder? "What ladder?"

"The rope ladder Twinkle keeps up in Castor's riding basket in case Pollux gets ornery about kneeling down. She does that sometimes."

God bless that saliva-spittin' dromedary. "That's just what we need, son. Good thinking."

By the time Will sent the rope ladder unrolling into

the coach's interior, Twinkle had awakened enough to help hoist herself up and through the doorway. She sat on the side of the coach while Gabe hurriedly followed and assisted her to the ground. Leaving Will to settle her beside the woozy Colonel Wilhoit, Gabe hurried back to Tess. She was still unconscious.

He knew that moving an injured person sometimes caused added harm, but he didn't see that he had a choice. "Honey, I'm going to get you out of here now. Hang on and I'll have you settled in a minute."

Holding Tess over his shoulder, he climbed from the coach. Will spread a blanket beside the spring and Gabe gently lowered her to the ground. He dipped his kerchief into the water, washed the blood from her face, then gently dabbed at the wound. Rosie plopped down beside the blanket, and Gabe would have sworn she looked worried.

"Are you going to stitch her up?" Will asked, his voice quavering.

"Not in this lifetime." Gabe's mouth dipped into a grimace at the thought. The very idea of poking her flesh with a needle had him breaking out in a sweat. "It's not bleeding so much now; I think it will be all right. She'll be all right." *Please, God, let her be all right.*

With Gabe kneeling on her right side and Will seated cross-legged on her left, they began their uneasy vigil. Helplessness clawed at Gabe and he continued to bathe her face. He never left her side, sending the boy to check on Twinkle and the colonel and to climb the butte to look for signs of Robards and his men.

Confounded Rangers. What the hell were they up

to anyway? Riding ahead. They hadn't needed to ride ahead. They just wanted to get away from the camels and Twinkle's singing. Gabe had heard Robards say it himself. *When I go to revamp the Texas Rangers, I'll see Robards transferred to the middle of nowhere.* The fact the man was already stationed in the middle of nowhere might complicate the task, but Gabe would by God see it done. "You know why they call West Texas God's country, son?"

"No, sir."

"Because no one else would have it."

The boy shot him a quizzical look. "What does that have to do with my mother?"

"I don't know. Nothing. Never mind me, son." Gabe was getting punchy with worry.

A few minutes later Twinkle and the colonel staggered over. Both looked very much the worse for wear and, except for advice, had little assistance available to give. Not that Gabe wanted any. It was his place to care for his wife. His and Will's.

Gabe's concern grew at a steady pace. It was past time for her to wake up. "Tess, enough of this now," he told her, holding the hand of her uninjured arm in one of his, stroking it with the other. "Come on, honey. Wake up. It's time. It isn't good for you to sleep so long."

He was tempted to pinch her cheeks to put some color in her pasty complexion. He wanted to shake her and scream at her to just wake up, dammit. "Open those eyes, darlin'. Please, sweetheart. You're scaring me."

"Please Mama. Do like he says." Will's voice trailed

away to almost nothing as he added, "I don't want to be an orphan."

"You won't be an orphan!" he snapped.

"But if Mama dies . . ."

"Tess isn't going to die and you won't be an orphan. Now, no more of that kind of talk, you hear?"

Gabe dampened the kerchief again, then trailed it across Tess's face. "Wake up, Tess. I need to see those beautiful blue eyes. I need you. Our son needs you. I love you, Tess. I always have and I always will. Did you hear that? I love you. Now open those eyes and glare at me for saying it. I love you, darlin'. I love you."

Tess's eyelids twitched and Gabe held his breath, praying for them to lift. Nothing happened at first, but then they twitched again. Had they lifted halfway or had he imagined it? "There! Did you see that, Will?"

When the boy didn't answer, Gabe flashed him a glance. Will wasn't looking at his mother. He was staring straight at Gabe, his gaze narrow and sharp enough to shave with. "You're him, aren't you?" he accused, betrayal shining in his eyes. "You are my father."

CHAPTER
15

"*Y*ou are my father!"

Will's bitter words pierced the haze of pain and confusion clouding Tess's mind. *Oh, no. Not like this. He shouldn't have found out this way.*

Her wits returning in the face of her son's distress, she ignored her throbbing muscles and pounding headache and forced herself to put aside the burning concern she felt for her friends' safety. She opened her eyes, wanting desperately to reach for her son and hold him, to talk to him and explain. To tell him how much she loved him.

Neither male noticed, their gazes locked upon one another, the air between them sizzling with tension and emotion.

Tess's heart gave a wrench. She had wanted to tell Will herself, or at least be cognizant enough to moderate the event. But now it was too late. Will had figured it out.

You are my father.

She'd never heard such rancor in her son's tone. A sense of urgency battled the drum corps playing in her head, and Tess tried to figure out what to do. It was so hard to think. Opening her mouth and speaking seemed an insurmountable problem.

But then, maybe that was a good thing. Maybe it was best that the two men in her life work out this situation by themselves. She allowed her eyes to shut and she listened.

"You're not Whip Montana," Will accused. "You are Gabe Cameron."

Tension added an edge to Gabe's firm voice. "I am your father, Will. But my name is Montana now. I've been going by it since before you were born."

"Why?"

The heartbreak Tess heard in that single word hurt her worse than the pain radiating in her head. Gabe took a long time to respond, forcing a curious Tess to peek at him through her lashes. Frustration hardened his jaw, but his eyes—oh, his eyes—held such anguish. *Oh, Gabe.* She wanted to reach out and squeeze his hand in comfort.

Gabe's voice was raspy with emotion when he spoke. "Just which *why* are you asking, son? I can think of at least a dozen. *Why* did I give up my name? *Why* did I give up your mother? *Why* haven't I been around to be your father?"

Will scrambled to his feet sending puffs of red dust billowing in little angry clouds. He clenched his hands at his sides so hard his knuckles turned white. With every word he spoke, his voice got a little louder, a little more desperate. "How about *why* the hell don't you get away from my mother! Why the hell don't you get out of here. We don't need you. And don't you ever call me son again. You changed your name. Well I'm changing my father. Doc is my father, the only father I want. You just saddle up and ride on out of here, mister. We don't need you!"

"Now hold it right there," Gabe snapped back.

Hearing the temper in her husband's tone, Tess decided to interrupt before the situation got out of hand. So she let out a little groan and gained both her husband's and her son's full attention. "Mama?" Will said. He dropped back onto his knees beside her.

"Tess?" Hovering over her, Gabe gently laid his hand against her cheek. "Tess, are you finally waking up?"

Bright sunlight stabbed like a cactus thorn when she fully opened her eyes so she shut them again almost immediately. "Oh, my head," she moaned, not needing to exaggerate her condition at all. She tried to sit up but both the pain in her head and the males in her life forced her to lie back down. A moment later, she again gathered her wits enough to ask, "What about Twinkle and the colonel?"

"They're all right," Will assured her. "Banged up a bit, but nothing too serious. The colonel's ankle hurts and Twinkle is seeing to that."

Relieved, she asked about the accident, and Gabe described the broken wagon axle and how the coach had rolled. "You were out a good five minutes. You probably have a concussion."

"Well, what are you, a doctor, too?" Will grumbled.

Gabe sucked in a deep breath and let it out slowly. The epitome of patience, he said, "You've a cut on your head—that's where all the blood came from. That's all I could tell. Do you hurt anywhere else, darlin'?"

Will's chin went up and out. His eyes narrowed pugnaciously. "Don't call her that. Her name is Tess. She is *not* your darlin.'"

"Yes, she is."

The boy's nostrils flared and his brow dipped into a fearsome scowl. "You are no hero, Whip Montana. You're a sorry sonofagun."

"Will, please." Tess struggled to sit up, ignoring Gabe's insistence that she stay put. Her head thrumming from the effort, she added, "Don't be like this."

"Like what?" He glowered at Gabe.

Then, the words flowing naturally, if ill-advisedly, from her tongue, she said, "Don't sass your father."

For the span of a heartbeat, Will froze. Then he shot her a look brimming with betrayal, and turned his head away. Rejecting her.

Tears welled up inside of Tess and despite her efforts to contain them, spilled from her eyes. Her whimper must have escaped, too, because Will darted a glance her way, then flinched guiltily. For just a moment she thought he might melt, but then the flame of anger rekindled in his eyes. "I've gotta go check on Rosie."

With that, he rolled to his feet and darted away.

The boy is so much like his father. Tess grimaced and looked to Gabe for something—support or comfort. She wasn't sure what.

What her husband offered wasn't it. "That bump on the head scrambled your brains even harder than I thought. Do you realize what you just said?"

"Yes." She sighed heavily and allowed him to wipe away her tears with his handkerchief. "But he said it first."

"You were awake?" The handkerchief slipped from his grasp. "You woke up and didn't tell us? Why, Tess that was downright cruel."

She stared at the white square of cloth lying in her lap and said, "The damage had already been done by the time I realized what was happening. He's devastated. This is just what I was afraid would happen if he wasn't properly prepared. Oh, Gabe, I'm afraid this accident broke more than an axle."

"What is it?" Worry colored his tone. "Your arm? An ankle?"

"It broke Will's heart."

"Ah, darlin'." Gabe sat behind her, pulled her back against him and wrapped his arms around her.

This was what Tess had wanted, him holding her. "Everything has happened so fast. I intended to tell him myself, to answer all his questions before he had the chance to stew on them. He likes you, Gabe. I watched the two of you together. If we could have done this right, he wouldn't have been so . . ."

"Mad as hell with the hide off," her husband's drawl rumbled in her ears.

Tess's head hurt, her muscles hurt, and her heart hurt as she recalled the last fuming glare Will sent her way before running off. "I don't know what to do now."

"We let him cool off," Gabe replied matter-of-factly. "We give him time to work the anger off."

"Are you sure?"

"Believe me, I'm an expert on the subject of being filled with fury toward your father."

"True." After a moment's pause she added, "I hope he doesn't take as long as you to get over a grudge. Aren't you worried that the old tenet 'Like father, like son' might come into play here?"

"No," he snapped. The muscles in his arms went hard. "I'm not. I didn't kill anyone Will loves."

Tess melted back against him. She felt just bad enough not to pick and choose her words, but spoke straight from her heart. "No, but in your son's eyes, you weren't there when he needed you. I never said a word against you, Gabe. Actually, I seldom talked about you much at all. It hurt too much. I answered what questions Will asked, but he undoubtedly had plenty more running through his mind that he didn't voice. He came up with his own answers, and now that he has figured out who you are before being told the why of everything, it's those perceptions we will have to overcome."

"You're saying Will hates me like I hate Monty Cameron?"

"I'm saying your son is almost as confused as you are where his father is concerned. You don't hate Monty, Gabe. You're angry at him and you've nursed that anger for years and years. It is my most fervent hope that once you meet with Doc and rant and rave until you've said everything you've wanted to say all this time, you'll be able to listen to what Doc has to say and forgive him."

"Forgive him?" Gabe gave a harsh laugh and moved away from Tess. He gently laid her back on the quilt, then stood and began to pace back and forth along the creekbed. He grumbled beneath his breath for a number of minutes. Then abruptly, he stopped. "Darlin', aren't you forgetting something? The man you want me to forgive more than likely broke a murderer out of prison, set up his own kidnapping, and allowed our son to travel across forty miles of desert all by himself to deliver a lie that led directly to the cut on your head and the spills Twinkle and Jasper suffered. Tell me, is that something you want me to forgive? Honestly, now?"

"We don't know that Doc is guilty. We don't know he's the one who wants you to deliver the gold."

"Yeah, well, we don't know for certain it won't snow in the Chihuahuan today, but it's a damn good guess."

Tess didn't argue any further. She blamed her reticence on her husband, but in all honesty, her own niggling doubts had something to do with it, too.

"Listen, Tess," Gabe said. "None of that matters right now. Doc is not our immediate concern, Will is."

Tess prodded gingerly at the gash on her head. "I think you're right about how to deal with him. The best thing to do is to do nothing for now. Until we settle the situation with Doc, ask our questions and get our answers, we can't settle our problems with one another. The way I see it, everything hinges on Doc."

Gabe knelt beside her and cleansed the cut once more, then braided the hair around it tightly in the old Indian way for pulling the scalp together. Then, he stood once more, his legs spread wide and his hands braced firmly on his hips. "Everything hinges on Doc, you say?" he repeated. "Then, by God, let's go find the sonofabitch."

They spent an hour salvaging supplies from the coach and setting up camp. Colonel Wilhoit appeared to have broken a rib and one knee was swollen to twice its normal size. In his condition he could sit neither horse nor camel, so Gabe decided to leave him and Tess here in camp with Twinkle to care for them. He and the boy would ride ahead toting the gold and keeping a sharp lookout for Jimmy Wayne Bodine and Doc.

While Tess attempted to sleep off her headache, Gabe gave Twinkle instructions for what to tell Captain Robards if Gabe and his son somehow missed the Rangers along the trail toward the rendezvous spot Bodine had specified. "We need one of the lawmen to ride back to Eagle Gulch and secure another coach and horses for the injured folks' trip home," he told the older woman. "I'm not chasing our runaway; he's long gone at this point. Robards and his other man can catch up with us. If we're lucky, Andrew will have fetched my friend Mack by now and they'll ride this direction. You can fill them in on the developments."

Twinkle agreed to the plan and Will voiced no objections. Of course, since Will wasn't speaking to Gabe that came as no surprise.

Knowing Tess as well as he did, Gabe chose to leave camp while she was sleeping. Despite her best efforts, not even Tess was hardheaded enough to overcome her injuries well enough to keep up. The accident had cost them time, and they'd need to ride hard to reach Dagger Mesa by Bodine's deadline.

Gabe rode out of camp followed by Will riding his sorrel mare and guiding the gold-toting Pollux by a rope lead. Will listened to the instructions Gabe gave him and followed directions, but never once did he reply. Gabe didn't press the issue. Tess was probably right. Get the Monty situation taken care of first, gather all the facts and separate them from the feelings, and then perhaps the other problems would solve themselves. At the very least, Gabe figured he'd have a better grasp on where he stood with his son once he had a chat with Monty.

What had the old sonofabitch told Will about Gabe? What dreams had the boy entertained about his father all these years? What dreams had today's ill-timed revelation destroyed?

With those hard questions on his mind and his silent son at his back, Gabe spurred his horse and increased their pace. They rode toward a dark and ominous range of mountains whose sharp red peaks rose into the sky like the jagged, rusted teeth of an extremely large steel trap.

He grimaced at the thought and hoped the image wasn't a portent of things to come.

They'd been riding an hour when Gabe spied a puff of dust on the trail ahead. Riders, coming fast.

He reined his mount to a halt, then pointed toward a jumble of boulders off to the left. "Will, take cover in those rocks."

His son spoke his first words in hours. Of course they were words of argument. "But I don't see why—"

"Now, boy!" Gabe's voice ricocheted like a bullet off the surrounding rocks, and with a glare, Will did as he was told.

Moments later Gabe identified the approaching riders as Captain Robards and his men, and blessed relief washed over him. He'd known from the beginning he didn't like having his son along on this adventure, but it wasn't until this moment that he realized how truly scared he was at the idea of Will meeting up with Jimmy Wayne Bodine. Immediately, he started thinking of ways to protect the boy.

The Rangers reined in their horses beside Gabe. He briefly explained about the accident and Robards immediately sent one of his men off with instructions too check on Tess and the others, then return to Eagle Gulch to obtain transportation for the injured. With that handled, the discussion turned toward Bodine.

"We've located the rendezvous spot. Tell you what, Montana, Jimmy Wayne Bodine might be a vicious criminal, but he's about as sharp as a marble. The place is up a steep, narrow trail. A footpath. Damned near inaccessible. No way are we going to get the gold up there. We'll have to leave it somewhere before we make contact with Bodine."

"But that's against his instructions," Will protested, having abandoned his cover when the Rangers rode up.

"This could be a trap," Gabe mused aloud. "The partner is an unknown in this equation. Bodine might pick a stupid spot for the rendezvous, but the person who successfully broke him out of prison is no fool. If that person was Monty and he chose the spot, then we can count on something fishy happening."

And I don't want my son anywhere near it.

Turning to the Ranger, he asked, "How close are we to Dagger Mesa?"

"Ten minute ride, tops."

Gabe nodded, feeling a sense of relief. Robards had handed him a way to protect his son. He'd intended all along to stash the gold before reaching the appointed spot, and a ten minute ride was close enough, but not too close, to his way of thinking. "Any chance anyone followed you back this direction?"

"No." Robards shook his head. "We'd have seen them. We all kept a sharp eye out, didn't we Lieutenant Blackwell?"

The remaining Ranger nodded. "Sure did."

Gabe made a slow study of the land surrounding them, then pointed toward a boulder-strewn area a couple hundred yards off the trail to the east. "There. We can't hide our tracks but at least the place is defensible. No one will sneak up on our men in the daytime, and I hope to have this mission completed by dark."

"But we can't leave the gold behind, I tell you,"

Will said. "The letter said to deliver it to Dagger Mesa. He'll hurt Doc if we don't."

"We have no choice, son," Robards told him. "Bodine will have to understand that."

It stuck in Gabe's craw to hear Robards call Will *son*, especially since the boy listened to the Ranger rather than argued. Ready to get on with the mission, Gabe tugged on his reins to turn his horse toward the rocks when Ranger Blackwell spoke up.

"There's a better spot to hide the gold up yonder a short ways. It's protected on three sides; you'd only need one man to keep watch."

Gabe sent him a sharp look. Was that an honest suggestion or could Blackwell be part of this conspiracy? "I like this spot just fine."

He really didn't, though. He was sitting on the horns of a dilemma long and sharp enough to make a longhorn bull jealous. Which was more dangerous? To take Will with him and risk him around Bodine or to leave him here alone or with a Texas Ranger who was, in effect, a stranger? Why the hell didn't the boy stay home in Aurora Springs where he belonged?

Because he's an awful lot like you. You wouldn't have stayed where it was safe, either.

"Let's get this gold stashed, shall we?"

They rode to the ring of boulders and started unloading the gold. Gabe eyed the sky and was glad to see it clear. Colonel Wilhoit had told him earlier that rainfall was higher this year than normal, much higher, in fact. The desert was amazingly green in spots with water available in the gullies and washes, a fact he took comfort in for the most part. The drawback was this spot he'd picked to leave his son, while defensible, provided little in the way of shelter. *C'mon, Montana. The boy's not made of sugar. He won't melt if he gets a little wet.*

Still, he couldn't help but fret a bit. Maybe this was part of what fatherhood was all about, worrying about things he shouldn't be worrying about.

Tucking that thought away for further consideration at a later time, Gabe removed the last bag of coins from Pollux's saddle, barely ducked a well-aimed spit, and deposited the money with the other bags. He was searching for just the right words to use to tell Will he'd be staying behind when the boy observed, "I knew this would happen. Ain't no way she'd stay behind."

Gabe followed the path of the boy's stare and felt his stomach sink. *How the hell can she stand to ride that hitch-gaited camel with the headache she is bound to be fighting still?*

Tess ordered Castor to kneel, then slipped from the dromedary's saddle. He was glad to see the color returned to her cheeks when she marched up to Gabe and slugged him in the stomach. "How dare you take my son and leave when I'm asleep. You have more nerve than a broken arm, Gabe Cameron, and I'm getting real tired of it."

"Montana," he corrected automatically, rubbing his stomach. "How is your head, darlin'?"

"Angry. All of me is angry."

"I don't see why. Every hour counts right now, Tess, and you obviously needed rest."

"Like I'd get any rest after being left behind while

you take my son into a potentially dangerous situation? I won't be left, Gabe. Never again."

"Our son." Gabe sighed. "I did what I thought was best."

"And isn't that what always gets us into trouble?" She punctuated her sentence with a sharp poke in the chest with an index finger. "And I don't care if we are smack dab in the middle of the Chihuahuan desert"—*poke*—"or in Aurora Springs"—*poke*—"or New York City,"—*poke*—"don't you ever run off and leave me without discussing it first, do you understand?"

Ranger Blackwell chuckled. "I think she means it."

Will said, "I told him you wouldn't like it, Mama. He just ignored me."

Gabe communicated his displeasure at the lie with only a look. He didn't need to do more because Tess rounded on her son and gave him the sharp edge of her tongue, too. The boy hung his head and took it, apparently no more willing to add to Tess's upset than was his father.

Finally, Gabe figured she'd had long enough to air out her lungs so he reached out and tugged her around to face him, then shut her mouth with a kiss. He intended simply to interrupt her rant, but right away the kiss turned into something infinitely more complex.

Her mouth was open so he couldn't help but take advantage of that little detail. He slid his tongue in and immediately lost his train of thought.

"Montana!" The protest in Captain Robards's voice eventually broke through the sensual haze in Gabe's mind. "We don't have time for that. Let the lady go and let's get on our way."

Tess broke the kiss before he did. "We shouldn't do this in front of Will," she said softly.

His gaze darted toward his scowling son. "I don't know. Maybe this is exactly what Will needs to see. I wish I had more time to pursue it."

"What's our plan?"

"Our plan is that I'm gonna leave and find Monty. I'm giving official notice." As her long, curled lashes narrowed, he led her beyond eavesdropping distance of the others, ignoring his son's glare as he did so, and added, "I have a confession to make. I'm awfully happy you felt like following us."

"You are?"

"I am." He quickly told her about the rendezvous spot and added, "From the way Robards described the terrain it would be nigh on impossible to protect Will. I mean for him to stay here with Blackwell and keep an eye on the colonel's gold, but I was torn about leaving him with someone I'm not certain I trust."

She shot a quick glance toward Blackwell. "But he's a Ranger. He's the law."

Gabe chided her with a look. "I'll feel better knowing you are here with him, Tess. Just in case."

"I guess I should be glad you trust me."

He stared deeply into her eyes. "Darlin', I could tell you I trust you with my life, but that's not nearly as important as the fact that I trust you with my son."

"Well, you should. I've kept him safe for eleven years, haven't I?"

Before he could answer, Ranger Blackwell called, "Montana? Daylight's wasting. Let's get a move on or are you planning to make camp?"

"Actually, I'm planning on *you* making camp, Blackwell. If one is needed, that is. I have every intention of being back here before nightfall."

"What are you saying?"

"I think we need someone to stay behind and guard the gold." He turned to Will. "Your mother's injuries are paining her, and she can't go any further. She plans to stay here and guard the gold, and I'm hoping you'll stay behind and help guard her. We shouldn't ignore the possibility that Bodine wants us to dump the gold before we meet up with him. Could be this is a ruse to get his hands on it without turning over his prisoner." *If Will's beloved Doc truly is a prisoner, that is,* Gabe silently added. "I can't see any way around splitting up, and I'll feel better if you're here to watch over the situation. Bodine wouldn't be . . . kind to a woman as beautiful as your mother."

Will scowled and lifted his voice in protest. "But what about Doc? Don't you need me—"

Tess manipulated the moment with a theatrical wince and sway, her hand pressed to her head. The little moan she let out didn't hurt, either.

"I'll take care of her," Will said, hurrying to his mother's side.

Minutes later, Gabe and Lionel Robards mounted up and headed out. Once he spurred his horse, Gabe purposely didn't look back. He was on his way to rescue Monty Cameron from the likes of Jimmy Wayne Bodine.

If he looked back, he might just turn around.

* * *

The uneasy feeling crept up Tess's spine like a desert centipede.

Gabe hadn't been gone ten minutes before the back of her neck began to twitch with a sense of menace. She wished Twinkle were here. For as little as Tess actually believed Twinkle's supernatural superstitions, she had to admit the woman knew what she was doing when it came to hunches. Tess wasn't nearly so adept.

Probably it's nothing, she told herself, scanning the desert around them with a keen eye. As flat as the land was and with such little cover, nothing bigger than a snake could sneak past three pairs of eyes standing watch. She was simply reacting to the seed Gabe had planted in her mind about a trap.

Lieutenant Blackwell certainly wasn't the source of her disquiet. On the contrary, his presence reassured her. He took his guard duty seriously, and his friendly manner toward both Tess and her son eased any concern that he might be a threat. If the man intended to hurt them, he'd have never apologized with such vigor as he had when he accidentally bumped Will, sending him sprawling into a fresh pile of camel droppings.

Keeping her eyes focused on the area she'd been assigned to watch, she tuned into what Will was saying to the Ranger now. Ah, it was the story of how Rosie had knocked the Hero of Cottonwood Hollow school flat during the state fair pig race. Tess bit back a sigh, wishing she could rewind the clock and somehow prevent his finding out about his father the way he had.

Blackwell displayed no reserve in reacting to the boy's story. In fact, his laugh was so mirthful that it drew Tess's gaze.

Just in time to see the red badge of blood splatter across his chest.

The sound of the gunshot blasted through her mind simultaneously, and then the moment seemed to pass in slow motion. "Will!" Tess cried, diving for her son even as the Texas Ranger slumped to the ground.

"Mama!" Will shouted, turning in circles and waving his gun with a shaking hand.

Tess got him down behind the shelter of one of the boulders. Fear pounded through her veins; her heart beat triple-time. She held her breath, her mind racing as she tried to decide what to do as she waited for another gunshot.

A voice threaded up from the other side of the boulder, menacing, threatening, and amused. "Scared you, didn't I? I love to do that. Now, throw your guns outside this here ring of boulders and I won't have to shoot the boy."

Will's arms grabbed her around the waist and he buried his head against her bosom. She could feel him trembling and she wanted desperately to tell him everything would be all right. But she wouldn't lie to her son, not now. Not when it might be the last thing she ever said to him.

Tess threw away her gun and instructed her son to do the same. Immediately thereafter, a face loomed up from behind one of the rocks. Black hair, thick, bushy brows. Mean green eyes that glimmered with an unholy light. Thin lips showing a smile sporting two broken teeth. "Jimmy Wayne Bodine."

"Yep."

Tess shuddered all the way to her bones. He scrambled over the top of the rock, keeping his Colt revolver pointed their direction. A dozen questions boiled in her head, and they popped from her mouth in no conscious order. "We didn't see you. How could we not have seen you?"

He grinned evilly. "That's 'cause I was already here. I've been watching for you. Expected you either today or tomorrow. Doc said you'd drop the gold, so I fixed hiding places in every logical spot. I was tucked beneath a wash of scrub in the gully here and every one of you walked past me half a dozen times. I wanted to laugh but I kept quiet. I've been watching you coming at me. You and your camels and that dead man Whip Montana."

"Dead?" Will gasped.

"Sure. He's been a walking dead man since I took my first step outside the Walls in Huntsville. Tell you what, I didn't like giving up my chance to kill him just now. But the boss, he wants it done a certain way. That Doc sure does like games, don't he?"

The boss? Doc? Oh, no.

"You're lying!" Will accused, recovering enough to unwind from his mother and stand alone once more. "Doc wouldn't kill my father!"

Bodine shrugged. "He's not planning to. That's my pleasure, and my payment for Doc's breaking me out of jail."

Tess felt as if her feet were sinking into quicksand.

No, she couldn't believe this. But the timing fit. The wanted poster fit. She didn't understand. *"Why?* Why is he doing this?"

"The boss?" Bodine gestured with the gun for Will to step away from Tess. When he added a glare, the boy moved. "I don't rightly know why he's after Montana, except for something he said about payback. Doesn't matter to me because my reasons are all I need to turn that sonofabitch into worm food." He gazed at Tess with a predatory gleam in his eyes and added, "And after seeing the way he ran his tongue down your throat, I'm thinking he'll especially hate what I have in mind for you."

Plans for me. Oh, Lord, help me.

"Boy," he said to Will. "I want you to start loading that gold right back on that monstrosity with the hump on his back. Handy of your pa to leave the camel here for me. We won't need to go fetch the travois I have stashed in the gully to move the gold to my hiding place. Go on, now. We don't have all day. I have plans for when we get to where we're going."

Fixing his gaze on Tess, he reached down and rubbed his crotch. "Special plans."

Tess shut her eyes as the knowledge seeped into her pores like a poison. Rape.

Fear fluttered through her, threatening to send her to her knees. But maternal instinct was mightier than fear, and as she turned her attention to protecting her son, her strength came roaring back. *Take it one step at a time, Tess. You'll know what to do when the time is right.*

Jimmy Wayne Bodine would not hurt her son in any way. Period.

"Do as he says, Will," she told the frightened boy.

It took them almost twenty minutes to get the bags properly balanced and lashed onto Pollux's saddle. Bodine sat and watched them, waving his gun, talking tough, and touching himself. Tess watched her son closely and saw the moment he realized what Bodine had in mind for her. The wild look on his face convinced her she must convince the criminal to leave her son behind. To that end, she began to talk.

"Don't be afraid, Will. You know how you get when you're afraid. We don't need to deal with vomiting and the other . . . well . . . I don't know that Mr. Bodine will allow you to change your britches. And you don't have that many extra pairs with you."

"What?" her son said, looking at her as if she were crazy.

Bodine scowled. "Are you saying the kid gets the trots when he's—"

"Upset or frightened or even just a little tense. It's a physical problem, and not something he can control. So, please, Mr. Bodine, don't take it out on Will when he becomes unpleasant to be around." Turning to her son, she said, "I know you'll try your best, honey, but when it happens, just make sure to stay downwind of Mr. Bodine."

Now she'd made the boy crazy. "Mama, what are you doing?"

"I'm sorry, honey. I know it embarrasses you, and I try to be extra sensitive of the fact. However, under the circumstances I thought it best for Mr. Bodine to know."

"Damned right," Bodine said rearing back and holding his hand over his nose. "I'm not taking a boy who shits his pants with me anywhere. Don't need him anyway. Get a rope, lady. We'll tie him up and leave him here." He scratched at his beard and added, "I sorta like that thought, anyway. He can give my message to Montana personally."

Bodine directed Tess to tie the knots so he need not get too close to the boy. "I will check them, though," he added. "So do them up right."

While she retrieved a rope from Castor's saddle, she kept her gaze on the ground, searching for the best sharp-edged rock among the many scattered across the desert sand. Making her choice, she dropped the rope to hide the act of scooping up what she intended to be a makeshift knife. Then, as she bound her son's hands, she whispered in his ear. "You are my best hope, Will. Try to get loose and get back to Twinkle. Maybe Andrew will have arrived by then. If not, she and Colonel Jasper will figure out a way to help me."

"But I can follow you," he whispered back. "Surprise him."

"No. I forbid it, Will. Do you understand me? You are not to come alone. I'll have your word on it."

Bodine said, "Hey, what are you mumbling about. No funny business, ya hear?" He took a step toward them. "Ya got him tied?"

"Yes."

Holding a hand over his nose, he approached Will.

His grimace told her he'd caught a whiff of the camel droppings ground into her son's pants during the earlier fall. The chiding glare he shot Tess told her she'd failed to sufficiently hide the laxity in her knots. "Get back over here and tie him again, woman." He put the barrel of his gun against her son's temple. "Do it right this time or I'll take care of the problem myself."

Tess tied good knots. Bodine checked them again and grunted his approval. "Damn boy smells like a goat. I can't get out of here fast enough, I'm telling you." He gave the rope a vicious yank, setting the knot even tighter, and backed away. "You won't be going anywhere now. You'll be here in case your pa misses the message we're leaving him up in the mountains. If that happens, see that he gets this." He removed a folded sheet of paper from his pocket and set it on the ground, weighting it with five gold coins. "Then give him a personal message from me. Tell him I've a hankering for a woman. Tell him while I'm waiting for his arrival, I'll be having me a right fine time with his wife."

CHAPTER

16

The Chisos Mountains rose to nearly eight thousand feet above the flats of the Chihuahuan desert. For comparison, if Gabe dubbed the lush, pretty little Aurora Springs valley as Eden, the area of the Big Bend wouldn't make a bad hell.

Robards had underestimated the length of time required to reach the rendezvous spot. It had taken them closer to twenty minutes to ride into the mountains to the base of Dagger Mesa. Though Gabe could see the needle shaped rock that was his destination, they still had a goodly climb to go before they would reach it. "This is shaping up to be a long ten minutes," he told the Ranger.

"Guess we made better time before."

Guess Bodine better not get too antsy when it takes longer than ten minutes to retrieve the gold to ransom Monty. If ransoming Monty was what this was all about, that is. Gabe wouldn't bet so much as a pebble on that being the case.

He eyed the steep narrow trail up the side of the mesa, noting the abundance of cover. "If Bodine is perched up high waiting to pick us off, he's had better opportunities elsewhere."

"I don't think that is his plan, do you?"

"No. He won't try to kill us until he knows for certain we brought the gold, and I intend to see and speak with ol' Doc myself before we let anybody know anything about where we stashed the stuff."

They conversed no more as they started up the trail. It was a slippery business and each man stumbled and skidded a number of times along the way. Gabe kept a close watch on his surroundings, on guard against ambush or other surprises as he climbed. Nothing untoward happened, and finally, the trail leveled out and a campsite of sorts was revealed.

Two items lay on display beside a ring of stones. Gabe identified the first item the moment he spied it. *My mother's locket.* His father had called it his most prized possession. That clenched it. Monty Cameron was involved in this plot one way or another.

The second item was a sheet of paper. Gabe picked it up and scanned the page.

"What does it say?"

"It's signed J.W. Bodine. Says he has moved his hostage to a place called Burro Canyon."

"Burro Canyon! That's at least a two hour ride from here. Maybe longer. In fact," Robards paused and rubbed his jaw. "Burro Canyon isn't far from where Doc has been working in those caves that have him so inspired."

Gabe's brow furrowed in thought. What was the

purpose of having them come this way to begin with? He felt like a miner lost in tunnels whose walls kept shifting. Somebody was playing with him, and he damned well didn't like it.

"So, do we ride on?" Captain Robards asked.

Gabe shook his head. "No. We go back. The rules on this game we're playing have just changed. We're going back for Tess and my son. Then we'll take the gold and head for Burro Canyon."

"You're taking a chance," Robards warned. "We'll be lucky to make it by dark and sunset is Bodine's deadline."

Gabe shrugged. "By sunset I expect Bodine will be dead, period. I'm gonna kill him."

With that profound statement, Gabe headed back down the hill. He led them away from Dagger Mesa and made better time than Robards going in. Upon reaching the flats, he spurred his horse into a gallop, a sense of urgency riding his shoulders, trepidation clutching his gut. Bodine or Doc or whoever played puppetmaster had sent them on a wild goose chase.

That knowledge was why, when they returned to the ring of boulders where he'd left his family, he wasn't surprised to find it empty.

Jimmy Wayne Bodine talked murder all the way to Burro Canyon. Starting with the playmate he'd purposefully drowned at the age of eight, he spoke in excruciating detail of the killings he'd accomplished. He threw in a robbery account now and then, and spoke of beatings and assaults. Mostly, though, he talked about death. Thirty-seven bodies.

Whip Montana, he told her, would be thirty-eight.

"I've been looking forward to this since the minute my friend Doc broke me out of jail. You know, I spent at least an hour of every day planning how I'd kill him when I had the chance. Thought up some great tortures." He chuckled with devilish glee and added, "For all my thinking, I never expected you. You are the best surprise I've had in a coon's age. Just think how it'll burn his ass when I plant ol' Dickory Dock in the pole hole."

His crudity served to insulate her from the fear and instead flamed her anger. Tess renewed her struggles to free herself, working the leather bonds at her wrists until her skin was raw and bloody. Tied to the saddle horn of the mule he'd provided for her to ride shortly after leaving Will, she was unable to loosen the knots at all. She was good and stuck on this animal until Jimmy Wayne Bodine saw fit to release her.

She tamped down her temper and forced herself to think. She'd be hanged before she'd let Bodine succeed at his cruelty. What she needed was a plan. Gabe had been scornful of Bodine's intelligence and she'd seen nothing that contradicted his low opinion. It didn't take smarts to be evil, and that's all Bodine had revealed up to now.

I'm bright. I can outsmart him. I'm not scared.

He turned his head and leered at her, licking his lips.

And rice grew in the Chihuahuan desert in July.

She lost track of the time they traveled, but eventually they arrived at a campsite deep in what he told her was Burro Canyon. Bodine left her tied in her saddle while he divested Pollux of his golden burden and stashed the bags in a brush-concealed opening in the rock. That he openly allowed her to view the hiding place told her without words of his intention to kill her.

"This area is riddled with caves," he explained matter-of-factly. "Easy to get lost in. When Doc first left me here, I went exploring one day and damn near didn't find my way out. I could've died in that maze."

"Wouldn't that have been a shame," she muttered.

With the gold stored, he approached her, carrying a bowie knife. Sunlight glinted off the long, curved blade, and Tess watched with an eagle eye as he sliced through her bindings, ready to take advantage of any lapse in attention. But he gave her no opening.

With his meaty hand wrapped around her forearm, he dragged her over toward a crate that smelled of onions and forced her to sit down. His gaze raked over her and lingered on her bosom. Heat flared in his eyes; dread washed through Tess.

"You sure are a pretty thing," he said. "I like women with big tits. Show 'em to me."

With his attention locked on her bosom, the big knife dangled at his side. *What the heck*, Tess thought. *A smart woman uses the weapons at her disposal.*

"No, please don't do this," she begged, the tremble in her voice dismayingly real.

"Pop those buttons."

"I can't. Not without standing up."

"Do it, then."

Tess slowly stood. Her mind raced as her fingers went to the buttons at her white shirtwaist. She fought to overcome the sick feeling sitting like a lump in her stomach and use Bodine's lust against him.

She made a show of undoing each small pearl button. Cowering and sniveling and pleading, she flamed the fires of his arousal. She recognized the danger in what she was doing. The man was stronger than she and sometimes physical strength did win out over superior intelligence. But Tess simply refused to accept that this could be one of those instances. Her buttons all undone, she pulled the blouse off her shoulders.

Bodine's eyes rounded as the fabric pooled at her waist. "Now the corset. Peel it all the way down to the skin. I want to see those beauties." His mouth widened in a hungry grin. "I want to see what Montana gets to see. In fact, maybe I'll go ahead and have me a taste. I'd figured to wait until Montana showed up, but now I reckon I'll go ahead and have me a snack while I'm waiting. Hurry up, there, gal. I like looking a bit before I get down to business."

She'd have to take off her skirt to get to the corset. Her stomach took another flip. Tess was finding this more difficult than she'd anticipated, but she made herself stay focused on the goal—unman him, unarm him, and make him *her* prisoner. To that end she unbuttoned her waistband and gave her hips a wiggle and both skirt and bodice floated to the ground. Her petticoat slowly followed.

Please let this work.

She stepped free of the fabric pooled at her feet, and stood before the criminal in her corset and drawers. Jimmy Wayne looked like he was about to swallow his tongue.

Come here, you murdering piece of filth. Come try to lay a hand on me.

"Faster," he rasped. "Go faster."

His stare was avid, but she needed his eyes glazed. She worked the hooks on her Primrose Path corset, then took a deep breath and tossed it atop her skirt and shirtwaist, leaving only the thin lawn of her chemise to shield her from Bodine's lust-coated gaze.

"Take it off."

No, she didn't think she would. This was where she drew the line, and if Jimmy Wayne Bodine wanted her naked he would just have to handle the task himself. Of course, she had no intention of allowing that to happen.

"I c-c-can't," she stammered and allowed tears to pool in her eyes as she brought her arms up to cover herself. *Come do it yourself, you snake-eyed whoremonger.*

When she interrupted his view, Bodine scowled and started walking toward her. Tess wanted to cheer when he absently sheathed his knife. Instead, she lifted her hands away from her body, acting fearful, but in truth trying to keep his attention on her bosom and away from her feet. She eyed the angle of his approach and shifted her body slightly, then balanced the majority of her weight on her left foot.

Bodine was four steps away . . . three . . . two . . .

Tess drew back her foot, then put all the force she could summon behind the weight of her riding boot as she kicked him square in the crotch.

He yelled out and dropped immediately, his hands cupped between his legs, his breath coming in a long, pain-filled gasp. Tess grabbed the pistol from his holster, and then the knife from the sheath. She backed away to a safe distance just as he caught his breath and let out a moaning stream of particularly vile epithets.

Tess shut him up by shooting at him. Not *at* him, actually, but in his general direction. Close enough to get his attention. As the sound of the gunshot echoed off the canyon walls, Tess told the stunned outlaw, "Throw me my skirt and shirtwaist."

He did and she struggled into them, careful to keep the gun aimed at Bodine. When she was covered, she said, "Now, take off your boots."

"My what?"

"Your boots. Throw them over here."

He pitched them hard, right at her, but Tess had expected that so she dodged them with little trouble. "Socks next."

"What is this? Are you trying to pay me back or something?"

"You'd have been better off having me take off my boots instead of my clothes, Bodine. Have you noticed the rocks beneath your feet? You will if you try to stand up. I guarantee it. Bare feet will slow you down enough to give me extra time should I need it. Which I won't, by the way. Unlike you, I am not easily distracted. Now, toss your gunbelt along with the socks, please. Just in case I need more bullets."

He growled at her, but was unable to manage anything more threatening as he met her requests. Tess was filled with a sense of empowerment and she had the silly urge to stick out her tongue at him and say, *I win.*

Instead, she glanced quickly around the campsite and chose a bare spot toward the center, out of reach of anything he might turn into a weapon. She pointed to it saying, "Move over there, Bodine."

"No."

She shot at him again. "Another thing. Don't think you'll annoy me into using up all my bullets. I give you fair warning, the next bullet will hit you, if not kill you. I'm quite good with firearms, you see. I spent a few years in Ireland with an avid hunter and when we weren't studying the stars, he was teaching me how to shoot. The gentleman was offended by the notion that any Texan didn't know how to use a gun. It ruined the Wild West fantasy for him, you understand."

Bodine stared as though she were speaking a different language. Tess waved the gun. "Now. Move."

He attempted to rise, but ended up crawling to the spot she had indicated. Tess grabbed Bodine's canteen and saddlebags, then took a seat atop a huge boulder, the position providing both a bird's eye view of her prisoner and unobstructed sight of the mouth of Burro Canyon where Gabe was most likely to enter.

Thus supplied, she settled down to wait.

Fear of this dimension wasn't a new experience for Gabe. He'd felt this gut-wrenching, mind-numbing terror previously in his life. Once. The night Billy died. But back then the fear had come on in a flash and ended quickly in despair. He'd never been this scared for such an extended length of time. It was a damned lucky thing Robards was with him, because he was having a hell of a time concentrating on the trail. One thought continued to override all the others in his brain, and it all but froze him into immobility.

Jimmy Wayne Bodine had his family.

Gabe followed Robards blindly through the rocky, winding trail of the Big Bend. In the few moments when terror loosened its grip on him, anger took its place. Fury at Bodine for being the bastard he was; anger at himself for bringing this danger to his loved one's door. Cold, violent rage at the man—no, the filth—who had seen Jimmy Wayne released from prison.

Was his father responsible? Had Monty Cameron become the animal behind all this grief? Despite himself, Gabe recalled the father of his youth, the man who had explored the world around him with such interest and excitement. Why would he do this? Why would he go to all this trouble? Had the years changed him this much?

Tess believes in Monty. Will thinks he hung the moon. If he's betrayed them this way, I'll kill him in a heartbeat.

Patricide. Gabe shuddered and shied away from the thought.

Sweat dribbled down his back despite the coolness of the day. He rode with grim determination, trying not to recall the carnage Bodine had left in his wake in times past. He reminded himself that had Bodine wanted Tess and Will dead, he'd have left their bodies back where Gabe had stashed the gold. No, Bodine or, more likely, the bastard's boss, had plans for Gabe's family. Otherwise, they'd already be dead. He refused to believe such an end might have already come to pass.

A shout interrupted his musings. "Montana," Robards called. "Burro Canyon is just ahead."

Gabe sent up a quick, silent prayer, then spurred his mount forward.

In the course of an hour, Jimmy Wayne made four rather feeble escape attempts. Tess was able to stop him with words rather than the gun, which was good because she didn't want to kill the man. But she had made the threat, and motherhood had taught her the mistake of making threats then not following through.

With the passage of time, Bodine's frustration built. She could hear it in the threats he made, see it in his choppy movements. She tried to distract him—and gain a little in the exchange—by asking him about his partner.

"That's right. Doc. Doc will take care of this, of you. He's liable to get a wild hare and come watch the show when I have my payback with Montana. You'll be in trouble then, missy. Doc is a mean sonofabitch."

"And that makes you . . . ?" she muttered. "Where is he now?" she called out.

"Probably on his way here. His caves aren't far, you know. That's where he spends all his time, down there counting his money. He's a real smart man. A scientist. Tells me there's all kinds of riches buried in these rocks."

A scientist. Oh, no. How could I have been so wrong about him for so long?

"He knows these mountains inside out, so even if you get away from me, you'll never get away from Doc." While Bodine spoke, he took small, ginger steps toward her. Tess winced at the thought of how all those rocks were biting into his bare feet. Just as she was fixing to raise the gun and send him back to where she wanted him, he let out a yell and lifted his foot.

The man had stepped on a cactus.

"Ow," she observed. "That'll teach you to stay where I said."

It was the wrong thing to say. Jimmy Wayne lost his temper. He charged at Tess, heedless of the sharp stones and the bloody trail his feet now left. He yelled with rage. "Goddamned rocks. Goddamned woman. You bitch! I'm going to kill you, you hear? I'm going to kill you!"

She aimed the gun, but he kept coming. She realized he wasn't going to stop and she wanted to curse right back at him. "I didn't want to do this!"

Tess pulled the trigger. The bullet hit him in the shoulder where she had aimed, and as he fell to his knees, she shimmied off the rock. "Curse you, Jimmy Wayne Bodine. This didn't have to happen. I didn't want to shoot you. I've never shot another human being, and I didn't want to do it today." She approached him carefully, keeping the gun trained on his rolling, groaning body.

"You murdering female," he moaned, swaying but not going down. "Help me, dammit."

Her teeth tugged at her lower lip as she tried to figure what to do next. The challenge was to staunch the blood flow without putting herself in danger. But how could she get near him without putting herself at risk? The man was a killer. Wounded, but still a killer. It would be stupid of her to get within ten feet of him.

But if you don't, then you'll be a killer, too. You should have thought of that before you shot him.

But what else could she have done? She'd had to protect herself. Jimmy Wayne Bodine had murder in his eyes and on his tongue when he ran at her, and Tess knew he would've killed her in a heartbeat given the chance.

She stopped just outside his reach, his every groan cutting her like a knife. "I can't let you bleed to death. I just can't."

Blood seeped through Bodine's fingers of the hand holding the wound. It scared Tess. This man truly could die and the responsibility would be hers.

She reached beneath her riding skirt and loosened the tapes of her petticoat, then pulled it off. Still beyond his reach, she set the gun onto the ground and set about tearing her underwear into strips. These she threw toward Bodine saying, "Wad this up and put pressure on the wound."

He sank back on his heels, his complexion gone pasty white. "My back. It's dripping down my back. You've killed me, girl. Kilt me dead."

Tess circled around him to get a view of his back. *Oh, no.* She covered her mouth with her hand as she realized what she would have to do. "You know, I am not ordinarily a stupid person," she told the outlaw as she approached him. "Don't make today be any different. I'm going to help you, Bodine, but if you so much as lift an eyebrow in a threatening manner, I will leave you for the buzzards."

As she reached out to touch him, Bodine jerked once, twice, three times. Bullets drove him backward, bloodstains bursting across his chest as he fell in a crumpled heap against the rocky ground and lay still.

Jimmy Wayne Bodine stared at the sky through sightless eyes.

Halfway down the trail to the bottom of Burro Canyon, Gabe tried to get his throat to work as facts flew at him like bullets. Captain Robards had shot Bodine. Tess stood by the body, apparently safe and sound. Where was Will? Ah, hell. Where was his son?

He gigged his horse, riding him dangerously fast on the uncertain trail. *Oh God, oh God, oh God.* It was a prayer playing over and over in his mind.

Then he was there and Tess was in his arms, murmuring words of thanks. She laughed with a tinge of hysteria and cried a little, too. Gabe urged her away from the corpse, away from the evil, and when he could drag enough air back into his lungs to speak he asked, "Where's Will?"

"He's not with you?" Tess pulled back to look up at him. Concern dimmed her blue eyes. "You didn't return to where you left the gold?"

"Yes, but he wasn't there. I expected him to be with you."

She shook her head. "Bodine left him behind; he left him tied up. What about Castor? Was she there?"

The camel? "No. Nothing was there."

"Good." Tess lay her head upon his chest. "He's fine then. Will must have gotten loose and gone back to Twinkle and the others. That's what I told him to do, and your son is good about minding his mother."

Since she appeared so confident, Gabe relaxed a little. He took his first good breath in what felt like days. The peace lasted only a moment, however, because he spied Tess's corset lying on the ground. Everything inside him cringed and he rattled off a mental string of curses. Outwardly, he nodded toward the discarded undergarment and asked, "Did he hurt you, Tess?"

She followed the path of his gaze and her body tensed. "No, not that way."

He didn't believe her. "Tess. Tell me."

"No. Really."

She made a quick summation of what had occurred after Bodine brought her to Burro Canyon. Gabe suspected she glossed over much of the story, and the parts she did tell him made him want to go kick Bodine's corpse. Before he went that far, Robards, having taken the steep, rocky trail slower than Gabe, rode up and dismounted. He sauntered over to the body on the ground and knelt beside it. "That was some darn fine shooting if I say so myself. I'm glad to see you're all right, Tess."

Watching the Ranger pat down Jimmy Wayne's pockets, Gabe asked, "Not that I'm complaining, mind you, but why did you kill him?"

Robards looked up in surprise. He slowly pushed to his feet, then walked toward them, his gaze focused on Gabe's wife. "Why, I killed him to save Tess. Montana here didn't think too straight once we heard the gunshot and spied you two from up top of the canyon. I kept my wits about me enough to watch for the opportunity to ensure your safety."

"But he was already shot," Gabe protested. "Couldn't you see that?"

Robards shrugged. "It was only a shoulder wound; it wasn't fatal. The man wasn't down. No telling what he might have done to her once she got close to him. Bodine was strong enough and big enough to strangle her with just one hand."

"I was being careful," Tess assured them. "I knew what I was doing." She glanced up at Gabe and added, "I had to try and stop the bleeding."

Tess hadn't wanted a man's death on her hands. Gabe understood that. He hugged her tight, then drew back and stared deeply into her eyes. "You didn't kill him, darlin', the Texas Ranger did. Remember that."

"I know," she replied, her warm gaze telling him she appreciated the reminder anyway.

Gabe was leaning down to kiss her when Robards cleared his throat and asked, "Where is Will?"

Tess explained her theory of where the boy might be, and Robards agreed she was probably on target. "I'm sure he returned to the others. I've come to know Will quite well, remember. He's a responsible young man. I'm sure he is fine. After all, he's traveled much farther across the desert by himself in the past, hasn't he?"

Gabe found himself wishing the Ranger would shut up. He didn't like being reminded that another man knew his son better than he did. It made him feel strange and the old saying of "like father, like son" reared up in his mind. Which brought his thoughts around to Monty. "Bodine had a partner, don't forget. The bastard has been pulling our strings for who knows how long." He hated to say it, but he couldn't ignore the possibility that plagued him. "The partner might have our son."

Robards grimaced and shook his head. "Doc won't hurt Will. He may have had us fooled about other matters, but he does love the boy. I've seen that plenty of times."

With that, Gabe had had enough. "Well, we can't be certain the culprit is my father, now can we? And we don't know what a stranger would do to *my* son. So I suggest we get busy trying to find the pair of them."

"You don't think Doc Cameron is the man who broke Bodine out of the Walls?" Robards asked.

Gabe wanted to agree, but he couldn't. The evidence against the man was overwhelming. Still, he waited for Tess to bust in with a defense of Monty "Doc" Cameron and when she didn't, he shot her a questioning look.

"Bodine said things. I don't want to believe it, but Gabe, I don't think it could be anybody else. Everything points to Doc."

Gabe closed his eyes, surprised at how her lack of faith in Monty managed to twist the knife a bit. Guess that when it came to dealing with parents, no matter how old a person got, a little bit of child inside him never died. *Hell, Daddy does it to me again.*

"Let's just go find the sonofabitch. We'll run out of daylight if we're not careful."

Of course, finding the puppet master was easier said than done since they didn't have a clue where to look. While they debated their next move, Tess suggested they bury Bodine. Neither Gabe nor the Ranger cared to go to that much trouble—they'd need a chisel to dig in this rocky ground—so they fitted the body into a crevice in the canyon wall and piled rocks on top of it. By the time they finished that unpleasant chore, they'd decided the most logical place to begin the search was the cave where Robards had found Doc working weeks before.

"It's not far," Robards told them as they mounted their horses, Tess trading in the mule for Bodine's bay. "I'll lead. It's a talent of mine."

Tess was tired, weary in both body and soul. This had been the longest day of her life and it wasn't over yet. More than anything she'd like to turn this horse around and head for home. Aurora Springs called to her like a little piece of Eden. *But here I am instead.* Today she was too tired to see the beauty in her surroundings. Today the Big Bend region reminded her of ugliness alone.

Lionel led them up out of Burro Canyon and along a winding path through the sandy, stony hills. Dread rode with Tess as she followed the two men, wondering what horror waited to be discovered up ahead.

Before she was ready for it, the Ranger reined in his horse. He pointed to a ridge off to the west a short distance and said, "It's there. I'd have never found Doc the first time if I hadn't caught up with him out in the open. The caves in this area are interwoven. He uses one for a campsite while he supposedly studies the pictographs in the others."

Gabe studied the hills with a careful eye. "So what's the best approach? On foot?"

"Yes, and we'll need to be quiet about it, too. Sound echoes out here."

Gabe glanced at Tess. "Honey, are you all right with this? You don't have to come with us."

"I'm fine. I need to be there, Gabe. I need to hear him admit it."

Robards shot her a look. "He might not admit it, Tess. You should be prepared for that. In my experience, criminals seldom own up to their misdeeds, even when there is a preponderance of evidence stacked against them."

"I need to be there," she repeated. Both men nodded and nothing more was said on the subject.

All too soon, they approached the mouth of the cave Lionel Robards had named as Doc's "lair." Lionel nodded toward Tess and Gabe, then drew his gun. Gabe followed suit. Tess took a deep breath and trailed the two men into the cave.

Doc Cameron turned at the noise and his jaw went hard. "Will," he said in a granite tone, "hand me that gun."

Seeing him like this shocked Tess's good sense right out of her. For a split second, she stared at her old friend, studying the lined and weathered face for signs of a wickedness she'd never spied before. Then his words hit her like a slap.

Oh, my. Her son was here with him, after all.

Protective maternal instinct propelled her past Gabe and Lionel, and she marched over to her son. "William Gabriel Cameron. What are you doing here? Didn't I tell you to go find Twinkle once you got yourself untied?"

"But Mama—" He broke off at the click of a gun being cocked.

"Doc Cameron, I'm placing you under arrest," Captain Lionel Robards said.

"No, I don't think so," Doc replied, his bushy salt-and-pepper brows dipping into a scowl. He glanced at Gabe and added, "Hello, son."

"Don't call me that." Gabe's gaze darted from his father to the Ranger and back to his father again. He held his gun aimed somewhere between Robards and Doc. "I swore off that moniker a dozen years ago."

Robards said, "Put down the gun, Doc."

Doc's expression grew scathing and his aim at Lionel Robards never wavered as he spoke to his son. "I'm innocent, Gabe. Will, here, has filled me in on what happened. We've been trying to figure out how to save his mother from Bodine, but since you're here, I assume he's dead."

Gabe nodded slowly.

"Good." Satisfaction swept across Doc's face before he continued, "Son, I want you to know that I've not left the Big Bend area since my arrival in mid-September. I never broke anyone out of prison. I never set any fires along the railroad spur, and I certainly never pretended to kidnap myself so my loved ones would believe they needed to rescue me."

He shot a glare at Captain Robards and announced, "But I know who did. What I don't know is why. How about an answer, Lionel? Why did you do it?"

"Me?" Lionel Robards laughed. "What nonsense is this? We have you dead to rights, Cameron. Bodine named you as his accomplice, and if that isn't enough the wanted poster out of Huntsville describes you down to the mole on your left cheek." To Gabe, the Ranger said, "Your gun needs to be aimed at him, Montana. Cover me and I'll disarm him."

"Point your weapon at him, Gabe." Doc's eyes narrowed to mere slits. "He's the guilty one. I don't claim to know how you managed it all, Robards, but you are the guilty party."

"Prove it."

Doc grimaced. "I can't. But since Will arrived and relayed his story, I have thought the matter through. You are the only logical suspect."

"Logical suspect." Lionel Robards shook his head. "Give it up, Cameron. You are a fool if you think anyone here will believe you. Even your staunchest supporter can't deny the truth. Right, Tess?"

She opened her mouth to deny the Ranger, but to her dismay, she couldn't. After all that transpired, she couldn't say she didn't have her doubts about Doc.

Tears pooled in her eyes, then slipped down her cheeks, significant for being the very first tears she'd shed this awful day despite all the trying events. Softly, she informed Gabe, "Bodine said his partner was a scientist who spent all his time studying pictographs in these caves."

"No, Mama," Will cried as Doc shook his head. "It's a lie. You're wrong. Bodine was lying."

He rounded on Gabe. Tears flowed freely down the boy's face as he faced his father and snapped, "You! What is it you've been asking me for days? To give you a chance? Well I'm saying you need to give *him* a chance. You give *your father* a chance, and maybe I'll give you one in return."

Tess sucked in a quick breath. "Will. Son. You don't understand."

"I understand this. If you point your gun at my grandfather, Whip Montana, then I'll never be your son again!"

I'll never be your son again.

It was like hearing words straight out of the past. Gabe's gaze went immediately to Monty. Yes, he could see it in his father's eyes that the older man remembered when his own son screamed the same six words during a violent fit of rage. He'd kept his promise, too. Never forgetting. Never forgiving.

Gabe spoke his first words since entering the cave. "Funny how the apple doesn't fall far from the tree, even if the tree lives in an entirely different world."

"Montana!" Robards demanded, "What the hell are you talking about? Hurry up, it'll be dark soon." He lifted his gun higher, pointing it right at Monty's head. "Put down the gun, old man."

Will sobbed in fear and frustration.

Understanding poured from Monty Cameron's gaze into Gabe's for a moment longer, then he shifted his stare to the Ranger. "You need killing, Robards. Go ahead and shoot me, but I'll get you, too. I'll go to my grave thinking it a job well done."

"Me?" the Ranger scoffed. He quit arguing with Monty and spoke to the rest of them. "If anybody needs killing it's him. He's the one who has been preying upon and making fools of his own grandson and the other people you care about." Tempering his voice, he added, "I know this is difficult for you, Will, and God knows I didn't want you and your mother to be here to see it. But son, you know what the evidence says. I'm a lawman. I must do my job."

"The evidence is wrong!" Will appealed not to Robards, but to Gabe. "Doc figured it out. Robards did it. Robards made it look the way it does."

"Why?" Tess asked.

"Because he's sweet on you, Mama."

"What does that have to do with framing Doc?"

Monty answered. "You've been sniffing after Tess for months, Robards. Once her husband turned up, you needed a handy way to get rid of him. Hence his old enemy. Bodine was supposed to kill my son, wasn't he?"

"That's the craziest thinking I've ever heard, old man. Your argument doesn't hold water. For one thing, if I wanted Montana dead, I could have killed him anytime. I wouldn't have had to go through such an elaborate game to make it happen. But what really shoots holes in your theory is the fact that I'm the one who killed Bodine. If I wanted him to get rid of Montana, why would I have done that?"

"I don't know. I haven't ascertained your motives

as of yet, although I am certain I will deduce them eventually."

"You're not gonna have an eventually if you don't shut up," the Ranger snapped in frustration. He fiddled with a clip on his gun belt, then tossed a set of handcuffs toward Gabe.

Gabe didn't catch them, choosing instead to let them fall to the ground. Despite all the evidence, despite his own long-nursed anger toward his father, he wasn't quite yet ready to judge him guilty. He needed the answer to one question first.

"Monty, why did you lie to me about knowing where I could find Tess?"

Monty winced, then heaved a heavy sigh and confessed. "I was selfish. When I ran into you that first time after so many years, I could see how much you hated me. I knew Tess still cared for you, and I worried that if you two got back together, you wouldn't let her and the boy have anything to do with me. I love them and I was afraid of losing them."

"Oh, Doc," Tess said sadly.

He brought his free hand up and wiped it across his mouth. "So when you asked me if I knew how you could find Tess, I lied. I knew what I did was wrong, and every so often I'd get to feeling guilty about it. That's when I'd go visit you again. Every time I'd plan to tell you. Every time I'd take the coward's way out." He paused briefly, then added, "I wasn't much of a father to you, was I, son?"

Will's eyes went round with disillusionment. "He asked how to find my mother and you told him you didn't know? And you were living with us?"

"It was a damned rotten thing to do," Gabe agreed.

"Which proves my point," Robards said. "Will, see what kind of man your Doc really is?"

The question hung in the air like a bad smell.

And Gabe made up his mind, shifting the aim of his Colt.

He aimed right at the heart of Captain Lionel Robards of the Texas Rangers.

"I do see what kind of man my father really is, Robards," Gabe said. "Monty isn't perfect; he never has been. But then, neither am I. My father is weak, true. But he's not evil. The acts that have brought us to this place at this time are just that—evil. Throw down your gun, Robards. I'm placing you under arrest."

Robards laughed. "What sort of nonsense is this? You can't arrest me."

"I just did."

"You're not even a Texas Ranger."

"Actually, I am. I recently accepted an appointment from Governor Ross and my job is to clean up the ranks of the corps. Guess I'll start with you."

Robards's eyes blazed. "This is ridiculous. You can't believe what that old man is saying. He's a liar."

"Yeah, but he's my father and I love him. If you love someone, you have to accept the bad along with the good. Now drop your gun, Robards, or I will blow a hole in you."

Will took a step toward Gabe, his expression filled with wonder and disbelief. "So you really do believe him? You really think my grandpap is innocent?"

"Of these crimes, yes."

"Wow." Will's face lit up and he altered his direction, headed for his grandfather, inadvertently blocking Doc's aim at the nefarious Ranger.

Robards took advantage of the opportunity. In a flurry of movement he took a shot at Gabe and launched himself toward Will, grabbing the boy back against him. Gabe, having seen the same opening, was already in motion so the bullet only grazed him, cutting a bloody, stinging path across his upper arm. He made a lunge for his son, missed him. Then stopped cold when the outlaw placed the barrel of his gun against the boy's temple.

"Get back," Robards shouted, his facade of civility dropping away like whiskers from a razor. "I'll kill him. I will."

Gabe heard Tess's whimper of fear, but he never took his gaze off Robards. "Let him go. Let's keep this between you and me."

"You and me? This has never been between you and me. You're a pawn, not a player, Montana. Yes, I wanted your wife, and using Bodine to get her was an enjoyable part of my strategy. But Tess wasn't the reason for everything. No woman is worth that much."

"Then what is?"

"The valley. The Aurora Springs valley. Once the railroad spur is completed and I'm able to transport items in and out of the valley, I'll have the perfect storage facility for my treasures. I won't need to make trips down to this armpit of the world."

"Now it makes sense," Monty said. "All that stuff in that tunnel is yours."

"So you found it, did you? Well, I knew it would happen sooner or later if I didn't either get you away from your Big Bend tunnel explorations or move my riches to a better spot."

Monty spoke to Gabe. "I found chest after chest of valuables in a tunnel not far from here."

Pieces of the puzzle were falling into place for Gabe, too, and he used the knowledge in hopes of distracting Robards enough for Gabe to make a jump for Will. "You're the bandit Mack Hunter is looking for. You're the fellow who runs the ring of thieves preying upon the railroad and stagecoaches that pass through West Texas." While he spoke, Gabe slowly moved closer.

Robards nodded as if accepting his due, then began backing away. "I've eluded the law for four years now. This time the game failed to play smoothly, but do you honestly think I'll allow you to ruin it for me?"

Tess spoke up from somewhere behind Gabe on his left. "We won't ruin anything, Lionel. We won't say a word to anyone if you'll only let Will go."

"Tess, Tess, Tess. I know you won't say anything to anyone. You won't have the opportunity. As much as the notion pains me, I'm afraid you'll be dead." With that, he took his gun away from Will's head long enough to fire once again at Gabe. This time, Gabe didn't get out of the way. This time he didn't have to.

Because the moment Lionel Robards shifted his Colt, Monty Cameron dove for him. He took the bullet that was meant for his son and fell in a heap at Gabe's feet.

Oh, God. Gabe froze at the sight of the bloodstain spreading across Monty Cameron's side.

In that distracted moment, everything happened at once. Will dropped to his knees beside his grandfather and hollered, "Doc!"

Robards lurched forward and grabbed Tess by the waist. She screamed and Gabe's head snapped up just as the Ranger dragged her into the yawning darkness at the back of the cave.

Gabe glanced from the spot where she disappeared back to his father. "Go after her," Monty said, his voice splintering with pain. "There's an exit to another cave. He'll take her into the maze of tunnels and we'll never find her."

"But I can't leave you to . . ."

"It's a flesh wound. Pressure will stop the bleeding. Go get her and bring her back to take care of me. Nobody nurses like our Tess."

Gabe blew out a harsh breath. "All right. Will, you stay with your grandfather."

"No, I'd better go with you. I know the tunnels a little bit. You could get lost."

"Go, both of you," Monty said.

And so they did. Pausing only long enough to light a pair of torches, Will led the way deeper into the cave, then through a half-hidden slip into a second cavern. At first they were able to follow the sounds of Tess's struggle, but as the chase continued, the way ahead grew disturbingly silent and increasingly dark. "Hold on a minute, Will," he said. "Let's stop and listen."

Gabe closed his eyes and listened hard. The air in

the cave smelled dank and moldy; the silence deafening. Still nothing. Just as he lifted a foot to take a step, the crack of a gunshot echoed like a nightmare off the tunnel's stone wall. "Son?" Gabe shouted.

"I'm fine. What about you, Pa?"

Pa. He wanted to savor the sound, but he didn't have time. He had to get to Tess.

If only he knew which way to go.

Fear fluttered like a million butterflies in his gut as they searched the tunnels for a good ten minutes until abruptly, they reached a dead end. "Oh, no," Will moaned. "I thought this was the way out. I got us lost."

"We're not lost," Gabe replied. "We just missed a turn somewhere. Let's retrace our steps. We'll find it."

He turned around and led the way back from where they had come, assuming his son followed on his heels.

It proved to be a dangerous assumption. When he spoke to Will a few minutes later, the boy didn't reply.

Somewhere along the way, his son had disappeared.

The instant Will emerged from the tunnel onto the dusk-darkened bluff, Tess took advantage of Lionel's momentary distraction and lunged for the gun.

"You bitch," he cried as she clawed and bit and kicked during the struggle. Then to her dismay, she felt her son join in the battle.

Lionel wouldn't hesitate to pull the trigger. He'd proved that a few minutes earlier when she'd jumped him the first time and he'd shot at her, but missed, thank God. Now, terror gave added strength to her movements. She would save her son from this monster if it was the last thing she did.

Will beat at Robards's back. Tess felt the cold steel of the Colt brush her fingers. The Ranger's grip on the gun was fierce, but a mother's protective instincts gave her strength she'd never known before.

She got a grip on the barrel. He landed a close-fisted blow to her face and her head snapped back. But she didn't let go. He hollered when Will kicked his leg out from under him. All three of them went down.

Then the gun went off. All three of them froze.

Tess felt no pain, but something warm seeped through her blouse onto her skin. She smelled the stink of blood. *Oh, dear Lord, please.* "Will?"

"Mama? Are you hit?"

"No. You, Will, what of you?"

"I'm fine."

Relief gushed over her like water from a barrel. Tess rolled off the bodies beneath her. Will scooted out from underneath the Ranger.

Lionel Robards didn't move.

"Aw hell, Mama. We killed him."

For the first time ever, Tess didn't correct her son for cursing. Two men dead. She looked away, noticing the sun setting in the west. This day couldn't end soon enough for her. Glancing down, she saw that blood covered her shirtwaist.

Will stood then helped her to her feet. She wanted to hug him, to pull him into her arms and never let him go, but she refrained from doing so. She wouldn't soil her son with the blood of Lionel Robards.

Getting away from the body, they walked to the edge of the bluff and stood looking down at the Rio Grande that flowed black and fast below them. "Lots of water in the river," Will observed, breaking the strained silence. "Must be all that rain we've been having. Look at it churn through the canyon."

"That's not the normal Rio," Tess agreed, glad to think about anything but the experience they'd just survived. "A person'd risk drowning if they tried to swim it now."

"Nah, not if they paid attention. I could swim it, I bet. I'm getting much better at swimming. I only had one close call all summer long, remember?"

Gabe's weary voice sounded from behind them. "Please tell me you're not going to try. I don't have another year of life span to waste on being scared. I swear that last gunshot took a full decade off me."

Apparently unconcerned about the blood, Gabe swept both Tess and Will into his arms and held them so tight that Tess could hardly breath. She didn't care. It felt so good to be held. Good to be safe.

How long they stood there, she couldn't say. Not too long; Doc was on all their minds. All she knew was that one minute she was basking in her family's love, and the next minute the nightmare had returned.

Maniacal laughter floated past them. They whirled around. Lionel Robards was on his knees, one hand holding his bloody abdomen, the other holding his Colt. "Guess what? I ain't dead yet. Joke's on you."

A spasm of pain flitted across his face, but the gun hand didn't waver.

"Robards," Gabe said, starting forward. "Let me help you. Put the gun down."

He laughed again, the wild sound of it sending shivers through Tess. Darkness was falling fast now, and the light in Robards's eyes glowed like something unholy. Which it probably was. "Don't take another step, Montana. Not before you make your choice."

"My choice?"

"I have one bullet left. Who gets it, the boy or the woman?"

"Robards, you can't . . ."

"Now, Montana. Who lives and who dies with me?"

"Me," he said. "Shoot me."

"No. Dying's too easy. You have to suffer. Pick now and I'll kill 'em quick. Make me choose and I'll gut shoot 'em like they did me. What's it gonna be?"

Horror twisted Gabe's features. "God dammit man, think of your soul."

"My soul? I gave it to the devil years ago. Last chance, Montana. I'm shooting on the count of three. One . . . two . . ."

One bullet. I can't bear to lose either one of them. Me, it must be me. Tess chose for her husband by pushing their son off the cliff.

"Mama!" Will cried as he went over the edge.

"He can barely swim, Gabe. Go after him. Save our son!"

"Three!" hollered Robards.

Gabe, aided by a shove from his wife, sailed off the bluff and jumped into the roaring Rio Grande.

Tess couldn't see them in the deepening darkness, but she kept her gaze on the water, her back to Lionel Robards just the same. Waiting for the bullet, she prayed for her husband and her son to survive the fall and the flooded river.

"You are something else, Tess," Robards said. "I always did admire a woman with courage. The game is yours."

The gun fired. She expected pain, but it never came. The bullet never hit.

Tess finally turned around. This time, Lionel Robards was well and truly dead.

A man stood at the entrance of the cave, smoke still rising from the gun in his hand. He looked vaguely familiar, but in her present state, Tess couldn't put it all together. "What . . . who . . . ?"

"Reckon it's past time we're introduced, ma'am." He tipped his hat. "Your husband and I are partners. My name is Mack Hunter."

Gabe couldn't see.

Cold water foamed and thundered around him, sweeping him downriver. With the high rock walls blocking what light remained in the sky, it might as well have been midnight as sundown. "Will!" he called out. "Will, can you hear me?"

The river bubbled and gushed. Perched on the canyon wall, a bird trilled and whistled.

Then, finally, above the rush of the river came the beautiful answering cry. "Help! Please. Help me!"

Sound echoed off the damn canyon walls, distorting the direction. *I need to see him, dammit. Dear God, help me see him.* "Will! Will! Where are you?"

"Here! He—" A gurgle cut off the word and chilled Gabe all the way to the bone.

The water slowed and Gabe realized they'd been swept beyond the canyon. But by now, full darkness had fallen and he still couldn't see. *He can't swim. Tess said he can't swim.*

Gabe shut his mind to thoughts of her. He couldn't deal with that now. He had to think of the boy. He had to save the boy. Their son.

Love for the boy warmed him, gave him strength to fight the water. He kicked his feet, boosting his shoulders out of the water, staring hard into the blackness.

But then it wasn't so black any longer. Light from the sky bounced off the water, lit it, and revealed his son's head right before it dipped beneath the inky surface. Strong strokes propelled him forward toward the spot where Will had disappeared. Gabe reached, searched the water. Found nothing but a rock to bang his hand against.

Now the water speed picked up as the Rio narrowed to flow into another canyon. But the light didn't die. The canyon walls stayed visible, the water surface visible.

There. Five feet ahead and off to the right, his son clung to a floating branch. *Smart boy.* Gabe reached, brushed his shirt. Grabbed and found. He spit out a mouthful of water and said, "Will?"

"Daddy, I knew you'd come. I just knew it."

Gabe thought his heart might just explode right there in the big middle of the Rio Grande. "I've got you, son. Now, let go of the branch and I'm going to turn you on your back. Don't be afraid, and don't fight me. I won't let you go. I won't ever let you go. All right?"

The boy nodded and let go the lifesaving cottonwood branch. Gabe hooked his arm around Will and, supporting his head, struck out toward the bank. It was only then that he happened to glance up into the sky and spied the light that had guided him. *Well, twirl my spurs.*

The Kissing Stars.

It was the Kissing Stars that had appeared and hovered over the river, allowing him to find his son. The Kissing Stars. Thank heavens he'd been able to see them. Thank Tess.

Tess. Up there alone with Robards. *Oh, God.*

His feet dragged the sand and he stood. "Here, Will. Dry land." Helping his son find his feet, Gabe never saw the big log that hit him in the head and knocked him flat.

He came to lying on his back in the sand. Something was lapping at his face. The events of the day came rushing back into his brain. *Must be the river. I never got out of the Rio Grande.*

It lapped again and this time he realized the wetness was rough. And it stank. This river smelled like a pigsty. It smelled like a . . .

Gabe lifted his head. "Rosie?"

The pig stuck her snout square in his face and licked

him right on the mouth. "Bleah!" he said, rearing up on all fours.

The laughter started then, sounding sweet as sugarcane syrup. And Gabe became fully aware of his surroundings.

Monty. His father. He sat beside him on his right, his face wreathed in a smile, his torso wrapped in a bandage. On his left sat Will, looking a little like a drowned puppy, but a happy drowned puppy, with one arm draped around his best friend, Rosie. And at his head . . . Gabe breathed a sigh of relief . . . at his head sat the most beautiful, courageous, infuriating woman on earth. Tess. *I'm going to make you pay for the stunt you pulled, pushing our boy into the water.*

Milling behind Tess he saw Twinkle and the colonel. And, to his surprise, Andrew and Mack. Hell, even Pollux and Castor were in attendance.

And that wasn't all. Above them, pulsing and glowing and burning in balls of gold and blue and green and purple and red—every damned color in the spectrum—above them shined the Kissing Stars.

Joy filled Gabe and he wanted to laugh and sing and shout out the love he felt for these people. For his family.

Instead, he climbed to his feet and dusted off his pants. Addressing the crowd in general, he said, "So, folks. What do y'all say. Think it's time we take home the bacon?"

EPILOGUE

Aurora Springs
December 1889

The star party was scheduled for six o'clock that evening up on Lookout Peak. The wedding party would begin at two down in the valley.

At quarter to one, Gabe ran a hand over his wife's naked buttock. "You're making a mistake. Rosie will steal the show."

"Well thank you very much." Tess nipped him on the shoulder. "That is just the sort of thing a bride loves to hear."

He laughed and when she punched him in the stomach, he laughed some more. He felt so damned good. "Now, Venus, don't get in a snit. Any woman who chooses to include a porcine princess as a bridesmaid at her wedding must anticipate sharing the limelight."

Tess giggled and stretched sensuously against him. "The veil is darling on her. Wait till you see it."

Gabe rose up on one elbow and stared down at his wife. "I'll only be looking at you, my love. Only at you."

Her sweet smile beckoned, and he lowered his mouth to hers for one more kiss. One kiss turned into a third bout of lovemaking for the morning that lasted until Twinkle banged on the bedroom door in protest. "Gabe-dear, I know you're in there even though it's the big middle of the day and you have a list of chores to do before the wedding."

With a devilish grin, he called out, "I'm working on the chores, Twinkle. I promise."

He returned to the business at hand, massaging his wife's nipples to hard, turgid peaks, until Twinkle interrupted again with a snort of disgust loud enough to impress Rosie. "Ten minutes, young man. That's all you get before I send Will in to get you. I don't imagine you want that, so hurry up. Tess needs a little time to prepare for the wedding."

"Will?" Gabe grimaced. "She wouldn't do that, would she?"

Tess shrugged.

Gabe focused all his efforts on finishing his "chore" in a timely manner. Eight and a half minutes later, pants and shirt buttoned but feet still bare, he exited their bedroom.

Tess indulged in a few more minutes abed. Deliciously sated, a smug smile of satisfaction stretched across her face, she simply felt too good to move.

Closing her eyes, she basked in these few minutes of pleasurable peace. They were likely to be the last such moments of the day. Invitations to a wedding

and a star party had gone out to every person in a
three-county area, and the Aurorians expected a
crowd.

Tess had protested calling this repetition of their
vows a wedding because she and Gabe had already
had one of those and she had fine memories of the
event—her father's shotgun not withstanding. Gabe
had overridden her arguments, saying he wanted to
marry her again and that was that and she needed to
stop whining about it.

She'd figured out part of the reason once Gabe suggested Doc give her away during the ceremony. Gabe
obviously appreciated the symbolism.

Fathers and sons. What a complex, complicated relationship that. Gabe and Will seemed to be finding
their way just fine. Over the past weeks the two of
them had grown close enough to share a button hole.
Her husband and his father, on the other hand,
weren't finding it quite so easy. They had come a long
way during the past month since the events down in
the Big Bend, but their relationship still had a little
ways to go before anyone could call it fixed.

Twinkle knocked on her door, reminding her of the
time. Quickly, Tess bathed and dressed. Sitting at her
vanity table pinning her hair, she reflected on how her
own relationship with her father-in-law had needed a
little doctoring, too. She felt terrible that she'd
doubted him, and even though he'd said all the right
things when she apologized, she could tell she had
hurt him. He hadn't quite managed to hide his pout.
Gabe had done them both a favor when he stepped

in and took them through the lies during their trip home from the Big Bend.

"Robards was a player, a strategist," her husband had said along the trail toward Eagle Gulch. "To win this particular game, he probably had three flags to capture, so to speak. One, he wanted Colonel Wilhoit's gold. Two, he wanted to own or at least control the Aurora Springs valley. And last but certainly not least, he wanted my wife. So, because he enjoyed the game as much as the victory, he concocted an elaborate strategy that didn't quite go like he had planned."

Doc added, "Don't forget he wanted me to end my pictograph studies. He didn't want me finding his cache."

"True. That's why he set you up to take the fall as the railroad vandal to begin with. Then when I showed up on the scene, he elaborated on the plan."

"Bodine," Tess said.

"Yep. Bodine. Robards intended for Bodine to kill me and threaten either you or Will or my father. Then he'd jump in and kill Bodine to protect his secret, but do it in a flashy save-the-day way and look like a hero. He undoubtedly figured you'd fall for him out of gratitude."

"Idiot." Tess sniffed with disdain.

"In some ways, yes, but all the evidence he planted against my father was inspired. He must have worn a disguise to look like Doc, and he made certain people saw him both when he set the rail shed fire and when he broke Bodine out of prison. He befriended both Will and my father, going so far as to take Will tracking through the mountains to make the boy think later that his grandfather had the opportunity to travel to Huntsville and back. And I'll bet if we looked close at that wanted poster he showed us, we'd find that the date of the breakout had been changed."

"He might not have even worried about the date," Doc confessed. "Everyone knows I lose track of time when I'm working. I know Will was gone for a two week period, but I couldn't tell you the dates of those two weeks to save my life."

"Maybe it did save your life," Tess observed. "If Lionel thought you paid closer attention to dates, he might have had you meet with an 'accident.' "

"You have a point," Doc said. "The man certainly tied up all his loose ends. Why, all that evidence might have made me wonder if I was guilty or not myself."

With that, all had been forgiven and the rest of the trip home had been made in happy company. At least, everyone had been happy until they reached Eagle Gulch and picked up Jack and Amy. Those two hadn't been at all happy to learn they'd missed out on all the excitement and Amy had demanded they make it up to her by throwing a wedding party the likes of which West Texas had never seen. Tess only vaguely saw the connection between a marriage reception and a life-and-death adventure, but she wasn't about to argue the point with Amy. Timid little Amy had disappeared. Empowered by her pregnancy, Amy made everyone think twice before saying her nay. Jack had taken to calling her Amazon Amy—in a loving way, of course.

A knock sounded on her door, jerking Tess back to the moment at hand. "Honey, are you ready?" Doc asked.

She took one last look in the bedroom mirror, pinched her cheeks and brushed a non-existent piece of lint from the shoulder of the white satin wedding gown imported from Fortune's Design in Fort Worth, and replied, "Yes, I'm coming."

She opened her bedroom door to find her parlor filled with Aurorians. Her friends, her family. Each of them holding a gift.

Colonel Wilhoit offered his first. "It's just a little bag of gold, Tess. I had hopes to hand you diamonds, but the mine is still evading me. Perhaps by the birth of your next child."

"My next child?" Tess repeated. How did he know? She hadn't even told Gabe.

He shrugged. "Amy said she could sense it. One mother to another."

Tess turned a look on Amy and Jack. He grinned sheepishly. Amy shot a look that dared her to deny it. When Tess settled for rolling her eyes, the younger woman smiled and brought a package out from behind her back. "This is Jack's and my gift. It's for now, not later."

The label on the box said Fortune's Design. "Not another wedding gown, I hope," she joked.

"No," Amy replied, her eyes twinkling. "It's a wedding *night*gown."

Tess peeked inside, saw filmy emerald green silk, and quickly shut the box again as the warmth of a blush stole into her cheeks.

Andrew laughed at her reaction and handed her a gaily wrapped package. It was a carving of a horse, a white horse. "Oh, Andrew, thank you. This means so much. Why, you know I love Regulus almost as much as you." The white stallion's strength that awful day had helped pull an unconscious Gabe up the bluff to safety after he'd saved Will from drowning. Tess had been feeding the horse an apple a day ever since. "I will treasure this always."

Next came Twinkle. Her gift was a small, twelve-inch by twelve-inch watercolor painting of the Kissing Stars. "Just in case you get homesick while you're living in Austin."

"Six months," Tess said, tears in her eyes as she hugged her dear, dear friend. "Gabe promised we'll be back in six months no matter what."

Doc appeared to have a tear or two in his eyes, also, as he watched from the doorway. Catching Tess's attention, he stepped forward and handed her a book. "A gift doesn't exist that's as valuable as the present you've given me, Tess. You've given me my son back, and for that I'm eternally grateful." He gestured toward the book and added, "I can't make up for those years with his son that your father and I stole from him, but this might help a little. I thought you'd like it, too. In my own way, I'm trying to do that for Gabe. It's a daily journal I've kept about Will since he was born. Tells a little of what the boy did each day."

Speechless, Tess could only hug him tight. When he hugged her back, she knew then that all had been forgiven. "I love you, daughter."

"I love you, too."

"Let's get on with the wedding then," Twinkle chimed in, her eyes bright. "The bridesmaid is already in the parlor waiting to ham it up going down the aisle."

The Aurorians offered good wishes and a few more kisses before filing from her home. A few minutes later, a french horn sounded the processional. Tess turned to Doc and asked, "Did you see the fellas? They're out there and ready?"

Doc nodded. "The groom is keeping an eye on the best man and Mack Hunter. Seems Gabe overheard his buddy tell his son something about whiskey and weddings and appropriate behavior for a young man when his parents are getting married."

"Oh, that Mack Hunter. Just between you and me, I'll be glad when he goes home. He is a bad influence on my men."

Doc laughed and held out his elbow. "Let's go rescue them then, shall we?"

They stepped out onto the front porch. "Oh, my," Tess said in surprise. What must have been a hundred people filled chairs, benches, and blankets on each side of a ribbon-marked aisle that led to a newly constructed gazebo with a beautiful view of Paintbrush Mountain.

Nervousness fluttered in Tess's stomach at the sight of all the people, but the butterflies disappeared the moment she got her first look at Gabe. He was so handsome standing before the preacher in his new black suit—a larger version of the one their almost-as-handsome-as-his-father son wore—that he took her breath away. And when he turned to look at her, love, fierce and forever, arced between them. In that moment, Tess was filled with joy. This was her dream. Her family.

"Get along there, Rosie," Doc said softly.

Wearing a poofed veil of yellow netting, a yellow ribbon around her neck, and an ingeniously designed and beautifully embroidered saddlebag contraption draped over her back, Rosie started down the aisle. Rose petals spilled from the bags with her every waddle, their fragrance blending with that of her rose-scented soap to perfume the air. She took her place before the preacher, plopping down on the feet of both groom and best man, and emitting a loud *oink*.

The titters of the crowd turned to sighs as the bride followed the bacon down the aisle.

Tess held her husband's gaze and smiled. *Oh, Gabe. I do love you so.*

I love you too, darlin', he told her with a wink.

Tess barely heard the preacher's words as he began the service. Not until the time arrived to repeat their vows did she focus her entire attention on the moment. She stood before God, her friends, and family and repeated the vows she'd sworn to this man what felt like a lifetime ago.

Then it was Gabe's turn. He squeezed her hands and said, "I, Gabe Cameron, take you Tess Cameron, to be my wife."

Cameron. Gabe Cameron.

Tess's heart overflowed.

Dear Readers,

I'm often asked what I like best about being a writer. Depending on my mood, I have different answers to that question—going to work in sweats and fuzzy house shoes always ranks right up there.

Of late, making research trips has been one of the perks of my job that I've thoroughly enjoyed. I always visit the places I write about and since I've always set my stories in my home state, I'm usually revisiting a place I've already been. However, for all the traveling I've done across Texas, before I wrote The Kissing Stars, *I had never made it to Marfa.*

Growing up in Texas I'd heard the legend of the Marfa Mystery Lights, unexplained balls of light that supposedly appeared hovering over the desert of far West Texas with some frequency. Then while researching one of my other books, I came across a reference to ghost lights dating back to the late 1800s. The idea that ranchers saw the lights before electricity or automobile headlights could explain away their existence intrigued me and sparked the idea for this book.

During the week between Christmas and New Year's in 1997, my husband and I loaded our children into our car for the long drive across West Texas to the Davis Mountain area. I had been told the lights appeared in the desert near Marfa shortly after sunset some two hundred days out of every year. Now, I'm not much of a believer in the paranormal, and I certainly never expected to see any strange phenomenon as we drove to the marked viewing area on a bitter cold December night. My purpose was to get a feel for the land where my story would take place. Imagine my surprise when minutes after the sun sank below the horizon, seven balls of light appeared in the distance.

We watched the Marfa Mystery Lights for the better part of three hours. They blinked on and blinked off. They moved together and separately, falling into lines at times and at others moving in no apparent pattern. We saw as few as two and as many as fourteen shining at the same time.

What were they? I'm certain there must be a scientific explanation, but after those magic hours in the West Texas desert, I honestly don't want to know what it is.

The memory of that evening and the fun my family had together while watching those intriguing lights dance across the sky is something I'll always treasure. I'll never forget the sound of my ten-year-old daughter's voice saying, "Look, Mom and Dad. The stars are kissing."

My fifteen-year-old answered, "That's 'cause they're trying to keep warm. Let's go, please? I'm freezing. Next time, Mom, set a book in Hawaii, would you?"

Happy reading!

Dealyn

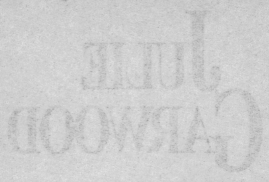

**Sonnet Books
Proudly Presents**

SIMMER ALL NIGHT

Geralyn Dawson

**Coming soon in paperback from
Sonnet Books**

**The following is a preview of
Simmer All Night. . . .**

San Antonio, Texas, 1883

I'm going to kill Christina Delaney.

While the bi-monthly meeting of the Historical Preservation Society continued without his attention, Cole Morgan reread the note the Delaney family butler had slipped him moments ago and tried to hide his outrage. The message was from Rand Jenkins, the third partner in the law firm of Morgan, Delaney, and Jenkins. It read: *Thought you and Jake would want to know. Tonight I went down to Military Plaza for supper and discovered a new chili stand serving up spice. Jake's little sister is San Antonio's newest Chili Queen. I may go back for seconds.*

Chrissy a Chili Queen.

His stomach twisted. He could only imagine the scandal this would create. The rebellious daughter of San Antonio's first family might well have gone too far this time. This could hurt Jake professionally. It could destroy their mother.

"I truly am going to kill her."

"What was that, Morgan?" a local businessman asked. "You said you'll go?"

"Go?" He jerked his head up. To Military Plaza? Did they know about Chrissy already? "Go where?"

"To England, man."

"England? Me?" What the hell had he missed? Cole crushed the note in his fist and quickly shoved it in his pocket. "Why in the world would I want to go to England?"

Elizabeth Delaney sighed as she smoothed a straying strand of graying hair back into her coiffure. "Cole, you haven't been paying attention, have you?"

That quickly, he was thirteen again, mortified at being scolded by the woman he held above all others. "I'm sorry, Miss Elizabeth. I'm afraid I got distracted by a message I just received." *Another sin to lay at Chrissy's feet.*

Elizabeth's tender smile offered both forgiveness and encouragement. "The Historical Society has unanimously chosen you to be our representative at the house party at Stanton Hall."

They what? Cole shot an incredulous look around Elizabeth Delaney's parlor where the cream of San Antonio society sat smiling at him. "Pardon me, but wouldn't that be a bit like sending a chuck wagon cookie to the ballet?"

"Don't be ridiculous, Cole." Elizabeth Delaney's elegant eyebrows dipped into a frown as she added, "You are every inch the gentleman—when you wish to be, anyway—and I am certain you will hold your own with my father's crowd."

"She's right," piped up the distinguished owner of

a local bank. "You're a homegrown aristocrat, Morgan. You ooze that Texan born and bred pride, but you do it within acceptable bounds for polite society. It's a talent, I say. One that will serve you well on this quest."

Aristocrat? His father had groomed horses. His mother had been a chambermaid, for God's sake. Before he could pose another protest, the butler nudged him in the back reminding Cole of the note. *I need to talk to Jake.*

But he needed to get out of going to England, too.

He shook his head slowly, then motioned toward his best friend, Elizabeth Delaney's son, and the new Chili Queen's brother. "Jake is the man for this job. He'll fit in just fine at Stanton Hall. Besides, the earl is his grandfather, not mine. He's the one who should go."

"No." Jake folded his arms and leaned back in his seat, eyeing Cole keenly. "Remember the new client our firm acquired last week? She's scheduled to go to trial in six weeks, but I intend to ask for a delay. This case could drag on for some time. I won't be going anywhere for the foreseeable future."

Cole scowled. He'd forgotten about the murder trial. Maybe it was kismet that he was reminded at this particular moment of the woman accused of murdering a family member during a fit of rage. *So I won't kill Chrissy. I'll just hurt her.*

He threw a pleading look to Jake, hoping for help out of this situation. "Maybe this . . . quest . . . could wait until the trial is done?"

Elizabeth Delaney shook her head. "This is the first

good lead we've had on any of the missing copies of the Declarations of Independence since we started looking two years ago. You'll need my father's help to succeed at this mission. He's an elderly man; we can't waste a day putting our plan into motion."

"You'll do fine, Cole," Jake said, a serious light in his dark eyes. "I agree with my mother. You're the perfect choice."

Fine. Thanks for nothing, friend.

As payback, Cole crossed the room and offered a handshake to Jake. "Thanks for the support," he drawled, allowing just a touch of sarcasm to enter his voice as he transferred the crumpled note to the other man's hand. Then, with his back toward the august assembly in the parlor, he gazed out the window toward the rose garden his father had planted for Elizabeth Delaney. England. Hell. His father would turn over in his grave.

But Elizabeth wanted Cole to do it. The woman who'd rescued the shattered child at the funeral of his parents and taken him in to raise as one of her own had asked this favor of him. Since he'd gladly lay down his life for the lady, he couldn't refuse this request. "All right," he said with a sigh, turning back to the assembly. "I'll go."

Maybe he could kill Chrissy, then escape to England and live under an assumed identity.

Elizabeth offered him that certain smile she reserved for special occasions, the one that made Cole feel ten feet tall. Suddenly, he found himself looking forward to the trip. He hoped their information was right and that he stood a chance of succeeding. It would feel damned good to find one of the missing parchments.

The Republic of Texas' Declaration of Independence was a historically significant document. Unfortunately, when the capital burned two years earlier, the lone copy possessed by the state of Texas went up in smoke. That's when the Historical Preservation Society of San Antonio decided to instigate a search for the remaining five copies that had disappeared after the Constitutional Convention in 1836. Cole believed the quest a worthy one, and he'd be honored to assist in returning the document to where it belonged. The fact that Elizabeth Delaney spearheaded the project made it all the more important.

At that point, a choked-off growl told Cole that his friend had finally gotten around to reading the note. Cole watched as Jake's complexion went red, then white, then red again. Seems he liked his sister's new avocation about as much as Cole did.

Watching Jake Delaney's temper build took the fire out of Cole's own anger. She was Jake's sister, after all. Let him take care of the termagant. He'd sure abandoned Cole to a British winter, had he not?

As the meeting's discussion turned to a question of what should be done about the deteriorating condition of the Alamo, Jake rose from his seat and slipped from the parlor and out of the house. Cole ducked out behind him.

This confrontation was one he damn well wanted to witness.

"I can't believe her!" Jake exclaimed when Cole caught up with him halfway along the stone path to the carriage house. "What was she thinking of? How could she do this? She's a Delaney. Delaneys have a reputation to uphold."

"Maybe you need to clarify *what kind* of reputation."

Jake made a growling noise low in his throat.

All of a sudden, Cole wanted to laugh. With blood-brother Jake taking responsibility for his sister, the burden was off his own shoulders and he could see past his immediate anger. How like Chrissy this nonsense was, actually. She'd been up to one sort of prank or another all her life. They should have known the last few months of relative peace wouldn't last.

"Look, Jake," Cole said, hoping to ease the tension a bit before they reached the square. If Jake lost control, he'd turn a scandal into a Scandal. "It could be much worse. She didn't steal a horse or rob a train. She didn't run off with a patent medicine salesman."

The first two might have soothed Jake a bit. The third got his goat. He knifed a glare at Cole. "We don't know that. You know who's in town, hawking his wares on the plaza? Dr. J. L. Lighthall, otherwise known as the Diamond King."

"The Diamond King," Cole repeated. "Isn't he the one who pulls teeth?"

"With lightning dexterity. Women are obsessed with the talent in his hands. He's a handsome scalawag and flashy dresser, and he gives a nightly speech from a gilded chariot that resembles a circus wagon, while his minions walk through the crowd selling Lighthall's so-called medicine."

And Chrissy had been spending her evenings listening to such drivel? Cole heaved a disgusted sigh. Looked like Christina Elizabeth Delaney had managed to do something exceptionally stupid this time. Considering her vast experience with idiotic acts, surpassing previous efforts took some doing.

All her life the girl had been a troublesome bit of baggage. She used to drive Jake and him crazy when they were children, trailing at the older boys' heels from the day she learned to walk. By the time she'd turned six, she'd grown to be such a pest they'd dubbed her "Bug."

Somewhere between the age of nine and twelve her adulation of her brother and his friend evolved into competition toward them. That's when the more serious trouble started. Dressed as a boy she once entered a horse race and ran against them both. Beat them, too, curse it all. He and Jake had a hard time living that one down. Then there was the time she played that outhouse prank on the headmaster of Royal Oaks Boys' School and set up Cole and her brother to take the blame. Such incidents went on for years until the night she followed them to the Gentleman's Club and got an eyewitness education of what the world's oldest profession was all about.

One good thing came out of that night, however. The Delaneys sent Christina back East to finishing school, and they'd all enjoyed three years of relative peace prior to her return.

Those Yankees had finished Chrissy, all right, Cole thought darkly. A tomboy had traveled north. A certified flirt made the trip back south. Over the course of the past five years she'd broken three marriage engagements, innumerable hearts, and now by the looks of things, the backbone of her brother's patience.

Cole didn't ask whether Jake wanted his help. Instead he climbed into the shotgun seat of the coal box buggy and waited for his friend to drive them to fetch Chrissy.

After a good five minutes of brooding silence as they drove, Jake started talking. "I can't believe her. Ever since Pa died, she's acted wild as a turpentined cat. Why does she have to be turned so damn different from other girls? Did my family make it happen? Did the Yankees do it to her? What do you think?"

What Cole thought was that he should choose his words carefully. Instead, as usual, he was blunt. "She's wild because you've let her get away with it. The girl's played you like a hoedown fiddle since the day we buried your father. You should have taken her in hand years ago, Jake."

"I know," he acknowledged with a sigh. "I just felt so damned guilty. Father sent Chrissy off to school because I told him she followed us to the whorehouse. She missed sharing the last three years of Father's life because of me."

"No." Cole resisted the urge to slap some sense into his friend and instead replied in a patient tone. "No, she missed sharing the last years of your father's life due to her own actions. You aren't responsible, Jake, she is. Don't forget it."

He shrugged, but sat a little taller in his seat. They rode in silence another few minutes until they passed one of the local Catholic churches. Cole's mouth slashed a grin. "I still say it could be worse. She could be at Frank Simpson's wedding causing a scene."

"Oh, God." Jake shut his eyes and shuddered at the thought.

One of Chrissy's old fiancés was getting married tonight. Cole wouldn't have put it past her to have waltzed into the church and told ol' Frank she'd changed her mind and wanted him after all. The fool would take her back, Cole knew, even at the altar in front of the priest.

Because Christina Elizabeth Delaney was beautiful. Punch in the gut gorgeous. Cole wasn't exactly certain when the gangly, gawky girl transformed into a well-rounded woman with thick, honey-colored hair, sparkling green eyes, and full, pouty lips that begged a man's kiss. All he knew was that one day he looked up and there she was, breathtaking and alluring.

It had been a damned disconcerting moment for Cole.

Thank God his knowledge of her true nature kept him thinking straight. He'd realized long ago that a good disposition in a woman was much more important to a man's happiness than physical beauty.

Ironically, Chrissy's own mother was responsible for the lesson. To Cole's mind, Elizabeth Delaney was as near to perfection as a woman could be. She was charming, witty, gracious and graceful. Her manners were impeccable. Her social skills unsurpassed. She was a Lady with a capital "L" and truth be told, Cole had been a little in love with her all his life.

He observed aloud, "Isn't it curious how different your sister is from your mother? One would think two females in the family would be a good deal more alike."

Jake snorted. "They're as alike as night and day. Of course, Mother was reared in England so that probably accounts for some of the difference. Remember those stories your father used to tell about my grandfather? Strict disciplinarian doesn't begin to describe it." After a moment's thought, he added, "You know, I've never looked at it this way before. It's amazing to think that Mother and Bug belong to the same family. I mean, can you even begin to picture my mother joining the Chili Queens?"

"About as well as I can picture Christina sitting down to supper with the Queen of England." After a moment's pause, he added, "That word makes me shudder."

"Queen?"

"No. The other one."

"England. It'll be fine, Cole. You'll track down our missing declaration. I have faith in you." Then Jake's mouth settled into a glum smile and he added, "Hell, I think you have the better end of the stick. You get to travel to England and see their queen. I have to say here and deal with ours."

Cole winced. Christina Delaney, Chili Queen of San Antonio, Texas. "It's enough to turn a man off beans, isn't it?"

Christina Delaney laughed as she whirled and twirled across the plaza to the tune of the Mexican street band. Wearing a white peasant blouse and a flowing scarlet skirt, she flashed a smile at the handsome vaquero who was her partner, and lifted her hands above her head to clap in time to the beat. She loved to dance. She loved to lose herself in music, to feel the rhythm of the song deep within her soul. When she danced, she felt free.

Chrissy especially loved feeling free.

The yen for freedom had been a part of her since childhood, and she suspected it had its roots in the innumerable times she watched her brother and Cole go off on an adventure while she was made to stay behind in deference to her gender. For a long, long time she hated being a girl. She'd tried to deny her femininity, to overcome the liability of being female. Then, in a series of experiences that began with a broken heart and ended with her first severed engagement, she learned the power of being a woman. After that, Chrissy embraced her womanhood with enthusiasm.

As the song ended, she hugged her dance partner, accepted his kiss on the cheek, then took up with another man for the next dance as the music started anew. She knew she acted reckless, knew she'd launch San Antonio society tongues wagging with the scandal, but she truly didn't care. Chrissy might be born to society, but she fit in better with those down here in the plaza.

Plaza de Las Armas, or Military Plaza, was an open air bazaar for hucksters, night-hawks, and peddlers at whose stands might be purchased everything from a pair of spectacles to a serape. But the features which made Military Plaza different from other city squares in the South were the open air restaurants serving chili con carne and other pungent Mexican dishes to customers seated on small benches around cloth draped tables. Lanterns and smoldering mesquite fires provided the light. Raven-haired señoritas waited tables and sang out customer orders to the cooks.

One stand, however, proved different from the rest. While most of the queens were of Spanish descent, Anglo-Saxon aggressiveness had asserted itself and as of this very night earned for a certain blond-haired, green-eyed woman the acknowledgment of queen of all queens. As announced by the official tabulator a short time ago, on account of her beauty, vivacity, aptitude of repartee, and of course, the superior quality of her food, Miss Chrissy Delaney had been voted Queen of the Chili Queens of San Antonio, Texas.

Chrissy had started to cry. Acceptance. What a delicious dish.

Then, the band had struck up the music, vaqueros tossed down their sombreros, and Chrissy began to dance. Forty-five minutes later she was still dancing, barefoot now, her eyes alight, her face flushed, her smile as wide as the West Texas plain. She swished her skirts, showed a little ankle, threw a few kisses.

Then glanced up to see her brother and that starched-shirt, disapproving, hypocritical friend of his, Cole "I'm-perfect-and-you're-not" Morgan.

In that instant, the night's magic evaporated and frustration took its place. Chrissy wanted to scream. She'd known they'd learn of her chili stand eventually, but she hadn't planned on that happening tonight. Her stratagem, involved sitting down with facts and figures in hand to help her present an unassailable argument why she should be allowed to continue the chili stand. The boys showing up in the midst of a barefooted hat dance wasn't on her agenda anywhere.

Just my luck. Why did it have to be tonight? Couldn't she have had this one evening of fun and freedom? "Apparently not."

"What did you say, sweetheart?" asked the monte dealer with whom she was dancing.

Ignoring the card shark, she glanced back toward her brother. He had that avenging angel look about him again. The words she'd heard all her life from him and from her mother and especially from her father echoed through her mind. *You're a Delaney, Christina, and Delaneys have a reputation to uphold.*

She turned back to her dance partner, smiled, and said, "I must think of my reputation." Then she grabbed him by the flashy satin lapels, yanked him toward her, and planted a kiss right on his lips.

The sound she heard behind her could have been a volcano blowing its top, but since San Antonio didn't have any volcanoes, she thought it might be her brother. Or maybe Cole.

She ended the scandalous public kiss with a flourish and flashed a saucy smile around the catcalling crowd. Then, adopting a regal mien in keeping with her newly crowned status, she glided over to her chili stand and took up her scepter, otherwise known as a ladle, and prepared to meet the enemy.

Look for
Simmer All Night
Wherever Books
Are Sold
Coming Soon
from
Sonnet Books